T0348987

The Colors of April

The Colors of April

FICTION ON
THE VIETNAM WAR'S LEGACY
50 YEARS LATER

EDITED BY

Quan Manh Ha & Cab Tran

THREE ROOMS PRESS
New York, NY

The Colors of April: Fiction on the Vietnam War's Legacy 50 Years Later
Edited by Quan Manh Ha and Cab Tran

© 2025 by Quan Manh Ha and Cab Tran

This is a work of fiction. Names, characters, businesses, places, events, and incidents are either the products of the author's imaginations or used in a fictitious manner. Any resemblance to actual persons, living or dead, or actual events is purely coincidental.

ISBN 978-1-953103-57-4 (trade paperback original)
ISBN 978-1-953103-58-1 (Epub)
Library of Congress Control Number: 2024951282

TRP-117

First edition

Publication Date: March 25, 2025

BISAC category codes
FIC054000 FICTION / Asian American & Pacific Islander
FIC003000 FICTION / Anthologies (multiple authors)
FIC123000 FICTION / World Literature / Southeast Asia
FIC082000 FICTION / Own Voices

COVER AND INTERIOR DESIGN:
KG Design International, www.katgeorges.com

COVER ILLUSTRATION:
Ann Phong
www.annphongart.com | instagram.com/@artist.annphong

DISTRIBUTED INTERNATIONALLY BY:
Publishers Group West: www.pgw.com

Three Rooms Press
New York, NY
www.threeroomspress.com
info@threeroomspress.com

Table of Contents

Introduction

FIFTY YEARS HAVE PASSED SINCE THE end of the war that has come to define Vietnam in the eyes of the world. Even now, the war remains deeply personal and politically divisive among the Vietnamese; no family was untouched by its haunting shadow, no one unmoved by its carnage or apocalyptic vision of hell on earth. Yet, it is never war that defines a country or its people, but the stories we tell each other, those we hand down from generation to generation—stories which we take and shape and make our own to pass down in turn.

In this expansive anthology, more than two dozen authors frame the Vietnamese experience through their own lens, each portrait capturing vividly the nuances of a history shared, then silenced by war, and now reclaimed. Among the contributors are a Pulitzer Prize winner and writers who are publishing for the first time, their stories standing together without regard for nationality, religion, politics—so long as they are Vietnamese. The stories vary as much in tone and style as they do subject matter. From the gritty realism of "Oakland Night Question" to the surreal quality of "What the War Left Behind"; the elegiac "Night" to the playful banter of "Bad Things Didn't Happen"; the narratives here contend with Vietnam's war-torn past and the ways we plumb the depths of memory to reconcile with it. These stories also wrestle with questions of identity, cultural inheritance, and how storytelling empowers a people to reclaim what has been lost to time and war. Individually, each story stands on its own, but together they show how the literal and ideological oceans that once divided the Vietnamese—separating those who left from those who stayed—are now finding common shores.

Since that April morning in 1975, Americans, Vietnamese of the diaspora, and those who remained in Vietnam have all grappled with the legacy of the war in different ways. For U.S. servicemen, their families, and the American public who watched the war unfold from their living rooms, the war's dramatic conclusion was for some a bitter pill. For many more, a squandering of resources and a tragic waste of human lives. In Washington, as political and military disasters piled up, the writing on the wall was clear: the war could not be won at the cost of more American lives.

In the years that followed, media narratives saturated public consciousness by repackaging and selling the war as a great American tragedy, complete with heroes and antiheroes struggling to do the right thing in the face of insurmountable odds—stories tailored for an American audience. Vietnam became little more than a backdrop, a stage for the American drama to play out on, with the Vietnamese themselves reduced to extras in the background, totally expendable, portrayed either as bloodthirsty communists from the North, who held little regard for human life, or as sympathizers from the South, subservient to the Americans, and valuing life only marginally more than their communist counterparts. The Vietnamese depicted across American media during the postwar decades were about as complex as a betel nut. But gradually, Americans have begun to seek out other perspectives on the war, gaining a more nuanced picture and greater understanding of the Vietnamese people.

For children of the diaspora, there is a whole generation of Vietnamese Americans who have grown up knowing little about the circumstances of their citizenship—why their grandparents fled Vietnam on overcrowded boats not meant to cross oceans, or why everyone, after making it Stateside, decided that Orange County, California, was as good a place as any to start over. But even the third generation after the original "boat people" are now reconnecting with their roots and the country that once held contempt for their parents and grandparents.

The Vietnamese who remained bore witness to the war's legacy in ways that neither Americans nor refugees could: battlefields and rice fields littered with the dead, millions of acres of land laid waste by napalm and dioxin—the latter a weapon of genocide which continues to cause birth defects three generations after the war. Now those who stayed are also learning about the trauma carried by those who left. Only by sharing stories can we hope to foster a deeper awareness for the struggles of the other. In the end, it is the stories we tell that bind us as a people. Only through the power of narrative can we bridge our differences, find common ground, nurture empathy, and seek some measure of closure—a way to transcend war and the suffering it brings, as storytellers have done since the beginning.

Long before numbers and written language, there were storytellers. These early narrators knew how to wield words to bring light to a dark world, create order out of chaos, and turn abstract ideas into tales of wisdom that even children could understand. These stories preserve cultures, a people's very soul, and as long as we keep telling them and listening to them, there is no fear that the past will fade from memory. So let us go back to the beginning, before war and its endless suffering, before time itself existed, when memory was but a pale fire in the din of our primitive brains. Back to those timeless words: *Once upon a time...*

Once upon a time, so the legend goes, the Dragon Lord Lạc Long Quân, guardian of both the natural and supernatural worlds, rose from the belly of the sea to meet the fairy goddess Âu Cơ—divine healer, giver of life, and the most sublime being in heaven and on earth—who descended from her mountain sanctuary. From the terraced highlands of Sa Pa to the mangrove forests of the Mekong, from the Trường Sơn Mountains to the beaches of Đà Nẵng—though worlds apart—somehow the dragon and the fairy found each other and fell in love. Their union gave birth to one hundred children, known as the "children of the dragon and the fairy," and from these one hundred children, descended the ancestors of the Vietnamese people.

We are defined not by the wars we fight, but by the stories we choose to tell.

—*Cab Tran & Quan Manh Ha*

The Colors of April

War's End

—Vũ Cao Phan—

IN THE EARLY MORNING OF APRIL 29, 1975, four of my soldiers and I stood outside a tall concrete tower behind a wobbly iron gate. "This must be it," I said. We called out at the same time, "Anyone home?"

A steward of the property came out but immediately went back inside when they saw us. We heard voices from inside rising and falling. Curious heads turned our way as a woman wearing a black nun's habit ambled into the courtyard.

"Good morning," she said. "You must be the liberation soldiers?"

"We are," I said. "May we come in?"

"Yes, of course."

After the woman opened the gate for us, I turned to her and asked, "Is this a church?"

"I'm afraid not, lieutenant. It's a school. But we've been closed all month. We evacuated from Orphanage G in the central region."

Although the nun called me "lieutenant," I wasn't wearing any insignia. She glanced at me furtively and said, "We escaped the bombing. Luckily, we found ourselves here. Some other soldiers were stationed here a few days ago, but they've already left. We're using this place as a temporary orphanage."

I didn't quite believe her and reflexively gripped the butt of my rifle. "Are there soldiers inside now?"

"No, sir. Of course not. They left days ago. Another group of soldiers passed through yesterday, but only to change out of their military uniforms before leaving."

I could clearly see the abandoned uniforms from here. The entire town was in the midst of an evacuation, so it was difficult to tell whether the area had recently been cleared, or whether it was still under the ARVN's control.[1] We stopped at the base of the tower, which looked modest and durable enough—but nothing like a watchtower at all. Why would a school need a tower like this? Could it have been used for surveillance? I ordered my men to remain vigilant while I inspected the tower.

Yesterday, our full-scale attack struck at the heart of Sài Gòn. Anti-aircraft units were ordered to shadow the infantry as we marched forward. But somehow our regiment ended up here, still quite a distance north from Sài Gòn. Our orders were to ambush enemy aircraft should they come in from areas outside Vietnam, which could happen at any time. As the reconnaissance team leader, I was ordered to find a watchtower for this purpose. It had taken us almost six hours to locate the property, using a map we had seized from the enemy yesterday afternoon.

"Up here!" I yelled to my comrades below. I gave them a nod to let them know that everything checked out. The watchtower was in an ideal location; we could see everything from up here. Nothing obstructed the view. I radioed the regimental commander and gave him an update on our situation. I informed him that I would start my assignment immediately. From that moment on, all our anti-aircraft guns were on standby and awaiting my orders. The commander had given me permission to give the order to fire at a moment's notice.

I told Mother Superior, the nun wearing the black robe, that my men had just been given orders to stay put, so we needed to inspect

---

1 Army of the Republic of [South] Vietnam, trained by and closely affiliated with the United States

the grounds and property thoroughly. She agreed with me, but something in her eyes told a different story.

Part of our mission was to recon the area, but the most important thing right now was to find a place for my men to decamp. We had been marching all night and exhaustion was setting in. I told Vinh, a veteran squad leader, to keep an eye on the watchtower while the rest of us followed Mother Superior.

The grounds were quite expansive, but there was only one building, the orphanage, on the property. The orphanage had maybe half a dozen rooms, most likely used as classrooms and play areas for the children. Although the nuns hadn't been here long, it seemed they had already fallen into daily routines. We inspected each room and did our best to be respectful. We saw innocent children of all ages. In one room, a little boy raised his arm and gestured his hand at us like a gun, pretending to pull the trigger. The nun standing at the front of the classroom displayed a look of distress. I smiled because I knew he was just a child. In another classroom, young girls were learning how to sew. When we got to the last room, however, we found it locked.

"Is this room usually left empty when it's not used?" I asked Mother Superior.

"No, lieutenant. This is the sacristy—the most sacred room here," she said quickly.

"I understand. So this is a Catholic orphanage."

I thought about where my men could set up their tents and camp for the night. It shouldn't be too difficult to find a spot. Then, as though she knew exactly what I was thinking, Mother Superior pointed at a tiny building not attached to the orphanage and said, "Why not take a look at that house over there? A family is living there at the moment, but we could make some sort of arrangement."

Three people lived in the tiny house: a young mother, her small child, and a sixteen-year-old girl. The young mother looked rather sad—and we knew exactly why. Mother Superior had told us that the husband was currently stationed elsewhere on a defensive line. When we entered, the woman greeted us and called out to the young girl, "Dịu Thơm, bring some hot tea for the soldiers, please."

The name Dịu Thơm, Scent, sounded so gentle and aromatic, as if the war had never touched this place. While the girl was preparing the tea, something occurred to Mother Superior. "Hồng, your family should stay with us so these liberation soldiers can use your house for a few days." Turning to us, she asked, "How long do you plan to remain here, lieutenant?"

"Until the war is over, Sister," I smiled. "The fighting is just about done, so we believe the war will be over very soon."

Mother Superior looked at me hesitantly.

***

FOR THE REST OF THE DAY, we took turns with guard duty atop the watchtower. Gunfire constantly erupted around us, seemingly from every direction, and this caused distress for my men. Even the sound of far-off, muffled gunshots reached our ears. Nobody knew when Sài Gòn would be attacked—maybe tomorrow, maybe the day after that, maybe—

An incident happened later that afternoon. Ruân, the first class private from Hải Hậu and a devout Catholic, approached me and said, "It doesn't make any sense to me. I asked Mother Superior about the prayer schedule, and at first, she pretended not to hear me. Then she asked, 'Why should a soldier like you, sent to liberate us, care about when prayers are held?' She added that they had the liturgy earlier. I told her I was Catholic, but because I had been stationed away from civilization for so long, I hadn't had a chance to attend Mass. We locked eyes for a moment, then she continued on her way without another word."

I found all of this odd. We had been on the grounds of the orphanage since early morning, and there was no sign that anything like a religious service had taken place. But before I had time to share my suspicion with Ruân, Vinh, our squad leader, walked in.

"Sir," Vinh said, "the enemy is hiding around here somewhere. While out foraging for wild vegetables, I saw a window that was left open at the back of the chapel, then heard someone slam it shut. So I went to investigate. I pressed my ear to the outer wall of the chapel and heard movement inside. That black lock on the door must mean—"

"I saw Mother Superior pass by that locked door," Ruân chimed in. "She was talking under her breath, and her eyes kept darting around like she was looking for something."

**

MY MEN WERE INCREDIBLY OBSERVANT. I had held my own suspicions about the orphanage ever since we got here, and with this new information, it all made sense: Mother Superior was hiding someone inside the sacristy. But who and why?

I had no reason to doubt Vinh's story. It wouldn't surprise me at all if more than one person was hiding inside. My thinking went that the enemy, for whatever reason, had left behind a squad of men after the rest of the regiment had moved on. Or maybe they were deserters from elsewhere. I quickly made the decision to cordon off the entire chapel based on two assumptions: as soon as it got dark, whoever was inside the chapel could use this to their advantage to escape or to prepare to ambush us. We only numbered five, after all, so the odds were already stacked against us.

In order to secure the area behind the chapel, I told Ruân to hang his hammock between two trees near the building. Even in the dark, this caught Mother Superior's attention. From a good distance, I saw her gaze in the direction of the hammock. Maybe she was wondering why we needed to occupy Hồng's house in the first place.

**

THAT NIGHT, THE SOUND OF DISTANT gunfire filled the air, lighting up the horizon. It made us tense and uneasy. While our comrades pressed on toward victory, we were stuck here carrying out our orders. The noise subsided around midnight, but none of us could sleep.

The ancestral moon, still hidden from view, had not yet emerged above the tree line. When I spotted a silhouette, I signaled to my comrades. The dark figure crept along the wall toward a tree that was about thirty feet from the chapel. The tree's canopy made it even more difficult to see. I knew exactly what was going on: the dark figure, whoever it was, either was trying to secretly communicate with the people inside, or was going to unlock the door and let everybody escape. Unfortunately, there was a clearing in front of the chapel, so the figure remained lurking in the shadows. After keeping watch for several minutes, the dark figure finally made for the chapel but lost its footing on the building steps and fell, causing a ruckus. Quickly, it got up and vanished. We decided not to chase after it.

***

IN THE MORNING, MY COMRADES FOUND an empty cassolette, food like bread scattered about, and a pair of sandals on the steps where the dark figure had appeared the night before. It occurred to me that there was a much simpler explanation for what was going on, so we left the items near the door. All that day, nobody at the orphanage walked by the locked door. Even the nuns seemed more anxious than usual. No morning prayer in the chapel. No Mother Superior anywhere.

When my superiors contacted me, they instructed me to be extra vigilant, as it was very likely the infantry division would march into Sài Gòn that same day. In my report, I informed my regiment commander of our situation and asked for permission to take necessary actions to resolve it.

"Do your best to capture them alive," the commander ordered. "Persuade them to surrender if you can. But everybody must be taken alive. This war is almost over." Then he asked, "Are there any children inside?"

I went looking for Mother Superior because I wanted to talk to her first. It wasn't because I wanted to proselytize or lecture her on politics and whose side she should be on, but to be upfront with her because I thought I understood where she was coming from. Catholic nuns were compassionate, and this orphanage was a testament to their kindness. I knew Mother Superior detested bloodshed, so we were on the same page about that, and I intended to tell her to persuade whoever was hiding in the locked room to surrender themselves—the Revolution would have mercy on them.

I was informed that Mother Superior was sick. Turning to another elderly nun, I firmly instructed, "Please get the key and unlock the chapel. We have to clear the building."

"Lord, have mercy!" she cried out. "Only Mother Superior has the key."

"Then please tell Mother Superior about our request," I said. "We'll be setting up a perimeter around the chapel grounds soon, preventing anyone from entering or leaving. Please ensure all the children and nuns are taken somewhere safe."

The elderly nun made the sign of the cross and quickly left. After half an hour, she still hadn't returned, but at least someone had taken all the children to the area opposite the building. I summoned my comrades, leaving behind a single sentry to man the watchtower. Vinh arrived, his face without emotion, and said, "The ARVN has surrendered. Here, take a listen," he said, turning up the radio strapped to his waist. ". . . *President Dương Văn Minh has ordered the ARVN to put down their weapons. . .*"

After hearing the news, I didn't know what to feel. I looked around at my men. "We have one last battle to fight," I said to them, even if I didn't know what was about to happen. I assigned each man their final duty. "Break that lock," I ordered, "and tell them to surrender."

"Look!" a comrade said. "It's Mother Superior—"

I turned around and saw her cautiously approaching us, holding a keyring. She was breathing heavily as she began to speak. We couldn't hear what she was saying until she was almost upon us.

"Lieutenant," she pleaded, "please don't shoot in there."

She looked weak and shrunken after only one night. As she bowed her head, her bony fingers searched the keyring for the chapel key. Her fingers must have gone over it several times, but she continued looking for it. Finally, her fingers latched onto a single key. She looked up at me. "Lieutenant," she said, "please allow me to open it."

Not a moment later, the unlocked door swung open. She made the sign of the cross and announced herself clearly to those inside: "It's me—your mother. You can come out now."

Mother Superior collapsed at my feet. Her voice choked as she begged, "God have mercy! Please don't kill them. They're all innocent."

From a dark corner three Amerasians—children of American soldiers and Vietnamese women—emerged. Two were half-black and one was half-white. They were hollow-eyed and malnourished.

"For the love of God, what did they do to deserve this?" she cried.

"Grab whatever you have in your rucksacks to eat and drink and give it to them," I ordered my men.

I bent down to help Mother Superior back on her feet. That was all I could say or do at that exact moment. Then, turning away, I walked off as quickly as I could—hoping no one saw the tears in my eyes.

—*Translated by Quan Manh Ha & Cab Tran*

In Silence, In Rain
—Trần Thị Tú Ngọc—

IN THE CITY, THE WET SEASON was finally coming to an end. Even the clouds, after months of weeping, had nearly wrung themselves dry. Walking through the last of the mist and rain, Phương felt a sense of resignation; no amount of rain from the sky could wash away the remains of earlier days. That afternoon, when she stopped by the secluded home of the celebrated photographer Vũ Thiên, she saw him sitting solemnly under a canopy made of wood, his wheelchair facing clumps of lilacs that seemed to bow in the rain.

"My husband's recovery from the stroke he had last year hasn't gone too well," Vũ Thiên's wife said sadly. Brewing tea for her guest, she continued, "He avoids everyone—journalists, his fans, even close friends from the art world. I appreciate you visiting, but he prefers to be left alone."

Phương leafed through the book in front of her and soon found herself on page 93, where she saw a picture of a village framed by a somber sunset. The sun seemed to gaze right through her with its probing eye. Trying to hide her uneasiness, Phương shut the book and managed a half-hearted smile.

"I was just hoping he'd autograph this artbook for me. It's no. 50 of the limited-edition copies. You know, back in those days, we studied these photographs so often that we memorized their composition and every detail." Those days weren't so long ago for Phương.

"You can just leave the book," the photographer's wife said. "I'll let my husband know you want an autograph once he feels better," she said, looking at Phương kindly. Phương jotted a few words down on a card, placed it in the book, then said goodbye. Outside, the rain began to let up. The lilacs were in full bloom along the path, the purple flowers hanging sadly in the rain.

***

DUY'S FATHER WAS THE YOUNGEST OF five children. At the height of the war, he studied literature at Sài Gòn University before emigrating to the United States. A relative in America had sponsored him. He became a father in his adopted country, and raised his child alone after his tumultuous marriage with another immigrant—a white woman—ended. Duy was cut from the same cloth as his father. He had his father's long, delicate fingers and the same eyes that constantly sought the past. Even in exile, he and his father carried their sorrow everywhere. Despite years in the United States, Duy's father never stopped grieving; he was never able to let go. In the cramped attic of his suburban home in New Haven, his father had kept an old, yellowing songbook with ink long faded, and a guitar that seemed to moan whenever it was played.

That summer, Duy brought his father's guitar back to Vietnam while working on a joint project by both Vietnamese and American cultural institutions. During this time, he met Lê Phương, a writer for the *Daily News* who penned the "Perspectives on Life" column. Phương was intelligent but also gracious.

***

PHƯƠNG LOVED SALTED COFFEE, Trịnh Công Sơn's music, and photos taken by Vũ Thiên. Duy was only familiar with the first two. On afternoons when it got chilly back in the U.S., Duy often saw his father sitting beside a cup of strong coffee and lost in thought, sometimes humming a strange and sad tune, one as moving as a prayer on a dreary night. The song, his father said, was sung back when the country was still at war. Sad, yet filled with hope, like a lover estranged from their beloved, as they were from their homeland.

Hearing Phương play the guitar and sing the song his father loved filled Duy with memories. His father often listened to that same song at an alleyway café. Since falling in love with Phương, Duy had come to enjoy the acrid taste of coffee. He taught himself Trịnh Công Sơn's romantic melodies, then understood why time seemed to stand still in discolored photos.

"Why do you enjoy Vũ Thiên's works so much?" Duy once asked Phương while she was reading a book.

"I don't know," Phương replied, her mind elsewhere. "Maybe it's because of the way he's able to capture people. He's famous, you see, because he was an independent war correspondent back in the 1970s, so he was able to show both sides of the war."

Duy listened to her while examining the photos closely. He was impressed by the photographer's technique. When they reached page 93, Phương suddenly turned away. The image—a village taken at sunset—was accompanied by a caption at the bottom. Duy had no idea a photo could evoke so many difficult memories.

The photo was taken at An Phụng Village, her ancestral home. Although many years have passed since then, for Phương the pain never quite went away.

***

As VŨ THIÊN LAY QUIETLY IN the dark, an unsettling dread grew until it subsumed his tiny room. The feeling, he knew, stemmed from the photo of An Phụng Village in that rare leather-bound edition of his book the young reporter Phương brought by. She stood out even among his devoted fans because she had sought him out many times. On significant dates, like anniversaries of historical events, major newspapers would clamor for an exclusive interview with Vũ Thiên. His camera during the war had made him famous, but Vũ Thiên knew that deep down he wished this period of his life hadn't happened; every photo contained an unhappy story, and this weighed heavily on him.

Phương was the only reporter who didn't ask questions that dredged up these old memories for Vũ Thiên. He was deeply grateful that she gave him enough space. Phương listened when he spoke of peaceful villages, of a happy child smiling through his lens, of tearful reunions at train stations, and of young lovers saying goodbye to each other. Capturing these photos was no easy task, as he had to make peace with the ghosts of war who haunted his subjects. Yet people got used to the idea of him on the battlefield, so they craved tales of conflict and sorrow. Phương avoided those topics in her interviews.

"I'm really sorry about that," she said guardedly on one visit.

Phương didn't go alone on that visit. Duy, a tall Vietnamese expat with brown hair and dark green eyes, accompanied her. Vũ Thiên listened to him and was surprised by his gentle tone and effortless Vietnamese, as if he had spoken it his whole life. When Phương started recording the conversation for an article in the *Daily News*, the young expat asked if they could conduct the interview in the garden. He seemed troubled and restless, as if he wanted to say something to Vũ Thiên but decided against it. After the interview, Vũ Thiên saw the couple off. As they walked by the lilacs, he heard the tall young man say softly: "It's strange, isn't it—that lilacs can mean both first love and separation? How can a flower be both beautiful and sad at the same time?"

***

WHEN SHE VISITED DUY'S GRANDMOTHER for the first time, Phương was surprised to learn that his family was originally from Sài Gòn but had been separated by the war. His grandmother was delighted to see Phương and insisted she stay for dinner. The ninety-year-old woman even went to the market herself to buy water lilies and carp for a special soup. She grew unexpectedly lively, telling Phương that even though Duy visited her once a year, this was the happiest she had ever seen him.

"I care for you both," she said, clasping their hands in hers. Duy just smiled, believing his grandmother was simply overprotective. When he and Phương explored the city together, the labyrinthine streets made anything seem possible. Phương awakened in him a love so extraordinary that it eclipsed even the early memories of his father. Duy stowed his father's old guitar in the closet. The overgrown bush in the yard was trimmed back. When the two had first kissed, sunlight poured over the veranda, casting petal-like shapes that fell gently onto Phương's hair.

But even in daybreak there lurked glimpses of darkness.

Their relationship began to unravel on a Saturday afternoon. Phương stopped by to give some documents to Duy. She saw his grandmother sitting on the porch, leafing through an old photo album. Her weathered hands hovered over a photo of an ARVN soldier with slanted eyes, a neatly trimmed mustache, and a distinctive mole on his nose. She told Phương that the man was Duy's grandfather who had died in the war a long time ago.

Phương gazed at the photo in silence. She noticed an uncanny resemblance between Duy's grandfather and a soldier in one of Vũ Thiên's journalistic photos of An Phụng Village. During a brutal raid in the dry season of 1970, Phương's grandparents and their four children were shot. Phương's father was severely injured, surviving only because he lay hidden under two corpses. He was twelve years old.

Duy surfaced from the house with coffee. Phương raised her head to look at him. To both, it seemed a fragile bond had snapped. The portrait of Duy's grandfather. The soldier in Vũ Thiên's photo. An Phụng Village in the bloody raid. Everything was interconnected, woven into a spider's web.

***

IN THE REAL WORLD, IT WASN'T uncommon for people to share similar faces. The soldier in Vũ Thiên's photo might have been Duy's grandfather, but it could just as easily have been someone else. Nevertheless, their uncanny resemblance troubled Phương deeply. She clung to the hope that it was just coincidence. She asked a friend at the Archive Center to search for documents related to the Scorpion Campaign of 1970, and cross-referenced those documents with the memorabilia from Duy's family.

Phương's friend sent over the results the following week: the full name, birthdate, military rank, even the unit number—and all the information matched. Duy's grandfather was the soldier who participated in the raid at An Phụng—the man in Vũ Thiên's photo wearing the camouflage uniform with a gun slung over his shoulder. Behind him, a village on fire, the sunset bleeding crimson across the sky. There were few documents about the event, the friend added, though some witnesses claimed that while some soldiers had deliberately committed the massacre, others had tried to protect the innocent. Unfortunately, there was no proof.

Phương made her way home. It seemed as if her father's solemn eyes were watching her from the altar.

Her father had died at forty-five following surgery. Phương was just eight. All his life, he rarely spoke of his past, how he grew up poor, all those killed during the war, the heart-wrenching separations. One time, while visiting their hometown to honor family graves, Phương asked why the tombstones of her grandparents and other relatives, along with many from the village, bore the same date. Phương's father stayed silent for a long time before he said, "Maybe when you're older, you'll understand."

Only now, looking back, did Phương realize the ghosts of war would never stop haunting people's lives.

***

THE BROKEN FRAGMENTS OF THEIR LIVES left deep wounds wherever they went. On very quiet nights, the grandmother heard Duy's guitar from upstairs, and maybe it reminded her of an off-key melody from a previous life, back when her youngest child left the university, torn between wanting to stay and wanting to leave, because he didn't know where history might take him.

Maybe seeing her grandson wandering alone made the old woman's heart clench. Once Phương was no longer part of this world, Duy's grandmother would no longer be by his side, and Duy would lose the final tie to his homeland.

"What's going on between you two?" his grandmother asked.

"It's nothing, Grandma," Duy replied, gently squeezing her knobby hand. "We're just really busy these days. And I only have a few months left before this joint project in Vietnam ends."

"And after that?"

The rain outstayed its welcome, soaking the city this late afternoon. Phương once said that if the rain could wash away everything, maybe we could all find peace. For the third generation after the war, what was left behind wasn't anger or bitterness, but an enduring sorrow that echoed from the heart.

***

DURING THE DRY SEASON OF 1970, amid the large-scale Scorpion campaign, a mixed regiment armed with overpowering weapons was ordered to land in An Phụng Village, where the Vietcong were suspected of hiding. They left at dusk after the first day of fighting, leaving behind a village burned to ashes and soaked in blood. From his vantage point, Vũ Thiên captured the scene. The photo, later published in a journal, sparked a tidal wave of antiwar protests. Many years later, Vũ Thiên still heard gunfire and saw human corpses in his dreams; the horrifying scenes kept replaying in Vũ Thiên's mind in slow motion.

Phương had written a private message on the postcard and inserted it into the book she wanted autographed. She sought information about a soldier who participated in that raid on her father's home in the 1970s, suspecting a connection to her current boyfriend.

Vũ Thiên looked at the photo thoughtfully. Each face seemed to silently gaze back at him. Whether they had died or were still living, these people had left their mark on the world in some personal way—a smile, gestures of bravery or cruelty, empathy or callous disregard. Throughout the war, Vũ Thiên had fulfilled his duty as a reporter by bearing witness, ensuring that events were not forgotten. For him, the past was already a closed book, even if for others the echoes of war continued on. Vũ Thiên was an artist; he understood what the young woman sought in his photo.

On another afternoon, after the rain had stopped, Phương returned to Vũ Thiên's house.

"I don't know what to say," the photographer said. His eyes looked sad as he asked his wife to push his wheelchair up to the window, so he could see the lilacs getting wet in the rain.

"I'm sorry to trouble you both," Phương said, her voice straining. "My father is dead, and all his fathers before him. How can we learn from the past if we don't even know how we got here?"

"I know it's been hard on both of you," Vũ Thiên's wife said softly.

Phương nodded, wanting to cry. Duy was leaving Vietnam tomorrow, and he wanted to see Phương one last time, even though he knew they had nothing left to say to each other. Had it not been for the incident, they might already be thinking about wedding photos in Thiên An.

Vũ Thiên turned to look at his wife. She held back a sigh, then carefully opened the locked drawer and took out a velvet-wrapped box. He looked at the faded box as though he were reuniting with an old friend and, after some time passed, he said to Phương, "This is what I witnessed that day—dead bodies, houses burning, all the ways the innocent can be killed by men. But there were soldiers who didn't follow orders, and they tried saving the wounded, protecting women and children from the massacre. I never published these photos because I thought it would only hurt more and divide people. But feel free to take a look inside if you think it will help you understand."

Vũ Thiên's wife wheeled him out of the room, leaving Phương alone. She looked at the box, unsure of how she should feel. The room was so quiet she heard lilac petals landing on the porch outside.

When Vũ Thiên returned to the room after Phương had left, the photographer found the box untouched. She hadn't opened it. Maybe she found whatever it was she needed to understand, in this city, on this afternoon, in that silent moment when the rain finally ceased.

—*Translated by Cab Tran & Hoàng Phượng Mai*

5A, 5B, DEST: SGN

—Andrew Lam—

HE TOUCHED HER, BARELY A TAP on the arm, and startled her. She turned from her window. So absorbed with the golden surface of the sea below she hadn't heard the flight attendant's solicitation.

"Ma'am, some more champagne?"

"Ah! So sorry. Please. A little more."

They were flying business class, secured, each in their own world. Passengers were listening to their music, or working on their laptops, or reading, and the atmosphere was at once elegant and lethargic.

But he recognized her accent, somewhere between California, Paris and Sài Gòn.

"I'll have some too," he volunteered. He had been drinking scotch. The attendant handed him a flute and he raised it to his seat companion. "Well, here's to the lovely sea!"

"Yes, to the sea," she raised her flute but made no gesture to clink his. She sipped politely, then turned once more to her sea below. The plane quietly hummed.

When he had boarded at Narita she was already there at 5C, leafing through an old issue of *National Geographic*. Between them a laconic concord, one that might have lasted for the duration, all the way to Hồ Chí Minh City, or Sài Gòn once upon a time, if he hadn't tapped her on the arm.

But now—now with several shots of scotch in him, he wanted to talk. No, he *needed* to talk. She, with her guarded air, however, presented a challenge.

He emptied his glass and cleared his throat. "*Có phải cô là người Việt kiều?*" he asked, a gambit—You must be a Vietnamese expat?

She looked at him and smiled. "Wow, you speak Vietnamese!" In a southern Vietnamese accent, she said, "*Việt kiều,*" and chuckled as if she hadn't thought about it herself.

"First time back?" he asked.

"First time," she said at length as if measuring the weight of its meaning. "Yes . . . But how did you know?"

"You seemed nervous," he smiled. "You've been reading the *National Geographic* for at least two hours and that mag is not known for its literary prowess."

She laughed. "Very perceptive," she said. "And a polyglot."

"Hardly. You speak French and English. You are too."

"But you don't have to. People like me, we learn another language to survive."

"I see. I have a few Việt kiều friends," he offered. "I know about their worries. But things have changed quite a bit as you may already know." Then through his American accent he added, "*Tất cả là tốt đẹp.*" All is good and beautiful.

"I doubt that," she said. A neutral and measured voice. "*Có cái đẹp, có cái xấu.*" There's good, there's bad.

A wrong thing to say, he realized almost immediately. In his line of work, it helps to act fast and redirect the flow. "You're right, of course," he said with sympathy. "There's so much that country needs to do in order to move forward." Then he changed the subject. "It's just that it's a vast improvement since I was a foreign exchange student there a dozen years ago in Hà Nội."

She stayed muted.

"May I ask if you're on vacation, or is it business?" he tentatively asked.

"My oldest son," she answered. "He's an architect in Sài Gòn working on a big construction project. He invited me. Plus I donated to an organization that protects and educates poor and at-risk young women. So I plan to see how they're doing."

She leaned forward and, with long, elegant fingers, straightened the back of her silk blouse. Her shoulder-length hair streaked with gray. Her perfume, the smell of intricate oils, water lilies and lady apples, reached his nostrils and his childhood memories surged—summer afternoons in the garden, a misty spray from a hose, the cheerful melody from an ice cream truck, and the sounds of his father's laughter.

Here was someone he imagined Thúy Lê would eventually grow into. Gray hair came but the beauty stayed, or rather, it was fading at its own leisure. He could easily see his seating companion as a young woman riding her bicycle along tree-lined boulevards in her white *áo dài* on the way to school. With those sparkling eyes and dimples, many heads must have turned.

"And you?" she asked. "Where are you from? Your Vietnamese, it's very good by the way. Even got a northern accent."

"Boston. Born and bred, but not the stuck-up, blue-blood kind," he said.

"Boston!" she said. "My second son is at Harvard right now, a political science major. He's thinking of going into law."

"Wow, Harvard man. I'm impressed. Only made it to Yale myself."

"Oh! What coincidence," she said, eyes widened. "Tommy, the one inviting me, he goes there! I mean, went there. You're alumni! I'll introduce you when we land."

"Wow," he said. He shouldn't have lied, a bad habit, but now it worked, hadn't it? He felt as if she were looking at him with new eyes, this new connection with her son. "I can't believe you're old enough to have children in college, let alone architects and lawyers."

She gave a little laugh. "Believe it, young man. I'm old. Like the old lady and the sea."

"Hardly," he said. "Hemingway would have retitled his master-piece as 'The Eternal Maiden and the Sea' if he wrote about you." Which made her laugh. "But you must be very proud. I mean, with such smart children," he added.

She studied her flute against sunlight. She hadn't sipped much since the second pouring. She was drinking now. "Sorry," she said. "I didn't mean to boast. What about you? What do you do? How did someone from Boston end up in Hà Nội?"

He looked at his Rolex: A good three hours from the destination. "It's too long a story," he feigned. "A story of broken romance, I mean. I don't want to bore you."

"Oh!" she said, sounding suddenly mischievous. "I don't mind, I love a good romance. Absolutely."

She started to arrange herself so that she could better face him, her back against the window, a pillow tugged between her and the armrest, the blanket on her lap. "I promise to not look at the boring *National Geographic* again if you tell your story. You talk. I listen."

"Ok," he said, matching her enthusiasm. "Not sure how good, but it's a sad one. And remember, don't say I didn't warn you." Then he raised his near empty glass above his head and shook it so as to catch the stewardess's attention. "Miss, we need a refill for the road."

Years ago, a young foreign student fell in love with a young Vietnamese woman in Hà Nội. The young man first saw the city as if in a dream; he had come with few expectations. But there he was, among moss-covered villas and sputtering motorbikes and squatting old men with unfiltered cigarettes dangling from their mouths, the languid city drenched in sunlight and the quiet nights lit by lamp lights and the old ballads sang through open windows from which incense smoke wafted. It was all like a mist on which he drifted, unmoored.

But then there was that winter, which was unexpectedly cold. No snow but the cold, through the humid air, got to the bones, the marrow. A morning in late November and he saw her in the lecture hall. He watched in fascination as the young woman rubbed her hands together. Wasn't it that moment, when she raised her hands to her mouth to breathe warm air through cupped fingers, that she stole his heart?

He knew it the way he knew he would always love raw oysters that first time he swallowed one at seven, that cool, lemony cool texture slithering down his throat leaving a salty-sweet aftertaste. Likewise, her hands rubbing in that cold morning sparked the amber into a fire in his heart.

"I hadn't fallen in love with anyone in high school, nor the two years in college, for that matter. Crushes, sure, and a few fell in love with me. But in my junior year in Hà Nội, of all places, love wrestled and pinned me to the ground, as the Vietnamese expression goes."

Why Vietnam? Maybe he always wanted to visit the place that haunted his father. Maybe he just needed to get away from stuffy Boston. In any case when the country opened up after the trade embargo was lifted, and he went in, backpacking first then he applied for the exchange program the next year. His father experienced horror in 'Nam but him? "I guess I found romance instead."

"She must have been very beautiful," the woman said.

"Oh yeah. Still is, I'm sure," he said. "Thúy Lê was so different. There was, I don't know, an inner peace, a stillness in her, and it made her extraordinarily beautiful. All the boys, and I think, some of the teachers, too, had crushes on her. But *I* courted her. I asked her to teach me Vietnamese in exchange for English lessons. A good bargain, there were very few foreign students at that time. She'd wanted to improve her language skill. She was ambitious. *And* she laughed at all my stupid jokes."

The woman laughed, too. "Well, humor's important."

But he was in love with the city too, and couldn't separate the love affairs from that delicious sense of displacement. How to describe the strangeness of living in a city that was shrouded in shadows after sundown and in many of its houses oil lamps and candles lit up crowded rooms; a barely lit city, cigarettes dangling from skinny old men talking, leaning over balconies. So much beauty in the austere life. In memories, he saw a stained tea thermos and a few cups, a cassette deck, shadows flitting against whitewash walls, a writing desk, a bed with a thin blanket and two pillows; his studio apartment. In memories, too, as in a still life, through an open window, he saw an old man mumbling prayers to the dead as he held a candle in front on his ancestral altar through an open window. On the street a few bicycles with burning joss sticks stuck in their wheel's pokes served as headlights as they rolled down near an empty street, and incense wafted air turned the entire city into a Buddhist temple. Somewhere in another apartment, a mother sang an old wistful lullaby to calm her crying baby. Elsewhere, an argument. How, indeed, to talk about that feeling of being so out of your elements, and yet it felt like swimming in some mysterious water?

It all still held him captive despite the years. The way they slow danced to folk music with the flickering oil lamp in his studio when the electricity was out, which was often—the monochord zither echoing nostalgically from an old cassette deck—and their shadows on the wall, and the furtive movement of the mosquito net in the night breeze, the window opened to the dark streets. So vivid were these flashbacks that he sometimes referred to it as post-romantic stress syndrome. But it sounded pretentious, he now told his seating companion, since it was his father who fought in that war and experienced trauma.

Then it all ended. Theirs, after all, was a coveted romance: On and off, they managed to live together for almost a year in his small apartment by Hoàn Kiếm Lake, hiding the fact from the authorities. Her two roommates lied for her. It was illegal back then to visit foreigners' homes overnight, and her parents, who lived in Thái Bình, didn't know. "She was really afraid of what her parents might do if they'd found out. That was our fight. She kept trying to hide us. I kept complaining of the secretive, restrictive Vietnamese ways. I'm afraid I said some mean things."

That and how Thúy Lê aggravated him by failing to tell him that she loved him each time he confessed his love. She often would just blush and turn away or say nothing. The last time he had said this, she'd wept. Then she said it: "I love you, too, Mark, very much."

That was the only time she ever said it, but the way she said it, it broke his heart. "What's wrong?" he'd asked, but she hid her face in his chest and sobbed. He came home the next day to find all of her belongings gone. She left no trace. She was back in Thái Bình somewhere and her roommates were no help. He didn't know where to find her.

"I should have said I wanted to marry her," he said presently, coming out of a trance. "Maybe that's what she wanted. But after what happened with my parents—their messy divorce—I wasn't too keen on it. I was too young, besides. I mean I was going to get my MBA after graduating. I didn't give her clear options. And I was leaving, going back to the States in a few months so I couldn't promise her anything. We didn't discuss it." What he meant to say was he could only see the world through his eyes, and failed to see what she saw, but he didn't say it out loud, this flaw: his cowardice, his centrality.

The woman said nothing but he could tell she was listening the way she looked at him; she was giving him permission. "So a few months after classes ended, and having failed to find her, my visa ran out. I came home, got my history degree, then got my MBA right after. Now, I'm based in Tokyo selling cosmetic products to wealthy Southeast Asians. I go to Vietnam often, but I've more or less stopped looking for her. I was told she was married and living in Paris. I mean, I have a Japanese girlfriend now."

The woman nodded.

"But then last week," he said. He paused to take a sip of the scotch. "... Last week, the phone rang. It was Thúy Lê. She said 'Mark?' and just like that, my heart nearly stopped. It felt like nothing had changed."

They didn't talk long. Indeed, she had been married and living in Paris, but got divorced last year. She said very little about it, but she was now living in Sài Gòn with her child. She met a mutual friend of theirs who gave her his number. She wanted to see him again.

"She said she had something to tell me," he said. His friend took a picture of mother and son. Her son, he said, looked a lot like him at that age.

"You're still very much in love with her," his seating companion said, but it was not a question.

He was going to deny it. But he looked at her. "I never stopped," he barely managed as tears brimmed in his eyes. True, he no longer searched for her, but he couldn't help being reminded of Thúy Lê each time he went to Vietnam on business trips. The nape of a slender neck in an open window, the peeling laughter of a young woman in a candle-lit restaurant, the silhouette of a devout worshipper burning incense in the Buddhist temple's hall—all led to memories of his first love. "I think Thúy Lê still loves me, too. But I don't know what to do. Michiko . . . . As open as we are to one another, I never told Michiko about the phone call. The photo. Thúy Lê is waiting for me with her little boy at the airport."

The woman nodded. Silence slowly reasserted itself. He lifted his glass but his hand shook. He put the flute back down and smiled apologetically while his seating companion studied him. "Well," she said finally, her tone upbeat. "It's a good story. I see now why you speak Vietnamese so well. But I can tell you that it's not a sad story. It's an unfinished story. And you deserve cold champagne, I think." She made a sign to the stewardess who was walking down the aisle with a tray of drinks. "I'm having some more, too."

"Thúy Lê's little boy's almost ten. His name is Laurent. She wouldn't tell me much but I couldn't help wondering if . . ." he said before stopping himself. "No," he said quickly, "better not get ahead of myself."

She handed him a tissue from her purse. "Thank you," he said. "You've been very kind to listen. I feel much better. *Cám ơn cô.*"

"*Không có chi,*" she smiled and briefly rested her hand on his wrist, but the sadness remained in her eyes. "It makes me feel better too. I'm glad to know that a happy ending is waiting at our destination."

He wanted to believe her. But he didn't dare envision it. He didn't want to think how the story would end and what it entailed. "Okay," he said and pretended to be relaxed and stretched his arms above his shoulders. "Enough about me. Now, we're getting to *your* story."

"My story?"

They were flying toward towering cumuli, a huge forest of luminous forms, and light streaked and streamed in from the windows to set faces ablaze. A few passengers pulled down their windows. "I bet you left on the first wave," he said, squinting a little to read her face.

"First wave? Ah, I see. Plane and helicopter people, right? Before the communist tanks rolled into Sài Gòn? No. No such luck. Boat person, I'm afraid. More like second wave. It would have been . . . ." She took a sideways glance out the window, her hand shading over her eyes. "Do you mind if I tell you later, when I'm ready?"

"Of course not," he said quickly. He knew of Vietnam's troubles, of course, its past horrors—refugees, boat people, reeducation camps. But the country he went to on regular business trips was one with shiny high rises and cyber cafes and neon-lit billboards selling Toyota and Coca-Cola and Tiger Beer. It didn't occur to him, considering her comportment, her slight French accent, her excellent English, that she was someone who might have experienced the worst of the Cold War era. It came to him then why she'd been intensely studying that sea.

"You don't have to," he said. "I mean if you don't feel comfortable, we can talk about . . ."

"No, no," she said, and he could see that she was trembling. But she gathered herself. "It's all right. It's only fair. I will give an abbreviated version."

The stewardess placed two small plates of mixed nuts on their trays and he was glad he had something to munch on so as to not look at her.

"After the war ended, my husband and I stayed, thinking that young, apolitical academics wouldn't be affected under the new regime," she said after taking a sip of the champagne. "Like you, I taught English. My father also taught it. He practiced it with Graham Greene, in fact, when Greene was living in Sài Gòn and working on that famous novel. My husband taught math. But soon after the war, we lost our jobs. The new government confiscated our house and sent a few of our friends to reeducation camps. We would be next, we figured, so we left by boat about a year after the war ended. Two boats actually, because there wasn't enough space in the first." She drank a little bit more champagne and gathered herself. "So my husband took our oldest daughter and left. He was always too logical. He wanted to make sure the statistics were in our favor –that we have a better chance at surviving. I was very mad at him and said some mean things. A week later I took Tommy and left with my cousin's family. I was pregnant with Phillip, my second son. The whole time, I prayed and I prayed. We made it to the Philippines. They ... didn't. No news. Nothing. An entire boat, over a hundred people, gone."

It felt as if they were suspended high above the earth, above the clouds, and not moving forward at all. He remained very quiet. He felt a little stupid, having gone on and on about his broken romance. "I'm really sorry," he said finally. "How awful."

"It happened a long time ago," she sighed. "Even so, my mind plays tricks on me. I sometimes fantasize that my husband is raising my daughter in another country—that he is mad at me for things that I said and decided not to find me, find us. Isn't that crazy?"

"No, not at all," he offered. "How else would we go on, I mean, if we don't invent something to hope for?"

She nodded and glanced briefly out the window. "When we were drifting, I missed the simplest things: the sounds of children's laughter, a cold drink, anything on the radio besides static," she said. But she straightened herself. Her voice was lighter, upbeat. "But that's an old story. I survived. My sons survived. I remarried. We went on."

"And now—now, you're coming home, after so many years."

"Now I'm going for a *visit* after three decades," she corrected him. "I also donated to an orphanage in the Mekong Delta, and shelters for returning trafficked victims. And I really want to see them, all those vulnerable, at-risk children."

He'd flown over this ocean many times, but it had never before taken on an ominous aspect. With closed eyes, he could see the woman and her son jostling for space on one of those decrepit, crowded fishing boats bobbing on the water, no land in sight. Then he imagined Thúy Lê, pregnant and alone. He imagined her taking the place of the older woman instead on that boat. He clenched his fist and shut his eyes for fear of crying—it came to him as a shock that his love had such depth.

"I didn't go to Yale," he said suddenly. "I don't know why I lied."

"Oh!" said the woman, surprised, and studied his face. But she quickly recovered. "Hey! that's okay," she offered and as if to prove it, she reached out to pat his hand and padded it repeatedly. He held it.

"We're screw-ups. My dad—me," he barely managed to say before he covered his face in his palm and wept. "I lied a lot to Thúy Lê. Maybe I knew I wasn't ready for marriage but I talked about the future in such a sure ways. Maybe that was why . . ."

The woman studied him. He still hadn't let go of her hand. "Listen," she whispered. "If there's one thing I understand well, it's how rare second chances really are. To fall in love with someone and have that love reciprocated, you're already blessed. To lose it and get another chance, well, you must act on it. It's no good for anyone involved if you don't."

He nodded repeatedly with his eyes shut, lest he'd embarrass himself by crying again. He continued to grip the woman's hand, however, as she talked, and only let go when he heard the sounds of a cart with its clinking bottles and squeaking wheels going up the aisle.

It was near dusk outside, and behind the clouds, the sun was crimson red. A warm glow spread inside the cabin, and the aromas of baked bread and grilled meat permeated the air. It was almost time for dinner. His stomach growled.

"You okay now?" She handed him another tissue.

"Yes," he smiled meekly at her. "You've been so kind. And you? Are you okay?"

"I'm fine," the woman sniffed, wiping her eyes. He hadn't realized that she'd been crying, too. "But a little drunk. Usually, I don't drink more than one or two glasses before dinner. But I don't even know if it's breakfast or lunch or what, back in San Francisco."

"Well," he deadpanned, "I hate to tell you this, but San Francisco's pretty far behind." She looked at him and laughed. "And," she added, "apparently, so is Tokyo."

The pilot's low, authoritative voice came on the loudspeaker, announcing the remaining time of their flight. "The humidity in Hồ Chí Minh City is 85 percent and the temperature 30.5 Celsius.

That's a cool 87 degrees Fahrenheit. I'll update as we near our destination." There was a collective groan in the cabin, followed by sporadic laughter.

"God," said the woman, shaking her head. "I don't know if I can take that heat." He laughed. But she looked at him. "You know," she said, her voice earnest. "I'm not afraid of the past. I made my peace. It's going back to a place that's gone on without me—that's a little scary. So many friends and relatives have scattered. I have more relatives in California and Paris than in Vietnam."

"Well, I have more friends in Sài Gòn and Hà Nội and Tokyo than I do in Boston. So welcome to the twenty-first century."

She laughed.

"We haven't been properly introduced," he offered. "My name is Mark. Mark Alexander. I went to Northwestern. An average student but a smart mouth. And I can show you around if Tommy's too busy working," he offered. "I know a great *phở* noodle soup place on the old Pasteur Street."

"I'm Phương-Anh Harris. But you call me Anne, easier on the tongue. And that's very sweet of you." Her smile was warm, but he wasn't sure if she was entirely convinced of his sincerity.

"Seriously," he said. He needed her to believe him. He wanted to make her happy, too. For he could see now what was at the destination: amid the milling, sweating crowd at the arrival gate, a woman in a green *áo dài* holding the hand of a shy, brown-haired boy in school uniform as she anxiously scanned the faces of arriving passengers. He felt breathless with anticipation. "What can I tell you—what can I do to make you feel more at ease?" he said. "Please—please ask me for anything."

Laws Of Motion

—Barbara Tran—

I LIVED FOR A TIME IN a small town in Michigan where people have neither black shoes nor black dogs. Buff is preferable in dogs, brown is acceptable. In shoes, brown is more common, as it's more practical, that is, can be worn appropriately in all seasons. There are two standards: oxford and loafer, Labrador and Golden. With choices limited to two, people are spared from surprise. As surprise can induce anxiety, it would be inconsiderate to be surprising.

Fran and her husband of three and a half years, Mr. Baker, adopted me. I was ten. This was surprising. Not my age, but the fact of me. And of my adoption. Not surprising to the Church. It was the Church that had encouraged the congregation to bring some of us into their fold. But *very* surprising to the rest of the Bakers. And to the Jansens, Fran's family.

Surprising, too, to put it tactfully, to the neighbors who were forced into the uncomfortable position of making small talk about— and with—the new arrival. It's not that the neighbors disagreed with the Church. In principle. They agreed that *someone* should save the children. But they preferred that that someone be someone they wouldn't have to make small talk with at the bank or at Diane's coffee shop on Sunday morning after Mass, someone who wouldn't prattle on endlessly about the challenges, the ongoing, unforeseen needs of a saved child. Someone who wouldn't confront them, as Fran did, with options for their own contributions toward broadening a saved child's life: teaching the child the game of tennis or about the world of broadcasting, taking the child to the carnival, or on a trip where they could introduce the child to the breeziness of floating on a lake in an inner tube.

Every option involved sacrifice on their part. And so it was, from the day of my arrival, I was considered inconsiderate. I had upset things. I had upset people. All before I was taught the words for: "Thank you for the Paczkis," or "Yes, I like snow."

Once again, inconsiderate of me. I didn't know how to respond appropriately to simple social niceties. I left the verbal equivalent of a hand extended (albeit begrudgingly so) hanging. I was the rude one. They went through the motions. The least I could do was to reciprocate with a word or two in their language. Inconsiderate.

This is not to say that I understood my transgressions from the day of my arrival. Far from it. I was a child after all, and busy thinking about childish things, such as how all mothers should be taught to prepare something other than ham from a can opened with a key, served with a side of soggy green beans (also from a can, this one without a key) prior to their being allowed to bring a child home. Anything else is cruelty.

Other cruelties: Sunshine yellow pants and polyester shirts in colors and patterns that (I, again, learned later) belonged in an American Independence Day display. It was almost good enough to be a ploy: Fran and Mr. Baker using visually (definitely not fire) repellent clothing to keep the other children away from me, so they could enjoy my undivided attention. This musing of mine was always short-lived. And then, I'd have to laugh, the logic being laughable. The other children needed no encouragement to stay away, and Fran had thought so far as "saving" a child but had not foreseen what said "saved" child's losses might look like. She couldn't predict my inconsolable palate, my insatiable longing for fermented anchovies, pineapple with chilis. She had no idea that in my ear—for years—would play that language I could no longer speak.

Another lesson I learned early on: when one is saved, one is expected to show gratitude. One is expected to *be* grateful. One is expected to believe. I did not. I acted the part but remained a non-believer. I wanted to believe. I wanted to be a believer. Fran was a believer. She believed in all things good. It did not hurt her. Instead, the world grew a protective layer around her, as if acknowledging her for the fragile flower she was. Mr. Baker recognized her too, and put a slate roof over head, and a knee-high, white fence and blush peonies around her yard. He made sure that what she believed came true: I was her daughter. Fran believed that, and believed no one would question it. Incredibly, no one did, not to her face or mine. At least not explicitly. Not while she was alive.

But remember, buff or brown, Lab or Golden. My hair is black, my skin brown. These were not amongst the choices. This went against the rules. If you go against the rules, it is presumed that you care not what society thinks, that you are thumbing your nose. If you thumb your nose, you cannot expect to be included. I did not expect to be chosen for dodgeball or invited to Melissa's sleepover. I resorted to more creative ways of entertaining myself.

In my thirteenth year, to Fran's flat-lipped disappointment, I convinced a classmate's older brother to ink my skin various shades of green and blue. It was an obvious way of ushering the discussion away from my inherited looks to my chosen ones. I dyed my hair fuchsia, then strawberry. It worked for me. I liked it. No one could predict what new design would adorn which body part, or what color my hair would be next. There was no longer a single dividing line. I could paint a new one any time, in my latest color of choice. I could decide what part of me people would stare at. I could make them stare more. I could be the talk of the town for $3.99.

It was as Fran was succumbing to lung cancer that I saw the horizon's edge. With Fran by his side, Mr. Baker could look at me as his daughter. Without Fran, he was terrified of me. He loved me. In his hands-off, polite-talk-at-dinner kind of way. But he was terrified. He wanted a daughter who could squeeze into a denim mini on Friday night, be grounded on Saturday, and descend the stairs, smiling demurely in a floral frock, in time for church on Sunday.

I wasn't that girl. And newly seventeen, I was about to be without my Fran, the only one whose disappointment in me couldn't last three minutes before she'd offer me a dry corn muffin or to braid my newly peacock-blue hair.

It happened on a Tuesday. She lay on a cot in the dining room, tubes plugging her nose, the beginning of home hospice care. I holed up in my frilly bedroom. I pinched the undersides of my arms. I wished I had asked for a black dog instead of a black bike for my birthday. I phoned my friend Benny. I tried to believe he could help me. In his car, I focused on the houses ripping past. Then, the odd light in the tunnel to Windsor. Benny was excited about partying on the other side of the border. I was consumed with finding a way to keep going. We stopped for gas, and Benny went in for cheese curls. I wrenched the keys and started the car. I put my weight on the gas pedal and like a sparkler in a child's hand swirled into the night. I thought of Mr. Mallow in Physics class, looking me in the eye and saying, "An object in motion will stay in motion, unless an unbalanced force acts upon it."

I never went back. I don't know how Benny got home. Or when or if he did. I called Mr. Baker, but our neighbor Mrs. Meijer answered. She apologized, *Dear girl,* for the loss of my mother and said my father would be home soon. He was in town, taking care of the arrangements. I drove myself to the next gas station, got out, and teared up. Smeared the mascara further around my eyes, so it looked more like a statement than a breakdown. By the pumps, someone was arguing with someone else. I caught none of what it was about. What I did hear was: "Where are you even from?" The response, if there was one, fell beyond my earshot.

I climbed back in the car and headed east. East until the sun came back up. East until I hit a different Great Lake. East until I was too tired to drive and got out and sat on a curb, elbows on thighs, palms desperately attempting to contain thoughts.

From under my hands, I heard jingling. An old Lab, milk chocolate brown, barrel-shaped, faded at the muzzle and paws. Tail, swish, swish, swishing. Just before reaching me, the dog sat. A hind foot reached forward and lashed at an ear with a degree of vigor that was surprising given the dog's plodding pace. Just as suddenly, the foot stopped its attack and plopped back down to the sidewalk. The dog's human was ready to move on and pulled at the fraying leash, but the dog melted into a puddle right there in the middle of the sidewalk.

In Mr. Mallow's class I'd wondered but never asked, "Am I the object in motion or the unbalanced force?"

As I sat on the curb, the answer grew obvious. I would get back in Benny's car. I would drive toward the tall buildings. I would drive toward the multitude of lights, the rush and noise.

Fran or no Fran, I'd been in motion all my life. No force, balanced or unbalanced, would stop me.

The Immolation

—Viet Thanh Nguyen—

THE DAY AFTER THE FUNERAL, Lộc and I rode our ten-speeds toward the reservoir, each of us steering with one hand and swinging baseball bats with the other. It felt good to take off a car's mirror or put a solid dent in someone's tin mailbox or nudge a kid off a skateboard. Lộc was angrier than usual, though, and when he saw Mandy Stein on her roller skates, Mandy who had turned him down flat for a dance at the spring mixer, he swung hard with the bat as he passed her and from a dozen feet behind I could hear the solid smack of wood on her ass like a hand slapping water.

"You son-of-a-bitch!" she screamed as I biked by, my black overcoat flapping in the wind. She was on her hands and knees, knocked off her feet from the blow, and she was starting to cry. "You freaks!"

I gave her the finger over my shoulder. Mandy was already a bit on the heavy side, and on her hands and knees she looked vaguely hippolike. Why Lộc asked her to dance, of all people, I just didn't understand.

We left her behind, Lộc going much faster than me. Eventually I caught up with him at the reservoir, a pool of water the color of cement, located in the middle of town and shored by sidewalks and barbed wire fences. I don't think anyone ever dreamed of drinking from the reservoir, but at least it did its job, which was to provide for things like fire hydrants.

Lộc sat on the edge of the concrete bank and dangled his feet over the water. I sat down next to him because there was nowhere else to sit that didn't seem rude. I was fourteen years old and I had no idea what someone should say to somebody else, even his best friend, when his father had just killed himself. Lộc took out a pack of cigarettes and offered me one and we started to smoke. I was glad I had learned to smoke because it allowed me to say nothing in critical moments just like this.

"My dad," Lộc said suddenly, cutting right through my fresh smoke and not giving me the chance to enjoy it, "is one fucked up asshole."

"Was," I muttered. I was already showing that precision that would suit me so well as a teacher. "Anyway, don't speak ill of the dead."

"Okay," he said, exhaling in my direction. "You're one fucked up asshole."

"I guess I am," I said, hoping to make him feel better. "That's what my dad says too."

Lộc sat silent for a few moments. From the streak of black mascara that was starting to leak from the corner of his eye, I could tell he was suffering. I knew he wanted to say something, and because he had three weeks of worry and anger and pain coiled up inside of him, I thought it would be something violent, and so when he did finally say something, the softness of it surprised me.

"Look at what he left me," he said, reaching into the pocket of his sweatshirt.

I looked at what he put in my hand. A fragment of a scorched driver's license and a set of dental X-rays. Mr. Bùi's X-rayed teeth were crooked and white like the Christmas lights he put up every year on the eaves of his house because his kids asked for them.

After that, we didn't speak anymore. We just watched the sun set over the shoebox homes that lined the reservoir. Smog obscured the sun, and as a result we could look directly into the sun's light, and we saw its rounded head glowing rich and warm like the tip of God's cigarette, shrouded in smoke.

That evening, we sat in his dark room listening to Joy Division, both of us with cigarettes and Lộc with a can of Aqua Net in his lap. We stocked Aqua Net like six packs of Coke, because it took a lot of hairspray to keep up a head of spiked hair. When Ian Curtis sang our favorite line—"Love, love will tear us apart, again"—Lộc lit a stream of Aqua Net with the tip of his cigarette, still in his mouth, and I saw his face enveloped briefly by a burning cloud.

"That was cool," he said, brushing away the tips of his burnt eyebrows.

"Here," I said, speaking tight-lipped around my cigarette. I thought I might look a little like David Bowie. "I want to try."

"No way, José. You're going to blow your face off."

"Oh, come on," I said. Maybe I whined. I had the tendency to whine back then, and Lộc had the tendency to keep things away from me like a big brother.

"Where do you think fire comes from?" he asked, ignoring me.

"What do you mean, where does it come from?"

"It doesn't just happen. Something makes it start."

"It's friction," I said after a while. I bumped my head against the wall to the beat of the music for a few seconds more while I thought. "Fire happens when things start rubbing together real fast."

"Exactly."

He reached underneath his bed and pulled out his journal, a converted chem lab notebook. The pages inside were covered with his poems and notes, and pasted with torn-out magazine pictures of far away places like Borneo. There were also torn-out pictures of impossibly stunning looking people. They weren't Charlie's Angels or anything like that, but people with spiked hair and pierced lips and body tattoos, from places with exotic natives like Los Angeles.

"What is in the match?" Lộc muttered, scribbling in his notebook. "What is in the spark that starts the fire?"

That was the way Lộc thought, like a kid, always asking questions. Most kids stop after a few questions, tired of asking. As a teacher, I measure kids by how many questions they ask before they finally give up and go back to the daily grind of their coloring books and Lego blocks. But every few years a kid will come into my class and remind me of Lộc, the kid with a constant stream of questions. He stops asking questions not because he has given up on the ultimate answer but because he has given up on me. Then he will turn away from me and walk to the window and look outside, ignoring the crayons and the finger paints the other kids offer him, and for a while he will be the only person in the room for me.

It was the summer of pushing our limits with our parents, and so after midnight we crept out the window and rode our bikes downtown, looking for fun and weed. We had some cash because of the odd jobs we did that summer. Where we lived wasn't the kind of suburb you see in Hollywood movies with wide quiet streets and no sidewalks. Parents around here gave their kids weekly allowances in the form of coins, and Lộc and I weren't even that lucky. Our parents had never heard of such a thing as allowances, and when I suggested to my father that perhaps he might give me some money for the chores I did, he said, "Fine. I'll just deduct that dollar from the twenty dollars I spend every week feeding and clothing your dumb ass. Now you owe me nineteen dollars a week. And get a haircut and look like a normal person. You look like a goddamn communist." So I spray painted "My dad is a jerk" on the side of Edie's Pawn Shop while Lộc watched the street. When I finished, he turned around and looked at my work, written in neat red cursive. Then he shook his own can of spray paint and scrawled directly underneath, "Future victim of society."

"Now look how it's done, for God's sake," he said, shoving me out into the street to guard for cops. I watched over my shoulder as he sprayed his message with medieval-like characters: "Fuel + Air + Heat = Fire." At the end of it, he put a skull and crossbones framed by a wreath of fire for a finishing touch.

We ran into the alley next to Edie's and crouched behind a dumpster. Lộc gripped the spray paint can like a grenade and stared straight ahead.

"See how it's done?" he said. "It can be like poetry."

"I don't see what's wrong with what I wrote," I replied.

"It's not poetry, it's not even graffiti," he snarled. "It's therapy."

"Well, my dad *is* a jerk," I snapped back, clutching my can to my stomach like a wounded animal. "That's the truth."

"Sure it is, Johnny Rotten." He held the can to his lips like a mike and whisper-screamed, "My dad is an asshole! My dad is an asshole! Oi!"

That broke us up for a while. After we stopped laughing, Lộc got the look in his eye again, the one that said he was starting to think with a capital T.

"You think fire comes from wood or coal or oil or whatever," he said. "But that's not so. When all those molecules that make up the wood or the coal or the oil start to heat up and move around, they start letting out gasses. It's the gasses that burn. What you got left behind after the fire is put out is just the stuff that doesn't burn."

We sat there and I knew he was thinking like I was about what was left behind after his father torched himself on the steps of the U.S. Senate. Whatever it was, the coroner and the mortician told the family they didn't want to see it, so Lộc's mom had the body cremated right away. The ashes were sitting around their house in a gold-plated urn until they could ship it home to Vietnam where Mr. Bùi's parents were still alive.

Eventually we noticed the smell of the garbage and the fact that we hadn't found anyone selling weed yet. We got up off our knees and Lộc reached into his back pocket and pulled out a Molotov cocktail made from a beer bottle filled with kerosene and stuffed with a rag. He lit it and threw it in the dumpster, and we ran to the end of the alley and looked back for a little bit at the bonfire we had made. The alley looked like hell with that burning garbage and the strange, scrabbling light and shadows it threw onto the walls of the alley. We smoked some cigarettes to mask the smell. We were fourteen years old and already we had a pack-a-day habit, which was a real bitch on a fourteen-year-old's income. We were hooked and we knew it.

In the early morning after coming home, I lay in bed and thought about his father spending his last few seconds absolutely alone under God's solitary eye. I was too embarrassed to say this to Lộc, but I believed in God, still, even if Lộc didn't have any use for Him or Buddha. If there was no God, who cared about Mr. Bùi's death, except for his family? That's a little sad, when you only count for your family, and in Mr. Bùi's case, I knew he wanted the world to care.

He was a history teacher back in Vietnam, and he was always trying to teach some history to Lộc and me. We were his only students, if you could even call us that much, since Mr. Bùi worked as the short order cook for the 24-hour diner on Highway One. Whenever I came over, he had a name or date or event for me.

"Sorry," Lộc always muttered, yanking me into his room. "What an asshole."

He was a thin, pale man, with a head of luxuriant platinum hair that made him look like he'd been electrocuted. His eyes didn't help, being the color and flatness of molten pennies. It was the posture, the hair, the eyes, the whole look of him that let people know they shouldn't start a conversation with him if they found themselves sitting next to him at a bus stop or standing in line, because he was clearly a man with a Theory.

"The communists are coming," he said to me one time when I was trapped in the kitchen between him and the open refrigerator, my hand inside and still gripping the peanut butter. "They aren't happy with just Vietnam. They wanted Cambodia. They've sent spies over here too. You need to watch out for them."

He was also a very religious man. Once, when I was little, he came outside and caught Lộc and I using a magnifying lens we found in a Cracker Jack box to set ants on fire.

"They're only ants," I said, watching him grind the plastic lens into a fine dust with his heel.

"You may be an ant one day," he said, grabbing both Lộc and me by the ears, "but only if you are lucky. If you were to die right now, I think you would come back as toilet paper."

He left two things behind when he took off for Washington with the family Pacer and an overnight bag. One was a note to his family. It said, among other things, not to be sorry or sad about what he was going to do. Death was only the door to new life, and he was convinced that he was about to do a great thing. Karma meant that his fate would be a good one. The other thing he left behind was a copy of a ten-page letter about the communist threat. He mailed copies to the newspapers and to our senators and representatives, too. All that translated into was two inches in the back of *The New York Times* and a long article on the front page of the town paper's local section. There weren't any photos of the event, so no one except the tourists, the office workers and the one or two Senators on the steps of the Senate will ever remember exactly what he looked like as he sat down quietly on one of those steps, unzipped his overnight bag and pulled out a can of kerosene which he tipped over his head. Someone started pointing and then shouting and someone ran toward him but it only took him a couple of seconds to reach into his pocket and pull out his packet of matches and light one—try to light one, because the kerosene had soaked through his pants and wet the matches. One after another, he ripped through them, searching for a dry one that he eventually found. There was the heat he needed, he being the fuel already surrounded by air. How bright the world must look from inside a bonfire of one's own body. I wonder when he understood that he was now seeing the world, not from under God's eye, but from inside it.

The next night we tried again to get some weed. We left the house and rode our bikes back in the direction of downtown. Lộc was sure the guy with the Grateful Dead T-shirt we had seen standing in one of the alleyways on a regular basis had weed for sale, and we felt like we were on a mission to get our first joint. We were halfway to downtown when we heard the purr of a car engine behind, and when we looked over our shoulders we saw a gold TransAm bearing down. It sped past us and then swerved in front, forcing us to stop, and when the driver's side window rolled down I heard Mandy Stein's voice say from the backseat, "Those are the slant-eyed cocksuckers that beat me up."

Freeze. This is the tableau that stays in my mind. I see everyone distinctly, their places and their faces, even if everything is lit by a slight orange glow like an aged Polaroid. Mandy Stein is standing by the open door of the TransAm, her mouth an open black hole. Lộc and I are contorted in impossible positions on the ground. Someone who didn't know any better could say we were caught in death throes or seized by some religious fervor. Mandy's brother and his three best friends are doing the storm trooper on us, kicking at us with steel-capped construction boots. I also remember quite clearly what was going through my mind at that moment. It was not utter, ball-shrinking terror (that would come just a little later). Instead, these questions were popping up like little white flags in my head: Was someone really going to kill us for slapping Mandy Stein on her fat ass with a Louisville Slugger? Were our gravestones really going to read *Here Lies a Slant-Eyed Cocksucker*? Was I fated to live and die in this shit-hole that passed for the heartland of America?

Obviously, no. They were happy with a lot of blood and screaming on our part. They capped everything by ripping out our earrings and spitting on us, and then as we lay there in our own piss and blood, Mandy Stein walked up and gave a final pronouncement.

"You stupid shits," she said, standing over us in her gold-lamé dancing top, lit up by the light of the street lamp like some high priestess. "Don't even think you're good enough to touch me. I'm not one of your kind at all."

Truer words were never said. Every time I see a woman naked, I remember Mandy Stein standing above me, arms akimbo, her mouth making words I know only from memory, not from sound.

Afterwards, we lay in his bed, naked and packed in ice like two half-dead fish.

"Bastards," I groaned. "Assholes."

"Nazis," he mumbled in response. His lower lip was split wide open. "Brownshirts."

"They were wearing plaid."

It was his turn to groan. He rubbed his forehead a little harder with his ice pack.

"We have to get out of here," he said. "They're going to kill us if we stay."

"They're not going to kill us," I replied. "They had their chance. If they didn't do it now, they're not doing it later."

"It's not them," he said. "It's *them*. Everyone else. The whole damn town."

"So they don't like us. Okay, maybe they hate us. Maybe everybody thinks we're freaks but it doesn't mean they're going to kill us."

"One way or another," he said, "we'll be dead here."

He leaned over the side of the bed and reached under it, painfully slow, and pulled out a Dutch Masters cigar box that he handed over to me like it was the Bible.

"You been holding out."

"Not the way you think," he said. "Those were my dad's cigars. Of course, he smoked them all before he left. Open up."

Inside were two neat stacks of bills, each an inch thick. I riffed through them and got the scent of cheap cigars and worn money. They were all one-dollar bills that looked about as old as my dad. The stacks felt good in my hands, the most money I had ever seen in my life.

"That's our ride out of here," Lộc said. "Bus tickets to anywhere, USA. Maybe even Mexico or Canada."

"Where'd you get all this money?"

"The old man was always kind of absent-minded," he explained. "A dollar here, a dollar there, it adds up after a few years. Anyway, I'm thinking of Los Angeles myself, but maybe New York or San Francisco or Toronto."

I could see it: cities full of people who looked like us, who thought it was fashionable to wear black in summer and dangle crucifixes from our ears, where British music didn't mean the Beatles and where *punk* was just another adjective. I spun the movie reel in my head and saw myself sipping an espresso in a Soho café, dancing half-naked in a Sunset Boulevard club, beating a drum in North Beach. I knew all of those places from the pictures that Lộc had clipped out and pasted in his chem book. Then I spun the reel some more and saw myself under newspapers on a Central Park bench, begging for change on a Hollywood Boulevard street corner, hustling in a Castro bathroom.

And all this time Lộc was looking at me, looking into my eyes as they projected those scenes. I didn't need to say anything. He just closed the lid on the cigar box.

The next week he called me from a pay phone to come down to the reservoir again. When I showed up, I found him sitting next to his bike on the concrete shore, dangling his naked feet in the water and leaning on two inflatable inner tubes.

"Glad you could make it," he said. "Look what I found."

We shed our clothes without any more words, and set ourselves adrift on the water with our butts squeezed into the inner tubes. For a long time we didn't say anything. I looked straight up into a sky that was, for once, blue and clear.

"It's good weather," I said after a while.

"Don't say that."

"That it's good weather?"

"There are two kinds of people in this world." He was starting to paddle with his hands and feet toward the center of the reservoir. "Those who talk about good weather and those who like bad weather."

He paddled hard, like we were racing, so I started paddling too, but I was already behind him and his wake slowed me down.

"Goddamn it, take it easy," I shouted. "There's nowhere to go."

He stopped paddling and coasted along. Soon he stopped altogether and so did I and we floated along like that in the middle of the reservoir, not talking and watching the sky change colors as the afternoon passed into night. Then I heard a match strike, and when I looked over my shoulder, I could see the light of his cigarette glowing like a very faint and far away beacon. I had left my cigarettes on the shore with my clothes. At that moment, nothing seemed like it could be better than to float on the water with a cigarette, smoking and looking up into a dark sky.

He was gone by the next day. My dad woke me up at dawn and told me there was a package for me on the doorstep. "If it's drugs, I'm going to kill you," he said, before stomping out to go to work.

It wasn't drugs. It was the Dutch Masters box, sealed solidly along the sides with masking tape and marked with my name on the cover in black ink. There was no note inside, just a solid frame of wood wrapped in newspaper. After I peeled off the wrapping, I looked at the frame and what it held for a long time before I could put it down.

It's been with me ever since. I leave it hanging over my bed, and it fits my image as a cultured, intellectual type. Some lovers are put off, some are impressed. I use it as a test of sorts, to figure out whether this lover is someone I want to keep around for the morning or would rather just dispatch after the festivities are over. I also play "Love Will Tear Us Apart" as my bedroom mood music, so they understand right away who they are dealing with. We make love in near darkness, the better to feel each others' bodies with, under the lone dim light cast by the dental X-rays in their backlit-frame above my bed. Inevitably, each lover will ask about the X-rays, and I tell them that it is a piece of modern art by someone I once knew. He didn't leave it a name, so I've given it one: "Portrait of the Artist's Father," three inches by four inches, white bone on black film.

A Rockfall Dream

—Nguyễn Thị Kim Hòa—

THAT NIGHT HAI KIM DREAMED OF a cloud of butterflies emerging, suddenly, from the cliffs east of Mount Devil Face. At first, they gathered into a buzzing yellow and black sphere, then unfurled like a carpet of wings. This tapestry would then drift toward the village. Their fragile wings fluttered noisily, like the crumble before a rockslide or the thunder of a raging storm.

"Maybe this heat is causing you to dream about rain," Kiên teased. "It rains only after we've harvested the green onions, never now." He grinned and wiped sweat from beneath his conical hat.

Shaking the dirt off the fresh onions, Kiên then put the vegetables into baskets for Kim to carry home. The baskets were tied to two ends of a bamboo carrying pole and balanced on Kim's shoulder. Her feet moved lightly, the baskets swaying a little, but all she could think about were the butterflies from her dream. It wasn't the first time they had appeared in her sleep.

Earlier that morning, Ba Sang had slammed the matriculation document from Đỗ Hữu Vị School down onto the table. "I'm going to head out to Thủ Đức Military Academy instead. These days, the militia is the only way to quickly move up the ranks." Sang said this without even looking at Kim.

The night before, Kim's dreams again filled with butterflies—though this time there were fewer than the night before. This swarm

46

formed a thin, yellow strip from the top of Dao's rock to the three great boulders on Mount Devil Face. Kim and Sang's uncle, the village chief, tapped the silver end of his cane on the floor repeatedly when he heard about Kim's dream. "You can't be serious," he said. "If it's true, then it's an auspicious sign—our ancestors are telling us that our village will produce promising leaders."

The day Sang left for Thủ Đức Military Academy, their uncle was so excited he considered setting off firecrackers. Ever since Mr. Tám's generation, it was rare for anyone in the village to finish high school with such distinction, or to follow Mr. Tám to military school. Mr. Tám had set a great example for everyone to emulate. While their uncle was optimistic about Sang's future, Kim was filled with sadness. It wasn't because she would no longer hear her brother's heavy foot-steps in the early mornings, or his snoring that sounded like a runaway train, or even when she discovered he'd misplaced his towel after a shower. It was because she knew she might lose him forever. Her anxiety grew as Sang's day of departure drew closer, especially when he put on his military uniform and committed to going.

Kiên, their youngest brother, was only eleven. His happiest moments were when Sang returned home to celebrate Tết, the Lunar New Year, with them. He would put on his elder brother's red beret he found on the bedside and run out into the street carrying Sang's Walther P38 pistol, which he'd snatched from his brother's pants pocket. Kim remembered chasing after him, shouting. A noodle vendor at the market had said she was terrified by Kim's shouting, reminding her of seeing her own son's battered corpse shrouded and dumped right in front of her house.

Kim had struck Kiên with a rod, then tied his legs to a bedpost with a dog leash. The more her younger brother cried and begged, the more resolute Kim became—she ignored his pleas and busied herself with cooking and other chores. Halfway through the meal, Sang lost his patience and said, "That's enough, sister! Please let him go. You can't keep him tied up like that forever."

Kim unfastened the leash and silently applied medicated oil to Kiên's bruised ankles. Her brother remained silent, not out of fear or anger, but because he realized she was crying, her hot tears mixing with each drop of the medicated oil she was gently massaging into his skin.

***

SINCE THAT INCIDENT, HER BROTHER KIÊN never touched anything that looked like a weapon, even when Kim wasn't around. When he joined the militia and self-defense forces and was issued an M1 carbine, he lacked the enthusiasm that filled his unit. He carried it only when he saw his uncle; otherwise, he left the gun with his friends.

Kiên would say he aspired to be a doctor, not a killer. Unlike Ba Sang, who was hot-headed and loud, Kiên was calm and cautious. Kim admired the way her youngest brother carried himself.

But why did Kim keep dreaming of butterflies?

Determined to find answers, she climbed to the Buddhist temple to speak with Monk Tuệ Tâm. Nestled on a mountaintop ringed by three other peaks, the temple was a place of quiet reflection. The guards at Văn Thánh Temple below, known for their teasing, remained respectful when they saw Kim. Sang's warning rang in their minds: "See this grenade? It's for anyone who teases my sister."

In her haste, Kim had forgotten to bring fruits to offer the Buddha and return the Buddhist scriptures to the monk. It wasn't until she reached the stone entrance that she realized she'd come empty-handed. The temple felt cold. Strong ocean winds billowed the canvas shelter on the temple's veranda, shredding banana leaves until they lay flat on the ground. A skinny apprentice monk with bright eyes heated the teapot, and Monk Tuệ Tâm took a sip as he calmly contemplated the gusting winds.

"You mentioned seeing a swarm of butterflies coming toward the village?" the monk asked.

"Yes, many of them. And wherever they went, I heard falling rocks, even in the village. Do you think it's a bad omen or a good sign?"

"That's irrelevant. What matters is *how* you respond to it."

Kim contemplated the monk's words but still couldn't grasp the meaning of her dream. So, whenever she heard footsteps on the village road, the squeak of a stopping vehicle, or a cry from a nearby neighborhood, she felt a whirlwind of emotions—from panic to calm, desperation to relief. The turmoil often left her feeling suffocated. Day by day, her heart diminished little by little. Even the slightest noise from the village gate made her heart tremble violently. She started to listen closely to the public loudspeaker nailed to a coconut tree next to her house.

Sang was stationed in some far-off place. One summer, he returned home and drove his jeep around with Kiên, at a time when the village was awash with grief, when phoenix flowers deepened from red to crimson. Kim was still haunted by the butterfly dreams. What if one day a truck stopped at her house, carrying a South Vietnamese flag-draped casket with Sang's body?

Kiên kept his routine, going to school every morning while Kim tended to her rows of green onions. But Kim began praying at her parents' altar more frequently and for much longer. The general mobilization order came to the village while Kim and Kiên were stooped low, harvesting their onions. She told Kiên about her butterfly dreams. From the public loudspeaker, Mr. Tám's voice echoed throughout the village, urging young men to volunteer and join the war effort: "Not enough blood has been shed in this war, and nobody knows when it will end."

Kim had never met the esteemed Mr. Tám. She guessed even her parents never met him in person. As the story goes, he had left the village as a young man, and in that time the villagers made him into a hero, a legend. Other young men who left the village to join the war effort never came back. On the same night they harvested onions, the loudspeaker fell from the tree during a hailstorm. Dogs barked. It was hard to understand the garbled announcement, then the loudspeaker, after a few seconds, went completely dead.

Due to their age, the uncle's two sons—Kim's cousins—were eligible for military enlistment. Both were married with two children each. "Grandpa! Daddy!" their children would cry in front of the closed door of the uncle's house. No one knew what the uncle was doing inside, but when he stepped out, he headed straight for the town's administrative building, saying, "Our village has a long tradition of producing heroes and leaders."

The noodle vendor at the nearby market spat on the ground when she heard his words. The uncle and his sons were taken aback; their faces revealed everything.

Kim hid Kiên in the underground bunker for two days. When the MPs arrived, she sat on a chair guarding the bunker entrance and said, "If you've come for Kiên, you can shoot me right here. Then you can go talk to Sang."

The MPs, familiar with the area, recalled how intimidating Sang had been at Văn Thánh Temple. Unsure of what to do after their search, they smoked, cursed, and drank at Kim's front door, while Kim continued to guard the bunker where Kiên was hidden. Kim's resolve didn't last forever. A few days later, her lips parched and her body emaciated, she was taken to a hospital. Meanwhile, Kiên was whisked into a military truck with other young men and left the village. Kim didn't see Kiên again after that day. At the entrance to the district's temporary detention, Sang, with a bushy, unkempt beard and an unhappy expression, greeted her. "I already told you not to keep him at home. It's pointless!" he said. Then, without making eye contact, "He'll come back, so don't worry so much."

***

KIM STILL MADE THE BED, COOKED a sour-flavored soup, and brewed morning coffee for Sang whenever he visited. Yet, when he looked around, he couldn't find his sister. Kim sat on a wooden bed in the dark, claustrophobic underground bunker, unsure why she had to be there—a place reeking of rat droppings and musty mold, the same place where Kiên, sweating profusely, had lain hidden for two days. She didn't know why her hands trembled as she put away his starch-white shirts, his new journals, and school bag into a box, items she bought with money from selling two towering baskets of onions.

The school year had just started, but Kiên wasn't around to say goodbye to her as he usually did when he biked to school. She didn't know where they had taken him. She felt the urgent need to keep the memory of him alive—away from the smell of gunpowder and the stale odor of blood that Sang liked.

"He'll come back," Sang said as she emerged from the bunker. "Don't be disheartened by this war."

Kim wasn't mad at Sang's terse words. She found it strange that he was so certain Kiên would return unharmed. She wondered if he was trying to convince her or himself. She hated the defiance and certainty in his tone, reminiscent of the loudspeaker before it fell from the coconut tree. Kim looked at Sang's shadow on the wall of their home. A rugged yet feeble shadow. How long could he keep believing?

Sang's jeep, along with his pride, had not been able to catch up with the military truck that took Kiên to Đà Nẵng. After traveling two hundred miles, the jeep's front tire blew out. He waited on the shoulder of the road, his jeep covered in red dirt, as a convoy passed by. Hundreds of young men with bewildered faces sat on the military trucks. As truck after truck in the convoy passed, Kim thought any of the conscripts could have been her brother, until their faces blurred into one another. What did war leave her and countless other women? Grief, another grave, an empty home, or loneliness? Before Sang could steady his sister, the bag of clothes she held slipped, scattering Kiên's white shirts across the red earth.

***

EVERY NIGHT AFTER THAT TRIP, Kim dreamed of Kiên and his stained white shirts. Around midnight, she would wake from her nightmares, screaming into the void. On nights like these, she ran into the front yard and sat dazed next to her black dog. Kim feared that if she stayed in her dark, quiet room, Kiên would appear, wounded and bleeding in his bloodstained white shirt, a ghost without any recognizable features.

One afternoon, without thunder or rain, the Dao rock fell. The colossal rock made a deafening noise as it pierced the earth like a knife dropped from the sky. Large fragments pelted the city mayor's house, terrifying him during a phone call. The village was buried under the earth, up to the roofs of houses, along with the human faces inside.

Villagers gathered and gawked at the rock fragments, shaking their heads in disbelief. In the afternoon, worms slithered from the rows of green onions and onto the road, where military trucks instantly crushed them, leaving green, oozy streaks. Then, butterflies filled the sky, just as they had in Kim's dreams. Peering through the cracks in their closed doors, villagers glimpsed the chaotic scene of soldiers. She saw men from the Central Highlands in their smoke-stained camouflaged uniforms and headgear, their guns scattered on the backs of vehicles. Some wore helmets askew; others had shirts half-tucked. Exhausted, unkempt, and hurried, they clung to their weapons. When the soldiers marched through the village, everyone recognized them by their clothes. Every household fortified their doors. Along the village road, even the dogs stopped barking. Huddled around the dim light of oil lamps, the villagers whispered of an evacuation.

"It's time to go," someone said. "The streets are deserted, and the town is already deserted."

"The communists are coming," another person chimed in. "We need to leave before the bloodshed happens. People here support the South Vietnamese government and their president in Sài Gòn. It's a lost cause now, so let's leave while we can. Three big families at the village gate have already boarded boats."

The uncle went to each village household, rapping on doors with his cane and gnashing his teeth. "Mr. Tám would never flee this village," he declared. "I'll kill anyone who leaves!"

Some villagers took the uncle's death threats seriously. Those who stayed behind dropped their heavy luggage and returned to their daily lives.

"See, Mr. Tám wouldn't abandon this place," a villager said. "Turn on the radio and hear for yourself. Our village is safe and protected like a steel shield. Our mayor is a coward for running away. He deserved to be struck across the face. Now our airport, our streets, teem with soldiers and tanks. Streets packed with infantry—Marines, Special Forces—and Sang's parachute regiment."

When the uncle reached Kim's house and rapped on her door with his cane, she ignored the man outside, too busy removing fleas from her black dog. The uncle continued on to a neighbor's house. Had Kim known he was outside, her fingers in the dog's fur would have trembled with more anger.

Kim remembered when her whole body shook after hearing news about Kiên. He was reported missing just three days after arriving in Đà Nẵng. Or when Sang, fully armed, parachuted from a C-130 Hercules and landed near her house, shouting, "Sister, where's Kiên? Bring that bastard out here! Stop hiding him! Did you know he deserted us and joined the communists?"

In that moment, Kim remembered, she was petrified by Sang's scowl and his gun as he tore through her house. Did he want to press the muzzle of his gun into Kiên's chest and pull the trigger? If so, Sang could have let her, Kiên, and their parents die when a stray artillery shell hit their thatch roof and set it on fire. But he didn't. What did it mean that he'd rescued them, yet now wanted to kill Kiên? Staring down the black barrel of Sang's gun and back at the rage in his face, Kim realized something about war's cruelest atrocities—that blood begets blood and could be thickened, spilled by the hand of one's kin, and that this fire of hatred didn't come from outside but from within one's own house.

Kim's mind was flooded with questions. Had Kiên actually joined the communist cause? Did he shoot soldiers on Sang's side without mercy? Did he still remember Sang as his older brother? Were they, as brothers, nothing more than ruthless murderers? And if they faced each other again as enemies, would they remember their bond and let the other go? Hearing the thunderous noise of artillery cannons from town, Kim's fingers trembled and her body convulsed, sending shivers down her spine. Her uncle had once said to her, "Men stand by their principles, their values, and see the bigger picture, while women waste away and shed tears over nothing."

***

SANG RUSHED HOME during a torrential rainstorm when he heard Kim was bedridden with a fever. Standing next to her bed like a shadow, he gazed at his sister with silent, vacant eyes. Digging in his pocket, he found a pill and forced it down her throat. Kim felt the pill at the back of her throat; it had a sooty smell to it, much like Sang. An odor that even the rain couldn't wash away. Sang had never come home before now, and he did so amid a downpour and screams of artillery. Without another word, and without looking back, he staggered to the front door.

"Sang," Kim said, struggling to sit up in bed. She wanted him to stay.

Sang paused at the doorway, turning his head. "I'm afraid it's too late, sister . . ."

She thought she saw his shadow nodding in her direction before quickly vanishing into the rainstorm. Kim lacked the strength to chase after him. Outside, she could only hear the growl of Sang's engine, the pouring rain, and the terrifying roar of the ocean.

***

AFTER THE SUDDEN RAINSTORM SUBSIDED, with the streets and the faces of its inhabitants still wet, the town was liberated. Braver villagers returned with stories of T-54 tanks, the grandeur of flowers and flags, banners and endless applause. The townsfolk paused their activities and poured into the streets, or stood on sidewalks watching the Liberation Army march by. A few teenagers craned their necks, curious if propaganda posters about liberation soldiers having tails were true. Older people smiled and said, "All propagandists are compulsive liars. Vietcong soldiers are fine and decent men, just like your grandchildren at home." Everyone stayed until the military parade through town ended. They returned home relieved, unlocking and leaving their doors open.

The villagers soon discovered that some of their relatives, thought to have escaped by boat, were still alive. Operation Frequent Wind, as it was called, hadn't left anyone behind. That afternoon, several liberation soldiers returned to the village, surprising everyone. The soldiers knew the village well, and the apprentice monk was among them. He went to the village chief's house to talk. Kim's uncle, his hair gone gray overnight, surrendered nearly a dozen guns. There were no great leaders or heroes here, only their myth, and only the bloodshed and victims that came as a result. Sang was someone who had believed in and propagated the myth.

***

KIM WALKED QUICKLY, as though she were scaling a steep, winding hill. She needed to ask Quan Yin, the Bodhisattva of Compassion, and the ancient stones on the mountain, why her life had been so painfully wretched, spun by the endless cycle of uniting and division. And why did her brother Sang live in exile on the other side of the globe? "Sister ... sister ..." called a voice from the bottom of the hill. It came from a man in a duckweed-shaped hat and green matching uniform.

Kim looked down to see Kiên smiling and waving his hand, his eyes just as welcoming. She wept as she embraced her brother, gone since that day she fainted above the bunker. Her tears seemed to fall on the ancient, jagged mountains and flow out to the sea. Tears shed for the obstacles she had overcome—tears for this pivotal moment in history.

***

SEVERAL YEARS PASSED. A granddaughter and her grandfather visited the newly renovated pagoda atop the mountain. The old man burned incense while the little girl played outside. She saw another elderly man, wearing glasses, slowly climbing the steps to the main worship hall. The man stood for a long while in front of the door adjacent to the hall. Her grandfather was in the hall praying to the dead. A photo on the altar caught the stranger's attention. Very slowly, he approached the altar and knelt down on the tile floor. The grandfather, mid-prayer, was startled and turned his head. Their eyes met. It had been years since they last saw each other; now they were both old men living out the final days of their lives.

The little girl was surprised when she saw the two old men crying, tears tracing the deep creases in their cheeks. The more she looked, the more they seemed alike. Her grandfather quickly helped the stranger to his feet.

"My brother . . . Sang . . . You've come back," the grandfather said. The two gray-haired men leaned against each other and, now united, gazed at the photo on the altar. Without a doubt, the girl saw Kim in the photo lower her head and smile.

—Translated by Quan Manh Ha & Cab Tran

A New Perspective

—Lê Vũ Trường Giang—

OVER THE PAST YEAR, DAY AFTER DAY, Job escorted his daughter to New York Harbor to gaze at the Statue of Liberty. To earn the credits required to be recruited as a combat photographer, he had once captured images from a Hughes OH-6 Cayuse during the war. Now, as he gazes out over the vast ocean, his thoughts drift to the distant land of Vietnam. He rummages through his pockets for a glass marble, the one with the tiny red flame at its center. Job holds the marble up to the sun and inspects it. In his mind's eye, within the marble, a village emerges out of smoke.

On the subway ride home, Job notices posters along the station's entrance, pictures of saluting veterans holding their guns. The posters are partly torn or damaged in some way, their faces scratched out; it's impossible to know who the men are. Someone had graffitied "Come home!" on one of the posters. Job overhears two students chatting nearby.

"I want to visit Vietnam at least once in my life," the first student says.

"Stop dreaming, Kil! There's a protest happening in New York every week," replies his friend with the pouty lips.

At home, Job's wife Lucy sets dinner on the table and probes gently, "Why do you spend so much time at the harbor?"

"It's a big part of my life," he answers.

"But why?"

"What else do you want me to do?"

Lucy gets annoyed by Job's rhetorical question. "You can't let go of the past, can you? What happened back then? What did you see? Why do you never talk about it? I wish you'd never gone to Vietnam. I wish you'd never picked up that camera before we got married."

Job doesn't finish his dinner. He stands up and goes to the porch, where he watches the unexpected summer rain. Again, he takes out the marble he brought back from Vietnam, holding it in his palm like a precious jewel. He taps the marble on the porch table in rhythm with the falling rain. Raindrops patter along the roof, on the canopy of old oak trees, then descend to the grassy earth and violets in bloom. The sound of rain is so familiar, as well as the smell of the earth, reminding him of earlier days spent in the scorching heat of military zones.

***

THE HUMIDITY OF CENTRAL VIETNAM was stifling. The first time he stood on a battlefield there, the temperature had dropped significantly due to a tropical storm. He used his poncho as a canvas to sit on, smoked, and looked out at the foggy mountains in the west, where the communist troops had organized. Over the past few days, Charlotte Company had marched tirelessly; they had raided areas suspected of hiding the Vietcong. They razed at least two abandoned military outposts and dozens of unoccupied thatched-roof buildings. Not a single Vietcong was found in the three bunkers marked on their maps.

When Job reported to Henry Richardson, the Captain of Charlotte Company, Henry was furious. "I'll gun down at least one hundred VC this month."

"Why?" Job asked, confused.

Henry's jaw clenched as he spoke to Job, who was in country for the first time, "Yeah, you should've known earlier. We need to wipe these goddamn VC out. Now your job is to use your camera to take winning shots of our Company during raids—the kind of photos people will remember about this war." Henry's face looked terrifying at this moment, and when he was this furious, no one dared disobey his orders.

Job had asked Henry several times why he harbored such deep resentment against the enemy, but Henry never gave him a satisfying answer. Once, howling like a wolf, Henry shouted, "Don't you remember how men from the Special Task Force unit were massacred at Ba Gia with knives and punji traps? Killed in their sleep! Our boys from Ohio lost their lives after less than a month in-country."

Before Job could mention that he had heard about the incident— that the unit had gone rogue and shot twenty-three unarmed civilians, mostly women and children hiding in an underground shelter—Henry had already turned away. He drew his gun and fired three shots into the air, then spat on a patch of burnt grass that was still smoldering.

***

EVER SINCE THEN, JOB HAS BEEN haunted by nightmares of inno-cent Vietnamese civilians massacred, and the crazed look in Henry's eyes. In his dreams, he holds the camera in his bloodstained hands, aiming it at the bloodied faces of those they had killed. Job would wake up screaming.

Lucy could never understand what Job experienced in Vietnam and why it had changed him since his return. One day, reading a newspaper article about the moral corruption of American GIs, Lucy reassures her-self that her husband, a former war correspondent, couldn't possibly have taken part in such atrocities. She asks him to share what he saw in Vietnam, hoping that by telling his stories, he would become more inti-mate and open with her, as he hadn't touched her since his return.

Job has trouble sleeping, but tonight, as he turns the marble over in his hand, he sees the tiny flame at its core glow more intensely. The marble slips from his hand and rolls across the floor, coming to a stop at the foot of the couch. Job picks up the marble, and as he looks up, he sees a sad Vietnamese boy seated on his brown leather couch, staring straight at him. Job lights a cigarette and sits down next to the boy. The boy begins to share with Job the story of his childhood:

My name is Đầu, and I'm eleven years old. Don't worry—you can keep my marble. I have no friends to play marbles with anyway. I'll never forget those sunny mornings in my village, the way sunlight filtered through the trees and morning glories. We kids loved playing outside. I used to follow a herd of water buffalo down a muddy road to the rice paddies. I loved looking at their black horns and hearing the laughter of the other buffalo boys. I loved seeing the strong, suntanned backs of farmers tending to their fields. I miss the village women, baskets in hand, chatting as they made their way to the early market.

My mom used to wake me up early, at five o'clock, and say, 'Go open up the buffalo pen for your dad, and fetch me some straw so I can start a fire for cooking.' I would rub my eyes awake, get out of bed, and go to the water tank outside to wash my face. The grass and flowers—even the weeds—smelled wonderful this early in the day. I would breathe in the air and feel thankful. Once, I took Mẹp, my water buffalo, out to a distant field in Cổ Lũy to pluck water lilies with friends. That night, I had dinner with my family, our final meal together. That's why I feel so tired now.

On Elephant Hill, we children flew kites and plucked wild rose myrtle fruit in the summer. From the top of the hill, I could see green rice paddies laid out like a chessboard, and small trails hidden among the coastal oak trees. I could see Mận Village and the blue ocean and its golden beaches beyond. But after the Americans came, they occupied the hill and built a military base there. They took away our playground. Worse, they shelled our village with artillery, shaking the ground beneath us. Helicopters hovered in the sky and when they landed in a nearby field, many armed soldiers jumped off and advanced toward my village. The bloodthirsty men looked demonic. They ransacked people's houses and searched our bunkers. Villagers were terrified and held up their arms, saying, 'We're not Vietcong.' They shouted and screamed; some cried, begging for their lives. But . . . they were dragged from their homes and shot dead anyway.

Job listens to Đầu's story and tells the boy what he remembers: "Your village was marked on our military maps as Plum Village. At that time, our commanders wanted to wipe Plum Village off the map because it meant they got a promotion. Captain Richardson, my superior—everyone called him 'Mad Dog'—he was the only survivor after his unit got ambushed. There was also Jeffrey Lee, the spiteful one. He had two friends he considered brothers: one died in Củ Chi and the other went missing in Quảng Trị. Both Richardson and Lee spearheaded the campaign in Suối Mơ after they were told that Battalion 48 of the Liberation Army of South Vietnam was hiding in your village."

Job tiptoed to the bedroom and soon fell asleep next to his wife. Henry's words ricocheted in Job's head: *Kill! Kill them all! Kill anything that moves! Don't let the VC take any more American lives!* Gruesome images of the massacre play again and again in his mind like a movie reel. Gunfire. The mountains of bodies. Limbs that had been blown to bits with bloodstained clothing clinging to them. Young girls and women who'd been attacked and sexually assaulted. Naked bodies left disemboweled, their throats slit. Homes in flames even as children dug frantically through the ashes for signs of their parents. Trees and vegetation shredded, burnt to the ground. After it was over, survivors buried the dead in mass graves.

Job screams himself awake and covers his face with his hands in horror. He mutters to Lucy, "I was there. I witnessed everything. Now I'm cursed with my guilt." Later, he unburdens himself, tells Lucy all that he had kept from her since returning from the war.

"You need to confess," she suggests.

That Sunday, they go and attend Mass at St. Paul's Chapel, and during Job's confession, the priest recites: "May your faith in God bring you peace. May you walk in the light for He is in the light."

Closing his eyes, Job prays, "Dear Lord, please forgive me for my sins. Help me become a better person, a man who knows what is good and what is evil." Even here, he sees Đầu appear next to him, smiling.

Back at home, Job reveals to Lucy how he got the marble: "I found a little boy in a corpse-filled irrigation ditch. He was still breathing when I found him. I saw the marble in the palm of his hand. A helicopter was thudding nearby—it'd come to stop the massacre—maybe save who was left. I carried the injured boy to Thompson, the helicopter pilot. The boy looked at me with gratitude and gave me his marble, still covered in his blood. It's just now that I realize he didn't make it. He told me his name was Đầu. I wish I had just shot myself in the leg instead, like Richard Carter did, so I wouldn't have blood on my hands."

"Honey," Lucy says, "there's an antiwar protest going on later this week." She looks at him knowingly. "It'll be led by students and veterans."

"Then we'll go," he says. "I know what I need to do."

***

AT THE ANTIWAR PROTEST, A MOTHER cries out, "I gave my country a good son, not a killer!"

The police struggle to control the crowd. Job imagines that Lucy has handed him a bouquet of flowers for the occasion. In this waking dream, he sees himself performing an act of kindness. Just the idea of this transforms him inside, knowing that men like him would eventually show the truth about the massacre to the American public.

One cold night, Job walks alone to the office of *Life* magazine and waits outside. He senses Đầu following him, smiling from the shadows. Job believes his wife and daughter will be proud of him. The editor-in-chief of the magazine is stunned when Job shows him sixty photos he'd taken of the massacre, telling Job, "My God, these are incredible. Thank you for bringing these in." He firmly shakes Job's hand.

Job goes home and writes a long, detailed account on the massacre for General Ian Reimer, a man of honor and pillar of the community. The report begins: *On March 16, 1968, in the span of four hours, American soldiers slaughtered approximately 500 Vietnamese civilians in Suối Mơ. I am ready to testify in court what I witnessed that day . . .*

The court martial unfolds in mid-November 1970 and stretches over several days. Lucy and their daughter grip Job's hands tightly as they listen to the proceedings. Job feels the comforting presence of the marble in his shirt pocket. Henry's eyes shoot daggers at Job and at the media, possibly wishing he'd had the sense to smash Job's camera and rip up the photos Job took while he had the chance. Jeffrey remains quiet and looks physically spent. Job envisions Đầu's spirit circling the courtroom, the boy's angelic face glowing. The spirit perches on the shoulder of the presiding judge for a better view of the proceedings. Job heaves a sigh of relief the minute the judge announces the verdict. That night, Đầu reappears in his dream, still smiling, and takes Job's hand. Together, they walk to the antiwar protest site and join Lucy and their daughter. In unison, they chant, "GIs, come home!"

—*Translated by Quan Manh Ha & Cab Tran*

A Vietnamese Arrière-Boutique

—Kevin D. Pham—

IN MY LAST YEAR AT THE University of California in Irvine, my grandmother passed away and, a few weeks later, so did my grandfather. They were ninety-three and ninety-two.

On a rainy May morning in 2010, as I stood with my family and watched my grandfather's casket go into the ground, it dawned on me that I had never had a conversation with either of my grandparents, despite visiting them every other week in Santa Clara before I left home for college, and for as long as I could remember. All my life, I'd arrive, say, "*Chào ông, chào bà*"—Hello, Grandpa. Hello, Grandma—and that was it. I had never asked them questions. What was it like living in Vietnam throughout the First and Second Indochina Wars? What did you think of colonialism? Of communism and communists? Which side were you on and why? What kind of country did you want Vietnam to become?

I was ignorant of my own family.

At the time, I was taking a course entitled "The Vietnam War." We read memoirs by American soldiers who fought in the war (Bill Ehrhart's *Vietnam-Perkasie* is a memorable one), Kennedy and Johnson's speeches justifying the war, and Americans—such as Martin Luther King Jr., Malcom X, and the Port Huron Statement—against the war.

We rarely heard from Vietnamese people, and, when we did, they appeared as one-dimensional caricatures of various roles: victims of or villains against America, or heroes of anti-imperial struggle, or puppets of foreign governments. On the first day, the professor showed us Peter Davis's 1974 documentary *Hearts and Minds*. In one scene, General Westmoreland stared into the camera and said, "The Oriental doesn't put the same high price on life as does a Westerner. Life is plentiful. Life is cheap in the Orient." And, as he went on about how Asians didn't care about life as much as Westerners, a montage appeared of Vietnamese children crying over the graves of their parents who were killed by American bombing.

I was furious at Westmoreland's ignorance.

But, in another way, I was also ignorant.

That morning in the cemetery, I decided I would live in Vietnam for some time after graduation.

***

I MOVED TO NHA TRANG, a quiet coastal town, and got a job teaching ESL. My real aim, however, was to relearn the Vietnamese language and learn about Vietnam's history and people. I talked with as many Vietnamese people as I could: people of my age, old people, street vendors. I asked them what they thought about the wars in the past and, bluntly, about their opinions on the various sides. Many were proud of the Vietnamese communists and saw Hồ Chí Minh as a hero.

When I had two or more days off work, I'd get on a bus or train with a backpack and go to another city.

In December, my parents, aunts, and uncles came from the United States and met me in Hà Nội. We visited our ancestral village, our *quê*, in the countryside of Nam Định. When I looked at our huge family tree on a wall, I saw my Vietnamese name, Huy, in small letters in a tiny box, and my cousins' names next to me.

With my newly gained Vietnamese skills, I could talk to my aunts and uncles. One evening, at our hotel, I asked my aunt, who was in her late seventies, "What was your life like in Vietnam before the war?"

"It was so nice, Huy!" she replied. "We owned a big house. We had servants. They did everything, so we never worked. I read books in the garden all day. Then, the communists took it all away! They're evil!"

I had expected to sympathize with her, but it was difficult to. It seemed natural, not evil, to me that peasants would feel resentful toward people like my aunt. How could she not see from the perspective of the communists? They were by no means perfect. But why couldn't my aunt realize that her description of life before the war—the inequality—was problematic, at least from the perspective of a Marxist? Did she think the inequality was natural? Or deserved?

Another evening, I had dinner with my uncles after touring on my own the Củ Chi Tunnels—the elaborate underground network of tunnels and booby traps used by the Vietcong during the war, not too far from Sài Gòn. I told one of my uncles where I had been.

"All fake," he declared.

He had served in the South Vietnamese Army, so maybe he knew something that I wasn't told on the tour.

"What do you mean *fake*? I was there and saw it all," I said.

"It's all fake propaganda. They made it up after the war. You don't know, Huy."

"American soldiers had first-hand experiences with those tunnels during the war. Do you mean that's *fake* too?" I retorted.

"Lies," he said, with a wave of his hand as if to shoo away the topic.

"What exactly did you do during the war?" I asked.

He paused, and then smiled at me and said in English, "Kill communists."

Yes, the tourist site was propagandistic, but to claim that the whole thing was a fabrication seemed absurd. Another time, as we were waiting for a bus, the name Thích Quảng Đức came up, the Buddhist monk who set himself on fire in Sài Gòn to protest persecutions of Buddhists by the South Vietnamese government. In that famous photo, my uncles and aunts claimed that he did not do it voluntarily but was drugged beforehand by communists.

Astonished, I turned to my cousin and asked, "Are they seriously saying this?"

"Well, maybe it's true. Who knows? We weren't there," she replied.

Confused and frustrated, I walked away from her and was silent for the rest of the day. Years later, I realized they were repeating what Ngô Đình Diệm himself had concluded about the incident. Perhaps the most shocking thing one of my uncles said, however, was that the massacre at Mỹ Lai was exaggerated propaganda.

As we visited family in the North, I was surprised to see statues of Hồ Chí Minh inside many of our relatives' homes. What puzzled me even more was that my anticommunist aunts and uncles saw the statues but remained friendly and smiley with the relatives. Were they on opposing sides of the war, and did the smiles indicate the achievement of reconciliation? On the car ride back, I asked them why our relatives had busts of Hồ Chí Minh.

"I thought our family *wasn't* on the communist side."

As if I had said something very naïve, they replied, "Of course they have statues of him. To show that they are loyal to the government, so that they don't get any trouble from the communists. They couldn't escape Vietnam, so that's what they must do to survive. Think, Huy."

For my aunts and uncles, our relatives in Vietnam with Hồ Chí Minh statues did not actually have warm feelings toward him but were faking it to appease authorities. Even if our relatives had declared aloud, "We love Uncle Hồ!" my uncles probably would have told me, Of course they have to say it out loud, too. But they don't really believe it. Their smiles did not mean reconciliation but a refusal to believe that their relatives could really love him.

I wanted to understand how my aunts and uncles understood themselves and their world. Their anticommunism was rooted in their own experiences. They suffered at the hands of those who called themselves communists, whereas I had great distance from the conflict, experientially, emotionally, and intellectually. Many of my friends in college called themselves "Marxists" and "communists." I prided myself on being curious, seeing from different perspectives, and having healthy self-doubt. But this meant that I had to remind myself that I could be wrong and they could be right, or at least partially. Maybe Thích Quảng Đức *was* drugged. Maybe aspects of the Củ Chi Tunnel *were* fabricated. Maybe Mỹ Lai *was* exaggerated propaganda.

I don't think they were.

But I don't have a God's eye view of truth.

On the last day of our trip, before my folks went back to California and me back to Nha Trang, I asked my uncle, the one who had fought for the South Vietnam Army, "The South Vietnamese were fighting *against* communism, but what were they fighting *for*?"

"Freedom and democracy," he replied.

Back in Nha Trang, I started reading about Vietnamese national heroes whose names were on the street signs, such as Phan Bội Châu, Phan Chu Trinh, and Nguyễn An Ninh. I read about the communists and Hồ Chí Minh to know about their ideas. "Freedom and democracy" (*tự do* and *độc lập*) were also the exact words that Hồ Chí Minh and his followers used to describe what *they* were fighting for. How could two sides use the same words to describe what they are fighting for and at the same time consider each other enemies?

I felt caught in between two sides that I sympathized with.

Frustration!

Around this time, I discovered Michel de Montaigne, the sixteenth-century French essayist who was a mediator between Protestants and Catholics who were killing each other in his country. Montaigne urged us to be tolerant, to doubt our own knowledge. He wanted us to be curious, to learn about different cultures and perspectives, and to embrace the fact that it's fine to change our minds. He thought that many conflicts happened over misinterpretations and misuses of words.

I identified with him.

I, the mediator between my anticommunist family and my leftist friends.

***

IN THE SUMMER OF 2020, I moved across the country to start a job at Gettysburg College. Not long after, I received a frantic phone call from my dad.

"Are you telling your uncles on the East Coast that you like Hồ Chí Minh?" he asked.

Puzzled, I responded, "First off, I didn't know we had any relatives on the East Coast. And second, I've never said to anyone that I 'like' Hồ Chí Minh."

"I'll call you back."

"Okay."

A few minutes later, my phone rang again. Dad calling.

Unbeknown to me, I had an uncle on the East Coast. He had heard about me from another relative and then found my website. On it, I described the book I was writing as "an exploration of the political thought of six influential Vietnamese thinkers," and displayed their pictures. One of them is Hồ Chí Minh. The uncle interpreted my use of the word *influential* to mean that I "liked" this communist leader. One can say that someone is "influential" and at the same time like or dislike them. After presuming that I "liked" Uncle Hồ, he called one of his cousins and asked, "Why does Huy like Hồ Chí Minh?" Then, that sibling called another sibling and asked the same thing; then that sibling called another sibling and asked the same question. So, by the time my dad visited his siblings—the first time he had seen them in months due to the pandemic—the first thing one of his brothers said to him was "Why does Huy like Hồ Chí Minh?" At that point, my dad called me.

They got into a heated argument. One of his aunts said something to the effect of "You and your sons are not like us. You all don't like Trump. You are all Democrats. They are communists! So Huy probably does like Hồ Chí Minh!"

Like many other Vietnamese Americans, my father's siblings supported Trump. Their anticommunism translated to a conservatism that led to support for the American Republican Party. Shortly after the January 6th riots, where some rioters flew South Vietnamese flags at the Capitol, my dad asked me, "Huy, should I take the three red stripes off my bright yellow convertible Mustang?"

"No. Just leave them on," I said.

When we drove in it, older Vietnamese people would stop as they crossed the street to salute us. Once, when he was in Westminster, California, Vietnamese restaurant owners gave his car special VIP parking. This is a flag of a country that no longer exists but exists in the minds of my dad and so many Vietnamese Americans.

The flag means different things to different people.

Months earlier, in the wake of protests following the killing of George Floyd, young Vietnamese Americans created Facebook groups as spaces to vent about their conservative parents.

As I read through the posts in one of those Facebook groups, I remembered old video footage on YouTube of the "Hi-Tek" incident. In 1999, thousands of Vietnamese Americans took to the streets in southern California to protest a Vietnamese man who displayed a portrait of Hồ Chí Minh in his video store. Several protestors threatened to set themselves on fire if he wasn't forced to take the portrait down. Some held up signs with Hồ Chí Minh's face next to Hitler's. Many had suffered during and after the war and, for them, Hồ represented all that was responsible for their suffering. At the same time, did they see the irony in claiming to love America for its freedom of expression while demanding the government to stop someone from displaying a picture of Hồ Chí Minh?

I thought of when I met a young Vietnamese scholar at a conference in the Netherlands. I asked her what she thought of Hồ Chí Minh. She smiled and said, "He's a hero. Sometimes I dream of doing what he did. Being like him. Leaving Vietnam to learn about the world and returning to help my country. Can you tell me all the books you've read on him? I want to learn more about him."

Her emotions were real, just as much as the protestors' in southern California. In a different time, their differences would have escalated to bloodshed. One of Montaigne's approaches to conflict, aside from being a mediator between opposing sides, was to avoid it. He is famous for retreating into his library, his *arrière boutique,* a "back shop," a private, mental (and physical) space to study, read, and think freely on his own—safe and away from political and ideological storms.

So that's what I did.

Retreat into a silent space where I can study Vietnamese thinkers and history.

Freely, on my own, I can discover how Vietnamese thinkers answer big questions. What is a good life? Who should rule and have power? How should one respond to conflict? What values are good for society?

And I can think about their answers and change my mind whenever I feel like it.

The Fish and the Banyan Tree

—Elizabeth Tran—

CHANGE HAPPENS IN DARKNESS, IN PITS, silent, underneath the ground. It happens in quiet, in dreams. It leaks a season at a time, until it overtakes, like sleep, like drowning. It was how people grew apart in Vietnam: the land between them grew a mighty river, an ocean to divide them.

This might have been one reason why the man's wife threw dirty dishwater on the banyan tree. In the past, when they had been happy in their marriage, the water she had thrown into the garden produced an abundance of fruit and vegetables—carpets of purple basil and green mint—velvet on the side the wind lifted—and sweet potatoes, cucumbers, and kumquats, sweeter than sugar cane. But then everything changed. The banyan tree had enough of the dirty dishwater, and it picked up its roots and fled to the moon.

The banyan tree, of course, was the heart of the land.

***

WHEN THE MAN WAS A BOY, his family lived in a modest house near the shores of the East Sea. The only thing they owned that was immodest was an enormous banyan tree in the front of the house, under which the boy left the girl gifts. Sometimes there would be a little rice cake with black sesame seeds; sometimes a ripe mango in a bed of *ngọc lan* flowers, to perfume her tongue as she ate the fruit. Once, he made her a necklace with a seashell pendant.

He had spent three weeks searching the beach for the perfect sea-shell. It was a brown-speckled spiral infused with yellowed ivory and bits of sunlight, and it appeared in the mouth of a great golden fish.

The fish told him he would marry her, but he would lose her (and then find her again in a different world).

When they got married, the boy, now a man, cut down the banyan tree to build a home for the two of them to live in. The seeds from that tree made a forest, through which a stream, like a silver ribbon, cut through the land. Another tree, identical to the one from his boyhood, grew by the stream.

As the tree grew, so did the stream.

As the water grew, so did its darkness.

One evening, as the man was sitting and playing his bamboo flute underneath the banyan tree, by the shores of the river, he noticed a fish jumping and playing in the water. He immediately thought of children jumping and playing, and he thought the fish looked a little bit like a child.

A leaf from the banyan tree, with green skin and veins larger than his hand, sailed down and floated into the water. The fish began nib-bling at the banyan leaf, and the man watched as the fish grew golden, brighter and larger before his eyes, until it rivaled the sun that hung over Âu Cơ's mountains. He looked up at the tree. Its ropy branches resembled long roots, as if the tree didn't belong above the earth but inside of it. He stood awhile, staring at the enormous tree breathing with life, and the brilliant sun-fish casting light in the water below.

The man was determined to take the tree with him. He took out his ax and cut around the roots of the tree.

***

THE MAN'S WIFE SHOOK HER HEAD from the window of the kitchen. She watched her husband drag an enormous tree along the path that ran through the rice field, from north to south.

As he moved the banyan tree along the path, she could see the blood on its roots, its soil not yet clotting the wounds her husband had made with his ax. It painted lines of dark red along the dirt, like open cuts in the earth. She imagined the severed roots left behind in the land, broken fingers and toes, half buried.

"It will grow here," he insisted, noticing his wife's expression.

And he dug a hole as deep as his spade would go, and buried his tree.

To her surprise, the banyan tree did grow. Perhaps it was desperate for a new life.

Or perhaps it was avenging its death, and dreamed of reincarnation.

Regardless of its mainspring, the banyan tree rendered glossy emerald leaves as if it had never been cut, bountifully, reaching from its roots to the sky like a creation myth. It grew like the woman's garden used to grow, in carpets and fountains and forests, in bouquets with inward spirals that were visibly endless. It blossomed like it was new and new again, drinking earth for the first time, seeing sunlight with new eyes. The banyan tree reached in all cosmic directions, calling to the winds of all realities.

One day, when the tree was especially full of leaves, the woman watched her husband fill his pockets with its greenery, and head to the village as if he were going to make his fortune.

And so he did.

Money or luck, stems or leaves, all came under the pounding of his stone pestle. He produced a healing pulp, and with it, he breathed life into everyone, from the sick to the very old, from the disabled to the paper souls to the damned. He brought everyone back from the brink of death, as fire that extinguishes its black blossom petals. Everyone in the village hailed him as a brilliant doctor, a savior.

In the neighboring village, an extremely wealthy merchant learned of the gifted healer. He sent word that his daughter, afflicted with a mysterious illness, had left doctor after doctor baffled as she grew sicker by the day. The woman watched again as her husband stuffed a new pouch with leaves from the great banyan tree, and put on his best jacket.

"How long will you be gone?" she asked.

"At least three days," he said. It's a full day's journey in each direction."

On the third day, her husband did not return.

In the ninth week, her husband still had not returned.

In the twelfth month—or it might have been the twelfth year, she couldn't be sure—her husband returned in a carriage painted in red and gold leaves, etched in feathers and dragon scales. Inside the carriage was the merchant's beautiful daughter, now wed to the man who had healed her.

The woman rushed out, ready to scream at her husband for his betrayal. She was shocked to discover that she had no voice. She searched the ground for the heaviest rock she could find. She realized that her hands were ephemeral, her body already disappearing.

Her husband and his new wife moved through her as if she were not there.

The woman turned accusingly to the banyan tree. But the tree had no answer made of words. It breathed with the wind; it shifted with the shadows.

Time moved through the woman's body, now made of the ashes of an ancient grandmother. Her husband and his bride did not, would not, see her. Her husband never spoke of her. If his memories held any part of her, he did not demonstrate so. They continued to live around her, as she moved through the rooms and the walls of her home. She would often press her hands and body to the walls, touch the furniture, useless efforts to prove her existence. She held nothing, and nothing held her. It was as if she had never been.

She went back into the forest for answers. All she found was the fish, now a shade, who had become too large for the ribbon-river. The river was drying up.

The fish wriggled its body around the river rocks, gasping for breath as the water level moved up and down in waves around its mouth. The fish, too, was losing its voice.

"The only way for your husband to see you again," whispered the fish, "is to water the banyan tree with water from the river."

"But I am a ghost. I cannot carry water to the banyan tree."

"You can," said the fish.

The woman looked at the river, its water level diminishing by the day. She said, "But you cannot spare any water."

"Then take me with you," the fish replied.

And so she did.

Just as the fish had promised, the woman was able to pick up the largest bowl in her house. She marveled at her hands and body. She had been without touch for so many years, she had forgotten what it was like to feel weight and texture. The bowl was cool in the warm, humid air. It pulled gently at her long, unused muscles. Her feet felt the soil; she delighted in the darkness of the crescent moons under her toe nails. She knelt by the river and inhaled. She pressed the edge of the bowl into the riverbank, making mud, taking earth, and with much effort, she filled the large, shallow bowl with river water. She scooped mud and let it run through her fingers. She thought of childbirth.

The fish wriggle-hopped into the bowl, as if it once had legs and remembered them. It took the rest of the water with it, until there was nothing left in the ground but a wound, its muddy scar quickly drying up.

As she walked back to the house, the fish said, "Your husband and his wife won't be able to see you."

"Why not?" she asked. "If I can carry this bowl, with you in it, why wouldn't he be able to see me?"

"Because he has forgotten you," the fish replied.

And so she entered her home, again, with great sorrow. She felt that the river, drained from the land, had taken its place in her body to run everywhere—her blood, bloating beneath her skin, became like the great sea of the East, rising to slow her every movement with the heaviness of her years. She could not stand. She moved to put the shallow bowl on the table near the kitchen sink, where the fish blinked at her with its mirror-eyes. She leaned her body into the walls and wished for true disappearance—a burial without memory, land without language.

A sound like a strangled cry startled her out of the hypnosis of her death wish. She looked toward the bowl she had set on the counter. Her husband's second wife was washing dishes in the shallow bowl, oblivious to the fish, who was choking on soap bubbles.

It gargled like a drowned child.

She moved swiftly, but she was too late. The fish sank into the soapy water and then surfaced like a leaf. Death was pungent and sour under the fragrance of the soap-water, durian and flowers and flies.

"Ugh," said the young wife. She pinched her nose. They both reached for the bowl, but the young wife grabbed it first. She rushed out of the house with it and, before the woman could stop her, poured the dirty dishwater over the roots of the banyan tree, fish and all.

A great rumbling, like thunder, sounded from under the ground. It moved the earth beneath the tree until the dirt bubbled, like the water inside a kettle over a stove. The roots shuffled their subversive branches. The leaves shuddered against a strange wind. Sunlight flashed for a moment on the scales of the fish, a thousand gold coins, a thousand years old. Its eyes reflected, for a second, all of the memories the woman held—of her husband, of her children, in the past and the future.

If knowledge could turn one to stone, the woman would have died that certain death. She imagined her bones expanded to liquid and then solid, filling her veins and arteries, rooting her where she stood. She was the second wife, her husband's second chance at their marriage. He had repeated their past with his banyan tree healing wish, going back into her youth without knowing he was leaving her behind.

The fish, silver in moonlight and golden in sunlight, dove into the ocean-soil. Its body stretched and dug, finding new water, an opening to Biển Đông, the East Sea. The fish was Lạc Long Quân, the sea dragon.

The roots of the tree were out of the ground now, thunderous, the sound of drums in her ears. It beat a steady rhythm from the center of the earth to its surface. It pulled itself out of the ground as its soul sounded. It woke her husband, who ran out of the house, shouting, "No! Not my tree!"

It woke everything.

The woman and the second wife, now seeing themselves at last, turned toward their husband, who was throwing himself at the roots of the tree as the tree lifted itself into the air. He scrambled to hold on, and then realized that it was too late to let go. The roots dangled miles long, longer than the branches that had reached skyward, now flying toward Âu Cơ's heavenly mountain realm.

He looked at his wife from that great distance, beheld one and then the other.

"I wished for us to be reborn," the man called out.

"You wished to forget," the women said together.

The tree lifted the man higher and higher. Rocks that had been buried deep between the roots were free to drop to the ground like hand grenades. Soil burst where they landed, and the wife, who was then two, ran in different directions to take cover.

The absence of the strong, intricate hold of the roots inside the earth loosened the ground until it broke. The people rushed out of their homes, only to find themselves separated where they stood. Where the tree had been, a great hole in the ground, now a ridge, now a canyon, cut deeply into the earth. What was grove became jungle; what was seashore became enemy lines. The tall, limber coconut palms cracked at the base of the earth. Their fruit tumbled like heads.

The tree was beyond the realms of Âu Cơ and Dragon Lord of Lạc now, with the husband like a particle of dust on the horizon. It found its rest on the moon.

Once, in a dream, the woman saw that the North and the South were husband and wife. They joined at the seashore, where land met sea, and their children were the fish. The land grew abundantly, as it always had, at the woman's lightest touch. The sound of her voice would call the seeds up from the ground; the brush of her hand begat gardens and forests. She dreamed she was Âu Cơ, and her husband was Lạc Long Quân.

She dreamed the world lulled her and her husband to sleep each night, into dreams where no war came.

The woman heard her husband's bamboo flute playing from the moon where he sat, on the roots of the handsome banyan tree, a tiny heartbeat in space.

The sea dragon, feeling the loss of the heart of Vietnam, sent nourishing water through the veins and arteries of the country until the land was heavy with it. He couldn't undo the divorce, or call the banyan tree back, but he could send the children and husband back to the woman, even if they ended up in a different world, or in a different form.

A veil dropped from the mountains of heaven, down to the dragon waters of the sea. The northern and southern regions of the land became strangers, and the two women, who had run in different directions, discovered they were pregnant.

Oakland Night Question

—Phùng Nguyễn—

NIGHT IS ABOUT TO END WHEN Đức and I get inside his decrepit car. Thiện stands underneath the arch of his apartment complex, waving goodbye. Yesterday afternoon, Thiện and Đức came to fetch me at my hotel. Thiện's hair, which goes past his shoulders, at first made me wary, but in truth Thiện is courteous, easygoing, and prone to daydreaming. Resting on a sofa in Thiện's apartment during the predawn hours, I let my mind wander along with his singing and guitar music. By and by, certain thoughts came to me, thoughts at first seemed fragmented, random, but in fact were related to Đức's question, posed to me hours earlier as if it were a natural part of the conversation, exchanged above foaming beers and plates of blood pudding at a restaurant in the town where we three congregated last night.

Đức and I would often get together in a city toward the southern part of the state, where neither of us lives. I have the sense Đức never lives long enough in any city to be considered a resident. He lives alone, has no real responsibility to anyone, travels often and anytime he pleases. That fact alone makes me extremely envious. On the other hand, I am older than Đức, old enough to kill and be killed legally before Đức had the chance to participate in the grown-up game we call war. The fact I was born and grew up in a poor village in the countryside, marked by omnipresent traces of bombs and bullets, has been enough to rattle him. Behind the high walls of an elegant mansion, sheltered from the dangers outside, people naturally have the luxury to ruminate. Đức told me about his complex, precocious thoughts about the war in a composition written in fifth grade.

Despite the great disparity in our childhoods and war experiences, I believe that Đức and I belong to the same group of people standing precariously on two planks floating in opposite directions, trying to keep our balance so we don't fall into the abyss of confusion below. It seems the piece of wood that keeps dragging me back into the past has more chances of success.

There are things in my past that will haunt me for the rest of my life. For several years now, I have gone backward rather than forward. Đức's friends, who are his age or younger, used to surprise me with their ability to speak, in Vietnamese, about other things besides *phở*, Huế beef noodle soup, and rice bits. Much later, after my surprise has faded, I wonder if this reaction might have come from the fear of losing my last lifeline of self-respect, namely my Vietnamese proficiency. When a person can no longer depend on certain things in life, the fluency with which he speaks his mother's tongue where such skill is not highly valued can mean a number of things, including the coy if desperate desire to profess both ownership of, and allegiance to, his dreary past.

But lately, when encountering Đức's young friends, I have come to expect from them the ability to express abstract thoughts not only fluently but also cogently in multiple languages. So I wasn't surprised when, earlier, I heard Thiện and Đức argue passionately about fresh assertions in a historian's recently published book. In Vietnamese, of course. And I wasn't the least bit surprised later when Thiện, hugging his guitar, sang his latest song in accent-free English until the early morning hours, in his clean and orderly apartment.

When the war ended, Đức was old enough to carry with him the ashes of the past, but also too young to cherish them as the only possession a person could own. It seems as if this bit of ashes occasionally gets stirred up by something or someone, creating a dust cloud that would choke Đức and make him cough. It wasn't a coincidence that he gave me Kazuo Ishiguro's *An Artist of the Floating World* when we visited his favorite bookstore near the heart of San Francisco.

After painstakingly pondering the novel's contents with my poor English, I conclude there are at least a few things that are troubling and will continue to trouble Đức for many years to come. I also believe that those worries, if my thoughts are not unfounded, have long since ceased to bother me. If I have to describe myself and my relationship to the war, I would often think of a man who has just lost a game of chess, embarrassed and unsure of what to do. The winner is determined not to erase the board and start over; it is thus useless to stand there and complain. So I take my leave with the consolation that I have at least finished the game, albeit badly played. Over time, the thought of having finished the game becomes a very effective antidote to many awkward situations. But not this time. When Đức's question came up, or rather, floated toward my direction above a table full of empty beer bottles and cigarette butts, I imagined catching something sincere and beseeching in his gaze. But I still ignored the question. I did not want to answer such a question. Perhaps because it has also been, for a long time, my own question. At any rate, I do feel I owe him an answer.

When his car turns into a road leading toward the freeway, Đức lights his first cigarette of the journey. He will smoke nonstop throughout this trip, and at times will be seized with hacking coughs. San Francisco is thirty minutes away. If I want my story to end before morning, I'd better start now.

***

THE WHOLE VILLAGE, INCLUDING ME—who was then a child—knew the story of how Mr. Thiệp hanged himself from his ceiling beam one summer afternoon. But why he did it, only a handful among the grown-ups would know. I was certain Little Kình did not know. Little Kình did not know a lot of things, including how to talk in full sentences. Little Kình was Mr. Thiệp's son, older than me by seven, eight years. If I called anyone else of Kình's age "little," my mother wouldn't have hesitated to whip my ass nice and good with her mulberry stick. But from childhood I had heard everyone in the village, including my mother, call him "Little Kình" or "crazy Little Kình." They said madness ran in his gene pool; Mr. Thiệp himself was far from being sane.

At the funeral, I stared at Little Kình. Wearing funeral clothes made of white linen gauze, on his head a white funeral band, his hands around a pot of incense, Little Kình walked behind the hearse, his face vacant. I was disgusted in seeing his thick, sheath-like upper lip fold over his lower, slobbering rim. My disgust was telling, since most village children, including my ten-year old self, were already shabby and filthy. While a poor village funeral was often a desolate, sleepy affair with nothing to stir anyone's interest, Little Kình at least made it bearable.

Little Kình did not go to school. He worked as hired help in the village, same as his mother—a weaver for Mr. Cửu Nhì's family.

The soil in my village was alluvial soil, mostly sand and gravel, not ideal for growing rice. People grew melons, peanuts, green and red beans, corn, tobacco, and mulberry, from which the leaves were harvested to feed silkworms. Alluvial soil was dry; to plant anything one had to water the soil constantly. Little Kình had the strength of a full-grown man, so he was hired to water the fertile patches. Both owner and hired help would collect water from a small pond using two large bamboo-woven buckets caulked with tree sap, then, carrying these buckets suspended from a wooden pole, would walk over the entire field. The pole, dipping and rising rhythmically from the worker's bent shoulders as he walked, would cause droplets of water to slosh around the rims of the buckets before spilling over the earth. And so it went, from morning to noon, from noon to dusk.

About two years after Mr. Thiệp hanged himself, my village became a bustling place. One day, the National Liberation Front showed up near dusk, rounding up the entire village council—representative, legal delegate, village registrar, secretary—and herding them like cattle toward the village's flagpole. The Front also ushered people from five surrounding hamlets to my village for a meeting. Each member of our village council was then singled out to be criticized, then released at the end of the meeting after each had sworn allegiance to the Front by not becoming collaborators for Ngô Đình Diệm or the Americans. It was a close call for these council members. Three days later, South Vietnamese soldiers came up from the district, in a confused hubbub of dogs barking and Garand rifles going off in staccato refrains. Then these soldiers retreated to Vĩnh Điện. The Front again rounded everyone up for a meeting. In spite of all these goings-on, from day to day the villagers continued to take up their hoes and carry their buckets to weed and water the field.

At this time Little Kình worked mainly for Uncle Tám Thơm's family. No one knew what had befallen Uncle Tám; he was always pale and sickly, all curled up on his wooden bed for at least twenty-eight days each month. Every morning Auntie Tám would head to the field carrying two hoes, followed by Sister Hạnh carrying two buckets, one containing an areca-sheathed lunch of rice mixed with reddish corn and the other a pot of steamed greens. Sister Hạnh turned eighteen that year. She had completed elementary school, and now lived at home to help her mother plant mulberry bushes and feed silkworms.

Each morning, Auntie Tám would slow down a bit in front of Mrs. Thiệp's house, call out "Little Kình, let's go," then continue on. Kình would quietly emerge, on his shoulders a pole tied to two old buckets and a large hoe. He would make loud, gurgling sounds to greet Sister Hạnh, his face bright and happy.

Three months after the Front had taken over the village council, the district sent out their people to take care of administrative matters. They came from either Phú Bông or Phú Bài. During the day they worked at the village headquarters, with guards standing at the gate outside. At night they retreated to their homes near the district for security reasons. From time to time the Front would show up for meetings, chiding the villagers, "Why do you let those good-for-nothings come by and boss you around?" Then the Front would vanish, sometimes for an entire month. Meanwhile the village registrar, Mr. Hồ Luyện, would make frequent visits to Auntie Tám's house "to be in touch with the people." No one knew the real reason for his visits, whether it had to do with Uncle Tám or Auntie Tám. When Uncle Tám fell dead after having a coughing fit that lasted for three days, the people weren't sure if the registrar's visits had to do with Auntie Tám or Sister Hạnh.

One morning, Auntie Tám was the one carrying the bamboo buckets containing an areca-sheathed lunch filled with thin slices of yam and a pot of steamed yam leaves. She stopped in front of Mrs. Thiệp's house, called out, "Little Kình, let's go," and walked on. Kình emerged from the yard, dragging his feet, his shoulders laden with buckets and hoes. He pursed his lips but stayed silent. Sister Hạnh was nowhere in sight to make him open his mouth and babble happily. Sister Hạnh was sick with no one knew what. But maybe Auntie Tám or Mr. Hồ Luyện would know. The village registrar had been coming to Auntie Tám's house for six, seven months at that point.

The next day, Auntie Tám repeated her routine, calling out to Little Kình then continuing on her way. After a while, she stopped and retraced her steps. Little Kình wasn't behind her. Little Kình wasn't in his yard. Little Kình wasn't in his house. She went back and forth. Then sitting on the sidewalk, dusty and covered with dry bamboo leaves, she cried.

Little Kình had gone away. Sister Hạnh's illness did not abate. She cocooned inside the house, seeing no one. Every morning Auntie Tám would carry her buckets and her hoes toward the field, all alone. In the summer I did not have to go to school, so during the day I would wander through the field, catching coal and fire crickets from under damp patches of grass and putting them in an empty milk can that I hid in a corner of the garden. If my mother found out, she would've surely whipped me. She often worried about me stepping on landmines or falling into some bamboo spike trap.

One day I followed a friend and walked all the way across the river to Thanh Châu to catch fire crickets. I didn't return home until dusk. I was worried about being whipped nice and good, but to my relief I found out the Front had returned that evening. My mother would need to attend the village meeting and wouldn't be around to whip me. The echoing loudspeakers were rallying the people to attend the trial of Hồ Luyện, evil collaborator of Diệm and the Americans. I nearly jumped with joy. I hated Hồ Luyện. My mother hated him, too. She often complained to my grandmother, wondering why there were men of his ilk who often preyed on orphaned, defenseless women.

That evening I pushed and shoved my way close the row of chairs where men of the Front were sitting. A guerrilla soldier, rifle in hand, was walking back and forth while yelling, to no avail, at a group of children fighting for seats. The trial began. The group of children, following the adults' lead, stood and saluted the red and blue flag next to a picture of the chairman of the Front. We were familiar with the ritual of saluting the flags. Blue, red, yellow—all flags were equally bright and cheerful. And those bigwigs in their portraits, compared with the dark-skinned village peasants, always looked so handsome and dignified, not unlike Vietnam's ancient emperors.

One man from the Front came up and said something that went on endlessly. I started to feel sleepy and nodded off against someone's dark, suntanned back in front of me. I didn't come to until Mr. Hồ Luyện's name was called. The man who talked for a long time was the prosecutor of the people's court. He cited a litany of Hồ Luyện's sins, any of which could have easily done him in. Finally, the prosecutor concluded that even killing Hồ Luyện three times over would not offset the blood debt he had incurred against the people.

But the evil Hồ Luyện was nowhere to be seen. Usually you would see the defendant, hands tied behind his back, sitting in a corner with a resigned and morose face waiting for his sentence to be read aloud. The younger kids started to whisper about Hồ Luyện's no-show, as did the grown-ups. Then the judge, who was also a member of the Front, stood up and told everyone why Hồ Luyện didn't show. It turned out the traitor was too cowardly to face the people. He had been shot dead at dusk by a member of the Front while trying to flee. The prosecutor said the warrior who punished Hồ Luyện was a blood relative of the people. He turned around and called, "Comrade Kình, please come and greet the people." Comrade Kình?!

Little Kình appeared, dressed in black pajamas like other members of the Front, over which he draped a brown oilcloth, and on his head a hat made of woven bamboo was also covered with oilcloth of the same brown. Carrying a long Indochinese rifle with an attached bayonet, he walked like a zombie with eyes staring straight ahead, stopping only when reaching the three-tiered steps leading to the forum. The light from a gas mantle shone on his blubbery, tightly-sealed lips, which looked as if he was trying to contain a large frog within. Suddenly Little Kình raised his left fist, shouting, "Down with the evil collaborators and traitors who work for Diệm and the Americans." Good heavens! Little Kình not only joined the Front but knew how to shout slogans. Perhaps the grown-ups were as shocked as I was, since no one repeated after Little Kình except for members of the Front.

Little Kình then shouted, "Hurrah for the National Liberation Front!" This time we all joined in. He shouted several other slogans, with hurrahs or denunciations, before abruptly falling silent. The prosecutor from the People's Court then stood up and escorted Little Kình toward the back. Out in the village's yard, we children were in a commotion. It was like market day. Everyone wanted to let everyone else know we were friends with Little Kình. I was truly impressed. Even a crazy one like Kình could learn to shout slogans after only a few months of joining the Front.

That night, I slept soundly and did not wake until noon the next day. As soon as I appeared on the threshold of the kitchen, my head freshly doused with water from the outdoor cistern, I saw my mother's angry face. She was holding her mulberry stick in one hand, and with the other hand the milk can that contained my crickets. Surely these crickets had made so much noise they caused her to lose her temper. I turned and ran out into the backyard, ignoring her scolding.

After climbing through an opening in a fence, I was inside Auntie Tám's garden. I was safe—for now. Walking along the side of Auntie Tám's house, I thought about seeking refuge at my uncle's house in the neighboring village of Định An until the evening. The sounds of people talking behind the bamboo walls of Auntie Tám's house unnerved me. Auntie Tám was still in the field, and Hồ Luyện had been shot dead—was Sister Hạnh talking to ghosts?

I looked through an opening in the wall and saw Little Kình's raft-like back. Little Kình was completely naked, his back and buttocks marked with lesions and pimples, going up and down on top of Sister Hạnh, chanting something nonstop as if in prayer. Sister Hạnh was lying face up, with eyes tightly shut. Her slightly tumescent belly rose and descended every time Little Kình's heavy, awkward frame pushed and pulled above her. They were doing husband-and-wife business. It was disgusting, Little Kình's voice was muffled by his labored breathing, so I had to listen closely before I could make out the words. He kept repeating slogans that had nothing to do with what he was doing. Sister Hạnh kept her eyes shut and never said anything. I grew bored, now aware that my empty belly was protesting loudly. I quietly backed away to the front gate, then ran at full speed to my uncle's house.

Sister Sáu, my uncle's daughter, took me home when it got dark. The Front was preparing to retreat, with Little Kình among the group, looking a bit lost, his confidence from the night before had disappeared. The next day my village would change leadership again.

This time South Vietnamese soldiers arrived from the province. There was also Mrs. Hồ Luyện, coming with the soldiers to retrieve her husband's body. When she arrived at Auntie Tám's house, Mrs. Hồ Luyện charged right into the yard, crying, cursing the slutty bitch who had killed her husband. Auntie Tám and Sister Hạnh must have been inside, but they kept mum. We children congregated around the house, watching the spectacle as if it were a circus.

The soldiers stayed in our village and nearby locations for a whole month, long enough for me to know almost everyone by sight. The summer went by peacefully. As long as the soldiers stayed, the cannons from the district would aim mainly at the mountainous area on the other side of Cái River. In the afternoon I would often visit the soldiers at their watchtower, listening to their rambling gossips. Not to be outdone, I told them about the shocking things that had happened in my village. Like how Mr. Thiệp had hanged himself from the ceiling beam. And his crazy son who followed the Front and was cured of his craziness. The soldiers laughed so hard, and asked why I didn't join the Front as well. I got mad, saying, "So you think I am crazy, too?"

The last days of summer were long and sad. Gone were my coal, fire, and iron crickets. Even the koi with their bright, showy tails had vanished beneath the irrigation canals. In a few days I would go back to school in town, sharing meals with my unruly posse at a boarding house.

One night, a pale, new moon appeared on the horizon. Without telling my mother, I ran to the watchtower at the edge of the village to sit dejectedly next to a soldier who didn't look much happier. Maybe he missed his family. From the direction of the wooden bridge, I heard the wind rustling among the bamboo hedges. I leaned back on the thin, filthy wall of the watchtower and drifted off to sleep. At midnight a loud series of *rat tat tat* jolted me awake. The soldier standing guard had shot at something beyond the fence of the strategic hamlet. From the village, other sounds came forth: the urgent, rhythmic knock-knock of fish drums; the lower-pitch rattling from tin barrels; the loud, echoing *woof-woof* of barking dogs. At first, these sounds seemed discordant, but gradually merged into a deep hum resembling the sound of locusts. By the district's order, we had to alert the surrounding areas with bells and drums when we sensed danger. I followed the soldier through the fence made of sharp bamboo spikes and came to a large, writhing form on the ground.

Under the pale moonlight, I recognized Little Kình. Blood glistened on his chest and belly. I screamed, "Oh, Kình!" and fell next to him. His thick upper lip was drawn back, drool mixed with blood giving his mouth an oily sheen. With glazed eyes toward the waxing moon, Little Kình babbled words and phrases that had nothing to do with what was happening to him. This was the third time I heard him utter these phrases. The last time was when I'd seen him naked with Sister Hạnh. He kept twitching, then finally became still. I looked up at the soldier. Little Kình was crazy, why did you shoot him? The soldier did not respond but turned away from me, the rifle on his shoulders hard and stiff like a dry log. That night, long, slow sobs could be heard from Mrs. Thiệp's house, and a baby's cries from Auntie Tám's. Sister Hạnh had given birth to her firstborn. A son, with a large, flat nose like Mr. Hồ Luyện's.

***

AT TWELVE, I WAS TOO EASILY distracted to learn anything from these events. Little Kình's death slipped through the sieve of my memory barely two weeks into the new school year. And after I reached twenty, I became saddled with too many worries to become concerned with things that now seemed so far in the past. Especially when these worries seem to be a lot worse than what had come before. Only much later, after the war had long been over and the wounds had become more bearable, did I begin to think, now and then, of Little Kình. Especially when I would hear, on this or the other side of the world, the shouting slogans similar to those I'd heard from his lips long ago. When Đức asked me what had caused people to stand on this or the other side of the battle line, I would think of Little Kình. So I thought I would share with Đức this story, full of holes and false starts, to see if he could find an answer that perhaps I'd also like to have. I am not an eloquent storyteller, and my story is clearly messy and erratic. Besides, my recollection, at best, could reveal only a tiny part of the whole, like drips or smudges bleeding into other shades in an abstract painting.

At one point, I thought I had found an explanation for Little Kình's tragic fate after learning the likely reason for his father's suicide. Several years before slipping his head through the noose made of coconut fiber, Mr. Thiệp had led at least two other men to their deaths. His uncle and this uncle's firstborn son were taken by the Vietminh[2] from their hiding place, brought to a camp in Châu Mưu on the other side of Cái River, and executed along with their comrades in the Vietnamese Nationalist Party. Their deaths were payment for Mr. Thiệp's safety.

My awareness of this history might have explained the reason for Mr. Thiệp's suicide, but it still has not, to this day, explained the strange relationship between Little Kình and Sister Hạnh or Little Kình's compulsive slogans. I have reasons to believe Little Kình never understood the true meaning behind those hurrahs and denunciations uttered by his misshapen lips.

In the car now filled with cigarette smoke, Đức remains stone quiet. I have no idea what he is thinking, but I know he has listened to the whole story. I begin to doubt myself. I have tried to answer Đức's question by telling him a story whose true meaning I'm not even sure I have grasped, at the same time hoping he would understand.

I know I'm not at peace with myself. It wasn't a coincidence that Đức suggested *An Artist of the Floating World* when we stopped by his favorite bookstore. Perhaps the detail I added to explain Mr. Thiệp's death—something I knew didn't make the story any clearer—has somehow bothered him. Is the finale Mr. Thiệp chose for himself—thirteen years after his relatives' executions at Châu Mưu—too brutal, too harsh, compared to the peace that awaits Masuji Ono at the end of Ishiguro's novel? Peace that represents a redemptive arc found in the bright smiles of young Japanese greeting each other in front of sleek skyscrapers erected upon the ashes and ruins of yesteryear? Was Ono's artistic dream—a floating vision, buoyed by an earnest but violent fervor to help the emperor create a New, Great Asia—less reprehensible or more forgivable than the savage ideology of my brethren?

---

2 A Vietnamese, communist-led organization founded in 1941 who fought against the French and the Japanese in Indochina

What has kept Đức and his cosmopolitan friends from disavowing the cheerless past that my generation, for lack of choice, has held on like an unalienable part of our lives? Why have I never asked myself this question when seeing young people holding hands, going to restaurants in bustling Vietnamese conclaves in Western cities, where they order *phở* or Huế beef noodle soup and greet each other with words and phrases from languages other than their (and my) mother's tongue? Is it because the younger generation has been exposed to movies about the Vietnam War made by foreign directors, with actors speaking Chinese, and scenery shot in Burma or Malaysia? Is it because they have read history books written by famous historians ten thousand miles away from the battlefronts where my friends and I shed our blood and bones? Is it the fear—my own fear of having to confront the younger generation's views of the war, constructed from these revisionist or alienating lens—that has made me avoid them?

I think about the loneliness that Đức and his friends must endure in their search for meaning from the exorbitant price that not only my generation, but also his generation, have had to pay for events that occurred long ago. Perhaps I owe him more than an answer to the question that hovered above the foaming beers and plates of blackish blood pudding in the restaurant in the city where we congregated last night.

***

ĐỨC LEANS OVER TO LIGHT HIS last cigarette of the journey. I open the passenger's window halfway down. Threads of smoke fly past me and dissipate into the damp cool San Francisco air. The car is heading toward Bay Bridge. Night and Oakland are behind us, now.

MIA, MIO; POW, POP

—Lưu Vĩ Lân—

KHÂM ĐỨC SWELTERS UNDER the unrelenting summer sun. A high-pressure system traps the heat, radiating it outward from the arid and barren Central Highlands. Winds from Quảng Trị whip through, blistering and dry, searing the soil or charring it to ash. Even the tired excavators, parched and breathless, feel the heat humming in their ears—a low buzz that reminds them of death.

Tâm collapses into his makeshift tent. He takes off his duckweed-shaped hat and bandana scarf, struggling for air. The sun's oppressive heat blurs his vision. But in this war-ravaged valley with its unforgiving climate, sunlight appears to liquefy into a mercurial haze that distorts eyesight. The light presses down, heavy as a dumbbell.

"Try these on, Tâm," Tom says, slipping the classic Aviator glasses over Tâm's sideburns.

"Wow, I can't even afford a knockoff Korean pair," Tâm says. But he shakes his head and returns the sunglasses to Tom. "I can't take something this nice."

"You've got to be kidding me," Tom says. "The sun's gonna roast your eyes!"

"Nah, but thanks."

Tom is taken by surprise.

"See those guys digging over there?" Tâm says. "Any of them wearing sunglasses? I'm just an interpreter. I don't need to look like some American general."

Tâm means General Douglas MacArthur, who always wore the same type of sunglasses. Tom nods. He has only one extra pair to lend his friend Tâm, who's the same age, though he's still surprised by Tâm's excuse.

Both were born in 1957, shortly after the Vietnam War kicked off, yet it would drag on for eighteen more years. Both survived the war, but the memories of it still haunted them. Now it's 1992 and they're back at Khâm Đức, west of Quảng Nam Province and the Hồ Chí Minh Trail, where a horrific battle took place in 1968. The Vietcong had targeted all the CIDG stations[3] that were put up to stop communist infiltrators.

"Our people don't have enough food to eat or clothes to wear, so who cares if their eyes burn too?" Tâm says this gently, without bitterness, realizing that the war ended long ago yet peace remains elusive; the postwar era feels like it's own kind of war.

Hundreds of Vietnamese workers from the mountains, made poor by the brutal war in the highlands, are digging with all kinds of tools in the valley. Under tarpaulins, they sift soil and sand through sieves to separate out the solid fragments, looking for the remains of American MIAs. Phước Sơn is a rugged area known for gold mining, but the diggers aren't after gold—just the sad past found in these human remains. The debates over the existence of these remains constitute their own sort of proxy war. Tâm's fully aware of this as he's the interpreter for the joint U.S.-Vietnam search missions for MIA/POW.

Tom, an American autopsy expert, makes Tâm wonder if he's with the CIA or FBI. Tâm knows that all the Vietnamese officials participating

---

3   Civilian Irregular Defense Group (*Nhóm phòng thủ dân sự không chính quy*) consisted of several Senators, consultants from U.S. Special Force and ARVN Special Forces commonly known as the Rangers, commandos of infantry battalions. Its main purpose was to infiltrate into the forest borders, scouting as reconnaissance, assassinate, and jammer.

in this mission are members of the national security forces. He got this job as an interpreter because of his clean record. The Vietnamese delegation is cautious of the Americans, a feeling that's mutual, but both sides still try to play nice. The relationship between Tâm and Tom is probably something like that too. Tâm has to be careful, even suspicious, of any kindness from Tom, including the sunglasses.

***

"CHICKEN COOP" WAS THE NICKNAME the children of the dilapidated railroad neighborhood gave Gonzalez. The locals, on the other hand, just called him Lết—much shorter and easier to pronounce. The railroad had been abandoned since the French stopped going through there to get to Đà Nẵng.

Lết first turned up in the neighborhood around 1970, and looking pretty scared. Tâm was thirteen at the time, and it dawned on him that not all Americans had soft, blond hair like in Phạm Duy's songs, or were giant, well-dressed men with pockets full of chocolate bars, who had a look about them that intimidated ARVN officers.

To Tâm, Lết wasn't much to look at but friendly enough, unlike most Americans Tâm had encountered. His skin carried shades of light and dark tones. His hair wasn't blond and he looked nothing like the black soldiers who frequented the brothels nearby. It wasn't until Lết started tutoring Tâm English that he heard Lết, who was Hispanic, use a derogatory term to describe himself. Lết laughed and told Tâm that his black and white friends did the same. "And you call a high-ranking military officer *The Man*. That's the slang black guys use."

Lết was an infantryman in Division 23, also known as the American Division, and his mission was mainly guarding some desolate expanse. Their HQ was in Chu Lai, just south of Đà Nẵng, with other divisions scattered in Hội An and Duy Xuyên District. Lết belonged to the 196th Light Infantry Brigade stationed in Duy Xuyên. The U.S. Army had built a strategic fence stretching from the base all the way to the mountains in the west. It sliced through the Hồ Chí Minh Trail and ended in a remote valley known as Khâm Đức.

In 1968, when the Vietcong attacked, Lết's unit was flown from Duy Xuyên to Khâm Đức to offer assistance to the besieged military base. Lết, a rookie and barely twenty, witnessed Khâm Đức turn to a hellscape, and showed him how firefights ended in Vietnam. Coming from a poor immigrant family, Lết enlisted hoping to secure a better future, not because he wanted to get injured or face death in this scorched wasteland.

A year later, Lết deserted and wandered into the railroad town. Its residents, refugees from the war, earned their living by serving American GIs—collecting trash from military bases, cleaning rooms, washing clothes, finding prostitutes, and setting up makeshift R&R spots for low-ranking GIs looking for some fun after each battle. He formed a bond with Hoa, a country girl who lost her home in the war. She had moved to the city, turning to prostitution to survive. Together, they built a make-shift home in the slum neighborhood, and the residents welcomed them and loved them. Lết was the first American deserter to join the community, which survived by serving the Americans.

Each morning, Lết put on his shorts, an old shirt, and a hat, and wandered the alleyways looking for work. He took on all kinds of handyman jobs—fixing roofs and furniture—just to scrape together enough money so Hoa could limit her exposure to prostitution. Known for his beautiful chicken coops, everyone in the neighborhood who raised chickens had one of them out behind their house. Before Lết arrived, the chicken coops were, much like their homes, poorly built. Lết, a farmer from Texas, used pallets from nearby American military bases to build ventilated chicken coops, equipping them with all the necessary things like nesting boxes, food and water trays, enclosed runs and access doors. Everyone thought the modern design of his chicken coops were impressive, and they saw for the first time how an American would build them. As a result, Lết earned the nickname "Chicken Coop." Beyond the war, military gear, and abandoned Amerasians left behind, Lết's American-styled chicken coops represented the first real "technology" common Vietnamese folks adopted.

Tâm only became closer to Lết after studying English with him. Tâm was only in sixth grade and found the new language difficult. His poor parents, who couldn't afford his tuition at the famous VUS English School run by the Americans, were thrilled when Lết offered to teach Tâm English. Their son could now learn the language from a native speaker instead of a Vietnamese instructor with a French accent. Later in life, when Tâm majored in English in college, he realized that the kind of English he had learned from Lết was far from standard.

When the American withdrawal began in 1972, Tâm's uncle, an ARVN staff sergeant, urged Lết to register for repatriation, knowing he couldn't stay in Vietnam forever. Lết remained silent on the matter.

The uncle shook his head and said, "Well, it's really up to him if he wants to stay."

At the nearby police booth, an officer who also lived in the railroad town chimed in, "I told him the same thing, but he wouldn't listen. So just think of him as a black ex-soldier who deserted to join the Vietminh."

A local female vendor added, "If he went back to the States, who'd take care of Hoa and their son, Little Dog? She quit her job after they got married and now works as a housemaid. Lết can stay here with the rest of us. There's no point in him going back—they'd just draft him for another war."

Lết confided in Tâm why he refused to repatriate: "If I report myself to the U.S. military, the MPs would arrest and throw me in LBJ right away. Do you know what LBJ is short for? President Lyndon B. Johnson, you know, the guy who started the war. Just kidding—it means Long Bình Jail. The Americans built a giant military base called Long Bình, south of Sài Gòn. The base has a detention center where American deserters and violators are held in custody. I'd be taken back to the States and court-martialed. They'd probably deport me somewhere, maybe Latin America, where I don't even speak the language."

After Lết said this, his hazel eyes darkened like the hot cocoa found in American GIs' rations, a drink Tâm craved but rarely had a chance to enjoy.

"Your sadness has a chocolate color to it," Tâm joked as he handed Lết a glass of iced tea. "Here, drink this. It'll make you less thirsty and help drown your sorrows."

By the end of the tutoring session, Lết was laughing too.

Years later, when Tâm was sixteen, he would take his girlfriend out for smoothies. As time went by, the image of Lết faded from Tâm's memory.

In May 1975, cadres from the suburbs, who had marched with the Liberation Army to seize Đà Nẵng, summoned Tâm to the ward's administrative office to meet with local authorities. Tâm had a clean family background: he was a poor, working-class citizen with some formal education, but no ties to the old South Vietnamese government or the ARVN. This meant he was eligible to become a local cadre while still a senior in high school. In fact, he turned out to be the most educated cadre of his ward. After attending several political training workshops and passing a thorough background check, he became a Party member and was appointed Vice Chairman of his ward.

Out of nowhere Lết reappeared. On a roasting afternoon in late June in Đà Nẵng, he saw Lết standing next to a chicken coop with his wife Hoa cradling their three-year-old son in her arms. They materialized in front of Tâm like three ghosts from the past, like an old scar on fresh skin. They seemed so out of place, especially when history would rather forget they existed.

"Lết!" Tâm said. "How come you're still around?" The two milled about and talked in the dark. They avoided going inside in case it would lead to trouble.

"He's got nowhere to go," Hoa said to Tâm. Lết remained silent because he had nothing to add to the conversation. He was a deserter, therefore an enemy of the American people. But where could he escape to? If he took flight like a bird, an eagle would catch him. If he swam away like a fish, a shark would eat him.

"How about this?" Tâm said after some thought. "Hoa, you're a war evacuee from the countryside. We know the government wants to send people to one of the new economic zones. Go to Kon Tum. You can register at the ward's office tomorrow. I'll help you with the paperwork. You should list three family members in your household. For your husband's background, just write down *mixed-race French*. If somebody asks, you tell them the French left in 1954 and your husband was left behind as an orphan. Tell them his name is Nguyễn Văn Lết. You both can start a new life there. They'll give you land to cultivate. People there are from all over and nobody knows each other."

With her son still in her arms, Hoa hugged Tâm. "Thank you for helping us find a way out. Ever since the liberation soldiers came here, my husband has been hiding out in our hut. I didn't know what to do."

Tâm wasn't used to this kind of gesture—hugging—which he understood was more popular in the West.

Many people were relocated to the new economic zones. Banners and slogans were put up for the farewell ceremony. As the three buses were about to leave, Tâm waved goodbye from the yard, a heartfelt gesture toward Lết, who sat at the back of the bus. Lết's cocoa eyes, often full of tension and sorrow, seemed to brighten with hope, as there was now a light at the end of the tunnel. When his bus made a slight turn to exit the gate, Lết raised his hand and waved at Tâm.

***

"OKAY, FINE," TOM INSISTS, "you take these ones, and I'll keep the Ray-Bans." He hands Tâm the cheap plastic pair he's wearing.

Tâm thinks to himself: Americans are so insistent on being nice, convinced that whatever is good for them must be good for the rest of the world. But it's too bad they don't read the *I Ching*. Asian people believe that a reversal of fortune happens when something reaches its peak. Extreme love becomes extreme hate; extreme kindness will turn into deep resentment. It's all tragic in its own way.

"Okay, Tom, I'll wear them." Tâm is moved by Tom's generosity. Afterward, they leave the tent and go down into the valley where the workers are digging. A wind blows through the excavation site and creates swirling dust devils.

"That high hill over there is called Ngok Tavak Peak," Tom says. "It's where the American and the ARVN Special Forces[4] were stationed. The NVA[5] attacked them for two straight days in May 1968. Some of our commandos were able to escape but were ambushed here. Three soldiers were shot and went MIA. The survivors told me about it. We're here looking for their remains."

"How sure are you the report was accurate?" Tâm asks.

"The U.S. Armed Forces write up reports after each fight," Tom explains. "Where else could these three missing guys be?"

Tâm doesn't answer the question. He knew the destructive and traumatic nature of war. The evacuations, desertions, surrendering. The wounded, paralyzed, disabled. The dead. But he also understood that the number of victims was uncountable; you couldn't categorize them. In this fleeting moment, Tâm thinks about Lết and wonders where he is now. When he had helped cover up Lết's identity, people from the railroad town whispered about it, though nobody believed the fabricated story and could care less about Lết. When gossip turned to accusation, however, Tâm was passed for promotion pending an investigation. He resigned from his position instead, giving the excuse of wanting to complete his education. He majored in English, just to compare the English he had learned from Lết with the more standard, school-taught English. Tâm bursts out laughing at how naive he was fifteen years ago.

"What's so funny?" Tom says.

"Oh, nothing. We Vietnamese laugh for all kinds of reasons." Tâm's tone turns serious. "Tom, do think there's MIA but also MIO?"

"You're joking, right?" Tâm's question takes Tom by surprise.

---

4 Army of Republic of [South] Vietnam
5 North Vietnamese Army

"Well, life's full of choices. If there's *missing in action*, there should also be *missing in option*. MIO. Maybe some people choose to disappear, and that's their choice."

Tom doesn't respond and waits.

"Here's more wordplay," Tâm continues. "Everybody knows about POW, but what about POP?"

Tom looks at Tâm, waiting for an explanation.

"During wartime, you're a *prisoner of war*, a POW. So in peacetime twenty years later, you can be a *prisoner of peace*, or POP." Tâm adds quickly, ending wrapping up their conversation, "Tom, that makes us both POPs."

Tâm continues on to the excavation site, leaving Tom behind to consider his words.

—*Translated by Quan Manh Ha & Cab Tran*

A Jarai Tribesman and His Wife

—Nguyễn Đức Tùng—

FROM A COFFEE SHOP NOT FAR from the 9/11 Memorial, I headed toward the Strand, where I bought a poetry collection by Gerald Stern and met Siu Kpa, a sixty-year-old Jarai man, and Dep, his wife. Jarai, Jrai, Gia-rai, Jrarai, and Chareye are all variations on the name of his ethnic group, within which he would be warmly received as *Anak Jarai*. Son of Jarai.[6] Both man and wife spoke Vietnamese, but his was better.[7] Actually, she belonged to the Ba Na, or Bahnar, which includes both highlands and lowlands people.[8] The couple had both lost their memory, but in opposite ways.

He lost his memory the way old people tend to lose theirs, meaning his short-term, while his long-term remained intact. In contrast, she could not remember important milestones in her own life story, but could remember things that happened recently. At times she would lose her bearings and certain words from the Ba Na lexicon. Likewise, he would forget his own name and important things like his address,

---

6 Jarai, which means "People of the Waterfalls," are an ethnic group from Vietnam's central highlands (i.e., Kon Tum, Gia Lai, and Đắk Lắk provinces), and the northeast Cambodian province of Ratanakiri. The Jarai were recruited by the U.S. military for covert efforts against the communists during the Vietnam War; and a few were resettled in the U.S. after the war's end.

7 The Jarai language is a member of the Austronesian language family, related to the Cham language of Central Vietnam, Cambodia and the Malayo-Polynesian languages of Indonesia, Malaysia, the Philippines and other Pacific Islands.

8 The Ba Na/Bahnar are an ethnic group living in Kon Tum and Gia Lai, and also along the coastal provinces of Bình Định and Phú Yên. The Ba Na language belongs to the Mon-Khmer language family.

the names of his loved ones, or his plans for the next hour. Yet he could recall his past in vivid, exacting details, especially if it had to do with his *plơi*, the village of his youth. He remembered the white loincloths with vertical stripes and the indigo headdresses with side drops of the Jarai men. He remembered the festive costumes of the Ba Na women, with abstract crimson patterns framed by white borders and flowing tassels.

They both remembered the sad and deeply purple mountains, sentinels that appeared more forlorn as one's gaze swept upwards.

They were not sitting inside the coffee shop but in front of it, on the ground. In New York, as you know, there is enough space on the sidewalk for squatters. The man and his wife were stripped of land, home, hearth. Like other ethnic groups from Vietnam's Central Highlands, they were forced into exile. Before this disaster, their relationship appeared like it would work out. Jarai society is matrilineal and insular, yet he had met a Ba Na woman, a rare enough occurrence. Ba Na people, while fiercely loyal, are free to marry outside their ethnic group and in the process adopt other groups' customs and habits.

The two were inseparable. They had a child, eight months old, who died in her arms during their flight from the mountains. Boy or girl? A boy, he said. A girl, she retorted. I asked for the child's name. Langanh, which she pronounced like *Nh'anh* – so it must have been a girl. But are you sure that's her name?

After their child was born, they moved from her parents' home to live on their own, in a charming cottage by a mountain spring. Hardworking and resourceful, they had chickens, three pigs, and even a horse. What color? A black horse. Black as ink. But maybe not. Black is an unusual color for horses in those parts of the country. A dog, too, yellow, with white spots, perhaps, that limped. In the aftermath of the Vietnam War, the couple's home, along with other ethnic dwellings, was seized or razed by Vietnamese settlers of the so-called New Economic Zone—vanquished Southerners forced to immigrate to the

Central Highlands to further the government's economic development policy. The highlanders' traditional customs, communal ways of life, beliefs, and principles of self-government were destroyed. Their ceremonial altars and gravesites were defaced. They marched in protest, in groups of tens, hundreds, and thousands. They were disbanded, harassed, and tortured by government officials.

And hunted. From Kontum down to Gia Lai onto Đắk Lắk. Hunted like beasts on the Cheo Reo Pass, the very birthplace of the Jarai. They ran into the forest. Were shot at. The muzzle of a gun ten, seven, sometimes only five meters away from Siu Kpa, spitting fire, behind the trunk of a *kơ nia* or wild almond tree, freshly felled, bleeding yellow sap. Yellow sap on his body bright as amber. Shrapnel pierced his right knee, causing him to walk with a limp, even now. Another piece of shrapnel lodged in his chest, close to his heart, grazing his *pericardium* like some kind of cosmic tease, before settling in his left lung's superior lobe. All his doctors left it alone, apparently not having the means or the inclination to remove it.

The couple reached Cambodia in 2001, stayed in a refugee camp, waited for three years, had their initial asylum interview, waited three more years, and went through more clearance procedures, before reaching New York in their seventh year of homelessness. She knew how to make fiber from cotton fruit, weave, knit, and embroider. He knew how to make cures out of roots, familiar as he was with all the medicinal aspects of plants. He recounted stories of collecting snails, harvesting young banana leaves, cutting down bamboo, finding the indigo plant and using it as dye. Whenever she missed their child, she would lie sideways, her legs pulled up, her head in his lap, her arms hugging a cloth bag as if it were a live infant. He would sing to her the *Xinh Nha* song of the Êđê people—their neighboring brethren in Đắk Lắk. He remembered the song by heart. Crying softly, she would keep her eyes tightly shut, refusing to let the light enter.

Imagine a person born and bred in the Central Highlands of Vietnam, in his *plơi*, each morning ascending the mountain with an ax in his woven bamboo basket to cut down trees, each afternoon descending toward his plot of land to make holes in the ground for seedlings, each evening drinking around the fire, living in the mythic world of the Cham oral tradition, at home in the wildness of Southeast Asian jungles, one day finding himself lost amidst the flashing green, red, and yellow lights of Manhattan, exposed yet invisible in the urban jungle. He could not go home. Did not want to go home. But never got used to his new environment. A person has to own something in order to live, but Siu Kpa did not own anything. For a long time, he had not owned anything, ever since the Vietnamese whom the ethnic minorities called the *Kinh* or plains people invaded his village and took away his home. They took away the village's ownership of the land. His wife lost her one and only treasure, the baby in her arms.

Now he worked odd jobs in the city's alleys and streets. As refugees, they were given shelter by the government, but Siu Kpa and Dep rarely lived there. They worked and subsisted by chance, not quite homeless but not quite settled. At sixty, they still looked fit and healthy. Dep is a Jarai name that he gave her while they were in the refugee camp. They both had forgotten her real name, a pretty name in the Ba Na language, a name without surname. One time, confused, desperate, mad, he threw himself underneath a moving truck but was saved. From then on, she never let him out of her sight. They spoke to each other in Ba Na, a language so close to extinction that no one could understand them.

No one cared to understand. After the endless rounds of interviews by humanitarian aid organizations in the refugee camp near the Cambodia-Thailand border, no one wanted to ask them any more questions once they arrived in the new world. What about the memories of her own village, the lovely trapezoid shape of the Ba Na's communal *Rông* house raised on stilts, of daily life on the plateau, festival days, of pitched gongs and ceremonial drums, the *t'rưng* bamboo xylophone? What about his memories of the *kơ nia* almond tree with broad, boat-shaped leaves and clusters of white flowers shivering in the soft spring rain, and long, deep shadows cast by ancient mountains and forests like cold, cernuous breaths upon their souls? Enshrouded, untended, all memories became obsolete. Time, too, becomes obsolete.

Anything that's obsolete will die.

At first his memory would slowly fade, becoming soft and fuzzy, before dissolving into complete darkness. Like a loss of vision. His cognitive faculties dimmed, occasionally sparked, like dying embers, sputtering, when someone sat down and asked him questions about his past. Questions helped unveil the flimsy screen of his memory, a fraction of the vast Jarai horizon, its heroic and tragic history, full of havoc and destruction wreaked by the Vietnamese against their mountain brethren.

She still remembered her horse and her dog, perhaps because they were fast animals. They ran faster than humans and therefore escaped death. Occasionally she saw her yellow dog in a trash heap on Lower Fifth Ave. She made her hands into a horn and cried out for him, but he would startle and run off, tail out straight behind him. One time an acquaintance alerted her attention to a horse grazing in a field across the Hudson River, under a blinding red sun. In an instance, the horse disappeared, then reappeared. Animals kept leaving, then returning, unsure if they were happy in their new country.

The light of a dying day, refracted from a skyscraper, soothed the couple's doubts and transformed them into shadows of a colossal, centuries-old banyan tree. Below that giant, swaying shade, in a vast courtyard, a white crane ambled that might have, at one time, landed on top of the now destroyed Twin Towers. The crane meandered among the rocks by a small fountain, cautious, alert. From eight meters away it stopped to listen to our conversation.

The air turned cold and damp. The clouds descended, casting their shadows on the water. There was a rustling of wings. The crane raised its neck, lifted its body, and drifted past the lighted windows of the skyscraper, then spread its wings, slowly as if to gather its strength and consider its position, then flapped its wings and flew straight up, away from the shadows of the skyscrapers, away from the pull of memory, away from the untamed and illusory mountains, before being engulfed by the vastness of the sky. We heard the crane, its guttural, raucous cry harmonizing with the high-pitched sounds of cymbals, gongs, *t'rưng* and *k'lông pút* xylophones, and the deep sighs of beings who understood the ways of life, who had begun to forget, or become confused, but had not quite lost their bearings. From this mélange of sounds, the laments of nature and a threatened civilization gradually subsided.

As his wife drifted off to sleep, I asked Siu Kpa about his *kơ nia* tree. He pointed toward a small bush next to a fence. It had delicate lavender flowers that resembled Japanese Ejitsu rose. I shook my head. He became flustered but refused to waver. It suddenly dawned on me that memory was not the only thing he had lost.

I asked him to estimate the distance between us and the flowering bush. At first, he could not do it, then guessed it was about five steps. After walking five steps, he extended his arm in an attempt to touch the bush, met air, lost his balance, pitched forward, and had to walk five more steps. Still missed his mark. The loss of the ability to measure spatial distance was a rare symptom among those already afflicted with selective memory loss. Five more steps and he finally reached the bush, hugging it tight, and, like someone returning home from years of travel, without hanging up his coat, ran headlong to embrace the cool smooth black surface of his house beam.

—Translated by Thuy Dinh

Country in a Glass of Water

—Vi Khi Nao—

THIS IS AN EXCLUDED PHOTO OF me and my brother. We have been, by now, expert Việt kiều, or expatriates, living in the States since 1989. Here, my brother is healthy. There is no pacemaker surgically embedded on his chest. Of my siblings, I feel the closest to him. Perhaps because he understands Vietnam better. There is a smaller age gap between him and me. He often sends me YouTube videos of Vietnamese songs prior to 1975, or *nhạc vàng*, to make my existence more meaningful. From this photograph, I can see why strangers and acquaintances assume that we are dating. There was no sexual event between my brother and me. Nha Trang has changed a lot over the course of twenty years. It no longer looks like this: with unmolested sand and vacated like this—maybe with just one-and-a-half hotels in the far distance. There appear here to be very few foreign investments, which this photograph has captured, and we would never see it come to reversed fruition again. Perhaps climate change and global warming have the ability to reauthor the conversation about beach resorts, about the infrastructure of a city, about my brother's body in relationship to himself and to me. I supposed in the 1980s stripes in articles of clothing must've been popular in America and I brought that popularity to Vietnam, where no one emulates or wishes to turn into a fashion statement. I am no model and no diva here. By then I could wear jewelry—golden bracelets and a watch and I don't care if my hair is disheveled. I don't care if I am squinting. The photo couldn't capture a few minutes later when I nearly drowned. None of my cousins know how to swim. But since my siblings and I are all American (Iowa City) educated, we are taught how to swim and had swimming lessons included in our classroom structure and perhaps lessons from summer camps or from the same place that Michael Phelps had his citizenship. My cousin, Hạnh, whose name means happiness or apricot tree, has gotten deep into the water and has clung on to me to keep herself from drowning. I, with a heart condition and a poor swimmer, could not keep both of us afloat. She wraps her whole body, long limbs—arms and legs, around my body, pressing me below the surface of the sea. I would try to hold my breath underwater for as long as I could to come back for air as I tried to bounce us back toward land. In my attempt, I had swallowed a handful of salt seawater of Nha Trang. I successfully did not drown us both. Once I was on sand again, I stayed there until we departed, probably to return to Sài Gòn. My attraction for water also repels my attraction for the sea. The Vietnamese word for country is nước. Have I, inadvertently, swallowed my former country? Is this why I crave salt so much? Have I lost my lungs to authenticity? Did I miss Vietnam that much? Have they confused themselves for a boat? Has water always navigated away from me? A few weeks after his photograph was taken, my brother will become severely ill. He catches something terrible. His fever becomes significantly high on our flight back to Iowa. My sisters and I take turns wiping him down with a cold cloth, with ice requested (shuffled into the cloth) from the incredibly hospitable flight attendants who serve us food every two or three hours, food my brother cannot eat. He continues to experience violent chills at various intervals of the flight. It is the first time I experience the fear that my brother may die on us and the terror remains in my memory still. What I remember most about that flight and about us taking turns caring for him is that he has a great sense of humor, cracking jokes while he suffers. I don't recall any of those jokes now and wish I could so I could share my amusement with you. When we reenter America, my brother continues to be sick for another ten days. Over twenty years later, his heart is broken literally and emotionally and there isn't a single thing I can do for him. Not even music, which we both love equally.

The Blood Lily

—Vương Tâm—

OVER THE COURSE OF SEVERAL YEARS, I would always run into her, the elderly woman, during the blood lily season. Usually, I was so mesmerized by the beauty of the flowers that everything else disappeared. I wanted to ask her name or why she didn't grow other kinds of flowers, but as I stood in front of the rows of potted blood lilies, I felt too overwhelmed to speak. Each pot contained only one flower that was just beginning to blossom, the vibrant red petals shyly starting to open. Each year, near the end of May, when the blood lilies began to blossom, I thought of this woman and returned to her stall to buy one of her flowers. Every customer seemed to return to her again and again, each of us thinking his or her own flower was the most beautiful and thanking her excitedly, as if she'd done us a tremendous favor.

She was a mysterious woman. I wondered why she always kept her face covered with a handkerchief, only revealing her sorrowful eyes. She had a deep, warm voice when she spoke, which made me assume that she was a woman with a strong spirit and full of love. Another strange thing was that, ever year, she added exactly one extra potted flower to sell. The most recent time I visited her stall, it was late in the season and she only had one blood lily left—the last pot, marked with a number 31, which I bought. This time, I couldn't resist asking her for an explanation.

"Mam, excuse me but could you tell me why there are thirty-one pots this year?" Then I added hurriedly, "Of course I feel very lucky to be the customer that purchased the thirty-first pot."

She seemed hesitant at first, as if she preferred not to speak. Then finally she said, "The pot you just bought marks the thirty-first year I have planted and sold blood lilies."

"But why don't you grow more to sell each season?"

"I don't need a lot of money. Anyways, goodbye for now. It's late in the afternoon and I'll be going home soon."

She reached behind her head to tighten the handkerchief around her face; then she began sweeping up the scattered leaves and soil on the ground.

"Mam, I wonder if you would mind teaching me how to plant a blood lily. Maybe I can walk you home?"

She was quiet again, then looked straight into my eyes and said, "Young lady, we can be friends—that would be all right. When you're free, come to Tân Khai Flower Village and ask for Ms. Huệ. That's my name. But for now, take the thirty-first pot and get going. It's late already. I need to do some shopping—tomorrow is the full moon. Goodbye."

I was surprised to see her walking so quickly down the busy street and vanish into the bustling crowd.

***

THAT SUNDAY, I DECIDED TO PAY her a visit. When I got to the village and started asking around about Ms. Huệ, I was surprised by how nice everyone was and how eager to give me directions to her house. One little girl in particular wanted to help me find the way to the house. She walked eagerly alongside me.

"Who does Ms. Huệ live with?" I asked the girl.

"Nobody."

"What about her husband and children?"

"I don't know," the girl said. "Ever since I can remember, she's always lived alone."

"Do you often go over to her house?"

"No."

"Why not?"

"Because of her black cheeks. Everybody says you shouldn't get too close to her, especially girls, because we don't want to get ugly black cheeks from her."

I knew right then why Ms. Huệ always covered her face with the handkerchief when she was in the city selling flowers. I'd been one of her most loyal customers for over ten years—this was the first time I had learned about the secret behind her handkerchief.

As we got closer to the house, the little girl turned to me and asked hesitantly, "Aren't you afraid of catching black cheeks from her?"

"No," I replied, firmly.

I pulled my hand away from the little girl's and knocked on the door. "Hello?" I called out. "Is Ms. Huệ home?"

After a moment, the door opened. An elderly woman stood in front of me. Her cheeks were covered in dark spots. I tried to act normal and looked directly into her eyes.

"I am Quý, your customer. How are you?"

"I'm doing fine," she said, recognizing me. "Please come in. I'm working in the garden behind the house. You can come take a look."

I followed her through the house and then out into the garden. She moved surprisingly fast. When I reached the garden in the back, I heard a melodious bird singing off somewhere in a corner. Her rows of flowers looked as if they were breathing. She must have recently watered them—threads of vapor rose from the pots.

She went over to a small mango-pine tree.

"I didn't pay attention to it yesterday, and now it looks so sad," she said, giving the tree some water. "Since early this morning, I've been petting each of its leaves and whispering to it sweetly. It seems a bit happier now."

Timidly, I came closer to the mango-pine tree, whose blooming burgundy flowers drooped over the stone planter. I was wondering to myself why this woman loved flowers so much, when suddenly she took my hand and pulled me to a corner of the garden. She pointed to a row of small porcelain pots.

"Those are your friends," she said. In front of us were just several pots filled with soil. She must have noticed my confusion. "Those are the thirty-two pots that have the blood lily bulbs for next year."

I looked up at her.

"But why do you count the years with the blood lilies?" I asked.

She stood there silently for a while, then replied, "Those are my loves. It has been thirty-two years of remembering. I don't know why I am telling you all this . . ."

She sat down on a round rock at the edge of the garden and sighed. I sat on the ground, ready to hear her story. Slowly, she began to recount her memories from over thirty years earlier.

***

THOSE HAD BEEN VERY SPECIAL DAYS spent in a forest along the Trường Sơn Trail. She had been a young female messenger whom everybody loved. The male soldiers treated Huệ like their younger sister. The jungle military hut they shared was always beautifully decorated with fragrant flowers. Every day the soldiers went into the jungle to pluck fresh flowers for her that they would then put into a vase. Everybody wanted to help her feel more comfortable—they knew she had grown up in the flower village. Meanwhile, she tried to help them with whatever they needed, from fixing their clothes to taking medicine when they were sick. All the messengers in the unit lived in harmony, like a tight-knit family, and the men insisted that nobody hurt Huệ's feelings, or even tease her.

One day, Thuận, a new recruit who was meek and the shyest person in the unit, brought back a palm leaf packed with soil. Seeing the pieces of string tied securely around it, the other male soldiers started to ask questions.

"Hey kid, what you got there?"

"A flower," Thuận said.

"So where's the flower?" one soldier asked.

"It's just soil you're holding," another said, dismissively.

Thuận ignored them. He walked over to Huệ and gentled placed the palm leaf in her hands. "This is for you," he said.

The other soldiers started laughing.

But Huệ said, "Is there a bulb planted in the soil that will eventually sprout?"

"Yes," he replied. "It's a blood lily. A village girl showed me this flower. And this is a mother bulb."

"Oh, I know this flower!" Huệ exclaimed. She was obviously very excited. "I will take care of it and wait for it to bloom."

Then she began to talk passionately about the beauty of the blood lily. None of the other soldiers were convinced because nobody had actually seen the flower besides Thuận and Huệ. As a shy person, whose face was often turning red with embarrassment, he had been lucky to find such a special gift for her. After that, they would take care of the bulb together, stirring and watering the soil, and eventually molding a clay pot to replace the palm leaf.

Time passed and everybody seemed to forget about the budding blood lily. The soldier's life they were all living consisted of hardships and important battles. One day, the enemy attacked and the infantry soldiers fought bravely to protect the entire region's communication system. All messengers were ordered to withdraw into an underground tunnel for an entire week. Once they were in the tunnel, Huệ suddenly remembered the potted blood lily back in the hut.

"Just forget it," the other messengers advised her. "You can't think about flowers in a situation like this."

"Just leave it there. When we win, we'll go back and enjoy the flower together."

"The blood lily won't bloom for another year. That's plenty of time. Just wait."

But when she wondered out loud what would happen if a bullet or a bomb shrapnel hit the clay pot, everybody was silent.

"I'll go up there and find the pot," Thuận said suddenly. Then, before anyone could stop him, he was running out of the tunnel.

"Thuận, do not climb up here," Huệ shouted up after him. "It's too dangerous!"

Gunfire, canons, and exploding bombs together made a deafening, brain-aching noise. Everybody except Thuận had followed the commander's orders and stayed in the tunnel. Time seemed to pass especially slowly as they waited for him to return. Huệ started to get anxious. The other soldiers stared at her coldly—they knew that she had won his heart, and if there was something special between them, then she would no longer be theirs. Huệ was fully aware of this, but what could she do? Everything was predetermined by the laws of fate.

Huệ felt restless. Looking up suddenly, she noticed a shadow hovering around the opening of the tunnel. The sound of gunfire was getting closer.

"Lie down!" everyone shouted.

But she was already running up out of the tunnel. As she reached the opening, a bomb exploded—she saw Thuận be thrown back from the force of the explosion. Then suddenly there were flames all around her and she felt an intense burning sensation on her face.

When Huệ came closer to him, she saw him sitting next to her holding a broken clay flower pot. She blinked and smiled, then cried out, "The blood lily is already budding!"

***

MS. HUỆ SUDDENLY STOPPED TELLING HER story and sat in silence. Her tired eyes seemed full of melancholy. Without saying anything, I reached out and held her hands. She must have been thinking about that broken flower pot from the war while looking at the pot that contained the mother bulb.

"So," I asked, "did the blood lily finally bloom in the tunnel?"

"Yes, it did. But Mr. Thuận was not able to see it, because a few days later he died heroically on the battlefield."

Ms. Huệ had started to cry. She wiped at her tears with a loose flap of her shirt.

"Since then," she continued, "no matter what it takes, I've been raising blood lilies." She pointed at the pots in front of her in the garden. "The bulbs in those thirty-two pots all come from the original mother bulb that came from Trường Sơn."

I was stunned. I hadn't realized that the blood lilies I'd bought from her carried the breath of soldiers as well as blood spilled in combat.

Suddenly, I was at a loss for what else to ask her.

"It's been thirty-two years since I parted from that person . . ." she said finally, her voice very melancholy.

I hugged her there in the garden. Finally, I understood why she added one extra potted blood lily each year. I told myself that I would buy the thirty-second pot from her next year.

—Translated by Quan Manh Ha

Bad Things Didn't Happen

—Gin To—

WHEN MRS. WORLD PUT ON HER face for the dinner party, she didn't expect it to be covered in vomit a mere three hours later. She did not expect the goo that used to be *bún bò Huế* to cake in between her thick slabs of foundation, for her green eyeshadow to drip all the way down her cheeks. She would look like half a clown, half blessed by Tinkerbell's fairy dust.

It was her son Louis' twenty-first birthday, apparently an important year given their new life in America. Lee—the man she fake-married for a green card—said so, said, *He been drinking and partying since ages ago; this just some American thing!* Lee was a man big in spirit. He laughed loudly. Manly jokes fell from his careless lips everywhere he walked, which wasn't very far these days. A meat lover whose gout had been flaring unbearably, Lee dragged his bad foot across their two-storied, four-bed Lincoln Park apartment like an elephant who stepped in its own shit.

Hồng, I'll be in my room. Don't wanna run into Richard! Lee teased.

Tonight, Mrs. World would be joined by her three lovers—

Lee, fifty-two, Vietnamese American, handsome with slicked back hair, swollen foot making him go hop hop; Richard Turner, fifty-five, white American, Mrs. World's ESL teacher from Harold Washington College, pathetic kicked puppy when begging for her love, her very own Uncle Sam, her big daddy; and finally, tan-skinned and curly-haired Linda, fifty, mixed Vietnamese and black, sweet and giving Linda, stodgy and plain in her cream-colored, long-sleeved polo and dark pants.

If Mrs. World had been more knowledgeable about American history, she might have felt bad about giving her rotation of Vietnamese guests the impression that Linda was her maid. Or not. There was no guarantee that one kind of downtrodden would be able to sympathize with another kind. After all, Mrs. World was hardly downtrodden. She had grown up poor in the countryside in central Vietnam, went to college away from family in the bustling Sài Gòn, discovered the power of her beauty and charms, charmed her way to the top. Mrs. World had been a Music Performance major in school. 'Til this day, she still entertained her dinner guests like a canary. No one knew about Mrs. World's lovers. In fact, "lovers" was a private word shared between her and her beloved(s), whispered between wet hungry lips, sheltered in the darks of nights, in between clean sheets. God, one would hope Mrs. World washed her bed sheets frequently.

***

DOWNSTAIRS, TWO GIRLS TUCKED THEMSELVES IN a tiny bathroom. No, a young woman and her cousin who identified as not-woman, but none of that was important. In this picture tonight, they were girls—sweet young things, beacons of hope, culmination of decades of postwar struggles. In the rapidly changing Sài Gòn of the early 2000s, they grew up like test tube experiments. A dash more of Western influence, a little less of Confucian patriarchy, more more more English, could never get enough of English, but then never forget your mother tongue. They entered the picture we are looking at when Louis, Mrs. World's son, fell in love with Moonshine. The three of them attended high school together, moved to Chicago one by one in 2014, 2015, and 2016. Mars, the not-woman, was the last to join. Tonight, Mars attended with her parents who were visiting from Vietnam.

"I think I'm gonna do it," said Moonshine, a cigarette between her fingers.

"Do what?"

"Break up with him."

Moonshine dated boys to try on different identities for herself. Currently she was playing the role of The Perfect Girlfriend—pretty as a doll, dressed to the nines only to walk back and forth, back and forth between the sink and the dinner table. Mrs. World had prepared an immaculate menu that night: *bún bò Huế*, spring rolls, papaya salad, sashimi bought from Joong Boo, steak, *chè* and pastries bought from Argyle then placed on crockery to look homemade.

"For real?" Mars was thrilled. She had *always* hated Louis.

". . . I think."

"Like, tonight?" Mars was sitting on the covered toilet seat playing with Moonshine's glittery eyeshadows and lip gloss and mascara and rouge.

"No," Moonshine scoffed, "I don't cause scenes."

"Yeah, that's more my thing." They snickered.

"How are your parents enjoying themselves?"

"Ugh."

Moonshine chuckled.

"I'm gonna come out to them," Mars said.

"Wait, really?"

Mars nodded, turning to show Moonshine her face. "How do I look?"

Moonshine made eye contact with her other half in the mirror. "You look . . . the same."

"Amazing."

"When? Tonight?"

"Oh my god, *no*. We're going to Gurnee Mills tomorrow. That's a lot of hours being stuck together."

Moonshine hummed, "Why now? I thought you planned to never come out." She was wrapping the butt of her cigarette carefully with toilet paper.

Mars said, "I'm graduating soon. Feels like the right time to be disowned. I'm gonna do it at the airport when I see them off."

"Mmmm," Moonshine reacted with toothpaste foaming in her mouth.

"Yeah, I'ma take them to the gate, stand in line with them, then before they go through TSA, I'm gonna be like, 'I'm gay, bitches, see ya never.'"

They laughed.

"That's a great plan."

"It is."

"Dude, we're doing it." Moonshine breathed into her hand then doused herself in perfume. "We are."

The tiny bathroom smelled like a nightclub. Soon, their secrets would have been filtered clean by the overhead vent. Moonshine told Mars to scoot so she could flush her tightly wrapped imperfection down the toilet.

***

MRS. WORLD WOKE UP PAST NOON today, had a light lunch, then made Moonshine give her a massage. Louis and Moonshine cleared the living room space, carried the couch out to the balcony (a great smoking spot designated for smoking men at the party, ironically though, Richard abstained from smoking due to a weak heart and Mars' daddy was a man without vices). At four or so, right as the temperature dropped from sixty to forty, Mrs. World had finished prepping the food and began to put on her face. She then, with the help of poor Moonshine, who had not had a minute of rest since past noon, squeezed herself in and out of seven different gowns to pick out the best ones for the party. Plural because Mrs. World enjoyed doing a sort of mini one-woman-fashion-show at dinner parties she threw. *I gotta perform my different outfits like brides at weddings*, she would say. The emerald green one with fake stones made of plastic was the one destined to be covered in vomit by the end of the night.

***

BACK IN VIETNAM, MRS. WORLD LOVED going to the market. Rich ladies in the city like herself had the options of local markets where vendors squatted on dirty cement roads or air-conditioned and well-organized supermarkets (Big C, AEON, LOTTE, Co.opmart, Maximark, and the newest chain Vinmart founded by the conglomerate Vin

Group). Despite countless news stories about rotten meat dressed in the five spices to cover its putrid odor at the local markets, Mrs. World had always preferred the shabby scene. It reminded her of childhood and of her mother's youth. But it also solidified how far she had come. From a wide-eyed music student arriving in Sài Gòn by herself, Mrs. World had grown into the epitome of glowing success by the middle point of her life. She loved to haggle at the market. It wasn't even that she didn't have the money to afford the overcharged prices based on her attire, skin tone, makeup, and diction. It was the *principle* of it all—Vietnamese people, regardless of wealth status, love a good deal. Rich Vietnamese people *especially* love a good deal. It is a skill they pass on to their children and then to grandchildren.

At the market, you want to look like you know your way around. You want to dress down (though rich people just have that something about them that distinguishes them from poverty, they do). You want to speak street, to code switch in a way that lets them know you are a self-made woman. Not a coddled china doll vulnerable in the real world. But not a moneyless woman either. Mrs. World loved the way street vendors looked at her with awe, envy, embarrassment. She loved the way they laughed at themselves in her presence, the way they asked her about her family, vacations, job, where her children went to school, the fancy meals of salmon and cold cuts and cheese no one could pronounce, not even Mrs. World herself. *The kids get bored of imported stuff. You gotta cook them Vietnamese dishes once in a while so they remember their roots.* The key to haggling is to go too low. If they say one hundred, insist on thirty. Then they would grimace, you would grimace. They'd pretend to decline service. You'd pretend to walk away. You make a round then come back and ask if fifty is okay.

***

THE GUESTS ARRIVED CLOSE TO SIX: Mars' mommy and daddy after visiting the Lincoln Park Zoo, the Shedd Aquarium, the Art Institute and the Apple Store off North and Clybourn all in one day; Nicky—Mars' white friend who taught yoga and worked at a tea shop; Richard

Turner in his best button-up; and Louis' minions in the form of two Vietnamese boys rivaling for his attention. Upon arrival, Nicky asked if he could help with anything but was told to sit tight because men weren't allowed in the kitchen. Nicky ended up nestled in between Mars' parents, wondering why they were asking him about his family income and medical history. Mars once told her parents that Nicky was gay, but her parents thought she was kidding and immediately forgot about it.

The Vietnamese believed in marriage, and obligation, and sexual/sociocultural reproduction. In other words, they believed in survival. And who could blame them? The homosexual agenda was so very counterintuitive, so based in desires and human frailty and spontaneous joy. They understood something Mars and her friends never could—the itch didn't always need to be scratched. Or if it did, have the decency to not advertise it publicly!

Besides, Mars' mommy—let's call her Dharma—didn't believe in bad things (which, in this case, homosexuality was a *very bad thing*). She was incapable of registering unpleasant experiences. This morning when Dharma was buying *phở* at Argyle, she saw a group of elderly men in uniform that was worn by the old Republic of South Vietnam, worn by people Dharma's VC daddy used to loathe. Dharma saw them and smiled her sweet Vietnamese smile, the one that united countrymen in a foreign land. They smiled back, slightly confused by the new face. She asked to buy a dish the restaurant didn't have, a dish no Vietnamese American would dare to sell or buy because the one key ingredient was pig's brain and, to Dharma's surprise, was not a thing Americans had the appetite for. Dharma walked away to find her daughter, not noticing the way smiles had turned cold.

***

"WHEN ARE YOU TWO GETTING MARRIED?" Richard tried to make conversation as he inspected the spread of exotic dishes.

Moonshine exchanged a meaningful look with Mars. "I'm sorry?"

"Hồng said that you and Louis are getting married soon."

"Nothing is set yet. We're just getting to know each other right now," Moonshine replied.

Mrs. World first brought up marriage when Moonshine and Louis started dating:

> They're getting married, I tell you. I'm taking them to Vietnam in the summer to greet Louis' grandma. Grandma is very strict. Picky old lady. She never thinks anyone is good enough for her grandson. You'll be good, won't you, Moonshine? The two of you go home and officially inform Grandma of your relationship, say, "We're getting married when Louis graduates from college." But for now, they're just good friends who help each other study!

It's been three years. And to be fair, Moonshine *had* been writing Louis' History and Religion papers so that wasn't far from the truth.

"How's your marriage, Richard?" Mars helpfully steered the conversation,

"Did you say she was Asian?"

"Hm? Oh, uh, yes, she's, she's Tha— "

"Everyone!" Mrs. World interjected obliviously, "We sing 'Happy Birthday.' We sing 'Happy Birthday, Louis.'" She picked up a chicken leg and placed it in Richard's bowl. Richard flustered and slightly bowed to her with palms pressed together like he had seen on TV. He didn't know that Vietnamese people had a million reasons to put food in someone's bowl—love and adoration, yes, but also: to change the topic, to accumulate social debt, to placate and manipulate you, to clear the last piece of food off the plate for cleaning, to avoid eating leftovers the next morning, for no reason other than a compulsive need to feed others.

***

AFTER A HORRIBLY OUT-OF-TUNE GROUP RENDITION of "Happy Birthday," Mrs. World asked Louis to bring out the electric organ. Mother and son then sang "Happy Birthday" again in perfect harmonies. They transitioned into a medley of Vietnamese children's songs, "Hotel California," The Beatles, "Hello" (by Lionel Richie, not Adele),

Vietnamese current pop songs that Moonshine and Louis' boys recognized but Mars didn't. The musical performance lasted too long. Nicky and Richard didn't know if they should give the duo their undivided attention or keep eating to show how much they were enjoying the food. Everyone clapped after the duo finished. Mrs. World blew her fans a kiss before disappearing to change. Her beauty queen smile and nasal voice made them all feel like gameshow guests. What else did Mrs. World have in store for them?

Then, it was cake time—a simple white cake with an assortment of fruits (slices of melon, peach, kiwi, maraschino cherries, strawberries) was brought out. "Everyone, cake. Cut the cake. Happy birthday." Richard came back inside after diffusing an unexpected situation just in time. Moonshine was on standby with a knife and a pile of dessert plates. Mars waited against the curtains with three iPhones and the weight of the world on her shoulders. Mrs. World directed everyone to sing "Happy Birthday" once again. Birthday boy Louis descended his knife to raucous cheers. Then Moonshine was forced to join him. *Smile! Trời ơi, you look like bride and groom!* Then everyone at the party was told to stab into the cake.

"Everyone, do it, cut the cake. Vietnamese tradition."

Now, like all cultures, the Vietnamese had their own idiosyncratic traditions that an outsider could only nod-and-smile at. But getting everyone at the party to stab the cake until it looked like the work of an axe murderer was strictly a Mrs. World's invention. The women (mostly Mars and Moonshine) loaded up each plate after everyone had a turn at stabbing, making sure to give away most of the frosting to those who didn't have to watch their figure. *Give frosting to the big white man,* Dharma giggled, *your dad and I, we have to be mindful of our cholesterol level!* Mrs. World chimed in, *give it to the boys, Louis! Hoàng! Thiện! You can get fat! It's okay.* Louis' minions tittered, arguing back sweetly that boys *also need to watch their figure nowadays.* Mars smiled along and imagined gobbling the whole cake down herself, cream and all. How shocking would that be. How inappropriate.

***

"SO, NICKY, HOW DO YOU KNOW Rose?" Richard asked, figuring he should be making conversation with his sole comrade in tonight's battlefield.

"Who's Rose?" Nicky asked, mulling over three different types of sauce and unsure which one he should use to dip his chicken leg.

". . . Rose. The host of the party?"

"Ohhh, her?" Nicky jerked his chin in Mrs. World's direction who was posing for candid pictures with a spatula. She was going to send these pictures to a journalist she knew so they could write an article about her throwing her son a fancy birthday party in America.

". . . Yes."

"Met her for the first time today, actually. I'm friends with Mars."

"Mar—oh, the, the, one of the young women."

Nicky decided to not get into the topic of gender identity, instead, deciding to dip his chicken leg in a thick and shiny red sauce with minced garlic. The two white men hyper aware of their outsider status in this scenario mmm-ed and hmmm-ed like bobbleheads.

"What school do you go to? I'm sorry, uh, are you in school?"

"Me? No, I graduated three years ago. I work at a tea shop now. And teach yoga."

More bobbling heads.

"And you work at—"

"Truman. Truman College."

If not for this party, Nicky wasn't sure he would give someone like Richard the time of day. Something about the dude reeked of MAGAism.

"Yeah, I teach ESL. That's how I met Rose!"

"Cool, cool, very cool."

More heads.

"You ever been to—"

"Truman?"

"Uh, uh, Vietnam, but also, yeah, have you ever been to Truman?"

"I ... uh, never been to Vietnam. Would love too! Never been to Truman either. I went to school in Florida briefly, then transferred to DePaul."

"Oh DePaul!"

"Yeah, yeahhhhh, yeah DePaul."

"Rose's kid, uh, what's his name, Louis? He goes to DePaul right?"

"Uhhh ... I, I don't know. Again, first time here."

"Right, right."

"..."

"So, you said you taught ESL?"

"Yeah, yeah."

"And that's how you met, you met—"

"Yeah, yeah."

"And her name is ... Rose? Rosa? Or—"

"Rose! A direct translation of her Vietnamese name. Isn't that pretty?"

It took Nicky everything to school his facial expression into a neutral one. Yikes, these two were definitely fucking.

"And then I heard people calling her something else too. Miss, miss something."

"Uhhhhh."

"Mrs. World," Mars injected from beside him, "Beauty pageant thingy," and shoved some spicy pickled mustard greens into his bowl.

Nicky hadn't even noticed Mars sitting back down. Moonshine and she seemed attached to the sink at their hips since he arrived.

***

CLOSE TO EIGHT, THREE DRESSES INTO the night (a fuchsia knee-length one, a sky-blue one with gold embroidery, and currently, a white wedding-style gown), Linda showed up at the door with a bag of kale.

"A bag of kale?"

"Why is she bringing kale to a party?"

"K-keo? Kheo? What is keo?" Dharma asked with a heavy accent. Mrs. World turned to whisper something unhelpful like *it's a type of vegetable* or *greens people eat* or *you don't need to know, we don't have it in Vietnam.*

Something had oozed and mutated that dinner—let's call it Love, a word pretty enough, meaningless enough, translingual enough that everyone could buy into without meaning the same thing. Richard Turner, the first white man Mrs. World had ventured into, wanted to leave his wife for her. The wife showed up at the door two dresses into the night and stood there in the forty-degree weather. Richard came out to beg her to leave. She stopped throwing a tantrum but stood there like a snowman until Linda showed up and asked if she was okay. Linda knew about Richard, about Lee, about Moonshine's second-class citizenship in Mrs. World's household, knew she was in love and only needed a tiny corner of Mrs. World's heart. Did she know that she wasn't the first lesbian Mrs. World had led on? Last year, in her first ESL class at Harold Washington, Mrs. World had befriended a lesbian photographer who was enamored with her for free high-fashion shoots.

Linda was still standing at the door, holding her bag of kale. It was weird. Linda usually blended into Mrs. World's grand painting so seamlessly that no one would notice her. People might note a tan-skinned woman with natural curls rarely seen on Vietnamese heads, but then would easily conclude that she must be Mrs. World's maid. When Dharma arrived last Wednesday, she mused, *Is she a Montagnard? Is she mixed?* but then had quickly moved on after Mars' simple answer—*she's Auntie Hồng's friend.* But today, Linda was at the door like an immovable mountain, drawing attention to herself. Mars and Moonshine peeped out from where they were washing the dishes at the sink ever so often to check and see if Linda was still there. At some point, Mrs. World dragged Linda into her bedroom to help her get into the fourth dress of the night—the emerald-green from Amazon.

***

THE EXPLOSION HAPPENED QUICKLY and without fanfare. Mars needed to pee, but Richard—whose delicate Caucasian stomach was reacting badly to Vietnamese cured pork—was hogging the bathroom near the dining area. Mars would have gone down to pee in the bathroom Moonshine smoked in earlier, but Moonshine and Louis were already down there fighting about God knows what. Her parents were yapping on and on about making Nicky their son-in-law. So, Mars decided to go for the one inside Mrs. World's bedroom.

Mars often thought about the way Vietnamese people used words. They said things they didn't mean and eluded the things they did mean. Big personalities like Mrs. World and Dharma used words like weapons, like boats, like water from a showerhead. It was as if language was not meant for comprehension. Or that communication wasn't necessarily verbal. People less showy like Moonshine and Linda would choose to swallow words. They made themselves small and unnoticeable. Mars was sick of it all. People like Mars made others uneasy.

Mrs. World and Linda didn't see her. Mars stood at the threshold seething. Suddenly, she wanted to be a forest fire. Fuck Louis' birthday party. Fuck Gurnee Mills. A strange air filled her up; she felt fearless and slightly cold. She was determined to open her big fat mouth and ruin everyone's night. But tragically, during the short walk back to the dining area, it dawned on her—What would this change anything? No one would believe her, certainly not her mother. She rethought her decision to out Mrs. World and Linda and herself and. Rethought the very act of coming out. Maybe she wouldn't even get disowned like she had hoped.

Mrs. World returned to the dining table in her green dress with Linda trailing behind. Before she could tap Mars on the shoulder, Mars doubled over violently. A shot of whiskey with Lee when she came over, sips of beer here and there, fruit punch Nicky brought even though it wasn't a potluck. Out go bún bò Huế and nem chua and sashimi and the image of those two sucking faces. People yawn when they see others yawn, right? Empathy something, something. Moonshine, who was a lightweight to begin with, joined the vomiting. At some point, Richard then Dharma then Daddy joined in. Mrs. World—the pro party-thrower—vomited plenty in private but never before in front of an audience. The novelty of it all was quite thrilling.

Oh my God, oh my God, I'm so sorry, Richard croaked. At least this act of vomiting on each other was unambiguous across cultures. For once, Richard felt solid in his footing. Nicky tried to escape. At least *something* came out, Mars thought to herself.

Moonshine didn't break up with Louis until two years later and Mars didn't come out until she was twenty-seven, in the days leading up to her mother's death. By that time, Dharma was too senile to fully comprehend what Mars was saying.

***

THAT NIGHT, AFTER EVERYBODY had gone home, (Mars in the Uber with her parents, reeking of vomit, Nicky with bags and bags of leftovers, the stuff that didn't get vomited on), Linda blitzed the kale she brought. Mrs. World hadn't eaten all night, determined to flaunt her ant waist in front of the guests.

Where did the kale come from? asked Mrs. World in the dark living room, where Linda had set up her air mattress for the night, too tired after cleaning up to go home to the Western suburb.

I was at the supermarket. I wanted to make hot and sour tilapia soup. But then I saw kale and thought of you. You told me you were on a no-carbs-diet, a low-sugar-diet, a 90 percent-green-diet, a fiber-full diet for a tiny ant waist. You saw the emerald-green dress and bought it a size too small. I didn't want to come at first because your lovers didn't like me and I hated them. If I were an American, would you marry me? Here, we can do that. Sometimes you're like a child—oblivious and excitable. You bite into powdered donuts like biting into an apple. You'd look so glamorous save for your dusty, white donut nose. I didn't want to come but I went into Jewel Osco and bought nothing but a bag of kale. I thought I was going home but found myself getting off the Fullerton bus at Southport. I was going to leave but then I saw her—Richard's wife—standing outside your door.

So, you decided to come in?

I decided to come in.

Good, good, I needed you to help me with the dress.

You could have asked Moonshine, or Lee, or even Richard.

It wouldn't have been the same. It wouldn't.

Maybe all that was dramatized for the sake of a story. The vomit, the secrets, the gross unsayables. None of that excretion happened. Because Dharma willed it so. Because collectively, they didn't register glitches. Maybe they went home to Vietnam and told of that time someone got really sick at a party Mrs. World threw. But that would be it.

Years later, someone writes a play. It starts at the end:

> *They vomit on each other, stunned, unsure how to*
> *move on. They finish the play covered in each*
> *other's vomit.*

Act 1, Scene 1.

Night

—Nguyễn Mỹ Nữ—

TWO WEEKS AGO, I ARRIVED HERE and wandered along the river, watching sampans carrying coconut and cork trees as they glided gently on the water. Seeking refuge from rain, I found shelter in the *porte cochere* driveway of a modern hotel. In this moment of solitude, my thoughts drifted toward her—a woman from my hometown who was displaced by the war.

Back then, my family used to own a storefront attached to our house, with rooms we leased out back. Phước rented a room for himself and his newlywed wife, a native of the parish at An Hiệp in Châu Thành, Bến Tre Province. The day she arrived, he eagerly drove his jeep to the airport to pick her up. When his jeep finally came to a full stop in front of our house, Phước announced, "Everyone, come out and meet my new wife!"

This piqued our curiosity, so we rushed outside to catch a glimpse of this woman, perhaps inadvertently making her feel self-conscious. She wasn't too tall or too short, her complexion neither dark nor fair, her looks not striking nor plain, and you couldn't tell if she was from the city or the countryside—she was just perfectly average in every way. Yet she caught my eyes the moment I saw her. I don't know why, but I felt immediately drawn to her, feeling that I could love and honor her for the rest of my life.

***

PHƯỚC WAS A RECONNAISSANCE OFFICER IN Regiment 41, Infantry Division 22. He wasn't home much because of his military duties, so his visits were often brief and sporadic. Phước was friendly, and when he flashed a wide grin, you could see a gold tooth in his lower jaw. The female tenants would tease him by saying, "Smile and let your gold tooth shine."

As Phước often spent time away from home, Night, his wife, would invite me over to keep her company. I was seventeen; she was twenty-two. She was easy enough to get along with during the day, but as darkness fell, so did her spirits. I would catch her crying when both the TV and the light in her room were off. She'd stand quietly at the threshold of shadows, her long hair cascading to one side. A pale yellow light from the next room flickered, casting shadows along the opposite wall that made her small frame appear even more fragile. Even now, all these years later, I still remember her lonely silhouette in that fluttering light.

I was named Daisy, after the common flower, though I never felt like a white daisy. If black daisies existed, that would be me—a girl whose skin was kissed by the sun. Night rarely called me Daisy, preferring Darling instead, her southern accent both lovely and a delight to my ears. But that name—I didn't associate it with the light of the sun, though I thought deeply about it. With my brows furrowed, I had said to her, "Your strange name is a mystery to me." And she replied, "Mysterious, yes, but also merciful."

I thought I understood *mysterious*, but it wasn't until much later that I fully grasped the meaning of *merciful*.

She shared stories with me, stories when we lay side by side—stories about herself, her parish, and its rivers. For the first time, I learned about a place called Kiến Hòa in the Mekong Delta—somewhere much farther than I could imagine. One night, she confided in me about Phước and their marriage, how it had been arranged by their respective fathers when she was still in middle school. Their fathers were friends since their school days, taking classes together, living together. Night's father, a military officer in Kiến Hòa, was a "stern figure," whereas Phước's father, a gardener, was soft-spoken.

Her father once threatened her, "You'll marry Phước, or I'll take my own life in shame before swallowing my pride."

Before getting married, Night had fallen in love with a young engineering student from the well-known Phú Thọ Polytechnic University in Sài Gòn, who participated in the student-led antiwar protests. When her father learned about this, he took his pistol and stormed out into the front yard. He fired his gun into the air three times, then came back inside and pressed the muzzle against his temple. In a rough voice, he threatened her, "You end your relationship now. I won't have a daughter of mine in love with a Vietcong."

Before she could call off the relationship with the engineering student, he was arrested and sent off to Côn Đảo Prison.

Then she married Phước.

Night recounted a tragic life story full of highs and lows, yet lacking any hint of anger and resentment. She even smiled at times, which I found rather odd. I've always seen myself as an extrovert, someone with a strong personality, and if I'd been in her place, things would've ended differently. I was captivated by her bedtime stories, partly due to her bewitching voice. Her stories transported me to her parish and church on Christmas Day and during Lent. She was native to Châu Thành, but she always went with her family to Chợ Lách, Phước's hometown, to attend Mass at Cái Mơn Church during important Catholic events. She spoke of nipa palms and the river's rising waters, of sampans and narrow canals hidden beneath green cork trees. With my eyes closed and lying still, I imagined being in her family's garden during harvest season—hammocks, cicadas, red rambutans—before drifting off to sleep.

***

BABYSON, A MIXED-RACE BLACK MAN IN his late-twenties who worked for R.M.K., rented a room next to Night's. He was nice and the wittiest American I'd ever encountered. Standing at five-foot-five, he had a small frame but attractive features, a charming smile, and a playful sense of humor. He liked to joke around and lie about his name and age, always giving everyone different answers. Night nick-named him Babyson, and it reminded me of the French song "Tous Les Garçons Et Les Filles."

Babyson loved this nickname, his beautiful face lighting up with pride whenever someone asked, "What's your name?" Since moving in next to Night's room, I rarely saw her alone by her door in the evenings. Instead, she and Babyson would silently stand together in the soft yellow light of her room, their shadows dancing along the opposite wall. Some nights, I watched them quietly from the dark. I felt a mix of fear and confusion without any clear reason, though it made me happy at the same time. Soon her bedtime stories included Babyson, tales of poor black communities in the United States, the ghettos of New York, Babyson's racist white boss at R.M.K.—and music. Night said both she and Babyson enjoyed country music and Christian hymns.

One cold evening just before Christmas, Night bought gifts in prepa-ration for her trip with Phước back to her hometown Kiến Hòa, where they would celebrate the birth of Christ. She had mixed feelings about the trip. That night, I saw her sit up and shift to the edge of her bed. From the adjacent room, Babyson's harmonica played a lonely tune. On December 22, Phước let Night know that he was involved in an impor-tant military operation and couldn't be with her for Christmas. She showed no disappointment, no sadness, when she received this news. Two days later, Night and Babyson pretended to look busy, and when I asked about it, Night said they wanted to surprise me.

Standing in Babyson's modest room, untidy on most days, I was surprised to see it bright and cozy. Christmas music filled the air and a Nativity scene had been set up in the corner, clearly made by someone who obviously understood Christ's story well. Across from the Nativity scene, a Christmas tree glittered with colorful, blinking lights, beautiful Christmas cards, and presents. In the middle of the room, a table was set with three chairs, candles, and wine glasses.

I don't remember having a more memorable Christmas. Before we sat down for *Réveillon*, Night and Babyson gave their present to me.

They sang "Silent Night," first in English and then in Vietnamese. I followed with "Jingle Bells" accompanied by Babyson on his harmonica. With her eyes shut and her hair set free, Night danced passionately to the music.

After a few glasses of red wine, I started to feel dizzy and sleepy. In my hazy state, I saw someone lifting Night up, spinning her around, and tossing her into the air. The candles and Nativity scene seemed to fly off into space. When I woke up the next day at dawn, I felt around the bed and realized that Night was gone. This repeated over the next four nights—she would vanish before I woke up. Over the weeks, tenants began to gossip about her affair with Babyson. They glared at her with disdain and whispered disgraceful things. My mother no longer allowed me to stay over at Night's place.

Phước paid an unexpected visit one night and caught her and Babyson embracing at the end of the hallway. But Phước stayed calm. Later that day, when I bumped into him in the hallway, he had a wide grin as usual. Before I could tease him about his gold tooth, he was already in his jeep speeding away. Night stayed remarkably calm after that. I slipped out to spend a few more nights with her, knowing they might be our last. She smiled, but tears filled her eyes whenever she talked about Babyson.

"Darling, let me tell you something. Babyson and I are both lost and homesick souls. We found a connection through songs, through music. We're lonely and mixed-up people exhausted by love. He's fed up with prostitutes and I'm unhappy with my arranged marriage. We long to share our comfort, to care for each other when we're sick. We started as friends and never imagined it would blossom into something like this. But now, it's too late to turn back."

"And Phước?" I started.

"You mean if he were to shoot me?" she said.

But Phước never shot her. When he returned to town, he didn't visit Night. Instead, he went with friends out to a bar and drank until he could no longer stand. His friends thought it was a bad idea when he insisted they drive him back. So he hitched a ride on a military truck to Quảng Ngãi. Because the truck was crowded, everyone stood. Phước tried to balance himself using someone's shoulder, but he fell off the truck when the driver suddenly hit the brakes. A jeep appeared out of nowhere and ran him over, killing him. When Night got the terrible news, she seized up and collapsed to the floor. The tenants were equally shocked. Phước's death cast a dark and haunting shadow over our house. Night's face lost its color, and Babyson's eyes took on a strange, red hue.

Night disappeared after that; Babyson stayed in his locked room drinking alone.

Night often appeared in my dreams, her long hair untied as she sat on a river pier in her hometown. Her shadow would take form, only to vanish behind the sipa palm trees. I saw her alone in a white voile *áo dài*, standing beneath the bell tower of Cái Mơn Church on her wedding day. I never saw Phước—or Babyson with his harmonica—in my dreams. Instead, I'd see a single gold tooth on a blurry face, a voice that said, "Night, is that you?"

***

TWO WEEKS SINCE MY RETURN. As I stepped into Châu Thành, my heart skipped a beat. Could I ever forget a woman named Night who lived here? On my first day in Châu Thành, I saw hyacinths floating on the water, how they seemed to sadden the river in the rain. A ferry skimmed by and memories of Night overwhelmed me. I said to myself, *Night, where's this woman I knew when I was only seventeen?*

In the morning, I wandered through some orchards, and soon found myself standing before a house I believed was Night's. The fence was broken, but the gate looked familiar. I entered through the gate and stepped onto the veranda. In the living room, beautiful chairs carved from the wood of coconut trees caught my eye. On the antique altar, in barely legible handwriting, were Lenin's famous words: *Learn, learn more, learn forever.* As I silently read them, I felt Night's breath near my ear. She must be somewhere inside the house; her voice was unmistakable. My throat suddenly tightened. I took deep breaths and continued exploring the back of the house. Different scenarios played out in my mind: *How was she now? Who was she living with? Did she marry someone else? Was it the engineering student she first loved?*

An old but kind woman greeted me. She peppered me with questions and offered me fruit she had grown herself. She gave me a bag of rambutan and jackfruit to take home. The old woman laughed and said nobody in her family was named Night.

"I'd never name my child Night," she said. "That's too strange a name."

We stood at the gate. Before saying goodbye, I asked her, "Who wrote the motto on the altar? The handwriting was hard to read."

"My husband, but I have no idea why he put it up there."

I thought I saw Night several more times, as if she were haunting this town. One morning at a church on the riverbank, I was startled to see someone I thought I recognized prostrating before an effigy of the Virgin Mary. But as I approached, it turned out to be a stranger. Another time, it was buying a cold coconut drink from a market vendor. Something about the merchant reminded me of Night. Sometimes, in the din of the busy market, I would hear someone call out "Darling" and swear the voice belonged to her.

Years have now gone by. I've never criticized or blamed Night for what happened, though I'm still troubled by all the terrible hardships she faced. I know I'll never stop loving her, and I hope I can do the right thing while I'm here. I'll always keep her in my memories, no matter where life takes me. Toward the end of my stay in Châu Thành, I became less anxious. The woman named Night, I realized, would always belong to her namesake, where she could seek refuge and remain hidden from the ordinary world. Though I miss her deeply, I've stopped looking for her—this enigmatic yet kind woman who belonged to the vast and endless hours of darkness.

—*Translated by Quan Manh Ha & Cab Tran*

Lost Love

—Vu Tran—

MY SISTER TELLS ME LU SHOULD not pay today. Three years I've been a driver for her and this is the first time anyone has ridden for free. I am to take him to Biên Hòa and wherever else he wants to go, all day if necessary, and if he insists on paying or even tries to tip me, I must still refuse.

"Lu is your oldest cousin," she's reminding me, "and this is his very first time back—the first time ever for his wife and kids. And he's done so much for us."

"But people tip for everything in America," I tell her. "He probably tips his mailman. It'd be rude of me not to accept."

Loan frowns at me. She's standing at the open window of my car (*her* car of course) with one hand atop the roof and the other on her hip, resembling our mother with that look of calm disapproval on her face. Years back, Lu loaned her a good bit of money to start her car service, and though she has since paid him back, gestures like today still matter. She reminds me of this as well, like it's an accusation.

"Remember the family you forgot to pick up at the airport last month?" she says, poking my shoulder playfully. "Consider today a down payment on your amends." When I don't laugh, she sighs. "I'm sorry your plans are ruined, Điềm, but Lu is the reason we can even do favors like this."

It's a mantra in our family: always pay your debts, no matter how much or how little, no matter how long it takes. This applies to everything in life, not just money. My granddad would've said it's simply the balance of things. I once asked him how we know when we've fully repaid a debt we can't measure, and he said, "Sometimes it just comes down to *this*," and tapped at his heart.

But I'm hardly feeling sentimental about my sister's gesture. It's me who's giving up an afternoon at the park with my girlfriend and working all day for practically nothing. The drive to Biên Hòa could easily take two hours today, and I still have no idea where exactly Lu wants to go. He told my sister he was still deciding, which probably means that from now until nightfall I'll be either stuck in traffic or waiting in one dismal alleyway after another.

"If anything, today can do you some good," Loan insists. "You'll both have a chance to talk."

I know she means for me to soak up Lu's wisdom or whatever it is that's made him so successful, especially with everything he went through before America. She likes to point out how easy I had it growing up after the war and the family's worst years, which is why I don't take anything seriously enough, like the job she's given me and the girlfriend I should've already proposed to. To her credit, she's always looked after me and the family, so whenever she reminds me of what I owe and where I fall short, I do the one thing I'm good at and stay quiet.

I drive away without saying goodbye. In the rearview mirror, I see her watching me with her arms at her sides. Before I turn onto the main road, I stick my hand out the window and give her a half-hearted wave.

At a quarter to noon, I arrive at the Rex Hotel in downtown Sài Gòn and see Lu already waiting out front in his sunglasses, smoking and ignoring a little girl who's pulling at his pant leg, pestering him to buy some postcards and cigarettes. It's a five-star hotel, and it occurs to me how wasteful *and* rude it is to stay here when he could've easily stayed with relatives. This morning, my sister showed me a photo of him and his two young daughters on vacation last year, smiling brightly in front of the Eiffel Tower. I assumed his wife took the picture.

In person, Lu looks even taller, a head taller than me in fact, his demeanor far from bright. I approach him and shoo away the little girl, and he turns to me with surprise, taking off his sunglasses.

"Is that you, Điềm?" he asks, squinting at me as he shakes my hand absently. I figure he's about to remark on how much I've changed, but he says, "I thought you were coming at eleven."

"Loan told me noon," I say, ready to prove it. But he calls out to the little girl, who comes running back. He takes a pack of cigarettes and pays her with a ten-dollar American bill, waving off change despite it being five times the price. Then he pats me on the shoulder, asks me where the car is, and starts walking there ahead of me.

He sits in the backseat, which only a stranger would do when they ride alone. I want to ask where his wife and children are (Loan told me his wife is half-white, half-Chinese, and very pretty), but as we drive off, he disappears into his sunglasses and gazes out his window.

Lu and I are first cousins, but he has a good twelve years on me and a few on my sister. He was twenty when he left two decades ago. All I can remember is him and his younger brother visiting our house every now and then and playing cards with my sister, and him cursing when he lost. I was too young back then to know all the details, but his father (my uncle) was an Army officer and spent time in the reeducation camps after the war, returned home with health problems, and died a few years later from a stroke. Shortly after this, Lu's brother fled the country but drowned at sea on a tiny fishing boat, no one knows how exactly. Lu made his own escape the following year and survived, but ended up languishing for three years in the refugee camp on Pulau Bidong, almost dying twice on the island before finally getting sponsored.

I see him now in the rearview mirror, smoking out the window in his crisp white shirt and his sunglasses, his slicked hair gleaming in the sunlight, and to me he looks like a man who's won more than he's lost. Even in my vague childhood memories, he was always the handsome cousin in our family, and middle age and wealth has only honed his good looks. He and his wife own a chain of restaurants in California and live in a six-bedroom house with three cars and a swimming pool. I'm not so naïve as to think these kinds of things ensure our happiness, but however much my cousin has suffered, I can't help suspecting that life tends to bend to his will.

We are entering the old highway that leads north out of the city, and traffic is as bad as I thought it would be. A bus fuming black smoke passes into our lane and nearly sideswipes us, and I hear Lu grunt in the back, unused to this kind of driving. He rolls up his window, so I also close mine. The air conditioner makes an embarrassing squeaking sound, so I put in a CD of Beatles music, which I often play for foreign riders.

Lu doesn't seem to notice. He's taken off his glasses and is staring thoughtfully at a stretch of high-rise hotels to the right of the highway, towering over the mess of new and dilapidated buildings below. I wonder if he can still see the old unruly Sài Gòn from his youth or if he prefers this newer alien one.

Traffic slows even more and I honk as scooters continue worming their way around us and through the congestion ahead. I see the problem in the distance: a truck full of caged chickens has stalled, smoke billowing from its hood. We come to a standstill, and a family of five on a Vespa stops next to us, the father driving with one child standing on the footrest against his chest and the other two sitting snuggly behind him and the mother straddling the rear. All three kids are crying for some reason, but the man and woman ignore it and stare off in different directions.

"You married?" Lu's voice startles me and I see that he's watching the family too.

"No, not yet." I give a small laugh, though I'm not sure why. I see an opening in traffic and dart forward, leaving the family and their wailing kids behind us.

"A girlfriend?"

"Yes."

"What's her name?"

"Tuyết." Then I add, "She comes from a family of jewelers, but she became a nurse instead."

I know he's asking out of boredom so I keep myself from also saying that she's smarter and kinder than any girl I know—that like my sister says, she's much too good for me.

"A good Catholic girl, I bet," Lu says with a whiff of condescension. "You love her, don't you? I can tell."

I can only smile and shrug as I keep my eyes on traffic.

"You're how old now—twenty-seven, twenty-eight? How long have you known her?"

"Two years. We've been dating for ten months." I don't feel like explaining that it took me over a year to ask her out.

"Can I tell you something?"

In the mirror he's looking straight at me. I turn down the music.

"If she loves you too," he says, "marry her as soon as you can. Make her parents love you, buy her a nice ring you can afford, and start forgetting all those impossible girls in your head."

I laugh to hide my annoyance at his sudden air of wisdom. He's being serious, but I can tell this has nothing to do with me. He just happened to guess right.

"Did Loan tell you to say that?" I ask.

His head has fallen back on the headrest, his eyes nearly closed, but he goes on: "I met my wife in the States, but before her, I nearly married someone else here. I doubt if you knew that back then, young as you were. She was the perfect person for me. And beautiful too. Flawless white skin—like a Japanese girl. Small pretty breasts." He chuckles to himself, his eyes still closed. "I wanted to propose, but then I thought I'd wait until things in the family got better, you know, after we lost my father and brother. She and I were both young anyway."

Lu takes off his seatbelt and settles deeper into his seat, sinking a bit from view. "Well then she went and fell in love with a good friend of mine. I'd known him since primary school and actually saved his neck once in a fight. They went on for months behind my back. I was so blind. That happens when you get too comfortable. But as soon as she confessed everything, I broke it off like that." and he snaps his fingers.

He speaks casually, flippantly. I'm not sure he even cares if I'm listening. But then he opens his eyes and stares up at the ceiling of the car. His tone changes: "That's the reason I decided to leave. Even if I drowned at sea like my brother did, it would've been better than staying." Again, he chuckles. "Once I made it to Pulau Bidong, I found out she was devastated that I had fled and dropped that friend of mine. She asked my family where I had gone and could she write to me. I told them that no matter what happened from then on, they could never tell her a single thing about me. To hell with her and her devastation."

He falls silent as if that's all there is to the story. I can't tell if he's offering it as a lesson, a confession, or something else altogether, or if he expects me to respond in any way. He seems uninterested in my pity, let alone my thoughts. He's back to staring out the window, so I turn the music back up. I think of his wife and wonder if she has any idea about this woman. What would it be like to know you were the next best thing?

We're approaching the new highway under construction, which is partly to blame for the stop-and-go traffic. But soon the drive to Vũng Tàu will take two instead of four hours, and I decide right then to take Tuyết to the beaches there next week to make up for today. I'll buy her a bathing suit, an expensive foreign brand, though I know she doesn't swim and might be too modest for the kind of bathing suit that Lu's wife probably wears.

"Good God, the traffic here," he mutters as if it's never been this way. He leans forward. "We're still downtown, aren't we? Let's stop somewhere for a bit. All this stopping and going is giving me a headache."

"Biên Hòa is still an hour away," I remind him, "maybe more."

"That's fine, that's fine. There's actually a little restaurant on Lê Duẩn Street I'd like to visit, if it's still there. Just a quick drink."

I sigh in my head and steer us through a throng of scooters toward the next exit.

Searching for the restaurant soon gives me the headache I thought it would. Lu doesn't remember its name or where it's located exactly. I offer to take him elsewhere, but he insists we keep trying. After half an hour of driving in circles, he spots a small café wedged between a computer store and an Italian ice cream shop. It's called *La Fleur Café*, which is not the name he's trying to remember, but he's confident it's the right place. Thankfully there's parking nearby, my first alley of the day. To my surprise, he insists that I join him.

The café is small inside but opens out into a crowded patio. As we approach the hostess, Lu says to me, "That girl I told you about—she and I used to come here and sit right there, under that tree. A lot has changed, and of course the tree is giant now. But this is it."

He tells the hostess he wants a table under the tree, and once we're seated, he keeps peering up at all the branches with a strange expression of pride.

The waitress comes, and without asking me, he orders two beers.

"I shouldn't drink, anh Lu," I say.

He waves that away and nods for her to go ahead. After lighting a cigarette, he offers me one. The beers arrive and he drinks half of his in one gulp before settling back and facing the inside of the cafe. His survey of the place is slow and complete, roving over the bamboo tables and chairs, the mint walls adorned with framed prints of the French countryside. Whatever memories are returning to him, it's like he's trying to recast them in a new light. That or he's just punishing himself.

"What was it like here back then?" I ask.

He doesn't reply and has turned his attention to the street. There's a beggar woman on the grassy median, swathed in a tattered *áo dài*, her face caked with makeup, doing a slow dance of some kind as traffic whips past her. From where we are, she looks like some impoverished kabuki actor, pushing invisible walls and drawing arcs in the air with a paper fan, her face alive with something only she can see. Lu turns to me, amused and a little unsettled. His beer nearly finished, he holds up two fingers to the waitress, who promptly brings over two more bottles.

"So where is it that I'm taking you?" I ask him. "Loan said you were still deciding."

He pulls a pen from his pocket and thinks for a long moment, then carefully writes on a napkin. He hands it to me. I don't recognize the address or that area of Biên Hòa. I tuck the napkin in my shirt pocket.

Lu settles back into his wandering gaze at everything and nothing, taking long swigs from his beer and pensive drags from his cigarette. There's no awkwardness in his silence. It's like he's forgotten me. I look at my watch and take another cigarette from his pack.

Two young women, likely Australian or European tourists, walk past the patio wearing shorts and halter tops. Lu eyes them and declares to me under his breath, as if imparting more wisdom, "Some American women—they're completely shaven down there."

I can only chuckle and drink my beer to hide how awkward I feel, which is less about the comment and more about its patronizing air. It reminds me that Tuyết is the only girl I've ever slept with, and of course she wants no one to know that we've even touched each other. That's when I realize that my annoyance with Lu is actually envy.

I say the first thing that comes to mind: "Where are your wife and kids today?"

There's another flash of amusement in his eyes. "I think she took them to that new waterpark. A waterpark in Sài Gòn! Who owns it, the French?"

"Malaysians, I believe. I'd like to take my girlfriend, but it's pretty expensive. Shouldn't we get going soon?"

Lu pats the air in front of me. "We have all day if we want." He sets another beer in front of me. "One thing I learned on Pulau Bidong is that there's always plenty of time for everything."

"Didn't you say I should rush out and marry my girlfriend?"

He grins and points his cigarette at me. "You're not as timid as I thought you were."

I try my best not to smile at the approval. "So what was Pulau Bidong like? I heard it was hard for you."

He shrugs nonchalantly. "I got hepatitis and spent six months in bed. Lost a third of my weight. Then a year after recovering, I got myself stabbed in a fight." He leans back and pats his abdomen as if he's full from a good meal. I'm expecting him to unbutton his shirt to show off the scar, but he only peers at the spot and declares, "Both times I thought it was the end."

"Which was worse?"

Lu shakes his head. "It's all the same memory to me now. Thing is, I remember very little about those months in bed, aside from how much I hated being helpless. And the stabbing, well, I can't even tell you how I got into it. Some idiot just decided he disliked me and he might've had good reason to. I don't know. I've completely forgotten his face."

"If some guy stabbed me, I'd never forget what he looked like."

Lu is shaking his head again. "Yes, but you've never had anything happen to you."

This time, I can't pretend to laugh or smile. I think of when I failed my graduation exam, or the morning my granddad passed away, or the day two women on a Vespa bumped my car and crashed into a truck, their crumpled bodies bleeding out into the street as traffic continued by. "How would you know that?" I ask him and put out my cigarette.

He pats the air again and cheerfully drinks his beer. It's like he's trying to test me. For what, I have no idea. I want to tell him he knows nothing about me—that no matter how much more he has than me, I'm the only one at this table who's at home anymore.

He flings his cigarette into the street, his smile fading as though he's changing his mind about something. He takes out his wallet and puts two bills under the ashtray. Leaning forward on his elbows, his face slightly flushed from the beer, he says to me, "You know what's funny? Of all the bad things I went through back then, before I left and after I left, the only thing I still think about is that old girlfriend cheating on me." He gives me a surprised look as if he only just realized this. "She sent me a letter two years ago. I have no idea how she found my address. She said she still thinks of me and still loves me more than she's ever loved anyone. And she apologized. Can you believe it? I had to hide the letter from my wife."

He downs the rest of his beer and gestures for us to go, suddenly as impatient as he was relaxed a few minutes ago. As I follow him out of the patio, it finally occurs to me that I'm taking him to this old girlfriend.

But then he stops and looks at his watch and walks back to the hostess. "You sell bottles of wine?" he asks her. "I want a bottle of red, whatever you have is fine." He hands her a fifty-dollar bill, far more than any bottle would cost here, and tells her to keep the change for herself. He adds, "Is the owner here? Can I speak to him?"

The hostess looks at me and back at Lu, unsure if he's an important person or some kind of swindler.

"I'm an old customer," he says, as if it should be obvious.

As he waits by the entrance, I ask for another cigarette and go smoke by the curb. Suddenly that beggar woman is beside me. It's like she just conjured herself here from across the street.

"So handsome . . ." she purrs at me with a toothy smile. She's even older up close, her face a dry white mask of crudely drawn eyebrows, rouged cheeks, and smeared red lipstick. I can't help feeling a little flattered though. At least she's not asking for money.

She notices Lu and starts approaching him from behind. I know I should get rid of her, but his comments are still gnawing at me. She stops a few meters from him, and sure enough, when he sees her, he nearly jumps back.

"Look how handsome . . ." she proclaims, turning to me for agreement. She's no taller than his chest and clasps her fan to her breast as if beholding some magnificent statue. "So handsome . . ."

Lu turns his back to her, the first time I've seen him act self-conscious. A man about his age appears with a bottle of wine. Lu takes it, shaking his hand and saying loudly, as if to drown out the old woman repeating her compliments, "Mr. Thu used to own this place, right?"

"Yes, yes! He was a friend of my father's and sold it to him fifteen years ago. I run it now." He proudly adds, "I've completely redone the place."

"I can see."

"You're from America? Did you know Mr. Thu?"

"His son was a friend from school."

"Oh, I see. The son ran things for a few years. It didn't go so well. That's why they sold it."

"How tall . . ." the beggar woman is now saying behind Lu with genuine amazement, turning from me to the people sitting in the patio, who all ignore her. "Look at him . . ."

The owner gives her a few distracted glances as Lu continues as if she's not there: "You know what Mr. Thu and his son are doing nowadays?"

"I haven't spoken to the family in years, but last I heard, the son served some time in jail for burglary. Sorry to tell you that. Very tough for Mr. Thu, I imagine."

"Must be," Lu mutters.

The beggar woman has come closer and is now mumbling right behind him. I can't help enjoying his discomfort.

He finally turns to her in exasperation, whips out a bill from his pocket, and stuffs it into her hand. "Here, now leave me alone, old woman."

The bill falls from her hand as she keeps smiling lavishly at him. She reaches for his wrist, and Lu pulls it away at once, glaring at her. When she reaches for it again, something flares in him and he shoves her away violently. She stumbles back and falls to the sidewalk, hitting the concrete hard.

I rush over to her, and when Lu does the same, I hiss at him, "What's wrong with you?" For the first time, he's not pretending to not care.

The owner snaps at an attendant to come fix the situation and seems unsure of who he should offer an apology to. People on the patio are staring as I help the old woman to her feet. She looks unhurt, and as the attendant leads her away by the arm, she starts mumbling to him and has already forgotten what happened, her face alive again with mad happiness.

Lu stands there gripping the neck of the wine bottle. He notices the woman's fan on the ground and the crumpled bill he gave her, picks up both, and after a moment hands the fan to the owner, who receives it with an awkward smile. I walk to the car without waiting for him.

We get back on the highway. It's not yet two, but it already feels like we've spent the whole day together. When Lu bought the wine, my first thought was that he was taking it to the old girlfriend's house, but within minutes of us moving again, I heard the cork pop and saw him bring the bottle to his lips.

He still hasn't said a word since we left the café, which I'm thankful for. I'm starting to feel complicit in some unseemly scheme, so the less he says, the better. I imagine Tuyết's reaction if I ever tell her about this. *Why betray your wife with the person who once betrayed you?* she'd probably say. *Lost love is just that: lost.*

But maybe Lu is also escaping something. Maybe he and his wife sit just as silently in their own car, hiding betrayals and secrets that the other already suspects. I'm reminded of his earlier advice and realize that Tuyết and I have not once argued with any passion. If I ever did betray her in some way, I can't imagine her leaving the country because of it, let alone returning decades later for whatever it was Lu was doing now.

Every now and then, I hear him kissing the lip of the wine bottle, and even as I find him increasingly pathetic and inexplicable, I can't help feeling a strange kind of envy. Was he planning to do this all along? Does the old girlfriend even know that he's coming? And why, after all these years, is he now returning to her drowned in booze?

Around three, we approach Biên Hòa. I exit the highway and find that we are going to a less populated area, beyond the tall buildings and city tenements. Patches of farmland with grazing water buffalo break up the stretches of dense neighborhoods and roadside businesses.

Lu asks me to stop somewhere with a toilet, his first words to me in more than an hour. I pull over at a roadside café, and he climbs out with the empty wine bottle. Five minutes later, he returns with a new pack of cigarettes, his face fully flushed.

Once we get going again, he asks me in a dull voice, "Will you be able to find this address?"

"We don't have much farther to go," I reply, and he returns to his silence and his cigarette.

He smokes continuously until we reach the entrance of the neighborhood I'm looking for. He immediately flings his cigarette out the window. I turn into a narrow, gravel road shaded by a wall of breadfruit trees. It is quiet here, hardly anyone outside. Small houses with dingy, stucco walls line the road, and my side mirror nearly scrapes their front gates as we slowly drive by. The road soon opens up into a shady circle of houses distinguishable only by the color of their window shutters. I check the address on the napkin and stop in front of a house with blue shutters, which stands half-hidden behind two giant plum trees.

Lu has yet to move. He is peering at the house as if making sure it's really there.

"Is this it?" I ask him.

"Must be," he replies softly. It appears he's never been here before. Opening the door, he turns to me and says, not unkindly, "Thank you, Điềm."

He trudges to the porch like someone just getting out of bed. No sooner does he reach the first step than he stops and returns, dipping his head through the open passenger window. He slips a hundred-dollar bill awkwardly into my hand and gapes at me with wide, bloodshot eyes. "I'm sure your sister told you not to, but take this and buy something for your girlfriend. And Điềm, don't talk about this with anyone in the family. Just tell them you brought me to visit an old friend." His words are soft and measured, his eyes lucid again. My gut tells me I should feel insulted by this bribe, but instead, for the first time today, I feel like we are actually cousins.

I lean over and ask, "Is this *her* house?"

He grins a little sloppily and says, "I won't be long."

He walks away more confidently now and mounts the porch, disappearing into the deep shade of the plum trees. I can hear a metal door sliding open and after some silence sliding shut.

I'm uneasy waiting in the car. A house on the opposite side of the circle has a small shop in its front room, and I wander inside. The shop sells everything from toothpaste to shoes. A pretty girl around my age sits on a stool by the front counter, reading a magazine while a small radio plays techno music. She looks up when I enter and nods, smiling shyly. She turns down the music and puts her magazine aside, glancing at me curiously as she shuffles some paper on the counter. She has short trendy hair, almost like a boy's—unlike Tuyết who wears hers down to her waist when she's not at the hospital.

I notice some leather handbags in the corner. They're very nice but I'm startled by the price.

"They're made in Italy," the shopgirl volunteers. "Real Italian leather. I promise you your girlfriend will love it."

She's lying about the leather, of course—or just doesn't know any better. Her smile is bright and confident now, and the certainty with which she assumes I have a girlfriend reminds me that she's merely doing her job. There's no shyness in her at all, which feels more deflating than it should.

I ask permission to use the phone on the wall and turn away from her as I dial Tuyết's number. She is not at home, but her brother is quick to mention that she was very disappointed about our canceled trip to the park. Before I hang up, I remind him to tell her that I called.

I glance over at the house that Lu walked into. It looks abandoned, engulfed as it is in shadows. I remember the day two years ago when I first met Tuyết at another cousin's wedding, and she asked me if I would ever want to live in America. I lied and told her no, that I couldn't imagine living anywhere else, which made her smile. It occurs to me that she still believes this.

I pick up the phone again and call my sister. She picks up, and I tell her that I won't know when I'll be back, but that everything is fine. She doesn't ask where we are, only if Lu and I are getting along. I say it's been nice, that we stopped for some ice coffee and he told me a lot about the past, good and bad things, and this seems to please her. She says she'll pay me a little extra today, so maybe I should buy Tuyết a nice gift. She must've said something to Lu after all.

Once I get off the phone, I decide to buy one of the leather handbags. I know Tuyết never expects such gifts and would probably want me to use the money for something more practical. Despite her family's profession, she isn't one for jewelry or fancy things or grand romantic gestures. I buy the handbag anyway, happy to use up Lu's payment for my silence.

But it's only as I watch the shopgirl wrap the handbag in newspaper that I ask myself, for the very first time, if what I felt for Tuyết was actually love. Had I just assumed it all this time? And what would have to happen for me to know? My mom would call these the kinds of questions only Westerners ask themselves, but what about someone like Lu or this woman who never stopped loving him?

The shopgirl is counting out my change when a high-pitched scream startles us both. I take a step outside the shop, and another scream rings out, definitely from the house Lu entered and definitely a woman's voice. There are crashing sounds, glass shattering.

As I hurry back to the house, I hear shouting, a man's voice now, then I see Lu's form from behind stumbling onto the porch. He straightens himself and someone shoves him back again, a stocky man in a white T-shirt, who's cursing at him and then smacks him brutally across the face. Lu staggers to the edge of the porch where he turns just in time to see it and goes tripping down the steps, nearly crashing into me right as I get there. I manage to keep him on his feet, but he stays keeled over, breathing hard and spitting blood on the ground.

The man is standing on the top step with his fists clenched, glaring down at us, wiping his bloody nose repeatedly with a finger. The last time I hit someone was in secondary school, and I lost that fight, but I surprise myself and take step forward. The man doesn't even see me, his eyes only on Lu. I notice a tattoo of a dragon running down his right arm and the deep leathery tan of too many days in the sun.

Faint voices come from within the house, and the man unclenches his fists and sighs as if the thought of throwing another punch bores him. Lu finally looks up at him, and the man shakes his head at him and mutters, with something like pity, "Lu, you idiot."

He trudges back into the house, and the metal door grinds shut. Behind me, Lu is already walking to the car.

It's not until I get behind the wheel that I see the neighbors staring at us from their own porches. Lu is now sitting in the front seat, his upper lip split open and bleeding into his teeth, his hair hanging over his eyes, his shirt spotted with blood.

"What did you do?" I demand a little too loudly as we roll away, already exasperated by the thought of driving him home in silence.

But his face breaks out in a grin and he starts laughing to himself, until his shoulders are shaking and he has to cover his mouth to keep from spitting blood on my dashboard. He wipes his hands on his shirt indiscriminately. I hand him the napkin that had the address on it.

"What's the matter with you?" I say, unsure if he might still be drunk. "Who was that?"

"The old friend, cousin—" he whispers loudly, looking at me with delight. "I bet I broke his nose. He thought I came to forgive him. He thought after all this time I had let it go!"

He holds the napkin to his mouth and bursts into another fit of laughter. For a moment, it's like he's laughing at me.

We exit the neighborhood, and I'm driving much faster than I normally would, desperate to get us back to Sài Gòn as soon as possible. A grin lingers on Lu's face as he watches the landscape go by. I want to ask if that's all there was to it, if his plan all along was just to come home and punch an old friend for betraying him twenty years ago—but asking anything about today would be like asking him why he bleeds.

At a stoplight, he holds the door ajar and spits blood onto the street. Once he closes the door, I finally ask him, "What am I supposed to say if Loan asks about your lip?"

He smiles wide again, dabbing at his lip with the napkin. "Tell her you were waiting for me in the car and napping, and as I was walking back to you, someone robbed me. I came back to you like this. I'll explain the rest."

He thinks for another moment and adds, "Tell her, they tried to rob me, but I didn't let them."

We're approaching Sài Gòn Bridge as the sun is setting. Lu is snoring softly, slumped in his seat. His upper lip is noticeably swollen and crusted with dried blood, which is also streaked across the front of his shirt.

On the bridge, traffic slows to a crawl. Pedestrians crowd the boardwalk, vendors prowling among them. Those who approach me, I shoot my meanest glare. A gaggle of them assaults the tall red touring van in front of me, waving their maps and books and drinks up at the windows. The van is carrying a large family of Việt kiều, the adults enjoying some story that one of them is acting out rather dramatically. I can hear their howls of laughter despite the closed windows.

Two little boys, about five or six years old, are sitting in the rear seat, both wearing identical baseball caps too big for them. They're staring at Lu with profound interest. When I ease right and come up beside the van, they move to the window right above mine.

One boy opens his window and shouts down at me in English, which I don't understand. He's pointing at Lu. The other boy interprets for me and says, "Is he *dead*?"

I hesitate, then shrug at them without smiling. "I don't know," I say and realize that I mean it.

Their eyes widen, and as I let the van pull away from me, they keep staring at Lu with a mix of awe and doubt. They're buried in youth, I think. They know nothing of what may come.

Traffic suddenly picks up, and when I shift gears, Lu's head falls onto his shoulder. He doesn't stir, his snoring childlike and weak. I wish I could laugh at how absurd the day has been, but I can't help feeling disappointed in Lu—that him righting this old wrong today was at my expense somehow. It's because of love, he'd probably say, though I'm sure the truth of the matter is at once as petty as what he did and much more profound than I can know. I suppose I've always imagined a kind of pain that keeps following people around like their shadow, despite whatever other sorrows they experience, despite reason and proportion.

We cross the Sài Gòn River, its calm waters burnished white by the sun, and I remember the handbag I left behind in the store. I realize, with sudden force, that it makes no difference to me.

Up ahead I see the red van again. Suddenly it swerves and darts around, weaving drunkenly as though it might tip over, nearly hitting a number of vehicles before it finally regains control. My heart leaps, and in that instant I imagine the van crashing into me, overturning on top of my car, my body pinned beneath its wheels as I hear above me the sound of laughter.

What the War Left Behind

—Nguyễn Minh Chuyên—

THE RESIDENTS OF HAMLET 7 in Quang Minh Commune often remarked, "The blind have a sixth sense for getting around. Somehow he always manages to find his way to the cemetery, navigating the winding dirt roads through the village."

Mr. Ngô, elderly and blind, often made his way to the cemetery, feeling through the darkness with his hands. He went there regularly to mourn the death of his son, and at night his sobs would reverberate throughout the village. He also grieved for his children who weren't dead, knowing that they would never get to lead normal lives.

One rainy night, in an inconsolable state, Mr. Ngô took a hoe to the cemetery. Despite the pitch-black night sky, he managed to find his first son's grave among the hundreds in the cemetery. Unlike other nights, he didn't break down emotionally. His clothes were soaked by the relentless rain, but he kept digging until his hoe struck the coffin lid. After struggling to open the coffin, he collected the remains and wrapped them in a length of cloth. When he got home, he placed the cloth bundle on a bed of straw in the kitchen and built a fire.

The next morning, Mr. Ngô went into his wife's room to wake her. "I just brought our son Nhân home," he said. "Do you remember the unusual shape of his head? I ate a piece of him and saved some for you. Please get up and eat."

Hearing her husband's nonsense, she was reminded of his mental illness. She sat up in bed before he dragged her into the kitchen, pointing to the ashes. "That's Nhân."

When Mr. Ngô's wife saw the heap of bones, the human skull, she screamed, "You've completely lost your mind! What will the neighbors think?"

The neighbors, hearing the commotion from outside, rushed into the kitchen. Mrs. Cam said tearfully, "What kind of person exhumes their son to eat him?"

"He did what?" an astonished neighbor asked.

"Come see for yourself," she said, pointing to the pile of bones. "Now my poor son will never rest in peace."

"Why did you dig up your son's grave?" the neighbor asked Mr. Ngô. "And why burn his bones like that?"

"Because he left me," Mr. Ngô grinned, "and I had to find him and bring him home." His eyes fell on the charred skull. "Isn't that right, my dear son? You've come home now."

Everyone was stunned. The toxic chemicals Mr. Ngô had been exposed to during the war had sealed the tragic fates for his three children. He had once believed that the effects would end with his children's generation, but they only continued. The dioxin robbed Mr. Ngô not only of his sight but also of his sanity.

***

MR. NGÔ HAD RETURNED TO HIS hamlet over thirty years ago with nothing but a rucksack. For nineteen years he fought on the battlefield, miraculously escaping every bullet and shard of shrapnel. He was lucky. After his discharge, he went back to his former life as a farmer and eventually married. When his wife gave birth to their first child, she reeled in horror at the sight of his dark face and hairy body, the stubby neck and deformed limbs, and his unusually oblong head. A year later their son, Nhân, swelled hideously, as though he were filled with water. Nhân died at the age of five.

A year later, Mrs. Cam became pregnant again and gave birth to twins, a boy and a girl. She cried out when she saw them. The boy had no birth defects, but the girl's skin was dark and covered in fur like a bear. Mr. Ngô named the boy Nguyên and the girl Thủy. The couple struggled to raise their children. By the age of ten, Nguyên began to show some signs of abnormality. He was sensitive to light and sometimes lashed out for no reason. His eyes had a vacant look about them. After everyone had fallen asleep, Nguyên would sneak out and sleep in the garden. By morning, when his parents couldn't find him, they would go looking for him, and see him snoring next to a peony bush. Sometimes at night, he would find himself in a water tank, and wait there for them until dawn.

Infected cysts as large as apples appeared on Thủy's fur-covered skin and gave off a revolting odor. For months afterward, Thủy cried out in pain from constant high fevers. Mr. Ngô and Mrs. Cam had to borrow money from friends and neighbors to treat their children's illnesses and deformities. They contacted various hospitals and even consulted with traditional herbalists, but nothing worked. Mr. Ngô gave up hope.

Despite her birth defects, Thủy grew up to be a relatively normal twenty-year-old girl. Behind the dark patches of fur on her face were bright, clear eyes. Her black hair was long and silky. The cysts on her body had receded and were now hidden beneath her soft fur. In contrast, her brother Nguyên struggled throughout childhood and became increasingly withdrawn and forgetful. He rarely displayed any emotion. Sometimes, he would wake up in the dead of night, humming a sad, silly song to himself.

When Nguyên finally reached the age of twenty, Mr. Ngô asked, "Do you want to get married?" Nguyên said nothing, giving his father a confused look. Mr. Ngô noticed that Nguyên's eyes looked abnormal, like those of deranged men or those burdened with deep-seated hatred. A month later, Mr. Ngô asked again, "Do you want to get married? I think it's about time you started building a new future."

Nguyên nodded. His parents were thrilled and a wedding took place not long after. Nguyên married Lan from the nearby village of Trực Nho. After getting married, Nguyên began to improve his communication, sometimes even conveying real emotions. News of Lan's pregnancy made Mr. Ngô happy, but it was also worrisome. He had heard about a man in Hà Tây who had been exposed to Agent Orange during the war, resulting in his son developing cognitive problems. After the son received treatment for his mental illness, he got married, but his young wife gave birth to deformed children. Mr. Ngô was concerned that the same thing would likely happen to his own son and his daughter-in-law.

On the day Lan gave birth, she fainted in the delivery room at the sight of her firstborn, who looked as beastly as his late uncle Nhân. Even more horrifying, the newborn had two sets of eyes and was covered in fur. He managed to live for three days before he died. A year later, Lan gave birth to another child and named him Linh. Linh could draw his neck into his body like a turtle, and the joints of his malformed limbs locked up as if he had arthritis. His head would occasionally loll about like a pendulum, and he cried incessantly. Nguyên and Lan took Linh to different hospitals, but it appeared that something inside him was causing the pain.

Due to his children's misfortune, Nguyên withdrew into himself again. Watching his wife weep as she held Linh in her arms, he felt an overwhelming apathy, as though all emotion had drained from him. Now and then, tears would fill his eyes when he saw his son suffering from seizures. But Nguyên would burst into demented laughter and his body began to wither and age much faster.

One day, people from the Red Cross visited Quang Minh Commune on a charitable mission. As they entered Mr. Ngô's front yard, they noticed a wizened and ailing man with gray hair sitting on a chair, his back propped against a pillar.

"Good morning," said Lộc, the group's leader. "Is Mr. Ngô home?"

Mr. Ngô said nothing, gazing vacantly at his guests before breaking into hysterical laughter. The delegation thought he must be hard of hearing, so they ignored him and continued into the living room, where they saw another old man covered in a blanket. This other man slowly sat up, got off the bed, and shuffled to the tea table.

"Hello!" Lộc called out. "Are you Mr. Ngô?"

It took Mr. Ngô a moment to respond. "Yes, that's me. Please, sit down and have some tea before it gets cold."

"Where are your son and grandson? The ones who were exposed to Agent Orange?"

Mr. Ngô closed the lid of the teapot and pointed at the man sitting on the porch. "That's my son," he said. He then began to explain Nguyên's health-related problems to his guests. When they had first entered the gate, the delegation had mistaken Nguyên for Mr. Ngô.

Nguyên slowly rose to his feet and went inside. He cast a steely gaze at the strangers around the tea table, said nothing, then retreated to his bedroom.

"You see, he's only in his twenties but he looks like a seventy-year-old man. Even worse, he talks to himself. He's got other mental issues as well."

"When were you first exposed to dioxin, Mr. Ngô?" someone from the delegation asked. Where did it happen?"

"Back on October 2, 1970," Mr. Ngô began, "my unit was stationed in a jungle around Quảng Đà. An American airplane flew over and dropped bombs, then sprayed Agent Orange all around us. I hurt my arm—it wasn't too bad—but the toxic chemicals made it hard to breathe. I blacked out. My comrades weren't hit by bomb fragments, but they passed out, too. We were rushed to a field hospital. Later, we learned that all the trees in the jungle had shed their leaves and died, so we moved on to another area. The U.S. Air Force had this campaign to clear vegetation by spraying herbicides and defoliants. Nine of my comrades suffocated to death not long after, and many more ended up in the hospital. Those of us who survived, we don't get to live full lives. We pass the toxin down to our children and grandchildren."

Mr. Ngô's voice trembled as he recounted his story, his emotions evident. He reached down and opened a tin trunk, pulling out a piece of paper. Handing over the letter, he said, "I wrote this to Monsanto, the company that made Agent Orange, and demanded they take responsibility for what they did and compensate Vietnamese victims of dioxin. Can you take a look and tell me if I need to make any changes? A young student from Hà Nội found their address online and gave it to me."

While the letter was being read aloud, commotion erupted from the bedroom. Nguyên stormed out with his teeth clenched, full of fury. He cradled his son in his arms and approached the tea table, making a motion as though he were about to throw the boy to the ground. Everyone rushed toward him to stop it from happening.

"He's losing it again," Mr. Ngô muttered.

Nguyên bent down and angrily hurled teacups and saucers onto the floor. He then placed his son on the tea table and fixed his eyes on Mr. Ngô. "Here, take care of your grandson. It's you who's making his life unbearable."

"Poor boy," Mr. Ngô said to his grandson. "Your father's losing his mind again."

"Exactly! I'm crazy, just like you. And do you know why? Because you've turned everyone in this house into lunatics."

"Blame the Americans!" Mr. Ngô said tearfully. "They're the ones who sprayed the chemicals, so it's their fault this happened to us!"

Nguyên's sanity completely shattered after that day. One rainy and thunderous night, he left home, abandoning his son and wife. He turned to the life of a street beggar, relying on the charity of strangers. A villager reported to Mr. Ngô that he had once seen Nguyên in the Hóc Môn cemetery in Sài Gòn, where he was living off the offerings left for the dead. Another villager said they had seen him wandering in Bến Thành Market and later at the Hòa Hưng train station. Whenever Nguyên recognized a face from his hamlet, he would scowl at them with tears in his eyes but refused to accept their handouts. That was the last anyone had heard from Nguyên.

Linh, his son, became sensitive to light and often crawled under his bed to hide. The family had spent all their savings on medical bills and received only a small government subsidy each month, just enough to cover Linh's injections for his seizures. Mr. Ngô borrowed money from neighbors and friends and sold most of his furniture. He even took out loans from loan sharks to save his grandson's life. At one point, he feared he might end up a street beggar, humiliated by the thought of having to carry Linh on his back. So he asked his wife to check the trunk for anything valuable to sell.

"Nothing, except for your war medals," Mrs. Cam said.

"You're right. I completely forgot about them. Let's sell them to antique collectors."

"Are you sure?"

"Yes, we need the money for our grandson's medical bills."

The following day, Mr. Ngô took his war medals to La Market. He put them in a basket and sat near the rice vendors. People passing by saw what he had to offer and began to talk behind his back.

"He shed tears and blood for those medals," someone would say. "Why sell them now?"

"Those medals aren't his," they said. "He'd get laughed at if he wore them. That's why he's getting rid of them."

Mr. Ngô could hear what others were saying about him but remained quiet. His friends suggested he sell the medals to discharged officers who were now civilians. They could use the war medals to impress future employers of their heroic deeds, which would help them get promoted quickly. But who would buy them in a small village market? Mr. Ngô decided to try a larger market the next day.

On his way home from La Market, less than a kilometer away, something strange came over him. His steps weren't heavy like usual, as though someone were lifting him up by his feet. Circles of light danced in front of him and the trees lining both sides of the road quivered, their green leaves turning red. The pebbles under his feet, the hyacinths in the pond, and the purple flowers all seemed to glow an unnatural red. He kept walking, but it felt like he was walking on air. Suddenly, he found himself plunging into water.

Passersby heading home from the market jumped into the pond to rescue him. They revived him before taking him to a nearby clinic. Mr. Ngô went blind after that. He could no longer see the pain and suffering of those he loved.

***

ONE DAY, MR. HOÀN, CHAIRMAN OF the local Veterans Association, paid Mr. Ngô a visit. Mr. Ngô explained that he had written a letter to the Monsanto Company but decided not to send it.

"Why not?" asked Mr. Hoàn. "Look at your family's disabilities. How can you forgive the enemy and their war crimes?"

"Please, calm down," Mr. Ngô said. "My family suffers, I know, but I don't want to file a lawsuit against the company. It would only cause more tension. Truth is, our country is at peace now, and we had to pay a heavy price to get here. No sacrifice, no peace. That's just how it is."

"On behalf of the Veterans Association, we're grateful to you for your sacrifices," Mr. Hoàn said. "Unfortunately, the local and national governments haven't done much to support veterans like you. The country's still recovering from the long war, you know."

After Mr. Hoàn left, Mr. Ngô fumbled his way to the ancestral altar. He found the letter in a tin box and took it, along with a box of matches, to the porch. Sitting down, he struck a match and set the letter on fire. Though he couldn't see the flames because of his blindness, but he could imagine the letter writhing and blackening, the ashes rising all around him.

***

E. JUM WALTE, AN AMERICAN SOLDIER during the 1960s, had sprayed toxic chemicals over the Central Highlands, Đà Nẵng, and the Sơn Trà Peninsula in South Vietnam. At the time, he believed these chemicals would strip the jungle bare, making it easier for the Americans to detect the Vietcong. When he returned to the States, he was plagued by PTSD-induced nightmares. In his dreams, innocent children with blurry faces and grotesque bodies chased after him, as though they wanted to eat him alive. As soon as he closed his eyes, they screamed and groaned in pain. Tugging at his shirt, they pushed him down, demanding their pound of flesh. Later, he learned that the chemicals he had sprayed were the cause of birth defects, realizing that the children in his dreams were the Vietnamese victims of Agent Orange. On April 30, 2005, he and his wife flew to Vietnam. They wrote "For Charitable Purposes" on their visa applications, but their true reason was to seek forgiveness.

After spending a few days in Sài Gòn, they traveled to the North and visited victims of Agent Orange, including Mr. Ngô's family. The sight of Mr. Ngô, his daughter Thủy, and his grandson filled Mr. Walte with dread. He feared they might lash out at him, attack him, or even unleash their pent-up fury out of vengeance, so he remained cautious and kept his distance. But after speaking with Mr. Ngô for an hour, Mr. Walte sensed no hostility. Both the host and his wife were courteous, despite the suffering they had gone through.

Mr. Ngô couldn't see the faces of his American guests, but he blinked as he spoke. "If we had met thirty years ago, I would've shot you dead. But you've nothing to fear now." He was quiet for a while, then said, "Even if I killed you, it wouldn't ease the pain you've caused my family. When you return home, tell the American people that we Vietnamese are willing to forgive their war crimes, but they must take responsibility for what's happened to us."

The interpreter conveyed Mr. Ngô's message to Mr. Walte, who replied, "Thank you from the bottom of my heart. Please let me take your daughter Thủy back to the States. I'll do my best to find good doctors who can remove her fur. You don't have to worry about anything."

Three months later, Thủy flew to the States. During that time, Mr. Ngô and his wife stayed behind with their grandson, Linh, who was still in constant pain. Meanwhile, Mr. Ngô became sick; his face turned pale, and his body and breath emitted a foul odor. Blisters erupted on his skin, oozing pus was like leech blood when they burst.

Confined to bed, he was plagued by nightmares in which he, a strong and fit soldier again, carried a rucksack and marched with his comrades. Their heads were oblong, their limbs skinny as bamboo as they hobbled along in their march. Terrified, he tried to step away, but his comrades picked him up and threw him into the air. As he flew alongside a rainbow-colored cloud through the blue sky, he began in his hallucinatory state, muttering nonsensically, his hallucinations driving him to fumble blindly to the cemetery to dig up his son's remains.

Thủy returned after a year of treatment in the States. Most of the fur that had covered her body was gone, except for a small patch just below her neck and from her knees down. She said, "The American doctors were kind and caring. The Walte family treated me like one of their own. I felt at home with them."

But Mr. Ngô couldn't see how his daughter had changed; he couldn't share her joy. He lived like a ghost in the shadows, saying and feeling nothing. Every emotion—from hatred and resentment to love and joy—was meaningless to him. Yet everyone else knew the truth—that he and his loved ones had suffered so others could live in peace.

—*Translated by Quan Manh Ha & Cab Tran*

Chị Nhàn at the End Time

—Thuy Dinh—

CHỊ NHÀN JOINED OUR HOUSEHOLD IN the fall of 1974, about six months before we left Vietnam with our maternal grandparents. The situation in South Vietnam was rapidly deteriorating. After my dad, a political columnist, was arrested by the South Vietnamese government, we left our house in Hàng Xanh, a secluded neighborhood in a semi-rural area, to move into my grandparents' house in a bustling alley on the edge of Sài Gòn Chinatown.

My grandparents, both sixty at the time, were now faced with the care and needs of six extra people: my mother and five of us children. My mother was also eight months pregnant with my youngest brother. To alleviate my grandparents' burden, my mother hired chị Nhàn to help with the cooking and cleaning.

In Vietnamese, *chị* means elder sister—a form of address that acknowledges our respect for an older person who is still our peer as opposed to someone in our parents' generation. *Chị*, or *anh*—its male equivalent—can also be used to address household servants or members of the service industry.

Chị Nhàn was mysterious. While her name, which means leisure and relaxation, and might have reflected her parents' wistful aspiration, her sturdy, 5-foot-seven build, considered giant by Vietnamese standards, did not seem to have been bred for delicate or leisurely activities. She was dusky and flat-chested, with large hands and feet, a longish, mournful face, heavy-lidded brown eyes, broad cheek-bones, a proudly flared nose, and thin, pale lips. Her beauty was esoteric, perhaps ahead of its time. Our previous housekeepers, chị Phụng and chị Đẹt—with milky skin, red lips and petite hourglass bodies—had long fled our household to explore better prospects with the Americans.

In private, my grandmother called chị Nhàn *con hộ pháp*—the temple troll—due to her imposing physique that reminded her of a *dvara*. I imagined chị Nhàn as an avatar reincarnated into human form. At once solid and detached, she seemed to be both earth and air.

It was not difficult to identify with chị Nhàn. At twelve, I struggled against my environment and began to judge the adults around me. Chị Nhàn's stolid elusiveness thus seemed reassuring, almost liber-ating. I remember hating a popular teen song by Phạm Duy called "Tuổi Mộng Mơ" ("The Wishing Age"), that played nonstop on the radio throughout 1974. It began with "Little one, what do you wish to become when you're twelve and thirteen? Oh I wish, I wish I could be a fairy princess . . ." It was such a fake and backward song. Many of my preteen friends were precocious, or had older siblings from whom they gained decidedly un-childlike knowledge. We were living in the aftermath of the Paris Peace Accords that heralded the end of the American military involvement in Vietnam. We knew about Watergate, Nixon's resignation, and desperate battle skirmishes in the provinces that did not get reported in the city papers due to the South Vietnamese government's censorship.

In the punishing Sài Gòn heat, my uniform—a long, white, man-darin-collared *áo dài* made of thick crepe polyester—became a symbol of oppression. I attended an all-girls' school, where an anachronistic code of virtuous maidenhood was zealously enforced by the adminis-tration. We were not allowed to wear clothes that hinted at our body shapes, flirt with boys, or be seen snacking in public. I bristled during the daily uniform inspection by our principal, who wanted to make sure we wore thick camisoles and rigid, cantilevered bras underneath our *áo dài*—protective gears that a famous male poet had nevertheless lauded as being more suggestive than the Western bikini.

On the whole I was restless, jaded, and without anchor. At twelve, I had gone with my mother to visit my dad in Chí Hòa Prison, where all prisoners mingled in a salty, bonhomie, almost festive atmosphere, as if imprisonment, whether you were innocent or guilty, was a normal everyday occurrence. Before my dad's incarceration, we would visit him in hotels or safe houses arranged by his friends—who said they were under "full CIA protection." During his years of hiding, and even when he lived at home, my dad sported a full beard to cover his features. My friends thought he looked ruggedly handsome, like Toshiro Mifune.

It was a time during which children, largely neglected, were free to create our adventures. I would cut classes with a handful of friends to go to the Sài Gòn Zoo or take the bus to Vạn Hạnh University, where we would run along the marble rim of the Turtle Fountain and furtively gaze at the objects of our preteen crush: male college students whom we called the Che brothers—after Che Guevara—mysterious, laconic beings with long hair, almond eyes, sensuous lips beneath earnest mustaches, and long thin fingers stained yellow by nicotine. The Che brothers, by their innate intelligence, or, more likely, through bribery and family connections, were exempt from the draft. They would lounge about the Vạn Hạnh quad and discuss French existentialism while languidly puffing on Bastos cigarettes.

From time to time, coming home from my truancy, I would spot the green dollar bills that my grandfather had brought back from work. He was a senior translator at the Department of Army's Defense Attaché Office (DAO) in Tân Sơn Nhất Airport. Toward the end of 1974, due to the volatile political situation and sky-high inflation rate, my grandfather had requested that his salary be paid in American dollars, instead of the Vietnamese đồng as of old. He would leave the green bills peeking out of a bank envelope, next to his leather portfolio on the counter. Chị Nhàn, if she paid close attention, would have seen those green bills.

Somehow, even before my grandfather said anything, I knew that our life in Vietnam was coming to an end. I became more and more disengaged. My grandmother scolded me, but in an airy, indirect manner, as if she was posing a riddle, "What kind of girl always has her head in the clouds? What kind of girl is slower than a turtle and lazier than a sloth?" I wanted to scream. My mother tried to talk to me, "You need to act like a big girl. As the eldest, you have to act on my behalf, to take good care of your siblings. You need to be helpful to your grandparents, for they're well past the age of having to put up with bratty children." Trying to contain my rage, I left the house to go sit outside. Chị Nhàn came to join me, saying, "Don't let things get to you."

From that day on I decided that a resigned, stoic mode was more efficient than rage. When my mother went to the hospital to give birth to my brother, I helped chị Nhàn take care of my younger siblings, waking them up in the morning, making them breakfast and getting them dressed for school. The younger kids had to attend school in the morning, but Long—my ten year old brother—and I, being older, would go to school in the afternoon. There was no school bus so we had to walk to the city bus stop, about half a mile from my grandparents' home, to catch the bus that would drop us off near the Sài Gòn Zoo, which was the nearest location to our respective schools.

One afternoon, we were running late and, seeing the bus heading toward our stop, my brother raced across the street without looking. A motorcyclist managed to avoid hitting Long at the last moment by deftly steering left and at the same time kicking my brother toward the curb with his right foot, hurling him, palms and belly down, across the asphalt. In a dizzying blur, I managed to pull Long safely to the sidewalk just as the bus was starting to leave. Neither the motorcyclist nor the bus driver had even bothered to stop. I was shaking. My brother had scraped his hands, almost his entire front, and both knees. His uniform of white shirt and blue pants were now grimy with dust and flecked with blood. The first thing he said, after calming down, was "Don't tell anyone."

We walked home. Luckily, only chị Nhàn saw us as we came through the back gate. My grandfather was still at work and my grandmother was upstairs praying with her rosary. Chị Nhàn didn't ask us what had happened, but simply helped Long clean up. Then she told him to put on a clean pair of long-sleeved pajamas and take a nap. At dinner we told our grandparents that Long was not feeling well and would have to stay home for a few days.

My mother came home with my baby brother after her standard weeklong stay at the hospital. Life went on mostly as before, but now chị Nhàn was faced with a daily heap of cloth diapers to wash, hang dry, and iron.

Events outside our house occurred at a dizzying speed. One day, at school, while we were exercising outdoors with our classmates, a rogue South Vietnamese pilot flew his plane and dropped a bomb on the Presidential Palace a few miles away. Southern cities, one by one, fell to the communists. Each afternoon we sang the South Vietnamese national anthem and solemnly recited the names of our fallen cities. No one dared mention the futility of such an exercise.

In early April, chị Nhàn disappeared for an entire weekend, from Saturday afternoon through Sunday. While she was free to do as she wished on her weekends off—being a single, unattached female domestic worker with no family in the city—she had never stayed out the night, let alone two nights in a row. We were worried but in the end decided not to contact the police. My grandmother said, "Who could ever hurt that giant temple troll?"

At dawn on Monday, chị Nhàn returned, her face distant and preoccupied. We did not want to pry but was hoping she would say something. Yet chị Nhàn remained quiet and simply went about her chores.

She disappeared for good on Thursday.

Later my mother found a letter tucked behind the banana hook in the kitchen:

Dear Mrs. Nguyen,

I'm really sorry for leaving so suddenly. One day I will be able to tell you everything but now I can't. I've had a heart condition since I was a kid. I passed out in the street Saturday night and when I came to I was in someone's house. I had no way of contacting you.

I feel bad that I have to leave, especially right after receiving such a nice raise and bonus. But I promise one day I will come back and explain.

Yours truly,
Lê Thị Nhàn

By now my mother had become fully convinced that chị Nhàn was a Vietcong spy, entrusted with a mission to infiltrate a Southern bourgeois family! We were deeply disturbed by her strange letter and the mysterious circumstances behind her departure, but other, more pressing concerns gradually took priority. Time became compressed. My grandfather then told us that his twenty-year career as a translator with the Americans would not bode well for him should the regime change hands, so for months he had negotiated with his superiors and secretly made arrangements for us to leave Vietnam by plane. He said to wait for his phone call from work. As my grandparents did not own a phone, he told us that he would call our neighbor's house to give us a coded order to evacuate. We received his summons on April 21, 1975.

***

FOR A LONG TIME, AND EVEN NOW, I have wondered about chị Nhàn. Was she hurt after passing out in the street and waking up in a stranger's home? What really happened? Was she really a communist spy, sent to study our Southern mores and capitalist shortcomings, or was my mother's speculation, no matter how disturbing, easier to accept than any other, unspeakable possibility?

If chị Nhàn was a communist spy, what did she make of us? Did we seem paranoid, pampered, and profoundly inept? We made up stories about my father's "overseas business" to justify his long absence to outsiders. But households with absentee fathers were fairly common in South Vietnam during the war, so we might have been fine with a simpler or more straightforward reason regarding his absence. The tense political atmosphere had made us wary of elements that we could not control, so over time we all learned to be fabricators.

Dissembling also became a defensive tactic in the public sphere. Our newspaper's front page was full of black space—newsprint columns that the government censors had blotted out but through this very visible act of erasure had confirmed the day's bad news. In a novel marketed to "Tuổi Hoa Tím" ("Purple Flower Age") suitable for readers age twelve to eighteen, I read about a young girl who commits suicide because she was raped and has no one to turn to. We thought we could be protected by silence or self-denial, but we had never considered safety—being free from harm—as a basic right.

Did chị Nhàn look into our desk drawers and closets? Did she think we were hopelessly sentimental because we preferred to look backward? My mother's main possessions were things created from love and happy memories, black and white photos of us as babies, love letters from my father, and her favorite áo dài—those she often wore during the best years of our lives—the blue and lavender with Pucci-inspired swirls, the bright coral that reminded me of sherbet, sunset, and salmon roe, and the cream Thai silk with black Rorschach blots that made me think of cubist sheep.

We also wrote letters to my dad that we hoped would reach him after we left Vietnam — letters that were more like diary entries. Here was one from me dated April 14, 1975:

Dear Dad,
We may have to leave Vietnam without you. Will they let you out soon?
This reminds me of Dr. Zhivago. In the movie after his release from
prison he came home to find out that his wife and children had left for
Paris. The war in Russia back then reminds me of this war. The ending
is too sad. Years after the war he happened to see his old girlfriend

Lara walking on the street, Dr. Zhivago was so shocked he died of a heart attack. I hope one day we will all be together, because it would be too sad if our story is just like the ending in Dr. Zhivago.

Assuming chị Nhàn was a communist spy, and if she indeed had inklings of our impending departure, did she mention it to her colleagues or superiors? Would our anticipated leaving lead her to dismiss us as cowards and traitors, because our desire for freedom did not align with hers, or that of her comrades?

Thinking about chị Nhàn also trigger my 1970s memories of my grandparents' neighbors, especially Mr. Ba with his black Fellini sunglasses who napped most days in his hammock under the milk fruit tree, oblivious of family members who occasionally had to step over his tumescent belly to reach the house. People said he napped to forget the death of his son Tiến, who died of a heroin overdose at seventeen.

Mr. Ba had another son, Hưng, rumored to be a draft dodger. One time I came over to their house to hang out with Mimi, Mr. Ba's youngest daughter who was around my age. We discovered Hưng's hidden stack of *Playboy* full of naked American women. These tanned, long-limbed models, with their standard sultry gaze or downcast glance over a shapely shoulder, seemed both matter-of-fact and opaque. Years later, I wondered if a naked body and a censored newsprint could somehow be analogous? Nakedness didn't always reveal, as censorship didn't always cover the truth.

There was also Mrs. Bảy—a self-proclaimed churchgoer addicted to gambling—whose shanty listed to the left of Mr. Ba's yellow stucco house. Mrs. Bảy often yelled at us for making a ruckus during her afternoon rosary. She had two paintings in her cluttered hut, the Good Death and the Evil Death. In the Good Death a dying man sees a heavenly vista filled with rosy-cheeked angels singing and blowing horns behind a blond, bearded St. Peter, whose long arm extends toward the dying man. The Evil Death painting, on the other hand, exults in terror and banishment. Even before the bad man draws his last breath, red devils with their pointy ears and long, anchor-shaped tails are already pulling his deathbed toward a blazing fireplace which signifies the gate to hell.

Mrs. Bảy had four tenants who lived in a dank, tube-like structure behind her living space: Mrs. Lê, the fried banana vendor, her husband Đức, and their two teenage girls, Xuân and Thu. Crude and short-tempered, Đức often hit his wife and cursed at his daughters. But on any Friday, a pint of cheap rice wine would render him utterly helpless. His wife and daughters would naturally seize this opportunity as payback time. They took turns slapping and kicking him in full view of everyone until he loudly sobbed for forgiveness.

What would chị Nhàn's communist comrades think if they read her detailed report on our family and neighbors? Would they consider these stories chaotic, sad, decadent, and absurd? And did chị Nhàn gain any personal insight while observing us at close range?

Sometimes I imagine chị Nhàn's abrupt departure from our family as reflecting her crisis of conscience. Perhaps she simply decided to renounce both Marxism and our daily surveillance once she had seen that our daily lives, while messy and baffling, contained rich possibilities. I also picture chị Nhàn leaving for a vibrant new world beyond Vietnam and America, where she would prosper as a capable and generous woman. In her own way, she had taught me a different kind of silence, something like self-possession—as a seawall against rage and confusion.

But these musings are indulgent and presumptuous. After nearly half a century, chị Nhàn remains an enigma, a mythic figure from the last chapter of our time in Vietnam.

A Mother's Song

—Annhien Nguyen—

BLUE SKIES AND A BRIGHT SUN halt at the black-tinted windows of
Café Võ.

The café is busy this time of day. Inside, middle-aged men with
salt-and-pepper hair punctuate their sentences with cigarette
smoke. Large TV screens, mounted side by side, show muted quarter-
backs commandeering teams in grass-streaked uniforms and shiny
helmets. Money is on the line for the men who lean in closer, who
don't laugh as hard after each play—their anxious gaze moving back
and forth between the screen and a prayer. Men come here to smoke,
to drink, to mindlessly look at young girls fresh from Vietnam.

This is the only respite the men get during the day while their
wives are at work. Nail salons. Restaurants. God forbid—offices. Most
have the perfect Vietnamese woman—hardworking, soft-spoken,
beautiful. She leaves home with heated curls in a cloud of Chanel and
returns smelling of long days and acetone. But she will have dinner
on the table ready at 6:00 p.m., and they will listen as her jade bracelet
gently clacks against the table.

It's easy to spot the young ones. They walk on heels like baby deer
breaking in their legs. Half these young girls dropped out of high
school; the other half are fresh from Vietnam. But they all ride the
high of waitressing at a cash-only business. The higher your skirt, the
higher your tips.

Sometimes the men accidentally call her *con*, or "child." Until they remember that the windows are tinted, and that behind them they can be someone else. It gives them courage to change *con* to *em*—"young maiden."

Hà fastened her apron. Her mother would kill her if she found her here.

On one of the screens inside the café, football was replaced by a woman in an elegant *áo dài*, the traditional dress of Vietnam. Slowly, the camera panned over the light chiffon fabric draping her ankles, following the embroidered flowers that climbed her body, and tracing the exposed skin at her midriff. Here the fabric clung tighter, until it reached the mandarin collar just below her jawline.

"Hà, turn the volume on," someone hollered.

Mai Lan, Hà's mother, was singing on *Paris by Night*, one of the most widely televised Vietnamese programs around the world, founded by refugees who escaped to France after the fall of Sài Gòn. She smiled as she faced a large, intergenerational crowd. Men in faded U.S. Army caps leaned back in their chairs, smiling to the songs they grew up with. Young children, dressed in their best clothes, squirmed with excitement next to their mothers. Song, dance, nostalgia—for a moment everything came together to unite a displaced community of people.

Mai Lan sang *cải lương*, a form of traditional Vietnamese folk opera. *Cải lương* was unmistakably Vietnamese and her mother's voice was made for it. Her voice cut through the hazy buzz of empty beer cans, reminding patrons of prayers that their mother, and their mother's mother, sang quietly at night.

A man in a beret broke the spell. "How can you listen to this? She's not even pretty."

The table of men roared.

Hà went to the back of the café. Away from the men making comments about the woman singing on the screen. The woman who, for a moment, had so effortlessly transfixed the crowd. The same woman who raised her.

Her mother would kill her if she found her here.

***

As Hà returned home after work, she was greeted by the familiar smell of incense and cigarette smoke. Bác Hòa was here—her mother's manager. His personality was as greasy as his pomaded hair, someone who laughed at his own jokes before anyone else had a chance to. He drove a two-seater BMW, held doors for women, and meticulously tailored the pants he bought from Goodwill. Many grandmothers thought him a fine suitor for their daughters, but Hà always thought of him as a leech.

"Your mother's voice is defiant," Bác Hòa said when he first met Hà. "You're American, so maybe you don't understand our history, but for so long we were owned. Our language itself was owned. Can you imagine? The Chinese, the French. If there is anything truly Vietnamese, I wouldn't know. But when I hear your mother's voice, I feel like it's owned by absolutely no one but her."

It was no surprise why her mother immediately hired him.

Inside the kitchen, Hà saw her mother and Bác Hòa at the table.

"What do you mean they don't want me to perform next year?" Mai Lan asked.

"It's the times, the new generation," Bác Hòa said.

A voice shouted from the other room, "I told you, but you never listened."

"Told me what?" Mai Lan said.

Hà's grandmother, Bà, walked into the room in her simple, gray praying attire. Every day, she prayed from six to eight, and prided herself on never taking a break. At the end of her prayers, she would ring a bell, slowly get up, and proceed to watch Korean dramas sloppily dubbed in Vietnamese.

"I told you to go to work," Bà said. "Get a decent job."

Mai Lan waved her away. "Aren't you supposed to be praying?" Then, spotting Hà, she asked, "When did you come home? Have you eaten? Stand up straight."

"Yes, mother."

"Yes, *mẹ*," Mai Lan corrected. "Out there, you speak English. But in this house, you speak Vietnamese, you understand me?" Her mother turned her attention back to Bác Hòa. "So what are we going to do about this?"

"Young people just don't listen to this type of music anymore. Especially not something like *cải lương*."

Mai Lan sighed. "Don't these parents teach their kids anything?"

He hesitated. "You know they're after a certain . . . look."

Appearance had always been a sensitive topic in their household. Starting when Hà was young, Mai Lan would tell her to stand up straight, to eat with her mouth closed, and to keep her legs crossed. Hà grew up terrified of the sun, especially because she was naturally tan, and anxious about furrowing her brows for fear of wrinkling her forehead. Her mother Mai Lan, on the other hand, wasn't what you would consider traditionally pretty. But whatever she didn't have in natural beauty, she made up for in other ways—and you couldn't help but feel that around her. She took care of her skin, her nails were always manicured. She learned how to sew so that she could tailor her own clothes. She did the best with what she had. Hà turned around to glance at her mother, her fingers turning white as she clenched the dining room door frame.

Back in the kitchen, Mai Lan leaned toward Bác Hòa. "Do you know how much money I invested into this? I didn't invest this much just to have them turn me away after two shows, with barely any upside or exposure. Is there really nothing we can do? What about marketing?"

"No," he said, shaking his head. "I had someone look into other options, but nothing's resonating." He paused. "We did talk about the procedure."

"You should focus more on saving whatever money you have right now and finding a real job," Bà said.

Mai Lan turned around and yelled, "Can you do anything but lecture me?"

"Are you just going to live off welfare for the rest of your life? What happens when I die? Who will take care of you then? You live paycheck to paycheck because of this stupid dream. When will you just let it go?"

"Does *Paris by Night* mean nothing to you?"

"So you got into the show, but are they keeping you? Who's looking out for you? After two shows, they want you to go. These people don't care about you. You need to care for yourself. You need to care for your daughter. Find something steady, stable. Find a job, any job. You can work at the nail salon, the restaurant. It's a steady income."

"I don't just want to survive. I'm working hard so that I don't just have to survive. So we don't just have to survive."

The faded kitchen walls seemed to sag from the heavy words her mother and grandmother threw at each other. She knew they had reached a point in their fight they couldn't resolve.

Bác Hòa, unfazed by the screaming, took another long drag of his cigarette. "Granny," he said. "Don't worry, your daughter is talented. We will be fine."

For a moment, the only sound was the ragged breathing of both women, tired from yelling at one another. Hà hated it when this happened. Anytime it was quiet, she knew they were up to no good. Before Bà knew it, her funds would be depleted. Hà wouldn't know how, but she knew her mother had something to do with it. Bà and Mai Lan would yell at each other in Vietnamese, and Hà wouldn't be able to grasp all the words they used. It was frustrating to only understand half of things. Her ears perked at the sound of the chair scraping against the hardwood floor.

"Goodbye Hà. Goodbye Granny," Bác Hòa yelled.

"Good riddance," Bà muttered.

Afterward, Hà helped her mother get ready for her show. Mai Lan asked Hà to brush her hair. Hà ran the hairbrush through her mother's thinning hair as she put on her fake lashes.

"Con," Mai Lan said. "What is your dream?"

Hà looked at her mother. "What do you mean?"

"I mean, what do you want to do?"

"I'm not sure."

Mai Lan looked at her. "Well. We're in America. We live in a place where you can dream. I always wanted to be here. Your grandfather would have loved it. You know how much people pay for their dreams here? I know someone who pays *Paris by Night* $60,000 USD to be on the show."

"$60,000?"

Mai Lan nodded.

Hà hesitated, then said, "You're not paying $60,000 to be on the show, are you?"

Mai Lan sighed. "It takes money to make money. I have to pay people to get promoted. That's how I got on *Paris by Night*." She turned to look at Hà. "You'll understand how this works one day."

Though her mother was only thirty-three, the years of stress that she filled with smoking and singing were beginning to catch up to her—leaving imprints in the deepening furrow between her brow, and the stains on her teeth that she couldn't afford to get rid of and had no healthcare for. She didn't think doctors did much anyway.

Mai Lan leaned back in her chair and stared at the mirror. "I'll be gone, just two days. There's a concert in Orange County I'm going to be singing backstage for."

Hà nodded.

"Don't look so sad," she said. "We have so much to be grateful for."

With that, Mai Lan got up and walked toward the front door, leaving a scent trail of perfume and slightly burnt hair. Hà watched as her mother opened the passenger door, the car light illuminating her thick hair that refused to be tamed. As Mai Lan shut the door, the light went away and all Hà could see was the faint outline of her mother's body. The rubber tires peeled from the driveway, and the car turned out onto the street.

Hà closed the door and stood there. As she shuffled down the hallway, she heard the soft buzz of her grandmother Bà's radio show: *The renaming of the Vietnamese district in San Jose, California, will be discussed this month with San Jose's first Vietnamese Councilwoman, Madison*

Nguyen. This shopping district is on Story Road. The Councilwoman will be a crucial vote in deciding the naming of the district. Many in San Jose wish to name this "Little Saigon" to remember the homeland they left behind due to the Vietnam War.

Hà entered the room and twisted the dial to lower the volume. She heard Bà snoring. Opening a history book, her hand hovered over a bookmarked page. Impulsively, she flipped through the pages until she got to the back of the book. Her fingers ran down the index page, the gloss dulled from years of use by other students.

Vietnam War, The

She flipped to the page and found what she was looking for at the bottom. The history book had a single paragraph on the war.

***

Her mother Mai Lan did the best with what she had. This extended to the men that rolled into her life. A flurry of cheap alcohol, hairspray, and cigarette smoke—her mother made do with the people that came into her life. She trained herself to let them go, to understand everything was fleeting—but sometimes, Hà caught her at her most vulnerable, and it was in these moments that she glimpsed the broken pieces inside.

"Why can't I find love?" her mother once asked Hà in a drunken stupor.

Hà wouldn't say anything as she took off Mai Lan's shoes. As soon as Mai Lan changed out of her clothes, Hà would run a face cloth under water, wring it out, then begin gently wiping away the makeup on her mother's face.

"Why won't anybody love me?"

"I love you."

Mai Lan wouldn't respond, crying herself to sleep. The next morning, the only trace that something was wrong were the red marks underneath her eyes..

***

THE DAYS WERE GETTING SHORTER AND the night air stayed crisp. One evening, Hà talked with her grandmother Bà while she was washing the rice, the water milky-white from the residue.

"Bà, what's your dream?" Hà asked.

"Every day we are alive and have a roof over our head is a dream."

Hà nodded. She had expected that answer. She asked her grandmother to tell her a story about Mai Lan, back when her mother was a little girl.

"I used to work for many hours," Bà said, "and I would save all my money in a small tin can. I didn't tell anyone where the can was except for your youngest uncle. Your mother had been asking me for weeks to help your uncles get new pants. But I wanted to keep saving the money. It was frivolous and their pants were still okay. But she wanted them to have new pants because she thought if they had that, they could make friends at school. I didn't see the point because I didn't know if our family had to move again. Your uncles' pants were getting frayed at the edges. And whenever they did, your mother would stay up late to sew patches onto them. She didn't know how to sew, and I wasn't home to teach her. So she went to the neighbors' house and would practice every day until she could get it right." Bà smiled. "Your mother sewed so many patches onto their pants that she began to call them TV pants."

Hà laughed.

"She kept sewing these pants," Bà went on, "but one day, your youngest uncle came home crying. The kids at his school are bullying him because of his pants. They tell him he's from a poor family and they don't want to play with him. Your mother breaks him down and finds the money. And she goes off and buys the pants."

"How did you react?"

"I beat her."

Hà didn't say anything. Then, "How did you feel?"

"What do you mean how did I feel? I felt mad that she took the money. She disobeyed me."

"I see."

Bà looked away. "I felt mad. And scared for her."

"Why did you feel scared?"

"Because in the middle of everything going on, when I was worried about feeding our family and being able to get your uncles and aunts to America, your mother cared about your uncle being bullied for his TV pants."

Later, as Hà was washing dishes, she heard a key turn inside the lock. She looked up. Her mother Mai Lan was home. She went to embrace her mother, but something was off. Hà stepped back to look at her. Mai Lan's face was wrapped in a scarf. "Mẹ," she said. It was rare that she called Mai Lan mẹ, or mother. "What's wrong? Why is your face wrapped?"

Mai Lan crumpled to the floor. Hà rushed down to brace her.

"I just wanted to be someone," her mother whispered. "I worked so hard." Her breaths became ragged. "I worked so hard. But it wasn't enough. I'll never be enough."

Hà's shirt dampened from her mother's tears. "Mẹ, you're crying, how are you breathing through that scarf?" She pulled down the scarf and gasped. Her mother was barely recognizable. Her lips looked like balloons, her nose was too slim, her eyes were no longer the same.

Mai Lan began to sob. "Bác Hoà told me that if I looked prettier, I could get work. I went to get the surgery and they messed it up. They took all of my money. All of it."

Hà couldn't breathe.

"Your grandmother was right. I shouldn't have dreamed. And if I didn't dream, I wouldn't be here. I wouldn't be here with these years of work that have done nothing for me. Nothing for me but a taste of what I could have had, and now I have nothing to show for it but this face. This ugly, ugly face. I gave everything Hà. I gave everything."

"But you're alive and healthy. You're here, and it's going to be okay."

"I'm here." Mai Lan began to laugh through her tears, "I'm here in this place where they say I can be anything I want to be. Where they say I can dream. But look what it got me Hà. LOOK WHAT IT GOT ME."

Her shrieks echoed across the room. She fell to her knees and her head dropped. "I'll never be more than this."

Hà held her mother's dejected body close to her. Looking up, she saw her grandmother Bà in the hallway. Together, they lifted and carried Mai Lan to the bedroom. Hà pulled the blanket over her mother while her grandmother Bà took the scarf and folded it into her lap. Hà sat on the chair next to the bed, holding Mai Lan's hand until her eyes opened. Together, they held each other and cried.

The Passed Season

—Bảo Thương—

WE RECEIVED A TELEGRAM FROM MY uncle about his pickup time at the Hàng Cỏ train station. It had been almost twenty-five years since my uncle was last living with us in 1954, the same year he left for the South with another relative, around when the Geneva Accords were signed. Grandma told my father she would be delighted to have my uncle around again, emphasizing, "You're both my children."

Now, as she carried laundry to the bedroom, she paused in the doorway to watch my father finish building the bed for his brother. She felt grateful for this gesture of kindness he was showing his brother.

"You're both my children," Grandma said again to my father. "The past is behind us, so let's focus on loving each other from here."

"Of course," my father said over the sound of his carpentry tools.

"We've lived through bad times," Grandma went on, "but we've also been blessed as a family." She sounded joyful, and reminded my father that both he and his brother were still alive. My father never made his feelings known, whether he was happy or felt differently. He kept focus on the bed he was making for my uncle. When he finished, Grandma was the first to test it out, as though the bed were a gift my father had built especially for her. She closed her eyes and smiled, filled with appreciation that my uncle was finally coming home.

***

THE WINTER AFTERNOON MY UNCLE ARRIVED, my father set out on his old bicycle to pick him up. Before coming home, my uncle had sent a photograph of himself with his letter: *I've changed so much and I'm afraid you might not recognize me. So here's a recent photo.* Attached to the photo is a diplomatic note, written as though by someone estranged from their family: *My return might bring challenges, but we'll do our best going forward . . .*

My father dressed in his finest clothes for my uncle's homecoming: a white shirt, khaki pants, and rubber sandals. He looked like a model civil servant back in the early years of liberation as he hurried to the railway station. Their reunion was marked by conflicting emotions: a mix of astonishment, elation, and uncertainty. After their emotional greeting, my uncle climbed on the back seat of my father's bicycle for the ride home. He wore a dark shirt and equally dark pants. His unruly hair flew everywhere.

"When was your last haircut?" my father asked. "And don't you have any less depressing clothes to wear?"

"With everything else going on," my uncle answered, "I didn't have time to think about getting a haircut. In the South, everyone wears dark colors. I thought it might be the same here."

"Was the reeducation program as tough as they say for former soldiers of the South?"

"Yes—it was really hard. Sometimes I thought I wouldn't make it . . ."

"Really? It couldn't have been harder than Uncle Hồ's soldiers marching through the Trường Sơn Mountains . . . ." My father was abruptly cut off when his bicycle hit a rock pile on the shoulder of the road. He sprained his ankle. My uncle's leg, pinned against the pavement, was bleeding.

A frigid wind whipped along the endless road, sweeping across the barren fields. It wove through the delicate tamarind leaves and chilled my uncle to the bone. Apparently, his dark shirt was too thin to keep him warm, and this caused him to shiver from head to toe. His wild hair didn't help his situation either. Even as they neared home, the cold wind never let up, howling down the empty road alongside the river.

***

GRANDMA GREETED MY UNCLE with a hug. She didn't care about his shirt or his disheveled hair. She only saw the son she remembered, the child whose bottom she washed and whose nose she wiped clean. Tears rolled down her cheeks as she embraced him. He wept too, and murmured, "I'm sorry, Mom."

With my uncle back in our family, the dynamics of our household shifted. He initially stayed in his room, reading the books he'd brought with him from the South. He read them over and over, until their binding fell apart and pages lay scattered everywhere. He would gather the loose pages and put them back in order. When my father asked about the books, my uncle replied, "Just some works by Albert Camus."

"You realize his books are banned here, right?" my father said.

My uncle shook his head. "We read these books in the South."

"I know," my father said in a sharp tone, "and that's exactly why they're banned. And because they're banned, you need to tell me why you're reading them now."

My uncle fell into a long silence.

A few days later, my younger brother Tí noticed the books went missing, so he asked, "Uncle, where did your books go?"

"I put them away," my uncle said. "Maybe when you're older, I'll read them to you." He affectionately stroked Tí's head.

With the books no longer an issue, my uncle turned his attention to the daily newspapers, drawn to the stories and poems, and to look at the pictures. One day, while my uncle was absorbed with his newspaper, my father approached and asked, "How's the Communist Party doing these days?"

"I don't know."

My father, looking for an answer, went on, "Don't you read those newspapers every day?"

"I just glance at the pictures and skim through the boring stuff."

"Hmm," my father said, "you don't seem to care about what other people care about."

"Sure," my uncle replied, his voice getting quieter.

After that day my father left for his government office, my uncle barely touched the Communist Party's newspaper again. In fact, he seemed to ignore it as he walked by.

***

WITH ANOTHER MOUTH TO FEED AND not enough money coming in, my mother came home one day with reams of colorful paper for our family's new venture: crafting paper flowers. My uncle threw himself into this creative activity, often skipping meals to experiment with different color combinations. He produced a wide array of exquisitely crafted flowers—roses, sunflowers, marigolds, dahlias, and many others. Each creation possessed a delicate sort of beauty that quickly established our florist shop as the neighborhood's finest. That Tết holiday, money flowed into our family. My mother was thrilled and showered him with compliments. He had, in her words, rescued our family from the brink of starvation.

The compliments didn't settle well with my father. "That's a strange way to go about it. How does a senior Party member let his family go hungry? Have you seen anyone living off things that are so *nguy*?[9] It's easy to miss what's sustainable and real."

I didn't understand that word *nguy* my father used. I wondered if it meant something else, or that he was simply referring to the fake flowers my uncle had been making to keep our family afloat. What I couldn't overlook, however, was the way my uncle's face changed at that moment. In the days ahead, he kept working and never spoke.

***

GRANDMA PASSED AWAY after the long winter, but at least it was spent with her second son. She hung on just long enough to see him

---

9 A derogatory term the Vietnamese communists used to refer to the former anticommunist South Vietnamese government, its people and military, or its arts and literature. The term can be a noun or an adjective. It is often translated as *puppet, illegitimate or fake*.

come home, then passed into the afterlife with her heart comforted. As she lay dying, she took my father's hand and gently placed it on my uncle's, saying, "Love each other, be kind to each other, and never let anything come between you."

At Grandma's funeral, my uncle was overcome with grief, like he'd been abandoned on this earth. The more unkind visitors pointed at him, while others spewed toxic words: "That traitor just returned from the reeducation camp in the South!" Anger clouded my father's face when he heard the gossip, while my uncle quietly kept to himself. The day we buried my grandmother in the field, my uncle wore a round straw headdress and held a bamboo stick. As he stepped backward from her coffin, he sent her off amid the hushed murmuring of onlookers.

After the funeral, my uncle withdrew into himself and rarely ventured out. My mother, concerned about his reclusive behavior, suggested finding a suitable marriage partner for him. But my father was skeptical, saying that my uncle had never shown any interest in a romantic relationship. She persisted, "If he's not open to the idea, then we'll find someone for him."

My mother asked around and eventually found a young woman who happened to be the daughter of my maternal grandfather's closest friend, a devout communist. My father doubted she was a good match, but my mother believed my uncle's past would remain buried. Still unconvinced, my father said, "Who's to say the past is done? What about *my* reputation?"

My uncle's bed creaked loudly when he heard those words. The next morning, he told my mother, "Thank you, but I don't want to get married. I'm happy living here with you and the kids. It's a blessing we're all together."

My father, saying nothing, retired to his bedroom.

***

IN THE DAYS THAT FOLLOWED OUR family discussion, my uncle became a bookworm, quietly retreating to his sanctuary of books. He often went to the public library and borrowed books, using the library card my father had gotten for him. He consumed a vast array of books on science, literature, economics, art—all kinds of subjects. He tutored my younger brother Tí in physics and taught me literature and chemistry. History was the only subject he refused to tutor, saying he never received any formal education on it. He simply advised Tí, "Go ask your father about history."

My father took Tí's textbook and read aloud, "The United States intensified the conflict in the North, conducted relentless bombings, and caused the deaths of many innocent people. They propped up the proxy regime of Ngô Đình Diệm, betraying the Vietnamese people by acting against our interests. They scourged and oppressed the South, and this led to widespread bloodshed and suffering. The cries of our countrymen echoed across the land."

Not understanding, Tí asked, "Who were the *ngụy*? Why were they so cruel to their own people?"

"They served the pro-American government of President Diệm," my father replied.

"So are they still with us?"

My father, his face flushed, was at a loss for words. "No—there're no *ngụy* here. Stay focused on your studies. I have to prepare for the upcoming Party Congress."

He hurried to his room and quickly turned on the light. At that same moment, my uncle sat illuminated at his desk, engrossed in a book he borrowed from the library. My uncle stayed there all night, his still and silent silhouette looming large on the wall. By the time the rooster crowed and woke me the next morning, his motionless shadow was exactly as it had been.

***

WITH INSTRUCTIONS GATHERED FROM VARIOUS BOOKS, my uncle tried to build a noodle-making machine out of leftover parts from a nearby factory. After six months of relentless tinkering, he successfully created a machine capable enough that could replace up to twenty manual laborers. Excited by its earning potential, my father ventured to the patent office to apply for a patent. We began dreaming of a factory for mass production. When asked who the patent holder was, my father named his brother, since as a civil servant, he couldn't claim ownership. My uncle brought his invention home. After my mother's homeschooling lessons, she tried making noodles with his contraption. Her noodles were not only the best in our neighborhood but also the cheapest, attracting a daily influx of customers. Word spread, eventually reaching the ear of our neighborhood leader. He came to our house and told my mother, "Don't undermine our old ways and take food from other people's plates. You're a teacher."

My mother abandoned the noodle-making machine venture. The contraption sat untouched in a corner of the house gathering dust. Every so often, my uncle couldn't help but let out a sigh when he glimpsed his neglected invention. My father settled the matter when he crossed paths with a junk merchant passing by our home.

***

MY MOTHER OFTEN REMINDED MY FATHER: "Think before you speak. Be careful what you say to your brother." After that, my father considered his words before speaking. One day, my father came home from work and told us to dress up for an event.

"What are we celebrating, brother?" my uncle asked.

"Just wear your best clothes," answered my father.

Tí, excited as though heading to a banquet, rummaged through his wardrobe for his best-looking clothes. I picked out a pink outfit, while my mother settled on a bright orange blouse, a pair of green pants, and a red hair bow. My uncle wore a white shirt tucked into black pants. He insisted on giving me a lift on his bicycle, boasting to me that we were the best-looking pair in town. He promised he would keep a watchful eye on me, his beautiful niece, and not let any of the bad boys flirt. I looked at him and felt giddy. It had been a long time since my family did anything together, especially after what we'd gone through over the last few months. Tí craved ice cream; I longed to revisit the Thủ Lệ Zoo; and my mother yearned for a relaxing time outdoors, especially after so much time spent just trying to make ends meet. My father promised us a good treat in town afterward.

"But what's the occasion?" Tí and I asked him.

"It's the anniversary of our country's reunification," he said. "We're celebrating the day the South was liberated!"

Joyful visions of the liberation vividly flashed in my mind. Tí clapped his hands together wildly, my mother's face brightened, and my father grinned, his eyes narrowing. But my uncle, stoic as ever, turned away to conceal his sadness. Pretending to fix his bicycle, he smeared grease all over his white shirt, using it as an excuse to retreat from the celebration. After our hysterical reaction, my father seemed to feel guilty, and my mother appeared even more remorseful. Hoping to make things right again, she suggested, "Okay, you better not go out in that dirty shirt. Stay home, read your books, and we'll bring back some delicious food for you."

***

MY MOTHER DIVIDED OUR FAMILY'S PLOT in half. My uncle set up a coffee shop on his inherited plot of land. He served coffee and waited on my father's friends, mostly retired veterans. The coffee shop, adorned with colorful slogans, buzzed with activity when the veterans gathered. They reminisced about the war, their close encounters with U.S. soldiers, and how they managed to wipe out entire cells of American and South Vietnamese spies. One of my father's comrades tapped my uncle on the shoulder and asked, "Where did you fight?" Before he could respond, my father interrupted, trying to put an end to the conversation: "He was exempt from the draft because of poor health."

"Really? He knows nothing about fighting then."

Everyone burst into laughter. Even my father, his face twisted, joined in. My uncle withdrew quietly and went to sit under a banyan tree by the lake. Each time he tossed a handful of rice mill pellets into the water, fish swarmed up to the surface to nibble the bait. The fish that failed to find any turned to attacking each other, hoping to steal the food. The tranquil lake churned with large waves. At dusk, my father approached my uncle and said, "Ignore them. They don't understand you, but I do."

***

ONE EVENING, MY FAMILY GATHERED AROUND the TV in our living room, our excitement building as the music show was about to start. My father called out to my mother: "Hurry up, a heroic song is coming on!" He closed his eyes and let the melody take him, singing along: *Here's a song I'll never forget, the song about my troubled country . . .*

"How many times have you sung this song?" she asked.

"What does it matter?" he snapped back.

The wind was raging over the magnolia tree, bringing with it the deep smell of night flowers, conjuring the souls of the long dead. My uncle came home and overheard the conversation between my parents. He plainly asked my mother, "Have you had dinner?"

"Not yet. Why are you home so early? No customers?"

"No," he answered. "I just came back for my book. I'm returning to work."

My father didn't see my uncle come in, still lost in the song on TV. He was reclined on the couch with his hands across his chest, letting the lyrics wash over his heart and soul, at times completely hypnotized by the gifted singer and the performance. With his book in hand, my uncle said goodbye to my father, who didn't hear him over the music. My mother looked at my father, shook her head, and went into the bedroom. He was left alone with the singer and the uniformed dance teams from both the North and South armies. The soldiers from the South, moving dizzily in a vain effort to maintain balance, all fell to the ground.

My uncle stumbled past a hedge of Thai tongue plants Grandma had planted long ago, and past the potted cacti my father cultivated. He couldn't smell their nightly fragrance. He only saw his fallen comrades and heard their dying screams, even as laughter poured from my father, a former soldier of the Liberation Army. Clapping his hands, my father burst into laughter again, not bothering to hide how happy it made him feel. "Get lost, all of you, go west!"

***

YEARS LATER, I GOT MARRIED AND took up teaching literature and coordinating social activities at a university. When preparing for a conference on the topic of postwar reconciliation, I knew I needed my uncle's perspective, his first-hand experiences. My father and uncle had a frank discussion on the topic, and I had never seen my uncle so happy. He shared his personal viewpoint with passion, eager to contribute to our country's great cause, and not just to give anecdotes to his niece. My uncle read over my conference paper, scanning each word and commenting in detail. In his gray eyes, I saw the same immense gray autumn skies, the muddy flash floods sweeping away everything in their wake. I saw the vast chasms, the deadly punji traps of wooden stakes, the sunset bloody in the western sky, and the rolling, dragon-shaped clouds. Most vividly, I saw Grandma in the curlicues of incense smoke as she repeated to my father: "I only have two sons. Any war must come to an end, and those separated will reunite once again. Brothers must love each other."

Three days later, my uncle passed away.

A few of his literary friends, some neighbors and patrons from the coffee shop, as well as its new owner, attended the funeral. My father stood by the ancestral altar and bowed, rose to his feet, then bowed again. It seemed he was trying to convey something to Grandma, or maybe even redeem himself. I saw her smiling in the smoke of the burning incense, as if to say a mother's heart is always kind.

—*Translated by Cab Tran & Đỗ Thị Diệu Ngọc*

Echoes

—Văn Xương—

AT THE WRITING RETREAT WHERE BOTH he and Thành had been invited to stay, Long had greeted Thành warmly. Though they didn't know each other, they were familiar with the other's work—enough to foster what Long felt was mutual respect. Long noticed that Thành had lost part of his left arm from the elbow down, the part missing replaced by a prosthetic limb. Long had lost his entire right arm, but left it the way it was, letting his shirtsleeve flap around freely. Over the following days, Long immersed himself in his work, a rare escape from demands—like providing for his family that usually took up his time—just so he could afford himself enough time to write. He imagined Thành lived in a similar world of ideas and emotions, but Thành was restless, someone who couldn't sit still, fidgeting with the pen in his hand but not actually writing anything down, as the blank pages in front of him showed. Something else was occupying Thành's mind, and Long wanted to know what it was.

Thành approached Long one evening.

"Sorry to bother you," he said. I know it's getting late. But how about you join me for a smoke?"

Long looked up and gave a friendly smile. "How's that story of yours coming along?"

"I think I'll be leaving early tomorrow before the retreat ends," Thành confessed. "I don't know if my pride can handle the embarrassment of not turning anything in," Thành confessed.

"What do you mean?"

Thành didn't seem as charismatic as when they first met. Instead, he came across as temperamental, as though he had a lot on his mind. "I've tried my best, but everything's a blur inside my head. Our prompt was to write on the revolutionary war, but I can't seem to come up with anything. It's like the writing judges are toying with me . . ." Thành's eyes lit up at the mention of *war*. "I know you can't change the past, what's already set in stone, but I want to write about the war from my own perspective."

Thành continued his philosophical musings. Long didn't pretend to understand, nor did he feel the need to argue. There wasn't enough time for them to really get to know each other, and besides, writers rarely held high opinions of each other's work anyway. But Long thought Thành did make a valid point. Long, like everybody else, abhorred war. What he really wanted was to spend the rest of his life writing about ordinary, everyday things.

To Long, Thành appeared sad. His eyes lacked enthusiasm and even his face seemed crumpled like discarded paper. Long could only imagine the scenes that haunted Thành's memory. But Long, too, was lost in his own thoughts, unsure of how to write it all down. He wanted to speak to the war, its carnage, to summon the courage to write about it with fresh insight but also truthfully. That was easier to say than to actually do. He'd attended writing retreats and won regional and national prizes in the past, but this topic left him more confused and uncertain than ever before. After Thành left, Long felt much lonelier. Night fell without him knowing. He lay in a trance staring at the ceiling, somewhere between the real world and the world of dreams.

***

AFTER THE CARNAGE, A DIFFERENT SORT of hell emerged. Long remembered how the smoke and stench of rotting bodies turned the air toxic—those who breathed it got sick. Untouched by the violence, ants and flies would swarm the battlefield and feast upon the mangled heaps of meat and bones, the puddles of blood. Somehow, the war didn't affect them. The more Long tried to forget what happened, the stronger his memories returned. In the trenches, rising water loosened the damp earth. Without warning, a shell hit the trench Long was dug in, killing two of his comrades. The blast threw Long against a concrete wall. He felt shrapnel piercing his thigh; his right arm went numb. Before he could regain his senses and escape, the muzzle of a gun appeared from behind an earth mound. A paratrooper from his platoon fell dead on the ground without knowing what hit him. Bleeding, Long dragged himself toward a partially demolished wall. Suddenly, the ground under his feet gave way and the earth swallowed him whole.

When Long opened his eyes, he found himself in a dark bunker. Nearby sounds drew his attention. In a moment of horror, as though time were moving in slow motion, he saw someone crawl into the trench. He realized, from the bloodstained camouflage, that it was an ARVN paratrooper. Long fumbled for his gun but couldn't find it. The unarmed soldier heard him, pulled the canteen from his waist, and hurled it at Long but missed. Long picked up the canteen and tried to swing it like a weapon, but didn't have any better luck. They fought like two animals whose only instinct was to survive. The fight didn't last long—both were too injured and tired to keep going. Soon, Long's vision blurred and he began to lose consciousness.

***

WHEN LONG REGAINED CONSCIOUSNESS AGAIN, he noticed two long fractures in the wall where feeble rays of light poured through. The enemy soldier sat up, struggled with Long using his good arm, but fell back down in pain. It occurred to Long that they had only minutes to live before the Ancient Citadel completely collapsed and buried them along with all their comrades. Would this bunker become their shared coffin, where they would lie next to each other for eternity? In the afterworld, Long wondered, would they still suffer? Would they still try to kill each other?

It was then that Long's mother appeared in his dream. He always believed that when you reached that place between life and death, it was your mother you cried out for. She didn't answer him, but her eyes held a sorrow beyond words. He was transported back to his idyllic childhood, back to his village with its river. As herons flew over the rice paddies, a lullaby filled the air, and the moon became visible above the village's communal house. He remembered the day his mother said goodbye and how she wept when he finally left for war. His two older brothers had gone to fight and never returned. He was the youngest, and what his mother told him he would never forget: "You're just like your brothers. So you do what you think is right. I can't keep you here any longer, so go do what you must do— but come back to me." Long once thought he understood what it meant to be a man, ready to fight this war, but in fact he was still just a helpless boy.

Long eventually returned from his near-death experience. He could still hear the rain outside. He took off his jacket and wedged it into the fissure where the rainwater was coming through. He said to the other soldier, "See if you can plug that other crack."

The soldier said bitterly, "We're both going to die, so what's the point?"

"Listen to me," Long said. "We have to live so we can return to our mothers."

The soldier didn't answer and quietly took off his jacket to plug up the other fissure. The bunker became dark as night. Afterward, he sat up with his back propped to the concrete wall.

Long felt his body begin to painfully swell up. His belly made a growling sound. He took out his rations and shared them with the enemy soldier, saying, "Eat this, and don't be so afraid of dying."

The soldier hesitated at first, but eventually accepted the offered rations. He devoured the food, then reached for his canteen, threw back his head, and guzzled. Afterward, he handed the canteen to Long, letting Long also quench his thirst. In that dark bunker, Long felt someone's cold hand brushing against his. But as he tried to reach out for it, he slipped back into unconsciousness. He felt lifted, as though airborne, carried out of the bunker and away to an unknown place.

***

LONG WOKE TO THE SOUND OF human voices. He opened his eyes and found himself surrounded by people in white coats. He didn't know if they were human beings or ghosts coming to take him away. Then a soft voice came: "He's awake."

He didn't regain full consciousness until days later. He realized he was in an ARVN field hospital. A nurse informed him that his right arm had been amputated due to a severe infection. At least he was alive. Whatever the future had in store for him, he would have to deal with it later. He thought about the ARVN soldier and asked the nurse if the man was alive or dead.

"I have no information about him," she said. Then she looked around to make sure no one else was listening. She went on, "But I've heard that you're a high-ranking communist officer, and we must save your life to get more intelligence from you."

A month later, Long was transported to a prison where he was detained and isolated from others. They interrogated and tortured him day after day. Finally, one day, he was put on a truck with other POWs and shipped to the North. The POWs got off when the truck reached the Thạch Hãn riverbank. On the other side of the river, several people were waiting and waving liberation flags. The POWs were overjoyed. They took off their prisoner clothing and stepped into a boat to cross the river.

As soon as the boat reached the far shore, people rushed over to help them off. The former prisoners and the helpers exchanged hugs and tears of joy. Only then did Long feel he was alive, that the war truly was behind him. Every time he looked into the blood-thick water, he saw his fallen comrades staring back from between the waves. Glancing up, he saw the Ancient Citadel on the far shore and mourned their deaths.

***

THÀNH CHANGED HIS MIND THE NEXT day about leaving the writing retreat, much to Long's surprise. Over the next few days, Thành grew more pensive and talked even less. Long didn't want to pry. They returned to their work, but took breaks to smoke together. Long felt as though writing had possessed him.

Eventually, both he and Thành finished their stories. They agreed to share each other's work, hoping to gain some insight into the other.

"How come our stories are so similar? Did you fight in Quảng Trị?" Long asked, handing Thành's manuscript back to him.

"Yes." Thành returned Long's draft and smiled. "I returned home just the other day, then went to Quảng Trị, where I almost lost my life thirty-four years ago. The Ancient Citadel is still there, but it's a war monument now."

Long nodded. "I also went to the Ancient Citadel, just before coming here. When I was wandering through the tall grass, I stopped to touch the ground, and it felt as though I were touching the bodies of my fallen comrades. I heard the wind whistle and imagined it was the voices of my fellow soldiers reading aloud letters from home. When I looked into the grass, I saw their faces rustling in the wind. I spent a night at the memorial but couldn't fall asleep. I was restless. I had nightmares. My comrades came to me in my dreams, and everything I envisioned reminded me of that life I gave up, of all the times I had to close their eyes before burying them." Long sensed that Thành wanted to say something comforting, but Thành had no words left to express his feelings.

—*Translated by Cab Tran & Lê Phương Anh*

Six's Sign

—Anvi Hoàng—

—Côn Đảo Island present

THE SNAKY ROAD SOUTHWARD TO Bến Đầm Beach has dangerous sharp turns. On one side, the mountains are thick with greenery, and on the other, endless open space ocean view. I will never have enough of this passage. Air. Rocks. Water. What makes them different from elsewhere? I pause. Sift the words out of my head: intense and dramatic.

I touch the glass to test the temperature. It's cool outside. I roll down the window for fresh air. We make another sharp curve. The window is halfway down. Soft breezes roll in and shake the two-piece air freshener crinkling. A partial crystal-clear view of the green thickets floods my eyes and entreats awe. The windowpane is fully down. Woodsy and sticky salty air infused with negative ions lightens me. Hmm, I wonder what you are going to say. White sand beach. Pebble beach. Rock beach. We pass them one by one. The waves look gentle from afar. Another sharp curve. The stressful me needs more happiness hormones, right, you would say. In some parts, the road is flanked by the rocky mountains and the woods beyond which a clear water beach beckons. Sharp turn. And another one. To my right is lust foliage. Amid the deep green there appears a white figure enveloped in a pinkish purple aura. Closer. I get closer. A woman stretches her arms out parallel to the ocean line and points her head northward. As I'm passing her, I notice she's wearing the white *bà ba*, the everyday suit of the locals. But definitely not in this color. White is very unusual. Local people often wear earth-tone colors. I wouldn't have peeled my eyes if it wasn't standout white. The aura is strange, too. I thought the alchemy of too much humidity, salt, oxygen, and a hint of mystique make it so. Her freaking long black hair entwines around her white-cladded body. The scattered hairs fly like wings and the tips like a tail behind her back. She looks like a human-in-snake-and-fairy form.

What's that woman doing there? I ask the driver.

What woman? He says.

Hahaha. That's a good one. I raise my voice and cackle, thinking he's joking.

I'm serious. He responds, not smiling.

What? I roll my eyes.

The driver laughs drily and lowers his voice. So you're one of them, huh.

I turn back trying to catch her again but we curve sharply. Too late.

No way. Not me. It's never happened to me before and never will. I'm not that kind of person.

Why not? You've been asking for a sign.

—ĐÀ NẴNG 2013

WHERE DO YOU WANT TO RETIRE?

I can be anywhere. I can be here.

You say so, but you won't like it.

What makes you think like that?

You cannot handle Vietnamese people. They will eat you alive.

—SÀI GÒN 2015

YOU'LL ONLY ENJOY IT HERE as long as you behave like a tourist.

Don't be so dramatic. I speak the language. I have the connection.

You say thank-you too often. The locals can tell you apart. You'll always be an outsider.

The thank-you-ing is fixable.

Regardless, the city is not yours anymore, you told me yesterday.

Sài Gòn doesn't count. It's too Western for Vietnamese overseas like us, the same way Tokyo is too fast for some Japanese descendants. I'll pick a small town. Besides, to set the record straight, I said it was mine and it was not. The not-part is reachable. With time, I will reclaim it.

With what?

With time! I told you. The long stay in the country will bring back the Vietnameseness in me in full, which will give me access to the entirety.

What's this *entirety* you're talking about?

You know. The mannerism, the logic, the people, the resourcefulness, the perseverance, the normalcy of humidity, the weirdly wonderful fusion street food, the ...

Don't forget the trickery, the stubbornness, the pragmatism that tops even the Americans, the grab-and-snatch culture, the mongrelarity that you prefer over mongrelization ...

Such a party pooper!

You, keep dreaming. Remember the closet trick. Anything you don't use for two years, give it up. It's been three years we've been visiting here. Give it up. You think you'll achieve the reachable part anytime soon? Another set of ten won't wait for you. Don't bet on an empty basket that your memory will improve next time, to where you want it to be. That's not how things work for folks our age.

—VĨNH LONG FOUR WEEKS AGO

I RENTED A ROOM AT THE Lodge that sits on the riverbank with its own dock at the end of the garden that hangs over the water. The last time I was in this country, I was a happily married person reconnecting with my birth motherland. That patchy memory's not usable anymore. Before I make a crucial decision that affects us both, it's necessary to revisit. We need to experience at least once the wetlands of southern Vietnam because of our shared love for the Mekong Delta. Centuries ago, a busy trading center. Last night, I came to the garden for dinner

to the view of the deep pink sunset. It was sinking in the water fast. I
didn't blink until gray darkness thickened. I stood immobile. Only a
cement floor separated me from the water underneath. I liked to think
that I was on the water. Dreaming. The Indian merchants. The Malay
and Ottoman spice traders. Getting off boats. Dragging their tattered
souls on the dock. Climbing to land. A stone's throw from me. All this
rich history to enjoy every day. I can sit and dream till oblivion. Why
not retire here and be a part of the hospitality we have heard so much
about. Southwestern Vietnamese are the most honest and kind. Too
many old traditions in the Central. Too many formalities in the North.
Too stuffy in Sài Gòn. Water is the currency in the wetland. Water
dominates and water provides a living. Which is why China has been
building dams left and right in Laos and Cambodia up the Mekong
River to control whatever and whenever water is released to Vietnam.
This belligerent reality was on my mind as I finished dinner in thun-
dering quietness. I doused myself with lemon eucalyptus oil spray to
deter the mosquitoes. Three skinny dogs surrounded the table, puppy-
eyeing me for food. They knew me well enough not to bark a single bit.
A few lights in the garden were turned on for me to see the food and
my way. May is a low season. I was the only guest in the compound. The
owner, an attractive woman in flowery *bà ba*, released all employees at
five and she herself cooked dinner for me. She also set the table. I asked
her to join me as the food was more than enough for two. She said *Dạ*
and sat on a chair three meters away to talk to me. People in the delta
say *Dạ* differently. They stretch the falling tone a long half second and
raise it back up, making it honey sweet so it sticks to your ears forever
once you hear it. Your guard is down. You are under their spell. I asked
her whether the Chinese-built dams upriver had affected the water
level here abnormally. Not so much, she said. Seasonal floods as usual.
A little hard this year, but she didn't notice dramatic changes. Huh,
how interesting that whatever news I read in the U.S. was so alarming.
The dams held all the water. Droughts in Southwest Vietnam. Saltwater
intrusion. Loss of crops. The dams release water at flood time. Severe

flooding in Vietnamese wetlands. Loss of livelihood and properties. I already know everything I read about my birth land in the news appears more electrifying. Never get used to that, though. Here I am again. I cannot explain or resist the pull of the motherland, online or in person. My heart complies every time. But now, I feel annoyed that I don't know things about my Vietnam anymore. Seeing how much I love water, my host was happy to arrange a tour to the floating market for me the next morning.

A motor boat waits for me at the dock. Only me in a boat for ten. The driver and I are alone in the canal but we don't have stillness to talk. The engine is too loud. Ten minutes later, he stops beside a sampan and asks me to climb over there. A beautiful woman stands anchoring on it, two paddles in hand. I'll see you on the other side, he says. I sit down on the raised wooden board in the center facing forward. I'm so close to the water like I'm sitting on a piece of paper. The thin and slim canoe glides on. I hear the water sloshing. We're the only two non-talking beings in the swamp. Sloshing. A great horned owl hoots. Water sloshing. A common loon laughs. A couple of light sheets intercept the carpet of trees here and there. A ruffed grouse drums. We slide in water. A common raven croaks and a crow caws. No wonder the Mekong Delta is one of the remaining richest biological treasure troves in the world. Sloshing. I tell the lady I admire her beauty, that it's befitting the delta women's reputation. She's delicate like stigmas of a saffron crocus, not muscular as I imagine a sampan paddler to be. The bà ba top hugs her body showing the taunting curves. Without shyness, she thanks me and says she's glad to have me. Sometimes, she continues, three big tall people are in the sampan. They step down, tilt it rocking and sink it deep. I struggle to inch it forward. Her voice commands and entices. I ask her for more. And sometimes the water is low I don't want to take a job. These giants insist I paddle for them. There are too many of them, I interrupt, why don't they rent a motor boat as they should? Because the engine noise disturbs them. They want to enjoy the tranquility of the wetland. She complains mockingly. Of course, they want the countryside for which they pay to see. I feel annoyed again. Pushing a canoe on mud is backbreaking. She's totally drained after a thirty-minute ride. At night, the muscles hurt so badly she can't sleep. I'm swimming toward her stories. A siren call couldn't be more captivating than this. I feel slight as an intruder in the swamp. At the mercy of water. Here's a makeshift embankment held up by a stretch of vinyl already twisted and torn. A new one has to be made to keep the dirt in place. Or else, water will wash away everything. There, a flimsy house easily swallowed up in flood tides. Only the mangrove trees take deep root. They're everywhere water and land meet. Their roots prop out and claw down water like stilts. They grow. They stay. In spite of water. The paddler says she has a motor propeller on board. It makes no sense to row back with near-strained muscles, she says. And sometimes she's lucky to have a new fare waiting at a homestay, she has to hurry back.

We're on the other side of a bridge and the boat driver's waiting. I get back onto his boat and we enter the river. Things on the banks become miniatures. More solid houses. A church. Cement embankments big and small. Some brand new, others badly damaged. A bigger church. The view opens three hundred and sixty degrees and keeps opening up. I'm inside the immense water. Its vastness inspires. Awe. Serenity. Humility. I edge near the side railings and dip my hand into the water. So close and so much of it. It swathes my mind and body. The river shrinks. The river expands. In some parts, there is only water around and ahead. This is the closest I can get to understanding how my fellow Vietnamese called *boat people* felt when they were in a tiny boat at sea. Fear. Is. Big. Here in the Mekong River, we are nothing. More worthless than a drop of water because we are the irregularity. We don't belong in it. We have no business building dams or levees to interfere. Embankments need reinforcement constantly. One moment of neglect and water can destroy everything and erase all our traces. Only water is durable here. The greatest feeling designated to us is smallness. Maybe that's just how I feel. Many people feel grand everywhere they go. I think about the three giants in a sampan. Do we matter in their eyes? Once they are inside the Mekong River as I am now, do they feel humble at all? Maybe not. They desire to own it and control it. For sure. The French did. I'm upset that my people get exploited. I'm tired that I feel too many things in Vietnam. Half an hour later, we arrive at our destination.

Mother f*ing sh*t! People at the Lodge, knowing full well there's no market, took a sh*t load of money from me to organize a non-floating-market tour for me. Such slimy people!

No floating market?

No! Only some random boats. I asked where's the market and the driver said there's no floating market anymore. Here's where it used to be.

They must be tricking you like they do enthusiastic tourists.

I have to give it up to the sweet-talking southwesterners. Do you think tourism and commercialization have become a way of life here? That's why service people learn to adapt to nasty and difficult tourists from big cities and abroad? But I'm not one of those people!

Well, intense economic growth in Vietnam the past ten years has brought on quite some changes. It's not that shocking.

I grew up believing the Saigonese who consider southwesterners to be the most honest, as if a hundred percent of them are. This attitude is bizarre. Or maybe it was I who wanted to believe so. Now I'm angry at myself for holding on to this credulousness for so long. The South is half my heart, my weakness. Maybe 99 percent of south-westerners were like that fifty years ago. But wars and intense peace, and most recently high maintenance northern Vietnamese and foreign tourists require them to be adaptive. Tourism could bring out the worst in people and do harm to local culture. I'm not blaming them.

—Sóc Trăng a week ago

Maybe I have to accept that I cannot handle Vietnamese people anymore, like you said. Ten years ago, I thought I reconnected with Vietnam. My fragmented memory only needed soldering. A bike ride around would keep my half-local, half-tourist perspective in balance. I was so proud to be a local with a tourist perspective. I want to protect that state of mind but that memory's slipping away. Remember the awkwardness when I talked to local tourists. Where're you from? An Nhơn. Where's that? In District 9. Where's District 9? Next to District 12. Where exactly is District 12? Where are you from? Trà Vinh. Where is it? I laughed at my own befuddlement, but they must have thought I was weird and clueless. I won't forget the steel eyes that shot my way. I am clueless. That's true. I cannot locate the districts of my hometown in my mind anymore. All the names sound familiar, yet so new. I swear I know all the street names. I mean, they sound familiar but I don't know where they are anymore. They sound familiar only because I speak the language. The names and places are deserting my body and relocating in my mind. Trying to locate them in there diffuses disorientation. Even when I drive past them, I don't recognize them. The new District 2 is like a busy American urban corner in a bustling city adorned by steel, glass, asphalt. It's perturbed to find exact Americanness in my birth motherland, in my head. The mixing and crossings within my two-homeland mentality breed more confusion than clarity. Most of what I remember about Vietnam is gone. I feel frightened at the realization, to lose a part of my memory, a part of me. This past four weeks tells me this time, it's permanent. I don't recognize the Vietnamese around me anymore. I talk like a local, but I neither understand nor accept the logic in their behaviors. Look, the Lodge owner in Vĩnh Long took advantage of me. The beautiful sampan paddler, who knows if her stories are real. Anyone who says Dạ like her would be suspicious. Does she really have a husband who drinks around, and does she have to work harder to raise their teen daughter? The boat driver smiled and took me to a non-existing floating market. I often say there are no pedestrians in most of America because it's a car country and there are no walkways. There are no pedestrians in Vietnam either, because the walkways are used as parking lots for scooters and reserved for street eaters. Whoever wants to walk does so on the street while intermingling with scooters and cars. What logic is that? What's the Vietnamese value or standard? I feel threatened by their assumed dishonesty all the time. I feel like they're all out there to get me. I feel like a tourist.

We're in a Khmer pagoda. It makes sense to feel a bit like strangers here.

I'm having a crisis and you're joking!

Sorry. What I want to say is now you know how I feel. You simply need to accept it to enjoy the visit.

I don't know. My state of mind is in transition. I hope it'll settle a score soon. So frustrating. If only there's an auspicious sign ...

No! Don't go there.

I know. I'm the last one to kneel down and pray. Nothing against prayers, though.

Only that if your prayer is answered, what to do about that?

I'm pushing a boundary I don't plan to explore. I know.

I've never seen you this desperate. If push comes to shove, do as the locals do.

What's that?

Remember the guard at the hotel you talked to yesterday, he said he didn't believe in prayers. He just went there and already acquired the peaceful feeling he was looking for.

You mean Côn Đảo?

—CÔN ĐẢO PRESENT

NOW I'M OUTRIGHT CURIOUS.

You're serious, you didn't see the woman in white back there? I press the driver.

Yes, I am. He says. I have a friend who sees things that others don't. This is Côn Đảo after all. He teases.

I'm aware that Côn Đảo is a site of pilgrimage. It was *the* notorious prison during the wars. Numerous executions happened here. The population of the untimely and unjust deaths in the island is more than twenty thousand. Larger than the living one that stands at five thousand now. The locals wear somber manners every time they mention the dead. We have to respect them. They are present. They answer prayers. They make miracles. They're watching.

This explains the pervasive enigmatic sense! A thrilling sensation surges in me.

Oh what the heck, when in Côn Đảo! I might as well visit the memorial where the most famous tomb is located. Local people call her Sister Sáu, meaning Sister Six.[10] The French executed the guerrilla girl in 1952 when she turned nineteen. Rumors go round that you can ask her for anything.

The memorial has a magnificent new gate. Two fresh, almost wet-looking, granite poles hold up the name board. The obelisk and many big statues occupy the immediate right hand quarter. A lotus pond shimmers our way there. In stark contrast, big shady trees and forlorn-looking communal and individual graves spread over the rest of space. At this twilight hour, I can still detect the overflowing greenness and luxurious space that shine respect and prestige upon the deceased here. They are anti-French freedom fighters, communists, supporters of the communist cause, unidentified soldiers and civilians. A ginormous copper incense-burning jar sits in front of the obelisk and some offerings lie around. A few visitors. Most people head toward Sister Six's tomb straight up the path deep inside. Way deep. Beyond where my eyes can reach is a dimming blanket, too dark and too far to form a picture.

The huge complex must be somber during the day. At night, droves of pilgrims turn it into a festival. They dress up. Many women wear the white *bà ba*, which is what Sister Six wore at the time of her death. Everyone carries colorful and beautifully wrapped baskets of fruits and flowers. Many carts in their offerings. They must have had great success since the last time, coming back to repay the blessing with larger offerings, asking for even more in return. That's the tourist cycle on the island.

I join the line of people moving deeper inside. From a distance, I see thick white air. 8:30 p.m. Can it be fog? 98 percent humidity and

---

10 Võ Thị Sáu (1933-1952), a Vietnamese teenage guerrilla in the First Indochina War. She is recognized as a heroine and national martyr.

36-degree-Celsius temperature cannot produce fog. Only sweats. The stickiness of my damp skin reminds me of Vietnam constantly. Unbearable. This cannot be what a Vietnamese really feels.

Five hundred feet away from a big crowd, I still can't decide what causes those white billows. Then it dawns on me. The incense burning.

Layers of pilgrims encircle Sister Six's grave. Mounts of offerings topple tables and shelves on one side and in the back. Difficult to see where the headstone is. More difficult to breathe. Condensed swirls of incense whiffs in the air, smoke tears out of my eyes. My nostrils repel such strong fragrance released from the bundle of incense in the burning bowl. A sign next to it says one stick of incense per person only. When the bowl is packed, one guard grabs the bundle and takes it away. People are waiting patiently for their turn to get close to Sister Six's picture and say their prayer. I put my flowers in the water vase on the side. Looking at the tip of her headstone, I'm thinking, if you're that sacred as people say, if it was you at the curve giving me a sign, please make another one. Forgive my skepticism.

I leave the crowd.

Wow, you are officially superstitious.

It's your fault that I am. Do you think these people really have their prayers answered? They've come nonstop.

How ridiculous! Sister Six fought to get rid of capitalism. Now people ask for her help to beat the globalization games to become successful capitalists.

Yeah, weird logic, right. I don't want to embrace it.

Stay here long enough, you are the same. Be careful.

So you've been warning me.

***

IT'S SO HOT IN VIETNAM I can take a cold shower. I hope to fall asleep after this long day.

Do you notice that the water here can never be as cold as it is in the U.S.? And yet, water's water everywhere.

Then why do you prefer to go swim in the Vietnamese ocean?

Because Vietnam weighs heavy in my heart. I know now that I'm not willing to reopen the well of Vietnameseness in me, I don't want to switch back to the Vietnamese personality. I choose not to.

Is Vietnam your home anymore?

Yes and don't know. My friend Kori moves around a lot. I asked where her home was. She said, I don't think about it. My home is every place I live. I was shocked to hear that. My thought about home came from the concept of diaspora. Home is a motherland we long for. In my deep-seated belief, home is where one feels belonging. I long for Vietnam and feel I belong there. I never question the concept. Now that you're asking, what do I really think about home? Can I really have an idea of my own? Instead of whatever has been seeping into my mind over time. Remember the thousands of immigrants who arrived in Bloomington, Indiana? I keep thinking about what they have to say about home. Is theirs the same diasporic concept?

I know. We've been talking about home forever. I'm exhausted. Should home become an overrated idea soon? So we can move on to something else.

I hear you. It'd be nice to be fluid like water. Home is where we arrive. This way of thinking would eliminate lots of pains and conflicts in me. Home is an exploration. A process of arriving.

You've been in Bloomington for twenty-five years. Is it home then? Like, to many Vietnamese Americans, home is California.

I feel at home in Bloomington, that's for sure. But when the snow falls, I think, I don't want to die here.

So home is where you want to die?

Yes, no, and what the heck. In my diasporic mind, my adopted home is in the United States, but a part of me wants to rest my bones somewhere with which a deep spiritual connection is unfathomable for a life on earth—my birth homeland. And yet, if I don't visit Vietnam often, it'll forever remain a perfect homeland I long for and am nostalgic about, but it won't be where I want to die. I'll continue to explore my home journey and arrive at the last minute. No matter where that is, I'm home. It could very much be Bloomington, or Córdoba ... Guacamole shoot! Did you just touch my shoulder?

***

A COLD SHOWER WORKS. At ease and refreshed, I fall asleep.

I find myself waking up at one in the morning feeling thirsty. I traipse to the liquor bar in the foyer right of the door. Open a bottle of water and have a sip. The back wall of the bar is a mirror. Against my back is the foyer wall on which a big mirror hangs. These two mirrors parallel and give me a view of myself back and front.

I leave the bathroom light on because I don't want to sleep in total darkness. The hotel room has ceiling-to-floor glass sliding doors opening up to an enormous balcony and a huge view of the ocean not too far away. At night, light from the moon gives a bright ambience in the room. Without the moon, light on the fishing boats in the dark horizon is an anchor for my eyes.

As I put the lid back on the water bottle, I see my front reflection. I lift my head up from the bar to turn away and see a glimpse of my back reflection as well. Tonight, it's the full moon. The view of my back is pretty clear. My eyes hit my shoulder and I gasp. It cannot be! I turn the foyer light on. Look at my back shoulder again. I shriek. OMG! OMG! No, it's not real! I can't believe it!

I'm so scared. I have to get out of here. Don't care what time it is. At least get to the lobby first. I grab the room key at the bar and rush to the door. The handle is stuck. I cannot open the door! No! I scream as hard as I can. I try the handle again. It doesn't budge. Why now? I panic. What the f*k is going on! I swear. I begin to sweat. I twist the handle again. Beep beep beep beep! The alarm goes off and startles me. I open my eyes and it is bright out. I'm lying in bed. Turning over I see the blue ocean beyond the balcony doors.

Shoot! It was a dream. My heart's still beating hard in my chest.

I get up and go to the bathroom. I'm not a morning person. My eyes are still half closed and I can only see enough not to bump into things.

I splash cold water on my face for a few seconds and tap the excess water with a towel.

I rented a car for a tour of the island today at seven. I'd better get ready.

I brush my teeth and get back to the bar for some water. Before I reach for the bottle, I look at myself in the mirrors and check out my back like I did in the dream. It was a hell of a dream. I have to check.

Macaroni f*king sh*t! The imprint of a hand is actually there.

By reflex, I eye the room. There's nothing out of place. All the doors are closed. Nobody can enter the room without me knowing.

I grab the only precious thing in the room and storm out the door. To be enclosed in an elevator is not a good idea. I use the stairs everyday as I'm on the third floor. They are right across from my room. The whole stairs are encircled by clear glass windows from the top to the bottom floors. I'll be in the light which helps ease the fear, I mumble. I aim for the stairs and fly down the steps. Reach the lobby and head straight toward the beach right outside the door. I run past the pool, march down the stone steps, toward the sand, to the chair under a thatch-roofed umbrella and sit down. The waves are coming in. Very gentle. There is only crystal blue water in front of me. I hear my heart pumping. It's slowing. The breezes are rising. Soft. One strong whoosh. Then soft breezes. There is only crystal blue water in front of me. Very gentle. The waves are coming in. Gentle. Water. Is. Soothing. I keep my eyes where the deep water is.

If this is Sister Six's sign, what the hell does it mean? I mutter.

A kid walks to me. She stares at me, then at my hands.

Pointing at my belly she asks, what are you going to do with that?

I look down and remember what I'm holding. And my responsibility.

An urn of your bones.

The Việt Kiều Casanova
—Tuan Phan—

The Store Owner

THIS VIỆT KIỀU[11] COMES INTO MY shop usually three, four times a week. He's in his thirties, I think, and each time, he brings with him a new girl, buys her a gift, and they leave together arm in arm. The girls are twenty somethings, freshly made up, with the new bodies we see now on Vietnamese women, a little fitter, curvier, with firmer butts. They're the ones I always see on Instagram making duck face selfies or at the gyms not breaking a sweat, flirting with the trainers, taking mirror photos. Some of them are probably part-time models, or Facebook entrepreneurs. I see them and I think to myself, God, it must be exhausting. It just seems like a lot of work for young women, nowadays, this primping and preening for a phone that's also a camera. I don't remember ever having to do so much at their age.

It takes a lot of time and effort for the Việt kiều too, taking a different girl to the shop each time. Imagine having to remember all you've told each girl, all you've said and done, with whom you said and did what with. How do you keep all those storylines in your head for all the girls?

My shop is on a busy stretch of Sài Gòn's new walking street. When I started it, my business partner, Linh, warned me there would soon

---

11 A member of the overseas Vietnamese diaspora, and in this context, a member of the first group that left by boat after the war

be construction. All of Vietnam is under construction. The government was turning it into a pedestrian friendly zone, she said, so be prepared for noise, and tough times, but if we get in right now, I promise you, she said, it'll pay off after. She was right, of course, but we didn't get any customers at first. The rare one would come in, sit down for one second, complain about the noise, and leave. But we stuck with it because we knew, once all the street construction finished, we'd do ok. A hip new shop and café was perfect here. The trick was to figure out when the construction would finish. The government promises completion dates for their projects, then they'd be delayed until the last bit of extra cash can be passed under the table, you know, to *speed things up*, or just to properly start. Inevitably, these constructions stretch into a future that never comes, and we owners wait in limbo. Linh and I took our chance, and then we finished the interior, we cleaned up the shop, distressed the walls, making it look inviting for photo filters, all the while checking our daily accounts and seeing them dip into the red. It's like the girls and this Việt kiều, if you think about it. Each of them playing a waiting game, waiting to see if there would ever be a return on investment.

When we finally finished, we thought we'd get a lot of teenagers coming in with their friends to take pictures, because our interior was colorful, and had that texture the young tend to like for their photographs. After all our work designing this shop for potential customers … I never thought it'd become what it turned into, a revolving door for expats and Việt kiều Casanovas!

Once, we saw two different regulars *shopping* for the *same* gifts they usually bought. They started out at different sections with their newest girls; the older white man in the far corner, looking at shirts, making his way to the bracelets section with his girl; the other, Korean it looked like, was making his slow way to the same area. Linh joked and told me that they should meet up at the register and trade seduction tips. I do feel bad sometimes, though. Conflicted. White expats, Korean expats, Việt kiều, they all bring their girls here knowing that I know too. They trust that I'll be discreet about what they do. I am, but feel like my discretion makes me complicit. Maybe that's in the nature of keeping a shop such as mine; you keep your mouth shut and smile, even if you want to say something. But the truth is, they're my best customers, these foreign Casanovas operating in the new Sài Gòn. They keep business humming. We haven't done a separate account category for expats and Việt kiều buying gifts for young Vietnamese girls yet, but I bet it'd make a good portion of our income.

I keep telling myself that *someday* I'll tell the girls, when the guys aren't looking. I see some of them getting really emotional when they get a gift, especially a bracelet, and I feel like grabbing them and saying: "Little sister, he's bought dozens for girls just like you!" or "Little sister, you're the third one that cried this month. Get over it already!"

My husband says to me, "*Trời ơi, em ơi!*[12] You don't need to tell the girls!" he says. "You're not deceiving anybody. In fact, I'll bet you anything that the girls know too. Like those Casanovas, they're playing along. And some of them, I guarantee you *em*, some of them have a *collection* of these bracelets, from *all* the boyfriends. Saigonese women, don't you know? You're a Saigonese woman yourself!"

I punch his arm and we laugh. I don't know if he's right or I'm right. Anyway, I never tell them. I keep the shop, and watch the routine happen, day after day.

Last Valentine's Day, a flood of them came in with their Casanovas and the bracelets sold out in minutes.

The Casanova

THE NORTHERN GIRLS WILL CUT YOUR dick off, man. If they catch you cheating. Or if they're mad at you for no reason. Sure, they're gorgeous, traditional, *kind*. But man, when they get jealous ... it's vicious! Girls from the South, here in Sài Gòn, are great! Easy going, friendly, cool. They're totally down with you hanging with other girls.

---

12 Good heavens!

But, they're all hustling, man. If they're hot, they're definitely seeing other guys, and then they'll be really into money, so it sucks if you don't have some. Gold diggers, bro. Gold. *Diggers.*

The girls from the middle region, from Huế? Damn man. I mean damn, they're the BEST! So innocent. Super kind. Kinder than the southern girls. But you can't understand what they're saying. I mean. Literally. Not a word. That accent. I got just enough Vietnamese to barely open the girls from the South as it is. *Chào em! Em đẹp quá.*[13] Blah blah blah whatever. But the girls from the middle region, shit, they might as well be speaking Chinese.

No one type of Vietnamese girl is perfect, you know? Which is why I'm still single at my age.

But I love it, man. Love it! There's not enough time in the day. They're my Kryptonite, man, Vietnamese women are my KRYP. TO. NITE. It's not just me though, all the guys visiting now got the yellow fever.

They were just skinny before, you know, but that's back in the 80s and 90s when my family left. I was the same too, man. Just a skinny, hungry little kid. But now they're all working out. Squatting at gyms building dat booty all day, know what I'm saying? Unreal!

Yeah, sure they see me and they see that ATM lighting up. Or they start hearing Alicia Keys' "concrete jungle where dreams are made off . . ." Whatever, man. I don't care. I'm from Garden City, Kansas. Podunk town in the middle of nowhere. My folks worked in the beef packing plants breaking their bones cutting cattle tendons for a living.

You hustle with what you got, right? Right now, I got a passport, so that's what I hustle with. You think I can swing this scene back in America? America? Where I'm round chop, ching chong, little dick ding dong? Fuck that. I got away from all that racist shit man. I'm killing it here and I'm never going back.

You know what you need to do? Take off those glasses, man. They might be 'hipster' or whatever in America but here you need contacts.

---

13 Hello! You're gorgeous!

Or get Lasik surgery. And maybe shave, and probably not wear those cargo shorts. Get some jeans man, seriously. Damn. I never needed to do all this shit when I first came back, you know, but now I just changed my whole wardrobe.

Everyone hustles here, man. Everyone. My family, once we got on that boat, we knew life was about hustle: 100 people on a fishing boat, man. We hustled our way onto it, we hustled our way off it, we been hustling ever since. Fresh off the Boat, baby! The Việt kiều that were born in the States, they got no idea. Soft ass motherfuckers.

Hey, at least I'm not some fat white dude with a mean looking but hot girl forty years younger, man. Right? I mean at least I dress decent and speak some Vietnamese, you know? None of that *Xin chào em*[14] shit.

The girls at this shop I go to here like the bracelets. They love them, the bracelets, man. It's how I test if they're into me for my looks and charm, or my money, you know? So, I get them these bracelets. They're cheap, but they look nice. I put them on and look into their eyes and I try to see what's up. Like what's up girl, are you a gold digger, or are you legit? Straight up.

And people here *still* think we got it easy in America, man. Like we rolled into the U.S. and everyone loves us, like whiteys just up and gave us jobs man. Seriously!

Oh, what's my field, what's my job? I'm an engineer. Knowledge, motherfucker! Worked bitch ass hard for my degree too. Been working ever since I graduated Rice University. Haha, yeah, my parents probably pushed me to go there 'cos it sounded Asian ... and safe, you know? They're so racist. Haha!

Let me give you my number, man. Yeah, hit me up. There's gonna be a party later on tonight. At the New World Hotel. Sweet scene. Pool party. You should come. Ditch the glasses though.

---

14 Hello!

The Girl

PEOPLE SAY THERE'S NO SERVICE INDUSTRY here in Vietnam, but here all women get ready to do in this life is give service. Service men. Service country. Service our parents. Maybe I'll get reborn in my next life and everyone will work for me for once. It probably won't happen this life. You probably don't know what I mean unless you've been raised as a girl here, or maybe if someday you have a girl of your own to raise.

There's nothing to look forward to. Marriage to somebody ugly and poor enough that they won't cheat on you? Hoping for marriage to someone too old and senile to hurt you? Neither option's good.

Speaking frankly here, the Việt kiều that left a long time ago, maybe you and your friends, come back thinking all the girls have been innocently waiting for you to come back, with your kindness and money, like we all need you, you know? The Korean and Japanese men who come here asking for a certain kind of girl in all these bars also all think the same way, that we'd been waiting here, waiting for them to come. My friends who work in Japan Alley, on Lê Thánh Tôn Street, tell me all about their clients. Make them feel like they never left their country, their bosses said, like they're still at their local Japanese bar or Korean bar, but a group of beautiful Vietnamese girls appear out of nowhere to pour their drinks and laugh and flirt with them. The food here is the same, the drinks, sake, soju, the same; we cut meats with scissors the way they've been told to from their cultures. The girls wear kimonos, speak the same Japanese greetings. *Irasshaimase!*

Some of my friends that work the Western bars tell me their bosses said to act like they don't know English. The customers, they'll like you better if you don't speak English, they say, or if you bumble and trip on the language. I know girls who are eager to learn it, thinking it'd help, but our bosses tell us there's no point. If girls can speak clearly, it just means less tips. The men get suspicious, so we pretend to speak in broken *Vinglish*. As for speaking Japanese or Korean, we never get beyond the few phrases we're told to learn. Why should we, when no one wants a conversation, when we're better off in the background, and chatting with them just takes a cut out of our paycheck?

My family? We're from Buôn Mê Thuột, high up in the mountains. I think I probably have some kinship from the hill tribes. It's so pretty there. The air gets cool, starting in October. It's quiet too, peaceful. And slow. But sometimes too quiet. There's not much to do for young people, so when I was done with high school, I came down to the city to find work with my sister. She came back, living back there now, raised a family, but I . . . just can't. This hot, bustling city. Sài Gòn. No, I don't think I can come back. I'll probably be here for a while.

I miss my family's cooking, though, the cool air, chatting with friends in cafes. All my friends who stayed in Buôn Mê Thuột never left. They're all married now. They tell me I'm too old to be single. You won't be beautiful for long, they say. But I don't see anyone I want to marry yet though, either there, or in this city. Maybe I don't see that kind of life for myself.

When I was a little girl, I saw a fight between two teenage boys while walking home from school. Other people gathered to watch it too. It was a fistfight at first, but then the two boys started grabbing bricks and flinging them at each other.

It must have been about jealousy, I think, the fight. Jealousy and love, they always go together. The girl they were fighting over watched nearby, she didn't know what to do. She was crying and concerned but she couldn't stop it. I couldn't tell which boy she was concerned about, though. Maybe both.

I was just in the crowd watching, but a brick they threw missed and nicked me on the side of my head. It happened so quickly that I didn't feel any pain, just a quick jolt. I touched my head and my hand was red.

I came home with blood dripping down my face. It soaked my shirt and stained the top of my pants. But it looked worse than it felt. I didn't cry or complain, or say anything. It just happened, and I was surprised, that's all. I just smiled. My mother took me in her arms and held me, and said, oh my poor baby girl, oh my baby girl, it'll be fine, it'll be fine, my poor little baby girl. She couldn't stop crying, but I was tough. I didn't feel anything. You can feel the bump now if you brush my hair apart, let me show you. Yeah, there it is.

The Past

ONE JUNE EVENING YEARS AGO, in the Galang Refugee Camp in Galang Island, Indonesia, a woman hanged herself.

She had been there for years, and her husband was still stuck in Vietnam. Her name was Liên, meaning Lotus Flower, and no one spoke to her during her stay to know her full story. There was a rumor that she and a friend who travelled with her had been raped by pirates on the journey there. Others on the trip corroborated what happened, and they both were silent shadows in the camp. Families, children, couples and singles were all waiting for families to arrive too, for lovers left behind to magically appear, everyone had their own concerns, everyone anxious and waiting. But when she hanged herself, the news spread through the compound and left a gloomy pall over everyone.

The Việt kiều of our story, our Casanova, was just a boy then, so he knew none of this. He could only sense the adults' restlessness around him, could feel the heat's oppression hover over the camp. Like them, he breathed the same air heavy with uncertainty and anxious waiting.

That night, someone had access to a radio and played music that echoed throughout the compound. Couples gathered and congregated to listen to popular American songs of the day, songs that were banned back in the old country. Sometimes the radio dipped back into the seventies, with disco and love ballads reverberating in the air. Families came out with kids to listen too; the barracks and compounds were steeped in sound.

Our future Việt kiều Casanova was nine. He was sitting in the hollow cavity of a tree trunk, with his friends perched on other branches. He hated being inside the barracks with all the other run-away families from his country. They were humid little shacks filled with the sounds of other people's chatter, with corrugated aluminum roofs that trapped the heat throughout the day, and only let it out at night. Infants born in the camp wailed all day, couples argued deep into the morning. No, it was better to be outside, roaming the dirt and clambering onto trees, testing the limits of the compound, wandering near the beach back to the ocean and sea, a sea that touched the wider, foreign countries beyond. Extended summer, no school, no homework, nowhere to go, days of kicking around the dust, shooting marbles, days blurred in a weird contentment that seemed to last forever.

That night, the boy had just finished a joyous afternoon winning four rounds of marbles against his friends, and now he rolled the crystalline spheres that were his prize winnings around inside his short pocket like a little monk shuffling prayer beads.

It had been a good haul, and as he and his friends relaxed, nestled on the tree's lower branches, sipping chilled Coca Cola in plastic bags tied together with rubber bands, the boy tried to picture which country his family would end up in. His friends had told him about people settling in France. There were Vietnamese people there who drank wine all day, eating baguettes, which were like *bánh mì* but filled with cheese. Others told him of relatives that settled in America, and snow, and kids that built little houses out of ice and played in them. The boy tried to imagine what was going on in his old neighborhood back in Sài Gòn, his apartment by the river, his school, his teacher and classmates probably fretting about, waiting for his triumphant return. When he gets back to them, rich after some years in America, they would all get together in the classroom, hands on chins, eagerly awaiting his stories: "Oh you were so brave, the bravest! How did you do it, cross the ocean so many have died in? How did you do it?"

The music started playing faster and faster. Young couples knotted themselves, limb layered over limb, bones and muscles locked stead-fast like tied lifebuoys set adrift on a disturbed ocean of sound, as if in the music's storm, entwined fingers, clutched hands, elbows and knees were all that kept them alive. On a nearby tree stump, the boy's friend Tu made the gesture of hugging a girl tightly to himself and moaned suggestively for effect. He and Tu laughed, but in a moment, the music's urgency turned them silent again.

No warm July

No harvest moon to light one tender August night

While the tune itself was upbeat, the music trippingly light, the crowd listening acted like it was music sadder than anything they had ever heard. The singer's voice and the amped resonance of the synthesizer lingered in the air, making the compound's wooden walls and aluminum roofs ache and sway. Indeed, the voice was sweeter than anything the boy had heard; it tasted sweeter than the cool sip from the Coca Cola bag he tasted, listening as he drank. Years later, he would hear that voice and the lyrics he had once heard but couldn't understand, playing on the airwaves of a classic soul station. Years later, when he was finally in America and had become a teenager searching for a way out of his own loneliness, he would listen to the song play on the radio and remember Stevie Wonder's voice echoing among the corrugated shacks of Galang, singing: *I just called, to say. I love you. I just called to say . . . how much I cared . . .*

Kinship

—Lại Văn Long—

LIEUTENANT COLONEL TRỊNH TÙNG was detained in the reeducation camp. His wife Vân Anh and their three children were evicted from their home in Sài Gòn, where they were staying in the Airborne Division Living Quarter, and had to move in with her parents in District 4. Because the house was already crowded, her parents, younger sister, and her brother-in-law weren't too happy with having four more people under the same roof.

Holding her mother's hand, Vân Anh pleaded, "At least let me use the front of the house for cooking. We'll eat separately. I'll look for work and feed my own kids."

The old woman was doubtful, but nodded.

Vân Anh had already sold all the furniture from her previous house, giving her enough money to open a small business. She and a close friend of hers, Hiền, whose husband worked as a judge in what was then South Vietnam and was later put in a reeducation camp, left their homes early in the morning and returned home every night when the bus made its final stop in Chinatown around nine o'clock. This was the period of "commercial restriction" across the country. Bars of soap, pairs of sandals, even bags of seasoning for food were considered contraband. Carrying a sack of rice, animals like ducks, or eggs and dried fish was illegal, even if you lived in the countryside.

One morning, after Vân Anh and Hiền made a little money but before they returned to Sài Gòn from Gò Công, they took all they had and bought three kilograms of dried shrimp and five kilograms of dried squid. They portioned out the dried seafood into smaller bags and hid the contraband on their body, securing the larger bags of squid around their arms and thighs. They didn't run into any problems at the first checkpoint, but at the second checkpoint Vân Anh was suspected of smuggling contraband, so she was escorted to the back of the station. She imagined being interrogated by a concerned cadre with a northern accent, but to her surprise it turned out to be Hai Mạnh. He had a trimmed mustache and was wearing a shirt that looked too tight on him. He smirked and made a pass at her, mocking her by using a southern accent.

"All that dried shrimp and squid you're hiding sure smells good," he said. "Because I have to search you, where should I check first?"

Vân Anh regained her composure and tried to flatter Hai Mạnh. "You're a handsome and assertive man. Women want to be with you. What if you found someone more attractive and left me?"

Hai Mạnh held Vân Anh and kissed her hair. She playfully cowered and said under her breath, "Not today though. I smell awful."

***

HAI MẠNH DROVE VÂN ANH ON his Honda 67 motorbike toward the Sài Gòn Bridge. He stepped on the gas as soon as they merged onto the Đại Hàn Highway. Feeling scared, she wrapped her arms around his waist firmly. When he throttled the gas, she opened her eyes and saw that they were turning onto a narrow dirt road. He pulled up to a two-story house with a large front yard, got off his motorbike, and unlatched the gate. Vân Anh tucked her purse under her arm and fixed her disheveled hair. Hai Mạnh shut the gate door, pulled her toward him, and kissed her madly ...

Vân Anh showered while he slept. She noticed the bright, white ceramic tiles of the bathroom walls, and in the shower caddy scented soap and a variety of shampoos, the ones she had often used before

1975. She found several long strands of hair in the drain and suddenly felt jealous. She wrapped herself in a towel, walked over to the bed, and shook Hai Mạnh awake.

"Who else is living here with you?" she asked.

Hai Mạnh opened his eyes, pulled her toward him on the bed, and said gently, "This vacation home once belonged to a former senator of the Sài Gòn regime. Now he's in a reeducation camp. His wife and children fled the country by boat. My friend, the chairman of this commune, let me have this place."

Vân Anh played with Hai Mạnh's mustache. "If you say so. But from now on this place is just ours. If you even think about bringing someone else here, you'll be sorry."

"You're my only fairy. I don't need another one."

"Are you married? Do you have any children?"

"I fought in the war for over ten years and didn't have time to get married."

"Then whose hair is that in the bathroom?"

"Must be from the former owner. I stay busy with four houses and don't have a lot of time to clean."

Vân Anh sat up and asked, "How'd you come to have so many houses?"

"People I know gave them to me."

"And here my kids and I have to live with my parents," she sighed. "We have to hear them complain all day."

"I can give you a house."

"Really?"

"I'll find you a good one. A house where you can open up a shop and earn a living, so you can feed your kids and help your husband in the reeducation camp. After they release him and you're both together again, you can keep the house."

Vân Anh pressed her body into Hai Mạnh. "You're a Vietcong, so why are you being so nice to a *ngụy*?"

He sat up and fixed his eyes on her. "That question came out of nowhere ... The communists fought hard and endured terrible things so we Vietnamese can enjoy our newfound independence, just as Uncle Hồ always wanted. The country is at peace now, and we're all Vietnamese. There shouldn't be a distinction made between the revolutionaries or *ngụy*. Go get dressed and I'll show you."

Hai Mạnh took Vân Anh on his motorbike to Chinatown. They pulled up to a three-story house on the corner of a crowded intersection. He opened the gate and the glass door. Vân Anh rushed upstairs. She stood on the rooftop and peered down at the vibrant, bustling streets. Afterward, she hurried back downstairs, hugged Hai Mạnh, and cried.

"Even when my husband was at his most successful, we never dreamed of owning a house like this. Are you sure this is mine now?"

Hai Mạnh ran his hand through her hair. "Whoever used to own this house has fled the country. So this and all the furniture is yours." He pulled out a stack of bills from his pocket. "Here's money for you to get your business off the ground."

She gently nudged him back to the bedroom, their eyes locked on one another, and she whispered, "This is an overwhelming gift. How can I show you what this means to me?"

He shook his head. "I was in the Special Forces and came close to death many times," he said sadly. "My comrades weren't as lucky—I survived the war. So let's not talk about gratitude here. Just tell me you love me."

"I can't do that," she demurred.

***

ONE BEAUTIFUL DAY AFTER MORE THAN three years without news, Vân Anh received a letter from her husband with a visit permit tucked inside. She was cautious, however, and didn't report to the authorities responsible for verifying her marital status. She was afraid they would seize her house and relocate her entire family to a new economic zone. This would also cause trouble for Hai Mạnh. She submitted paperwork to the commune chairman about her address before 1975 when she lived in the Airborne Division Quarter in Bà Quẹo.

"The ARVN paratroopers were all cruel. They killed both my younger siblings and raped my older sister before they shot her. So why should I sign off on this document for you?" the chairman said angrily.

Vân Anh was speechless, stunned by his accusations. She shuddered, as though suddenly cold.

A cadre wearing a faded military uniform overheard the conversation coming from the back room and walked into the main office. With a northern accent, he said to the chairman, "Keep calm or you'll lose self-control."

"As the Secretary General, you fought in all the big battles. You couldn't possibly understand what it's like to carry out clandestine activities while living among the enemy. Or what I've experienced with these bloodthirsty killers."

"The war's over," he said to the chairman. "The Party has new policies in place for *ngụy*." Then he turned toward Vân Anh and said, "Where do you live now? There's nothing left of the Airborne Division Housing Quarter."

"My children and I live with my parents in District 4."

"Then go to the local authorities there and have them verify your status."

After learning about her situation, Hai Mạnh helped her with the paperwork and bought two roundtrip train tickets, which were extremely difficult to purchase at the time. Since moving into the new house, she'd opened a business selling food and drinks. It earned her more than enough money to take her first trip to the North to see her husband.

After they had dinner, Vân Anh and Mỹ Dung, her daughter, carried two oversized bags and a duffel to the Hòa Hưng train station to catch the seven o' clock evening train. The car was packed solid with passengers, their belongings, even chickens and pigs, their dogs and cats. Many didn't have tickets, so they bribed the conductor to let them sit on the floor. After passing the Bến Hải River, the passengers got rowdy as they jostled for a view of the bridge and river. Vân Anh also craned her neck to get a glimpse of the sad river that had divided her country for over twenty years.

Another day went by. An old woman wearing a shawl who sat across from Vân Anh and Mỹ Dung announced excitedly, "We'll be arriving at Hà Nội's Hàng Cỏ station shortly."

The train slowed down. Seeing the city move backward, Vân Anh felt as though she'd entered a foreign land. Most passengers had gone their separate ways after thirty minutes, leaving the platform almost empty. Several women and their children, who dressed in city clothes, stood at a corner and waved at Vân Anh and her daughter to join them. She soon learned that these women also made the trip to visit their husbands in Hà Nam Ninh, where the Ba Sao reeducation camps were located. Mrs. Tuyền—a chubby middle-aged woman who wore a purple *bà ba* outfit and had a mountain of hair—was the oldest in this group, the wife of Special Forces Colonel Trọng. Mrs. Tâm wore brown pants, a white shirt, and had a pixie haircut; she was the wife of Lieutenant Colonel Khánh, who worked for the ARVN's General Staff. But the youngest and most beautiful one in the group was Miss Thanh, fiancée of Major Luyến of the 23rd Infantry Division. Each woman was accompanied by a family member: Mrs. Tuyền by her teenage son, Mrs. Tâm by her daughter, and Miss Thanh by her nephew. They seemed delighted by one another's company because they had all been on the same boat. They hired separate pedicabs and headed to the bus station, where they would go sixty kilometers from Hà Nội to Phủ Lý.

In the evening, after arriving in Phủ Lý, they paid a buffalo cart driver twelve đồng to take them to Ba Sao Camp. The man held up a hurricane lantern with eight Saigonese people in tow.

The hoped-for day finally came. In the waiting room, the visitors were nervous. A cadre slowly turned the pages of each dossier. The crinkling sound made the visitors even more anxious as they waited for their names to be called.

"Mrs. Nguyễn Thu Tuyền," the cadre said.

"That's me, sir."

"Call me *cadre*, not *sir*. Understand? Is your husband Colonel Phạm Trọng?"

"Yes, cadre."

"He's stubborn and often makes trouble. He's being disciplined at the moment, so no visiting hours this time."

Mrs. Tuyền let loose a squeal and nearly passed out. Vân Anh and Mrs. Tâm quickly rubbed some medical oil on her forehead and pulled her hair back to help her regain consciousness.

Mrs. Tuyền rested her head on Vân Anh's shoulder, clasped her hands together, and pleaded to the cadre, "Please let me send him these gifts. My son and I have gone through a lot to get here."

"I'm afraid you can't," the cadre said.

Mrs. Tuyền sobbed and said to Vân Anh, "Please take my son back to Sài Gòn with you. I'll die here to please the cadre if I have to."

The cadre banged his fist on the desk, stood up, wagged his finger at Mrs. Tuyền, and berated her, "Do you realize how many families in the North had to wear mourning headbands because of crimes committed by the puppet regime? I've lost six family members. What do you think of that? The Party has been merciful to your husband. What else can you possibly want?"

This terrified Vân Anh, Mrs. Tâm, and Miss Thanh, and they told Mrs. Tuyền to be quiet. Her son hugged her, begging her not to do anything foolish.

The cadre was still furious. He sat back down and sipped tea to calm himself. Then he called out, "Mrs. Lê Thanh Tâm.".

"I'm here."

"Is your husband Lieutenant Colonel Tống Văn Khánh?"

"Yes, cadre."

"He's sick but being taken care of. Go ahead and send him your gifts. If you brought any pills with you, put them separately so he can take them first."

"Please let me and my daughter see him. Give us just a few minutes." Mrs. Tâm got on her knees and begged. "If something happens to him and he dies, then at least we'll get to see his face one last time."

"That would go against regulations," he shouted.

Mrs. Tâm cried and sluggishly got to her feet. Vân Anh helped her stand up, then guided her back to her seat.

The cadre then called Miss Thanh and asked about her relationship with Major Dư Đình Luyến. When she said she was his fiancée, he smirked, "Lucky you!"

"So can I see him now?" she beamed.

The cadre jerked his chin up. The lieutenant, who was sitting next to him, said to Miss Thanh, "Come over here and sign this document."

She moved quickly to the desk and just as quickly signed where the lieutenant was pointing. But when she returned to her chair with the document and read it, she fell in a heap on the floor. The document read: *Certificate of Death* . . .

Mrs. Tuyền and Mrs. Tâm forgot about their own problems; they rushed to Miss Thanh's side and helped her up. Miss Thanh bit her lip and said, "At least allow me to visit his grave."

The cadre stood up and said loudly, "Mr. Luyến died because of illness. He was buried behind the mountain. You can't go there because the road is dangerous."

In the end, only Vân Anh and her daughter were allowed to see their loved one. They heard the sound of footsteps on the loose, pebbly ground outside. Two police officers led Trịnh Tùng into the room. It startled Vân Anh to see her husband again. He bowed to the cadres at the desk with deference and said, "Please let me talk to my wife and daughter."

The lieutenant pointed at a long table and said, "Have a seat there. Do you remember our regulations?"

"Yes, cadre."

"You and your daughter can sit across from him," the cadre said to Vân Anh. "You have thirty minutes."

However nervous or elated Vân Anh initially felt, her heart sank when she saw her husband's thinning hair that made him look bald. That haggard, sunbaked face, his missing front teeth, those dry, cracked lips. Even his frightened eyes looked tired above his hollow cheeks. His skin was pale, and his dry, calloused hands were shaking. Feeling overwhelmed, Mr. Tùng wiped his tears away with a hand and asked the little girl, "You must be Mỹ Dung. You're a big girl now. What grade are you in?"

"I'm in sixth grade," the girl said. She looked at her father innocently. "I'm the second-best student in my class but the school didn't give me an award."

"Why not?" Mr. Tùng asked.

"My teacher said I'm a *ngụy*'s daughter. She even said it doesn't matter how well I do in school, I can't go to college. She said *ngụy* people are betrayers of the motherland."

Mr. Tùng stared at his daughter without moving his eyes away. He bit his lip and wiped tears away with the sleeve of his shirt. Vân Anh held his bony hands and gently rubbed them, calluses and all, as though the act would help quell the storm of sadness brewing in her heart. Mr. Tùng became clumsy. His eyes flicked between the two cadres sitting at both ends of the long table. He pulled his hands back, and said in a somber voice, "I've heard that the residents of the Airborne Division Living Quarters were evicted. So where do you and the kids live now?"

Mỹ Dung spoke on behalf of her mother, "We live in a much bigger house. Uncle Mạnh gave it to us."

Mr. Tùng frowned and asked his wife, "Who's this Uncle Mạnh?"

While Vân Anh searched for an appropriate answer, Mỹ Dung quickly added, "He likes to carry a gun like those two policemen over there. He takes me and my sisters to the cinema and likes to buy us things. He gives Grandma money and bought the train tickets for us to come see you."

Mr. Tùng's face grew even paler as he looked at his wife with disbelief. His hands continued to shake. The two cadres, smoking now, seemed astonished by the girl's story. The room grew quiet. Vân Anh lowered her head and sobbed.

"You have no idea what our kids and I have gone through," she said.

Mr. Tùng held his tongue to control his anger. Maybe in a previous life, he could have pulled the trigger and shot his unfaithful wife. But now, he was like a tiger who'd been trained for the circus—disciplined and in control of himself—for fear of beatings. He swallowed his anger and jealousy. His eyes wandered to the ceiling. The veins along his neck pulsed as tears fell from the corners of his eyes.

His wife bit her lower lip. Their eyes locked and she said, "Did you know that I once cooked a pot of porridge and thought about pouring into it a bottle of pesticide? Then the three kids and I could eat it and die. But I've always thought about you and I ... Go ahead and ask your daughter."

One of the cadres banged his hand on the table and interrupted her, "Ma'am, are you blaming the revolution for what happened?"

"No, I just blame our poor circumstances."

Mr. Tùng was moved by Vân Anh's story. After he listened to her, his anger suddenly subsided. He loved his wife and children more than anything, and there was nobody to blame for their misery except himself. "It's my fault," he said. "You're not to blame. What you've gone through to raise the kids—but does this mean you're someone else's wife now?"

"Forgive me, and let me still be your wife."

"But you're now the wife of someone from the winning side, while I'm a prisoner from the losing side. Take back your gifts, go back to Sài Gòn, and don't ever visit me again." Then he got on his feet, faced his daughter, and said wryly, "And you return to your kindhearted uncle so he can take you to the cinema and buy you ice cream and nice clothes. Tell him I'm dead and that he can take whatever he wants from me."

The cadre stood up and pointed his finger at Mr. Tùng, saying, "Nonsense. Stop accusing the revolutionaries of stealing your wife and children from you."

235

"I want to die. Go ahead and shoot me," Mr. Tùng barked, beating his chest with his fist.

Vân Anh grew dizzy, lost her balance, and fell to the floor. Their daughter Mỹ Dung wailed, "Mommy . . . Daddy . . ."

***

A WEEK LATER, VÂN ANH met Hai Mạnh again in Sài Gòn. They sat together on a bench in a park at Bạch Đằng Port. She told him what happened at the camp visit, and he listened attentively while smoking.

"We were treated horribly back there," she said, resting her head on his shoulder.

He rubbed out the cigarette with his shoe and asked her, "Are you finished with your story?"

"What did you want to tell me?"

"Do you think the ARVN wasn't cruel? They shot my father, raped and tortured my older sister. She died in Phú Quốc Prison. They arrested my mother and beat her until she was coughing blood." He cried. "They have to pay a price."

"You seem different today," Vân Anh said with concern in her voice.

"When I think about what happened to my family, my heart fills with resentment."

"If you dislike *ngụy* so much, then why love me—a mother of three kids?"

"That's just karma," he sighed.

"If you're so fed up, why not just leave?" She then whispered, "I wouldn't blame you."

"I'll never put you in a situation. After they let your husband out, you can join up with him again. I won't get in the way."

For the first time they wept together.

***

AFTER THE NORTH TOOK OVER THE SOUTH, Hai Mạnh, a law graduate, became a trade supervisor thanks to the recommendation from Mr. Sáu, a high-ranking NVA officer. Hai Mạnh was accused of moral

236

corruption and having an affair with a married *ngụy* woman. Mr. Sáu was worried, so he arranged for Hai Mạnh to be the cadre in charge of legal issues in Chí Hòa Prison, hoping that his "protégé" would not make more mistakes in his new working environment.

Hiền, Vân Anh's close friend, was put in jail for smuggling. She begged Hai Mạnh to let her visit her three small children for a few hours, promising him that she would return after they had been sent to their grandma. He let her borrow a police uniform and helped her take care of her family business. But Vân Anh escaped and didn't return. Hai Mạnh was imprisoned for a year for colluding with the detainee. Upon release, his Party membership was revoked, his various properties confiscated, and his former comrades kept their distance. He took a risk and fled the country with Vân Anh and their three-year-old son, Cường, on a small fishing boat, leaving behind her three daughters, Mỹ Dung, Mỹ Diệu, and Mỹ Giang.

Vân Anh left behind a note to her daughters that read: *Dear my beloved daughters, Uncle Mạnh has taken great care of our family for the last five years. I blame myself for what's happened, and there's no future for him in this country. I also can't leave him. I've sinned in terrible ways. Please forgive me and goodbye.*

A year later, the daughters received a telegram from abroad, saying that Vân Anh had died and was buried on Bidong Island. They weren't sure if Hai Mạnh had sent the telegram. Trịnh Tùng was released from the reeducation camp earlier than expected due to good behavior, but he decided not to emigrate to the United States through the Orderly Departure Program. He couldn't leave the graves of his parents and ancestors in Huế unattended. He devoted his time to raising his abandoned daughters.

***

IN AUGUST 2022, AFTER THE COVID-19 pandemic was finally under control, Mỹ Dung, along with her husband and daughter, flew from Sài Gòn to Kuala Lumpur, Malaysia, and joined a group of thirty expat tourists in Terengganu, where Bidong Island was located. Most were in their sixties or seventies, and they had stayed in the refugee camp on this island several years earlier, before they were granted asylum to the United States, Australia, or Europe. They cried as they saw what was left of their houses of worship, their schools and hospitals, the markets—places that evoked in them strong memories of what they had gone through, and their perilous journey out to sea. At one time, they had resisted the "liberators" and harbored vehement desires to subvert the communist government, but now they returned back to their homeland to do business, participate in entertainment events, or to find a young partner to marry, or just to enjoy retirement. Those who once saluted the South Vietnamese flag now thanked the Party for welcoming them back.

***

MỸ DUNG WAS THE CEO OF a company that exported rice and chicken, and since 2015, she had come to the island many times to search for her mother's grave. A Chinese Malaysian and a hotel owner named Yeh Feng knew the area well and helped her find Vân Anh's grave, which was hidden beneath the overgrowth. Her tombstone read:

Trang Nữ Vân Anh
born 1943
died September 21, 1983

Mỹ Dung respectfully put fresh flowers, fruit, and paper offerings on the grave for the dead, burned incense, and thanked Lord Buddha and the gods. She also burned incense at other nearby graves—all were refugees who'd lost their lives on the island.

While she was pulling weeds from around her mother's grave, an elderly, gray-haired man and a young man walked quickly in her direction. They were also carrying offerings for the dead. The old man looked at her and his voice trembled when he said, "Who are you? What are you doing at my wife's grave?"

It dawned on her who the elderly man was . . . Uncle Mạnh!

She made a video call to her father so that the octogenarians could talk to each other. They saw each other on the video feed and cried.

"Thank you for taking care of my family while I was locked away," Trịnh Tùng said. "Without your help, they might not have made it."

"I've lost my loved ones. On a small fishing boat forty years ago, six former ARVN officers and I fought off Thai pirates to save our families. By the way, my son Cường just met your daughter Mỹ Dung, her husband, and your granddaughter. Cường is now a lieutenant colonel in the U.S. Navy."

Trịnh Tùng said, "My granddaughter you just shook hands with is now the district vice-chairwoman."

The two men spent a long time catching up. Then, Hai Mạnh said to Mỹ Dung, "Tell the gravediggers to get going. We'll take your mother's remains back to Vietnam, and let's all of us meet up in Sài Gòn."

Mỹ Dung hugged Hai Mạnh. Choking up, she said, "I consider you a father from forty-seven years ago. My sisters and I have two fathers."

He knelt down in front of the grave and prayed. "You've been interned here for over forty years. It's time we sent you home, my dear. Please find a way to let go of the pain of the past, to set your soul free."

Mỹ Dung wanted to ask Hai Mạnh how her mother died, but hearing the sincerity of his prayer, she realized that maybe some things might be better left unsaid.

—Translated by Quan Manh Ha & Cab Tran

American Grass

—Nguyễn Thu Trân—

BEFORE 1975, THERE WAS A TYPE of grass that grew ubiquitously around the high hills in the South called "American grass." It was tall and few dared to step on it because of its sharp blades, a type of grass that could cut people and make them bleed. In the dry season, the grass would turn yellow and cause wildfires. During the wet season, it had green leaves and was impossible to eradicate completely. Some often compared the grass to the Amerasian children in the South because both were unwanted and stubborn.

I

I RAN AWAY FROM HOME at eighteen, not because I was pregnant in my first trimester, but primarily because I wanted to escape troubles that happened during mealtimes. I was frightened by my father's hostility, along with how rare it became for my family to make eye contact whenever we sat down to eat together. I would ask myself if my father was typical of other fathers, and my conclusion was he wasn't. That year I left home, Grandma was seventy but looked even older. She was also traumatized by my father's brash and unpredictable behavior, but resilient enough to put up with his volatile nature.

On the day I left, I looked him straight in the face and said, "Can't you be a decent person? Grandma and our family have suffered enough."

He slapped me across the face and said angrily, "Once you leave this house, don't even think about coming back. A daughter like you can only make a living by having affairs with American GIs." He was referring to my mother, who had run away to escape her abusive husband.

Whenever I was beaten for any reason, I would scamper to a corner of the house and cry. Grandma would find me and sit next to me. Running her fingers through my hair, she'd comfort me by saying, "Your father might be mentally unstable, but at least the evil spirits didn't take him away with your uncle Hai."

My grandmother led an unhappy life. When she was pregnant with my father and Uncle Hai at the same time, Grandpa disappeared soon after, leaving behind the unborn twins for her to take care of alone. Every night during the last month of her pregnancy, half-awake in bed, she often saw a ghost whose face was as round as a serving platter and with fangs that reached down to its knees. It would stand at the foot of the bed and ask her to give up her baby. This terrified her and caused her to wake up in a cold sweat. She began hiding a machete under her mattress, believing that the sharp weapon would scare the ghost away. But in the early mornings, when the roosters crowed noisily in the neighborhood, the ghost would reappear, asking for her baby.

My father was the younger twin because he came out of her womb after Uncle Hai. Grandma had a shaman cast a spell on the front and back doors of the house to keep the ghost away. But it didn't work. She draped amulets around my father's neck and limbs, thinking that the ghost was after her younger son. On the night Uncle Hai had a fever, a strong wind rustled the roof. Grandma gave him medicine and rubbed a tincture made from lemons all over his body, but that didn't alleviate his fever. The other twin would wail loudly and Grandma would see the ghost stand at the foot of her bed again. Filled with anger, she grabbed her machete and attacked the ghost with all the strength she could muster. As soon as it disappeared, Uncle Hai took his last breath. Grandma later regretted that she hadn't also given amulets to her older son.

Raising my father was a challenge for Grandma because he was prone to throwing temper tantrums, but she remained patient with him. He married at nineteen, and Grandma was overjoyed when she heard that her daughter-in-law was pregnant. In the last month of my mother's pregnancy, Grandma was afraid the ghost would come back and take the baby away, so she again had the shaman cast spells all around the house. But the ghost never returned.

My father was drafted to fight in the war. A year later, when I was just learning how to walk, he lost his left leg and returned from the battlefield on crutches. From then on, he became a cruel man, quick to anger, and someone who was impossible to live with. After my mother gave birth to two sons, Đạt and Út, she ran away. This was the reason for my father's deep-seated misogyny, even though his hatred for women was directed at Grandma and me, his only daughter, who was the spitting image of him.

My education only lasted until the seventh grade, so I knew nothing about menstruation and pregnancy. I also didn't know who the father of my baby was. I had been raped one night while sleeping on a bench in a park after running away from home. I didn't want to upset Grandma, so I didn't tell her about the incident. I named my son Việt, a handsome boy who was nothing like his unattractive mother. I decided to keep him instead of giving him up for adoption to a rich and childless family.

My job cleaning after the marketplace barely earned enough money to raise Việt. Ms. Xuân, a *me Mỹ*,[15] often gave my son milk and helped me get another job at the American military base where she was working. She said, "Working for the Americans will give you a bad reputation, I know. But you'll make enough money to raise the boy. Isn't that what really matters?"

---

15 A derogatory term referring to a Vietnamese woman who had an intimate, often sexual, relationship with an American man (or men) for financial gains during the war

I sent Việt to an orphanage but registered him as still living with a single mother. This meant I would pay the institution a monthly fee and retain permission to visit him. I thought this was wise because at least he didn't have to be alone in my tiny, fly-infested house near the squalid market where I worked. My father didn't know about my new job—working for the Americans. If he had, he would've ended my life.

***

NEWLY HIRED, I WAS ASSIGNED TO clean restrooms in a section occupied by black American GIs. At first, I was scared, so I kept my head down and focused on work, not daring to look at anyone. Later, I realized that many black soldiers were kind; they taught me how to say a few simple English phrases and sometimes offered me chocolate, which Việt loved. But there was one tall black soldier who often took his showers after lunch, and he liked to stare at me. One day while cleaning the men's room, he locked the door behind him, pushed me down to the floor, then covered my mouth with his hands so I couldn't scream—

A few months later, I found out I was pregnant. I asked Ms. Xuân if she could recommend me for cleaning and laundry work in another section of the military base. I was still hoping to earn extra money. I gave birth to Kẻng, and he had healthy bronze-colored skin. I loved him as much as I loved Việt. I took maternity leave for several months, and when Kẻng was five months old, I sent him to the orphanage. I didn't know the name of his father or the other members of his unit, and I was told that the men had moved to a different region. It didn't really matter after all, because when you give birth to Amerasian children who were unwanted in this country, it would be pointless to track down who their father was.

My coworkers at the American military base were Vietnamese women who came from war-torn families. I lied to them that I was homeless and that my parents and brothers had all been killed in bombing raids, so that I didn't have to answer any questions about my background. I was as good as dead to my family anyway because I worked for the enemy.

After saving some money over time, I went back to visit my family but didn't enter the house. I stood under a freshwater mangrove tree, waiting for my brother Đạt to come home from school. When I saw him, I pulled him aside next to a sugarcane vendor and asked how everybody in the family was doing. He said that Grandma and my father were doing fine, and that my mother hadn't come back. Đạt was in the fifth grade, Út in fourth. I was heartbroken and said to Đạt, "Take this money for Grandma—for you and Út, too. but don't tell Dad we met up."

Đạt refused the money, saying, "You work for the Americans, so I can't take it."

"Who told you that? I'm a waitress at a noodle restaurant. I'm *not* working for the Americans."

"Grandma said someone saw you in a miniskirt with all sorts of makeup on. I don't know many waitresses who dress up like that."

I lowered my voice and asked, "Does Dad know about this?"

He rubbed his eyes and shook his head. "No. If he knew, he'd burn our house to the ground."

"If you cared about me at all, then give Grandma the money."

"You know I can't do that. If it's true you're selling your body to the Americans, we don't want your money." Đạt left quickly after that.

I would spend all day every Sunday with my sons and the other orphans. These were some of the happiest moments for me. If it weren't for Việt and Kẻng, I would've already joined the monastery. Later, I thought my life would feel more complete if I had a daughter. She and my two sons would be the yin and yang of my life.

Then, Leo Smith came to mind. He was a handsome sniper corporal with a great sense of humor. He also had won a lot of medals. I washed his clothes, so in the evenings we often went to a bar for a drink, then rented a hotel room to spend some intimate time together. I wasn't sure what Leo thought of me, but every time we made love in a candlelit room, he felt more and more like my husband. Like the other GIs, Leo could care less about who he slept with, because like them, he didn't know if he would outlive the war.

Since my daughter Kim was born out of wedlock, Leo had become more attached to me. When he returned from battle, he would eagerly go looking for me. Afterward, he would give me a generous tip, even recommending me to his fellow soldiers. Ms. Xuân often joked, "Leo must be addicted to your body odor. The way melon fields smell under a scorching sun. The odor of nature!"

My time with Leo was pleasant but brief. I don't know why, but I started developing strong feelings for him. His friends also tipped me generously, and I soon became obsessed with the greenbacks. My popularity brought me new clients, and I was able to buy more things for my children at the orphanage. Other women working there treated me like royalty—a rich mother of three whose children had different colored skin.

Before returning home to the States after his tour in Vietnam, Leo asked me to let him meet Kim, his one-year-old daughter. I didn't want him to meet her, so I lied to him about never having a child with him.

***

ĐẠT BROKE NEWS OF GRANDMA'S DEATH with a written note: *Grandma will be buried in the field tomorrow. If you come, you shouldn't get too close or let Dad see you. He said he would desecrate the body if he saw you coming.*

I still didn't understand why things between my father and me were getting worse. Did he have something against women? I arrived just in time to see the funeral procession. I quietly knelt down on the side of the street to bow and pay my respects to Grandma as the hearse went by.

***

ONE DAY, WHILE I WAS IRONING clothes I'd just washed for a group of American GIs who had just come back from a battle, Ms. Xuân caught up with me and said, "You won't believe this, but the MPs just dissolved the orphanage. Take a day off work and we'll go there and see what's going on."

Ms. Xuân's Amerasian son, Jerry, also lived there, just like many other children born to GIs. When we arrived, a huge bulldozer was knocking down the gate. Two tall pillars made of solid concrete fell down and violently shook the vicious jaws of the bulldozer. Inside, the orphanage was a pile of rubble and debris. I walked around to look for my children's pink house, but I saw only clouds of dust. In a panic, I shouted, "Where are they? Give me back my kids!"

The orphanage was destroyed because the MPs suspected that there were communist spies on the executive board. After several days of searching, Ms. Xuân found Jerry. I was heartbroken when I learned that my three children had been sent away to the States. Việt was five years old, Kẻng three, and Kim two. Would I ever get to see them again? They were now on the other side of the world and oceans away.

Being separated from my children traumatized me to no end. I became dispirited and despondent. After three months of treatment for emotional disorder in a mental hospital, I gathered all the money I had saved and returned to where the orphanage had been. I set up a tent, opened a vendor stall that sold beverages, and waited for my children to return to find me. Ms. Xuân thought what I did was foolish and invited me to come live with her, hoping that I would eventually find a way to learn the whereabouts of my children. But I declined her offer because I didn't have the same optimism she did.

Some time later, I was told to ask for help from the U.S. Embassy in Sài Gòn, but I didn't know anyone there or what to do. I was merely a *me Mỹ* with little education, someone just awaiting a miracle. My three children were born in different situations, but I loved them equally. I was most worried about Kẻng, who was half-black, because he would more likely be the target of racial discrimination wherever he went. In my sleep, I dreamed about my children's future—especially for Kẻng. I would give him a good education and find him a decent Vietnamese wife who loved him sincerely and who would give birth to beautiful and healthy children.

***

TWENTY YEARS PASSED.

While living a solitary life in a tent, my brother Đạt appeared with some news. My father had died, Út became a schoolteacher and was married with three children, and Đạt was working but still unmarried. He told me that before Grandma and Dad passed away, they had asked him to send me their apologies. I asked why he waited so long to deliver their messages, and he replied, "You've had a difficult life, and I hesitated telling you ... but you know what? Even though Grandma was a daughter-in-law of a wealthy family, her life was full of sorrow. Any time she broke something that belonged to her rich husband's family, they forced her to sleep in a graveyard. The ghost with the flat, round face followed Grandma around for years, and that's why her marriage was so unhappy. Grandpa left when she was pregnant with Dad and Uncle Hai. After the ghost had taken our uncle away, she became more frightened and thought the ghost was after babies. When she was looking for a wife for Dad, Grandma wanted him to marry a woman who was already pregnant, so that the ghost would steal the out-of-wedlock baby, rather than her biological children."

I covered my face with my hands and burst out crying. Why was Grandma apologizing? Had she used me as a scapegoat? After the ghost rejected me, she loved me more than she loved her grandsons. Although I wasn't my father's biological daughter, the older I became, the more I took on his appearance. Now I understood why he hated Grandma, my mother, and me, and I forgave him for having treated me so cruelly. I built a shrine in the front yard for my father and Grandma, and I prayed for their eternal sleep, one without suffering.

***

NOW I AM SEVENTY AND FULLY prepared for death when it comes. In these last days of my life, ever since I've had serious heart problems, Đạt has moved in and waited with me for the return of my three children. He'd injured one of his legs in a traffic accident, and he's currently making a living by selling lottery tickets.[16] On my deathbed, the ghost finally appears to take me with him. I don't resist or push

---

16 In Vietnam, lottery ticket vendors are primarily socially and economically disadvantaged people who struggle for survival. They are mostly the handicapped, poor elderly people, orphans, and destitute people moving from the countryside to a city to eke out a living.

him away. If he becomes a human in the next life, perhaps the ghost would suffer as much as Grandma and I had.

II

MY NAME IS KỂNG AND I was born in 1970. I'm an Amerasian.

I don't remember much about the days when my siblings and I were at the orphanage because we were too young. All I remember is that Việt, Kim, and I got along very well and never fought one another. Then one day, our orphanage was demolished for unknown reasons. We orphans were sent scrambling. All three of us were put on an airplane that flew to America, where we were adopted by three different families.

In the beginning, we were allowed to visit each other once a week, but as years went by, our visits became less frequent and then rare as we drifted apart and became more accustomed to our new lives. I finished high school and left home when I went to college. I first experienced racial discrimination when people refused my handshakes and when my friendliness was returned with glares and smirks. Even Helga, my classmate, whom I helped with schoolwork, ignored me when she was with her white friends. This caused me a lot of frustration. Sometimes, I would pound a wall with my fists until my knuckles bled and shout, "But I'm Vietnamese." Helga could care less about my situation. One day, a girl named Nam Kha standing behind me spoke to me in Vietnamese, and we started to become close friends after that.

Since meeting Nam Kha, I've thought about my mother and about Vietnam more often. But I also hated my biological mother more. I wished I had never been born. Some questions kept invading my thoughts. Why did she give birth to me? Where was she now? Was she even alive or was she dead? Did she think about her three children who were airlifted out of Vietnam?

When I shared my life story with Nam Kha, she said, "I'll teach you Vietnamese. Your Vietnamese is horrible. But after you understand the language and culture, maybe you'll blame your biological mother less and even love her."

Nam Kha came to America on a Babylift program in 1975, three years after I did. She was three or four back then. She was fortunate to be adopted by a Vietnamese family, so that's why her Vietnamese was much better than mine. In college, she excelled in her sophomore year, whereas I struggled to get through my classes. I finally dropped out of school and found a job as a janitor at a supermarket.

Nam Kha had a large network of friends of her age in Vietnam. She shared with me the information about the orphans who had come to the States through the Babylift program before the war ended. With her help, I was able to find the location of my orphanage. I started to collect information about my biological mother, hoping that one day I'd return to Vietnam to go look for her.

Nam Kha suggested that I go find my biological father in America first before making a trip to Vietnam to find my mother. I couldn't sleep for several nights, wondering why the United States had organized evacuation flights for orphans like us, and why they then found families to adopt us. Did this have anything to do with a national guilt related to the war?

When we, the Amerasians, came to America, our fathers never attempted to find us—because we were the result of their affairs and illicit relationships with Vietnamese women. Even if they looked for us, they would reject us as their children anyway. Even after we became naturalized U.S. citizens, that feeling of loneliness and rejection never went away. The Vietnamese at home were suing American companies that had manufactured the nerve agent dioxin used in the war, which had caused birth defects. The Amerasian children, however, didn't become physically handicapped like children who were victims of dioxin, but the Amerasians, nevertheless, encountered psychological and emotional trauma.

"Maybe we need to sue our American biological fathers for abandoning us," I said to Nam Kha.

"That'd never work!' she said. "If you can't find your father, find your siblings instead, Việt and Kim."

After some research, I only managed to contact Việt's family, but Kim was nowhere to be found. Việt was married with two children and worked at a gun range. One fateful day, without warning, he grabbed a loaded gun and shot himself in the head. His wife said she didn't understand why he committed suicide.

I felt the urge to visit Vietnam and the site of the orphanage. After I got off the plane at Tân Sơn Nhất Airport, I put a piece of laminated paper on my chest that read *Tôi là người Việt*—I am Vietnamese. As though it were a miracle, everyone treated me kindly, as though Vietnam had always been my home.

***

I STOOD FOR WHAT FELT LIKE an eternity in front of an international company that was built on the land of where the orphanage used to be. An elderly man selling lottery tickets asked me, "Are you looking for the orphanage?"

"Yes," I replied.

"It's been long gone, I'm afraid. Just last week, an old woman who'd been waiting for her children to return finally passed away on a stormy, rainy night."

"Did she happen to have three children—all with different skin colors?"

He nodded, then looked at me. "How'd you know?"

I forced a smile without trying to give anything away, not wanting him to probe deeper into my background. "I've some Vietnamese friends here, and they told me about her and her kids. I'm sorry to hear she's dead."

"She worked for the Americans, you know, so she was a victim of the war. After her children were airlifted out of the country, she opened up a vendor booth, a beverage stall right here. hoping that one day they'd return to find her."

"Does she have any living relatives?"

"A brother."

"You said earlier that she was a victim of the war," I said. "What do you mean by that?"

"Vietnamese women who worked on U.S. military bases servicing American men often concealed their real identities. Many of them gave birth to Amerasian children and this brought disgrace to their families. Are you one of the Babylift sons coming back to find your mother? If that's the case, you're in the wrong place. No orphans from this orphanage were airlifted out of Vietnam ... But I've said enough already. How about you help me out and buy some lottery tickets?"

I took out some money from my wallet and bought a dozen lottery tickets. Without saying goodbye, the elderly man lowered his head and walked away, leaving me standing alone in the tropical rain. How was it possible that he knew so much about my mother? So much more than what little I knew about her?

From the depths of my memory, my childhood rushed back to me. I remembered how we used to cry with joy whenever our mother visited us on Sundays. I didn't remember her face clearly, and the only thing about her that was etched in my memory was the sweaty smell of her skin when I pressed my face into her body and begged her not to leave us.

Here I was standing on the soil of my mother's homeland, naive to think that this country could also be my home. The grass under my feet was soaking wet. It dawned on me that I still had a long way to go, before I could reach a place called *home*. But what did it mean to say *home*? Was it a real place? Did it exist or was it only a figment of my imagination? The rain started to come down more heavily. A strong wind flipped over the piece of laminated paper I was wearing on my chest. I carefully straightened it around my neck. I mustered up all the feelings of love and gratitude I could, so that my veins would be filled with compassion before the blood made its way into my heart.

—Translated by Quan Manh Ha & Nguyễn Huy Cường

A Small Dream for the Year 2000

—Ngô Thế Vinh—

THE MAN, A FARMER, WAS FORMERLY an ARVN soldier. Twenty years had passed since his days in the military, and he was now a middle-aged person. Though not yet fifty, he had been made pallid, old and decrepit by a life of unrewarding hard labor. He had lost his left foot, ironically after his military service had terminated, when stepping on a mine right in his own rice field. One did not have to be a doctor to know that his body hosted various illnesses and diseases: malnutrition, chronic malaria, and anemia. Whatever energy and dignity he retained was revealed in his bright though rather sad eyes, eyes that always looked directly at those of the person he talked to. Today, he came to this field dispensary for another kind of complaint. It concerned a bluish-black lesion on his back that was not painful, but had been oozing an ichorous discharge for a long while. He had sought various treatments, but found no hope of a cure. First, he had been made to wait in a district's health service station where a communist doctor had eventually given him a few Western medicinal tablets; then a traditional herbalist had treated him in turn with an herbal concoction and acupuncture. Despite all that, the disease refused to go away, even as he was steadily emaciating. Hearing that a group of healthcare workers from overseas had come to offer volunteer services, he decided to come to them at this dispensary and try his luck. With good fortune, he hoped, he might even be able to again meet the doctor he used to know—the chief surgeon of his Airborne Ranger Battalion in the past, who presently lived and worked in America. But it turned out that all the faces he *saw were young and unfamiliar. Nonetheless, he showed them his back for examination. From the team of young doctors came an audible gasp of surprise. The heart of Toản, the team leader, seemed to miss a beat. Without the necessity of engaging in complicated diagnostic procedures, he immediately recognized a form of malignant melanoma, which certainly would have had metastases spread to other parts of the body. The disease, of course, could have been cured if discovered earlier. Unfortunately, this present case, being at an advanced stage, could not be treated even with the most elaborate and sophisticated medical technologies available in the U.S. It was not the patient, but the young doctor who expressed sadness: "You've come too late; this disease otherwise could have been treated successfully." Betraying no embarrassment, the soldier-turned-farmer patient looked directly at the young doctor, his eyes darkened with anger and sternness: "I've come too late, you say? It's you doctor, who has come late, whereas myself, like all my compatriots, have been here forever." Flatly refusing to wait for anything else from the group of unknown doctors, the man turned his back on them and walked out, limping along on his bamboo crutches, his eyes looking straight ahead, accepting his miserable lot with the same courage he had shown as a soldier in a time past.*

***

DURING THE PRELIMINARY MEETING HELD IN Palo Alto to set up the agenda of the Convention, it was decided that the upcoming Fifth International Convention of Vietnamese Physicians would be changed to one of Physicians, Dentists and Pharmacists. After all, intermarriage among Vietnamese practitioners of the three branches of medicine had been a very popular practice. To Chính, that was good news reflecting the strength of unity amongst overseas Vietnamese medical professionals.

The last discussion in Palo Alto did not conclude until past midnight. Even so, the next morning, as was the habit of a person advanced in years, Chính woke up very early and got ready for his one-day trip to Las Vegas for a visit with his son. Toản, his eldest son, in a few months would complete his four-year residency in general surgery. The younger man's plan was to subsequently go to New York, where he would spend four more years studying plastic surgery. This was a medical specialization which Toàn once had remarked that a number of his father's friends and colleagues had abused and degenerated into "prostitution of plastic surgery," transforming it into something like a pure cosmetic industry which helped its clientele acquire more beautiful features like a high-bridged nose and fuller buttocks. Toàn was strong and healthy, taller and bigger than his father. He lived very much like a young man born in the United States, quite active and aggressive in both work and play, his thoughts and actions uncomplicated. Not only Toàn and his peers' way of thinking, but also their manner of identifying legitimate issues of concern, differed greatly from the perspective of Chính's generation. To be born in Vietnam but live abroad, and to be a first- or second-class citizen, had never constituted a problem or issue to Toàn.

Even though father and son had only one day together to talk, Toàn insisted on driving Chính to a ski resort very far from the entertainment district of Las Vegas. Along the way, Toàn confided in his father that it was not accidental that he had chosen to study plastic surgery with a central focus on hand reconstruction. It was not the artistic inclination expressed in his being a notable classical guitar player that made him treasure this part of the anatomy. Rather, to him, the function of the hands was a highly valuable symbol of a life of labor and arts. Unlike his father and his peer friends, Toàn was endowed with golden hands, as was the observation of his mentor professor. Indeed, from routine to challenging cases of surgery, through each and every economical slit and cut he made, Toàn always came out with results that were judged state of the art. For a long time, Toàn had been inspired by the example of the English orthopedist Paul Brand who worked in India. Not only with talent, but also with faith and enduring dedication, Dr. Brand had contributed enormously to the field of orthopedic surgery specializing in hand reconstruction, essentially to help people with Hansen's disease, or leprosy. His work brought hope to millions of people afflicted by that malady, and what he had accomplished for the past four decades intrigued Toản a great deal. Recently, Toản was also deeply moved when reading for the first time a book written in Vietnamese and published abroad by a Catholic priest, a book which describes the wretched situation of leprosy camps in Vietnam, especially those found in the North. Thereupon, Toản vigorously reached the decision that it would not be Dr. Brand or any other foreign doctors, but Toản himself and his friends, who would be members of Mission Restore Hope bound for Vietnam. He mused upon the dream that the year 2000 would be when Hansen's disease no longer posed a public health issue in his native land.

Toản related to his father that, lately, he had received in succession of letters and telephone calls from Colorado, Boston, and Houston inviting him to work in Asia, Vietnam being top priority, under very favorable conditions: a starting salary of six-digits or over a hundred-thousand dollars a year, coupled with guaranteed fringe benefits including tax-free privileges when working overseas. Toản had a res-olute response to the offer: if the sole purpose was to make money, he did not need to go and work in Vietnam. He was told by those contacts that groups of Vietnamese American doctors, not merely the vocally loud group led by Lê Hoàng Bảo Long, but also others comprising "more brainier" physicians, had quietly gone back to Vietnam to pre-pare a network of market-oriented medical services. It was said that, in their vision, the first base of operations would be Reunification Hospital in Sài Gòn, which would be renovated and upgraded to American standards, and doctors serving there would all have been trained in the United States. However, what would remain unchanged was the hospital's adherence to its priority of treating high-ranking Communist Party officials. The only difference and "renovation" it would succumb to, so as to be in line with the market economy, was to admit foreign clientele from around the world, who were rich and in possession of expensive medical insurance coverage. They would be from South Korea, Taiwan, Hong Kong, America, France, Australia, Canada, and other countries. The main point was to guarantee and safeguard their health to the highest extent possible, so they would have the peace of mind to work and invest, as well as to enjoy their lives, in all corners of Vietnam, from Nam Quan Pass in the North to Cà Mau in the Deep South. And, undoubtedly, all this would also promise fat profits, which were greedily eyed not only by American insurance companies, but also by a certain group of Vietnamese American physicians who were eager to "go back and help Vietnam."

At the age of thirty, Toàn had his own way of thinking, clear and free, and showed self-confidence in the path of commitment he had chosen. Chính did not exactly agree with his son's view, but at the same time he knew only too well Toàn's firm and independent nature. Certainly, Chính did not entertain the thought of clashing with Toàn for the second time over the same issue of whether or not they should go back to Vietnam and engage in humanitarian services. On the brighter side, Chính felt relatively calm when considering that whatever choice Toàn made was prompted by pure and noble motives, which set him apart from the opportunistic crowd. And in a certain fashion, Chính felt a little envious of Toàn for his youth, and even for his gullibility, which was almost transparently obvious. At this thought, which sounded rather absurd, he shook his head and smiled to himself as he drove back to Palo Alto.

***

FROM MONTREAL, CANADA, CHÍNH HAD MORE than once visited California. Despite his familiarity with the area, every visit seemed to have given him the impression of seeing new Vietnamese communities with expanding renovations and animated activities. Instead of the slightly-over-an-hour flight, Chính had decided to rent a car from Hertz at the airport and drive from Palo Alto to Little Saigon in the heart of Orange County. The trip was toward a young city of the future, but simultaneously it was for him also a journey backward into the past, a trip taken in part to contemplate a time lost. To confront future problems faced by Vietnam at the threshold of the twenty-first century, even against the cold, hard background of political reality, one needed not only to utilize one's brain, but also to pair it with one's heartfelt emotions, he thought. Chính recalled a joking statement made by Thiện, a friend and colleague, that kept haunting him: "The evil demon was seen not exclusively in the communist specter; it was lodged in our own hearts, hearts that remained callous."

Tongue in cheek, Thiện had said that if a fanatic were to shoot and kill Bảo Long, labeled pro-communist, how desolate Little Saigon would certainly become. Then perhaps a second Bảo Long would need to be found to take his place in provoking anticommunist sentiment among the diasporic Vietnamese community, for without anticommunist fervor as a stimulant, Little Saigon would not be able to retain its liveliness. The only thing was, it was not easy to pin down the communists, their target ever shifting and treacherous; and given that tricky situation, unwittingly, communist hunters were also made to move in pursuit, only to voluntarily come full circle in no time at all, and naturally from the first round of shots verifiable losses were counted among their very friends.

Chính planned to meet with Thiện, author of Project 2000. The aim of the project, which Chính thought bold and appealing, was to coordinate all circles of overseas physicians with a view to "exploiting and transforming the abundant talent and energy existent in the world into resources available to Vietnam; opening the hearts of people to tap a sector of the world's prosperity and channel it to the land of their birth; shaping the destiny of Vietnam by modern technologies prevalent all over the world." The plan was to establish a non-profit co-op group wherein each doctor, each dentist, and each pharmacist would contribute U.S. $2,000.00, merely a very small tax-deductible amount set against very big income taxes paid every year in their adopted countries. With participation of the thousand members, the acquired budget would come to a sum of two-million dollars in cash. Given that financial potential, there would be nothing that the International Association of Vietnamese Physicians, Dentists and Pharmacists could not do: from responding immediately to urgent matters like aiding fellow-countrymen caught as victims in violent disturbances in Los Angeles or helping victims of floods in the Mekong Delta; to long-term projects like building a Convention Center together with a Vietnam Culture House and Vietnamese Park adjacent to Little Saigon; participating decidedly, and in timely fashion, in a health project designed by WHO, the World Health Organization, for eradication of leprosy in Vietnam by the year 2000. Chính was aware that right in the heart of Little Saigon alone, among the silent majority, there existed many kindhearted and sincere souls.

There was the colonel, former commander of an Airborne Ranger Group, who had just arrived in the United States after fourteen years in a communist prison. Paying no mind to the care of his own failing health, the colonel had immediately sat down and composed a letter to Chính requesting that Chính, on the strength of his good reputation, help motivate Vietnamese immigrants to recreate the sculpture called *Thương tiếc*, Mourning, so that soldiers who had lost their lives for the freedom of South Vietnam would not be forgotten. The original large statue was a well-known work by Nguyễn Thành Thu, featuring a soldier sitting on a rock, his rifle in his lap, his dejected expression suggesting a deep sorrow widely interpreted as representing his mourning for his fallen fellow fighters. It had been placed in front of the National Military Cemetery midway between Sài Gòn and Biên Hòa. Hours after the fall of Sài Gòn on April 30, 1975, the communists had pulled down the sculpture and destroyed it.

Then there was Tiến, Chính's former collegiate fellow, who had taken the oath as a member of the Boy Scouts of Vietnam at an assembly on Mount Bạch Mã, or Mt. White Horse, near the city of Huế. He held but two passions: to restore the organization of the Boy Scouts of Vietnam abroad for the benefit of youths, and to establish the first Vietnamese hospital in America.

Of special note was Nguyễn, Chính's former senior colleague. Almost sixty, he still remained single. For so many years, Nguyễn had continued without fail to be a devoted friend to Indochinese boat people, and also a physician, gracefully free of charge, serving circles of writers and artists, as well as HO families—those who immigrated to the United States under the Orderly Departure Program. Liên, another doctor who had come to the local scene rather late from a refugee camp on an island, was determined to fight, against all odds, to undergo intensive retraining so as to be able to practice medicine again in his new homeland. Even so preoccupied, Liên did not give up on his ardent dream of bringing into existence a monumental sculpture of Mother Holding Her Child plunging into the immense ocean and drifting to another horizon, which art work would symbolize the huge exodus of two million Vietnamese who were on their way to creating a super Vietnam in the heart of the world. Chính could think of numerous other symbolic characters and noble thoughts, yet at the same time he asked himself why, in spite of all that, he and his friends continued to lose touch with one another in the darkness of "arrogance, envy and delusion," to use Thiện's words.

For a few decades now, Chính had remained a tormented soul, an intellectual witnessing tragedies in a time of turmoil and of glittering and bright deception. In the midst of so much noise and the reverberation of depraved words and expressions, surrounded by false political realities, very often Chính wanted to retreat into tranquility and quietude, doing away with tortuous thoughts that only caused personal distress and did not seem to do anyone any good. But he would not be himself if he chose to walk that path. Forever, he would definitely be himself, a man of strong conviction. To use electronic computer terminology, he had been programmed, and, as such, there could be no question of change or alteration in his pattern. The only possibility he could imagine was that he might try to become more sensitive—to the extent that he would feel amenable to dialogue with viewpoints different from his own, all of which he believed could come together in the end, even though the result would be a rainbow coalition. But, after all, multiple forms and colors are the ferment of creativity, he thought. Chính realized that the number of people who were still with him and supported him was dwindling with time. Not opposing him openly, the others simply detached themselves from his sphere and each chose to walk his own way. As for Chính, certainly for the rest of his life, he would continue on the straight path he had drawn for himself, no matter how deserted it grew. The ready forgetfulness and compromise exhibited by overseas Vietnamese—which Chính considered damaging to their political dignity and refugee rights—together with the extreme joy shown by people inside Vietnam because of the so-called *Đổi mới*, or Reform, only served to sharpen his heartache.

In the end, everyone tries to accommodate himself to new circumstances in order to survive, Chính told himself. A life abounding in instinct is ever ready to shed old skin, to change colors, and to proceed with fervor. The very few people who were as highly principled and constant as himself seemed to be facing the possibility of becoming an endangered species.

Chính's mother, hair completely white with age, still lived in Vietnam. One of his dreams was simple: that real peace would come to his homeland, so he could go back to see his mother before she passed away, and to visit his old village and watch children play in the village schoolyard. What a great happiness it would be if he were able once again to provide medical care to familiar peasants who were ever honest and simple, from whom the fees he had received sometimes were no more than a bunch of bananas, some other varieties of fruit, or a few newly laid chicken eggs. His dream was seemingly not so unattainable, yet it still appeared beyond reach and far into the future. The reason was, he firmly told himself, because he could not, and would not, return to his country as a mere onlooker, as a tourist, or even worse, as a comprador shamelessly flaunting his financial success. Though he longed to see his mother, Chính could not by any means return to Vietnam in his present state of mind and current external circumstances.

***

SINCE THE MIDDLE OF THE 1970S, following the fall of South Vietnam, there had been a massive influx of Indochinese refugees spreading all over the United States, the greatest concentration of them being in California. Difficulties faced by those who had arrived first were not few. To their camps, like Pendleton and Fort Chaffee, humane and generous American sponsors had come to give them aid and moral support. On the darker side, there was also no shortage of local residents who discriminated against them, who held ill feelings toward them and wanted to send them back to where they had come from. *We Don't Want Them. May They Catch Pneumonia and Die*, so went a slogan. Among that first mass of refugees were Chính's former colleagues. Currently, the number of Vietnamese doctors has reached 2000 in the United States alone, not counting smaller numbers living in Canada, France, Australia, and a few other countries. Out of a total of about 3,000 physicians in the whole of South Vietnam, more than 2,500 had exited the country. This was not unlike a general strike staged by the entire medical profession, a strike that had prolonged itself from 1975 until the present. Chính knew for sure that he himself had been one of the few who had effectively mobilized and led that endless and unprecedented strike.

Chính had a clear itinerary in mind. He would visit various places: San Jose in Silicon Valley, valley of high-tech industries; Los Angeles, the city of angels that ironically was about to become a twin sister of Hồ Chí Minh City; Orange County, the capital of anticommunist refugees, in which is located Little Saigon; and San Diego, known to have the best weather in the world. All these locations were full of Vietnamese, and their population kept increasing, not only because of the newly arrived, but also due to the phenomenon of a *secondary migration* of Vietnamese from other states. In the end, thus, after having settled elsewhere, they chose to move to California, a place of warm sunshine, of familiar tropical weather just like that in the resort city of Đà Lạt in Vietnam, as they told one another.

Eventually, the Vietnamese immigrants embraced standardization, a very American particularity. Big and small, cities in America all look alike, with gas stations, supermarkets, fast food restaurants like McDonalds. Likewise, entering crowded and bustling Vietnamese shopping centers on Bolsa Avenue, one readily sees, without having to spend any time searching, restaurants specializing in *phở* beef noodle soup, big and small supermarkets, pharmacies, doctors' offices, lawyers' offices, and, naturally, newspaper offices, given the insatiable Vietnamese appetite for news in print.

Chính's colleagues had been among the first group that arrived in this land. They represented a collective of academic intellectuals most of whom, with help from a refugee services program extended to all refugees like themselves, had quickly returned to practicing their profession in extremely favorable conditions. After that, if only every one of them had retained good memories about their initial feelings and emotions when forced to abandon everything and to risk their lives departing for an unknown destination, they would have conducted their lives differently in exile, Chính began silently grumbling to himself. Engraved in Chính's memory were those days in an island refugee camp where Ngạn, one of Chính's former colleagues, once and again had confided, "I only wish to set foot in the United States someday, having no dream of venturing to any further place. I hold no high hope of practicing medicine again. Happiness and contentment for me will be no more than breathing the air of freedom, living like a human being, starting all over from the beginning to set up a home solely by manual labor, and sacrificing myself for the future of my children." Luckily, reality had turned out better than what Ngạn had expected. With his intelligence and relentless energy, and, of course, with luck as well, only within a short period had he become one of those who resumed their medical practice. To work as physicians in America meant to belong to the upper-middle class, and, therefore, the status and position accruing to this group of newly certified doctors was a dream even for many native-born American citizens.

But Ngan and a number of others in the profession had not felt content to stop there. And, eventually, what was inevitably to happen had happened. Concerted police raids on a number of Vietnamese doctors' offices uncovered what was labeled as "the biggest medical fraud in the history of the State of California." The news made headlines in newspapers and television networks all over the United States. By then, only nine years had passed since the fall of South Vietnam, a traumatic occurrence which was still an unmitigated nightmare for its displaced people. And these same displaced people had to face the humiliating February 1984 medical scandal, a second nightmare of an entirely different nature. The name Vietnam had never been mentioned so very often as it was in the entire week that followed. Nor had the past ever been so cruelly violated. This event was indeed an ignominy to the past of South Vietnam and its people, a past defined by many sacrifices for a righteous cause. The image of a horde of Vietnamese doctors and pharmacists, Ngan among them, handcuffed by uniformed police, seen in the streets, exposed to sun and wind, had been thoroughly exploited by American newspapers and television networks. All members of Vietnamese communities felt their honor damaged by this scandal, which instilled in them a feeling of insecurity and fear. In fact, immediately afterward, there had arisen a wave of abuse which local people flung at Vietnamese refugees in general. In factories and companies, some insolent employees in a direct manner rudely referred to their Vietnamese co-workers as thieves, while others in a more indirect fashion stuck American newspaper clippings, complete with photos of the event, on the walls around the area where many Vietnamese worked. Those average honest Vietnamese citizens, who had come to the United States empty-handed, who were trying to remake their lives out of nothing except their will and industrious hands, suddenly became victims of a glaring injustice projected by discrimination and contempt. Choked with anger, a Vietnamese worker screamed to the absent academic intellectuals that even way back in the old country, anytime and anywhere these intellectuals had been happy and lucky, so it was about time they showed their faces in his workplace to receive this disgraceful humiliation they themselves had brought about.

The scandalous event of almost a decade ago appeared as though it had occurred just the day before, so heavy was the flashback that flooded Chính's mind. He tried to liberate himself from stagnant residues of memory about a woeful time in the past. He pressed a button and automatically the car windows were rolled down, admitting from the ocean a strong breeze which flapped noisily against the interior of the car. Blue sky and blue ocean—it was exactly the same deep blue spreading over the two opposite shores of the Pacific Ocean. The sight brought to mind a Chinese statement Chính had learned while in prison without knowing its origin: *The sea of suffering is so immense that when you turn your head you cannot see the shores.* Freeway 101 along the Pacific coast triggered his memory of National Highway 1 in the beloved country he had left behind on the other side of the ocean. Over there was seen the same great sea formed from the tears of living beings, the same stretches of glistening sand, the same fields of white salt, the same rows of green coconut trees. The homeland in memory would have been absolutely beautiful, if not for the intrusion of flashback-like film strips projecting scenes *along Highway 1*, showing the *highway of terror* and *bloody stretches of sand* during the last days of March, 1975.

***

LITTLE SAIGON, HIS DESTINATION, IS ALWAYS considered the capital of Vietnamese refugees, Chính reflected. In a certain sense, it is indeed an extension of the city of Sài Gòn in Vietnam. On the other hand, if one cares to look at historical records of this geographical area and its people, one will note an irony of history, which is that the first Vietnamese to live in Orange County was an ugly Vietnamese named Phạm Xuân Ẩn, a communist party member. On the surface, he was known to work for ten years as a correspondent for the American *TIME* magazine. What nobody knew then was that he was at the same time a high-ranking spy for Hà Nội. Supported by a fellowship from the Ministry of Foreign Affairs of South Vietnam, Ẩn went to the United States to study in the late 1950s. After graduation, he traveled all over America, and ended up settling in Orange County. Subsequently, Ẩn returned to Sài Gòn where he worked for the British Reuters news agency, then for *TIME* until the last day of South Vietnam. Only much later did one learn that Ẩn had joined the Vietminh, Vietnamese Independence Brotherhood League, very early on, in the 1940s. Initially, he had worked as a not-so-important messenger and guide, and finally had become a strategic spy who, under the cloak of a correspondent for the prestigious American magazine, had escaped detection by various CIA networks. Now, in the 1990s, Ẩn lived quietly in Sài Gòn, witnessing first-hand the failed revolution which he had loyally and wholeheartedly served for more than forty years. In the meantime, it was estimated that about three hundred thousand Vietnamese lived in Orange County, where Ẩn had previously established his residence. If Ẩn had a chance to come back, he would not be able to recognize the area at all. From a dead place with poorly developed orange orchards, it had become a youthful and bustling Little Saigon. In spite of all the hardships they shared with their parents as the first generation of Vietnamese immigrants, many children proved very successful in school and at college, and helped raise the standards of local education a step higher. They graduated in every field of study. This was more than what could have been hoped for from Đông Du, the Go East Movement, in the first decade of the twentieth century, which sent Vietnamese students to Tokyo for modern education. After a period of less than two decades in the United States, the Vietnamese produced for the future of Vietnam a whole stock of experts who could serve all areas of Vietnam's social and economic life.

In his life of exile, not being able as yet to directly contribute anything to his homeland, Chính nonetheless nurtured a small dream for the year 2000. After attending many conventions, he had the impression that he and his friends and colleagues were still like homeless people, even though they were lodged in no less than four-star hotels. In view of that, he decided that during this present field trip to California, the first item of construction he would campaign for was not merely a home base for the International Association of Vietnamese Physicians, but more extensively, a cultural park complex comprising a convention center, a museum, a culture house, and a park. It ought to be a representative project of great scale and high quality, which would be given utmost attention in various stages of construction. As much as the village's communal house symbolizes the good of the village, the proposed Culture Park complex would be an embodiment of cultural roots, indispensable roots that should be jealously safeguarded by generations of Vietnamese immigrants from the first days they set foot in this new continent of opportunities. The complex would be like a common ground for the currently very divisive Vietnamese diaspora, and would help younger generations advance with pride in their adopted country, while looking toward Vietnam for their true identity. It was envisioned that the Cultural Park complex would be built in the southwestern part of the United States, specifically located in a large area south of Highways 22 and 405, adjacent to Little Saigon. It would be a place conducive to a lively introduction to unique Vietnamese cultural traits, through attempts to reenact periods of history, both glorious and tragic, of the Vietnamese people since the establishment of their country.

This project would not solely be the job undertaken by a Special Mission Committee composed of the cream of the diaspora, drawn from all areas of social activities, Chính thought. Rather, it had to be a work of the whole community of free overseas Vietnamese, without discrimination on the basis of differences displayed by individuals and various camps. To begin with, if each immigrant simply contributed a dollar per year, Chính estimated, there would be more than a million dollars in addition to the two million expected from the

Association of Physicians, Dentists and Pharmacists, and whatever else from the Society of Professionals and business people. Three million dollars per year was by no means a small amount with which to build the foundation for Project 2000. The first five years would be spent in identifying and acquiring a piece of land big enough to meet the requirements for the Cultural Park complex. Of the buildings, the convention center would be the first to be erected, for it would serve as a cradle of community activities in culture and the arts. Thinking these thoughts, Chính at the same time could not forget how many times he had heard the so-tiresome refrain of dismissal that Vietnamese were incapable of constructing works of great scale, because so many destructive wars, in addition to the humid weather of tropical Asian monsoon, would not allow any great man-made work to survive. But like himself, they were in the United States now, and he wanted to prove the fallacy of their argument. After all, the essential element was still man. As long as he had a dream worthy to be called a dream. Then what was needed was a cement substance to bandage and join broken pieces in the larger heart. More than once, Chính had proved his ability to lead an intellectual community that had consistently done nothing for the last two decades. Now he was confronted with a reverse challenge, that of mobilizing the strength of the same collective to do something, if not inside Vietnam then outside, within an end-of-the-century five-year plan, before the twenty-first century arrived. He dreamed of a five-year period significant with planning and action, not with a passive attitude of simply watching things run their course.

But reality told another story, Chính reminded himself. After, but a few tentative first steps of sounding out others' feelings, Chính had come to clearly realize that it was indeed easy for members of the Association of Physicians to agree on non-cooperation with the Vietnam government in everything, including humanitarian aid. On the other hand, it was a much more complicated problem when it came to a concrete plan which demanded participation and contribution from everyone, resulting in numerous questions of "why and because" issued from the very people who Chính thought to be his close friends, having walked a long way with him. Given this state of affairs, Chính thought, the upcoming Fifth Convention would be a challenging testing ground for the willingness, not only of himself but also of the entire overseas Vietnamese corps of medical professionals, to commit themselves to this meaningful cultural project.

From Chính's point of view, instead of standing as onlookers from the outside, the International Association of Vietnamese Physicians should play a pioneering role, getting directly involved from the beginning in the construction of the Cultural Park complex. The building of it would be a rehearsal, serving as the blueprint of a model for the museum of the Vietnam War envisioned by ISAW, Institute for the Study of American Wars, an American NGO. ISAW was planning to build Valor Park in Maryland comprising a series of museums dedicated to seven wars in which the Americans had been directly involved since the foundation of their country. Of course, among the seven was the Vietnam War, the only war of just cause lost by the United States, along with its South Vietnamese allies. Providing correct facts and searching for answers to the question of causes would have to be the proper contents of this future Vietnam War Museum. Surely, two million people who had left their native country in a huge exodus could not accept a second defeat, an eternal one at that, at Valor Park, imposed upon them by a repetition of falsified historical facts, manipulated by the communists as usual. In fact, if things went according to ISAW's plan, the museum would exhibit incomplete, one-sided testimonies that would show, for example, that the war was between the United States and North Vietnam, ignoring the role of South Vietnam in the conflict. It was not simply a matter of who had won and who had lost. Rather, it involved the political personality of two million refugee immigrants who were struggling for a free political system in the land of their birth.

Furthermore, Chính believed that the process of constructing the Vietnam War Museum by ISAW had to start by drawing from the planned project of the Vietnamese Cultural Park complex of 2000, to be located right in the capital of Vietnamese refugees. This Park was to represent an overview and a selection of images, data, and testimonies related to various historical periods of the Vietnamese struggle for independence. It was intended to be a place where younger generations of Vietnamese immigrants could get help to look toward Vietnam in search of a lost time, to fully understand why they were present in this new continent. In such light did the envisioned Cultural Park complex constitute Chính's dream.

***

BETWEEN CHÍNH AND HIS SON TOÀN there transpired a silent conflict with regard to the battlegrounds of their dreams. Toàn's dream was thousands of miles away, back in the native homeland. But then, Chính asked himself, what dream can't one dream, inside the country or out? Realization of any dream did not depend solely on the brave heart of one person; it had to be based on the will of a collective whole that together looked in one direction, together cherished and longed for the joy of a fulfilled dream. As for Chính personally, what he was wishing for was not a temple to worship in, but a warm sweet home for "A Hundred Children, A Hundred Clans"—Vietnamese descending from the mythological union of the fairy Âu Cơ and the Dragon King Lạc Long Quân. This home base would be a location where values of the past were collected and stored, a gathering place where the ebullient spirit of life in the present was demonstrated, and a starting point from which to challenge the course of the future. It was to be, above all, a pilgrimage destination for every Vietnamese no matter where in the world they lived.

The Return

—Christina Vo—

TONY SCANNED THE *SAN FRANCISCO CHRONICLE* travel section, his eyes drawn to the article on northern Vietnam. The vibrant photos of Hạ Long Bay's jutting landscapes and Hà Nội's picturesque French colonial architecture seemed to leap off the screen, captivating him. Images of the capital's sparkling lakes, nestled amidst the bustling city, ignited a spark within him—one that he had known existed.

Sitting at his desk at the pharmaceutical company where he worked, thousands of miles away from the exotic destination, Tony knew he had to go there—to Vietnam. The longing to explore this intriguing corner of the world consumed him, and he could already feel the anticipation of the journey ahead coursing through his veins.

Tony had dutifully followed the path laid out by his Vietnamese parents, who had always emphasized the paramount importance of education. They had encouraged him, with unwavering conviction, to forge a brighter future for himself by pursuing the venerated professions of medicine, law, or engineering, as if these were the only beacons of success in an otherwise uncertain world. They yearned for their eldest son to construct a future that outshone their own—as Vietnamese refugees who arrived in America a few years after the war's end, Tony's parents, Mai and Phú, felt constrained by their choices. His mother worked in a nail salon, and his father had first been a mailman and then found a stable position at a Goodyear man-ufacturing plant in the Central Valley. They dreamed of their son owning a lovely two-story home in the suburbs, of their grandchil-dren attending a Montessori school and seamlessly integrating into the fabric of American culture. They envisioned a life for him that they could not achieve on their own, in a land that regardless of how long they lived here, remained foreign to them.

After taking a year off of school to work at a pharmaceutical com-pany, Tony was scheduled to start medical school this coming fall. He thought the year of work would allow him to save money and prepare for the subsequent years of his education, little did he know that this brief detour would lead him to question everything he had planned for his future and everything that his parents desired for him.

Tony picked up his phone and texted his mother, *I think I need to go to Vietnam.* He watched the ellipsis as his mother must have been tex-ting furiously. He imagined what she was thinking in her broken English: *What? What do you do in Vietnam? You have to go to school.* Instead, there was no response.

A few hours later, as expected, Tony's father called as he was on his way home from the office. "Your mom says you're going to Vietnam. But you have a plan, Tony. Why do you want to go there?"

"Chill, Dad, I'm just going for a vacation for a few weeks, maybe a month, this summer before school starts. I'll be back," Tony explained. "There's nothing to worry about. I still plan on going to medical school in the fall."

"So where do you plan to go? The South for a few weeks?"

"No, Dad, I'm actually planning to go to Hà Nội."

"Hà Nội? Why Hà Nội?"

"It looks beautiful there. I want to visit Sa Pa and Hạ Long Bay. I saw an article online about northern Vietnam, and that's where I want to go."

"It doesn't make sense to me, son."

"I know. Maybe one day it will."

Phú couldn't fathom why his son would be interested in returning to Vietnam, and how he had the audacity to decide on Hà Nội, and not the South where Phú and his wife were from. As he paced back and forth in the living room, he couldn't understand WHY. He had fled Vietnam in the late 70s after two failed attempts and finally made his way to California with support from some of his family members. In Vietnam, Phú was educated and he thought, had it not been for the war, he would've been successful there. But the war, in his opinion, ruined everything for him. He spent two years in a reeducation camp. How he survived, he doesn't even know. Maybe it was that he had friends there that helped each other get through the days. Once he and his friend, Đạt, went fishing in a small lake. It was one of the most memorable days for them, but when they returned, they were punished and it was demanded of them that they never do that again. For those years, the basic pleasures of life were sucked dry. Lifeless. Now, he could not understand why his son would want to return.

Once Phú arrived in the States and lived with his family in the Central Valley, where the heat was different from Vietnam's heat. But hot nonetheless. Phú landed a job in a tire plant near their relatives' home. The manager learned about Phú's engineering background from Vietnam and was generous enough to offer him a desk role, so that he would not have to be on the floor. But with his limited English skills, Phú thought the role would be too onerous for him, and declined the manager's offer responding that he'd rather just work on the floor. Now, more than two decades later, Phú still worked at the tire plant. He often wondered how he managed to get through his days, but somehow he did.

Phú was proud of his son's accomplishments. He'd graduated from a reputable public university; he was admitted to medical school. His future was so much brighter than Phú's—why would he return there when everything, including his family, was here in front of him.

Phú regretted that he and his wife never spoke about Vietnam, and didn't even teach Tony to speak Vietnamese, but they had bigger concerns on their minds. They were focused on survival in this new country. One time, Phú remembered when Tony was in high school and returned from a field trip from San Francisco. He was so proud to give Phú a small Vietnamese flag on a little stand, but it turns out he picked up the current Vietnamese flag—the red one with a yellow star in the middle. He had no clue that in Phú's mind that was *not* the Vietnamese flag. Phú still honored the yellow flag with three red stripes which represented the Republic of South Vietnam—his home. Giving him that flag, along with his decision to live in Hà Nội, not Sài Gòn, Phú viewed as small betrayals of his son.

A week before Tony's departure, he visited his parents who had planned a going-away dinner for him with relatives—many who still had not returned to Vietnam. Tony struggled to grasp this; he understood the war had created trauma, having taken a course on intergenerational trauma in college. He'd even studied basic Vietnamese for a semester, but the language, though he heard his parents speaking it, didn't seem real to him. He couldn't understand the hold this country had on people—those who left, and vowed never to return, yet still held this deep and abiding love for that country, Vietnam. He remembered on the weekends growing up hearing his father play Vietnamese videos on YouTube. He could sit for hours in his room just watching those videos.

Growing up, Tony did everything he could to be more American than Vietnamese. He only dated white women, including his current on-again-off-again girlfriend, Zoe, whom he met in college. Zoe was well-versed in trauma studies, having majored in psychology, and one of the reasons he felt connected to her was because she seemed to have this insatiable desire to understand people's trauma. Tony had a more direct path to healing, though he didn't see it that way at the time. He figured by facing the country, by stepping foot on that soil, he could help his family heal.

At the party, Tony wondered why they were even hosting one since he was only planning to leave for a few weeks, a month at most. His relatives asked what he felt were dumb questions and made seemingly offensive comments. They mentioned that he wouldn't like the bathrooms, that the water was dirty, that he wouldn't get by without speaking Vietnamese. From what he'd read about Vietnam, much of what his relatives were saying seemed false. Tony knew Vietnam was growing rapidly, even one of the fastest-growing countries in Southeast Asia.

As Tony passed plates of Vietnamese food, from *bánh cuốn* to *bánh xèo* to *chả giò*, he found his father sitting there talking to one of his brothers. In front of others, Phú was proud of Tony and somewhat jovial, but the disconnect between them was palpable.

"Tony, what's the first dish you'll eat in Vietnam? You think *phở*?" Phú asked.

"I don't know, Dad, maybe something different like a snake," Tony responded, slightly joking.

Phú gave Tony a book, *Catfish and the Mandala* by Andrew X. Pham. "That guy also went back to Vietnam. Maybe his travelogue will inspire you," Phú encouraged.

Tony was thankful for the gift, but what he wanted more than anything was to know his father's thoughts about his return to Vietnam. About his life there. He wanted to ask about the box of photos he found in the basement. The ones of his parents in Vietnam. Ironically, they seemed so happy in Vietnam at their wedding, when they were younger. Their smiles in Vietnam seemed to say something completely different than their half-baked smiles here in the States. Tony wanted to know why.

Tony stared at the itinerary on his computer. San Francisco—Seoul—Hà Nội. In a few days, he'd be departing and he already felt he was there. Everything seemed to be changing, slowly and quickly at once. He hadn't been responding as quickly to Zoe's messages, despite her demands and clinginess. He could sense that the relationship was somehow ending with his departure to Vietnam. His parents didn't say much; his mother, in her typical fashion, used enthusiasm to cover any unsettling emotions. She simply kept repeating through text: *I'm so happy for you.*

He noticed his father had been a little more distant than usual, unaware of how much time Phú had been replaying this idea of "returning to Vietnam" in his head. For a moment, Phú thought he should simply fly back with him—that would be better than Tony going alone. But Phú didn't know Hà Nội at all, he didn't understand northern Vietnam. He wouldn't be helpful to Tony. He also knew he had to let go of his desire to control this journey. This was Tony's choice after all. It was Tony's life. This was simply the chasm between them, but Phú also couldn't understand why, when faced with his son, he could not share all the thoughts in his mind. He knew Tony admired his friends' parents who were more American; the fathers who expressed their love and emotion more readily than Phú and other Vietnamese of his generation. But the love was there—right in front of them, not invisible, present in their every action. The biggest decisions of their lives, including the one to flee Vietnam, were all made with the desire for the next generation to have a better life. Didn't Tony see that? Phú's mind spiraled as he kept asking himself why. After all this sacrifice, his son decides to return to the country that he fled?

Tony's parents drove him to the airport. Phú pulled one of the suitcases, while Tony grabbed the other. His mother had tears in her eyes.

"Don't worry, Mom. I'll be back in a few weeks, a month at the most," Tony tried to reassure her. The simple fact that Tony hadn't bought a return ticket was already a sign that part of him wanted to stay in Vietnam. For how long, he didn't know.

Tony's dad handed him a crisp $100 bill. By this point, Tony had learned to accept the money as a gesture of love, even though his father probably needed that $100 more than Tony did.

"Thanks, Dad," Tony said as he firmly shook his father's hand. He also had to hold back his own tears. His parents waited until his bags were checked and walked him to the security gate. They watched until he made it through security, and they waved with smiles on their faces and tears gently rolling down their cheeks.

Before boarding the flight from Seoul to Hà Nội, Tony noticed a group of students on the plane who seemed to be traveling together. He saw a couple of them glancing at a Hà Nội guidebook together. One of the girls sat next to him in the boarding area and mentioned they were spending a semester in Hà Nội. Tony envied their group dynamic for navigating this new world, feeling both liberated and frightened by his solitude. He exchanged email addresses with the girl, and said they'd meet up in Hà Nội for coffee, or something.

On the plane, Tony simply wanted to rest his eyes and fall asleep, but he was seated next to another Vietnamese American who introduced himself as Ben. Ben was chatty, almost too talkative, and told Tony he had graduated three years ago but couldn't find a stable job in the States. He'd applied to twenty or so marketing jobs and didn't land any of them. After doing a number of odd jobs, working at coffee shops and bookstores, Ben decided to return to Vietnam to teach English.

"It's not easy to find a good job now, and I'm not sure I want to be on this corporate path in the U.S.," Ben explained. "And who knows, maybe not finding the right job is a blessing in disguise. Maybe I don't *need* to be on that corporate ladder." He added that a friend had already returned to Vietnam and made a decent living teaching, while also having the time to enjoy life.

"I don't have to worry about jobs yet because I'll be going to med school later in the year," Tony shared, although he recognized Ben was more interested in sharing than listening.

"We'll see about that," Ben responded. "I have a feeling you might stay. You know, my grandfather came to California in the early 80s, and then when he turned eighty, he decided to move back to Vietnam. He said life isn't as lonely there and it's visible."

"Visible life," Tony reiterated. "That's interesting. Who knows, maybe I will stay there."

Landing at Nội Bài Airport, Tony found the customs process intimidating, with officers in military green uniforms looking serious. He'd considered his uncle's advice to slip a $20 bill in his passport but decided against it, passing through relatively easily. Outside, he found taxis as expected, knowing roughly the cost for the forty-minute drive to Hà Nội. As he exited the airport, the sea of Vietnamese faces felt oddly familiar and strangely like home. For the first time, he wasn't part of a minority but the majority. Tony smiled, feeling both perplexed and at peace: how could this foreign country feel so much like home? Was it truly the Motherland?

Tony had arranged to stay at an affordable hotel in the Old Quarter for the first week while he got his bearings, intending to explore neighborhoods and decide on further travel plans. His first week in Hà Nội flew by as he absorbed his new environment amidst preparations for the Mid-Autumn Festival. The city was alive and vibrant in a way different from the Bay Area. He savored northern dishes his parents likely never heard of, admired the French architecture, and found the lakes as romantic as imagined. He stayed out late with the foreign exchange students, even having a one-night stand with the girl from the plane. Feeling guilty afterward, he messaged Zoe to break up, surprised by her easy agreement. He also faced the glaring reality that in order to stay in Vietnam, he needed to learn Vietnamese and enrolled in a class. While he could easily get by on his lack of Vietnamese language skills, to fully immerse in this culture, he wanted to be able to speak to the local people.

Fully immersed in his new life, Tony rented an apartment near Lenin Park for just a few hundred dollars a month. He zipped around town on a rented motorbike, feeling completely free. One morning, sipping *cà phê sữa đá*, iced milk coffee, on the street, he realized he needed to tell his parents he wouldn't be returning. After considering a call or text, he decided on an email:

Dear Mom and Dad,

I am really enjoying my time here in Vietnam and have decided to stay indefinitely. I know this might surprise you, but something about being here makes me feel at home and I need to understand more about this country and our family. I hope you understand.

Tony

He imagined his parents' shocked reactions, but Phú simply responded hoping Tony would enjoy his time in Vietnam and stay safe. Phú knew that his son would not return once he stepped on Vietnamese soil. He wasn't even sure how he knew this but somehow he could feel this in his heart, and he needed to accept that his son's path would be different than what he expected or planned. Tony wouldn't go to medical school. Tony might live the rest of his life in Vietnam. Phú smiled to himself as he thought that his wife would be happy because Tony might marry a Vietnamese woman, but then her grandchildren would be in Vietnam and not in California. Too many thoughts passed through Phú's mind; too many to even consider how this story might end. Just as he reconciled having to flee Vietnam decades ago, he made a firm and resolute decision to accept Tony's choice as well. He had to trust that his son could navigate his own heart and mind. He could hear his son's heartbeat though, and Phú knew, for whatever reason, in Vietnam, Tony's life had finally begun.

Editors

QUAN MANH HA was born and grew up in Đà Lạt, Vietnam. He came to the United States at the age of 22 for graduate studies and completed his doctorate in American literature at Texas Tech University in 2011. He is currently Professor of English at the University of Montana, where he teaches and researches American literature, Vietnam War literature, multiethnic U.S. literature, and literary translation. He is the co-translator of *Other Moons*, *Hà Nội at Midnight*, *The Termite Queen*, *Longings*, and *'Light Out' and Modern Vietnamese Stories, 1930-1954*. He lives in Missoula, Montana.

CAB TRAN was born in Vietnam and emigrated to the United States with his parents during the diaspora. He holds an MFA from the University of Michigan Helen Zell Writers' Program and teaches fiction for Gotham Writers Workshop. He has received fellowships from the University of East Anglia, Elizabeth Kostova Foundation, The Writers' and Translators' Centre of Rhodes, and elsewhere. His fiction and nonfiction have appeared in *The Iconoclast*, *Black Warrior Review*, *Distinctly Montana Quarterly*, and elsewhere. He is the co-translator and co-editor of Bảo Ninh's *Hà Nội at Midnight*. He lives with his wife Lindsay Tran in Helena, Montana.

Contributors

BẢO Thương is the pseudonym of Giáp Thị Thủy. She teaches literature at a high school in Bắc Giang, a province in the Northeast region of Vietnam. She is the author of the novel *Mùi hoàng kim*.

Thuy DINH left Vietnam in April of 1975 and grew up in the Washington, D.C., area. She received her BA in English and French literature from the University of Virginia, and a Doctor of Law from the same university. Dinh is a bilingual critic, literary translator, coeditor of the Vietnamese webzine *Da Màu*, and editor-at-large for the Vietnamese diaspora at *Asymptote Journal*. Her works have appeared in *NPR Books, NBCThink, USA Today, Prairie Schooner, Unbroken Journal, Rain Taxi, Pop Culture Nerd, diaCritics*, among others.

ĐỖ Thị Diệu Ngọc, co-translator, holds an MA in applied linguistics from La Trobe University (Australia). She is a lecturer of English at International University, a member of the Vietnam National University System in Hồ Chí Minh City.

Anvi HOÀNG grew up in Vietnam and came to the U.S. for graduate studies in American studies and history. A bilingual writer in Vietnamese and English, she enjoys exploring the in-between worlds in which she lives. She lives in Bloomington, Indiana.

HOÀNG Phượng Mai, co-translator, graduated with a BA in literature from Fulbright University Vietnam, where she was the co-founder and editor of the student *LIT Magazine*.

LẠI Văn Long was born in 1964 in Đà Lạt. He is a news reporter for the *Hồ Chí Minh City Police News* and has won many awards for his work as a journalist. The English translation of his award-winning short story "A Moral Murderer" is anthologized in *Other Moons*.

Andrew LAM is journalist and a prolific writer who often writes about the Vietnam War, the refugee experience, and transnational identity. He is the author of *Perfume Dreams: Reflections on the Vietnamese Diaspora*, *Birds of Paradise Lost*, *East Eats West: Writing in Two Hemispheres*, and *Stories from the Edge of the Sea*. His fiction is widely taught in Asian American literature courses, and he often contributes articles to NPR, PBS, and the *Huffington Post*. He lives in San Francisco.

LÊ Phương Anh, co-translator, graduated with a double major in literature and art & media studies from Fulbright University Vietnam. Her co-directed film *Saturn* won the Best Short Movie Award at the UOWD Film Festival organized by the University of Wollongong in Dubai in 2023.

LÊ Vũ Trường Giang holds a doctorate in history and teaches at Huế University, Vietnam. He is the editor of *Sông Hương Literary Magazine* and author of seven books. In 2022, he received the Young Writers Award from the Vietnam Writers' Association.

LƯU Vĩ Lân is a journalist living in Hồ Chí Minh City and the author of the trilogy *Mật đạo*, *Ngẫu tượng*, and *Nghiệp chướng*. The last one won the First Prize for Fiction in 2021 in Vietnam. He states, "Writing should be reconciliatory. That's my only intention as a writer. If writing is intended to hurt people's feelings and to open up newly healed wounds, that's a pity."

Vi Khi NAO, a cross-genre writer, is a graduate of the MFA program at Brown University. Her books include *A Bell Curve Is a Pregnant Straight Line*, *Sheep Machine*, *The Old Philosopher*, the story collection, *A Brief Alphabet of Torture*, and the novel, *Fish in Exile*.

NGÔ Thế Vinh graduated from Sài Gòn Medical School and came to the U.S. in 1983 after having spent three years in a reeducation camp. He later did his medical residency at SUNY Downstate Brooklyn and currently lives in southern California. He is the author of five novels and one short-story collection.

Annhien NGUYEN is a debut writer hailing from San José, California, home to one of the largest Vietnamese American communities. Passionate about fostering intergenerational relationships and capturing diverse narratives, Nguyen finds inspiration in listening to others' stories. When she is not immersed in writing, she cherishes moments with her family, dabbles in photography, and enjoys playful moments with her two cats in Brooklyn, New York.

NGUYỄN Minh Chuyên graduated with a BA in literary studies in Hà Nội. In 1967, he enlisted to fight in the war against the Americans and was sent to the Southeast region. He is a writer, a movie director, and a victim of dioxin, which damages 40 percent of his health.

NGUYỄN Huy Cường, co-translator, holds a doctorate in education from Michigan State University and teaches English at International University, a member of the Vietnam National University System in Hồ Chí Minh City.

NGUYỄN Thị Kim Hòa is a young, emerging writer from Ninh Thuận Province, Vietnam. Her fiction has won prestigious national awards. In 2021, she was recognized as one of the twenty inspiring women by *Forbes Vietnam Magazine*. The English translation of her award-winning short story "The Smoke Cloud" appears in *Longings: Contemporary Fiction by Vietnamese Women Writers*.

NGUYỄN Mỹ Nữ lives a quiet life in Quy Nhơn City, Bình Định Province. Her short fiction has won many awards in Vietnam. She has published ten books and writes for both adult and teenage readers.

Phùng NGUYỄN was born in 1950 in Quảng Nam Province, Central Vietnam, and resettled in California in 1984. He had been editor-in-chief of *Hợp Lưu Magazine* before he co-founded the online literary magazine *Da Màu* with Đặng Thơ Thơ and Do Le Anhdao in 2006, and functioned as the magazine's web manager and nonfiction co-editor.

NGUYỄN Thu Trân grew up in Đồng Nai Province and lives in Hồ Chí Minh City. She is the author of several novels and short-story collections, and she writes for both adult and children's readers. The English translation of her story "The American Service Hamlet" appears in *Other Moons*.

NGUYỄN Đức Tùng is a Vietnamese Canadian poet, literary critic, translator, and physician based in Vancouver. After fleeing Vietnam as a boat person, he settled in Canada in the 1980s. He often contributes fiction, memoirs, and poetry criticism to Vietnamese literary websites, such as *Da Màu* (*Multitude*), *Tiền Vệ* (*Vanguard*), *Văn Việt* (*Vietnamese Arts and Letters*), and *Thế kỷ 21* (*21st Century Forum*).

Viet Thanh NGUYEN is Aerol Arnold Chair of English and Professor of English, American studies and ethnicity, and comparative literature at the University of Southern California. His novel *The Sympathizer* won the Pulitzer Prize in 2015. Nguyen is also the author of *The Committed* and *The Man of Two Faces*, among others.

Kevin D. PHAM is Assistant Professor of political theory at the University of Amsterdam (Holland). His research explores theories of colonialism, identity, freedom, and democracy through cross-cultural analysis that challenges and enhances the way we understand the canon of political theory. Pham was born and grew up in California, and he is the author of *The Architects of Dignity: Vietnamese Visions of Decolonization*.

Tuan PHAN graduated with an MA in literature from Middlebury College, and he is a Vietnamese American teacher of literature currently splitting his time between Sài Gòn and Taipei. Phan was born in Vietnam and left in 1986 with his family as part of a second wave of Boat People refugees. His memoir, *Remembering Water*, about his family's departure and return to Vietnam, was published in 2023.

Gin TO *(she/they)* is a writer, visual and performing artist currently based in San Diego to pursue an MFA in Creative Writing at the University of California in San Diego. Her writing can be found on *Kaleidoscoped* and *diaCRITICS* (by DVAN).

Barbara TRAN was born in New York City and earned a BA from NYU and an MFA from Columbia University. She is the author of the prize-winning poetry collection *In the Mynah Bird's Own Worlds* and coeditor of *Watermark: Vietnamese American Poetry & Prose* and *Beyond the Frame*.

Elizabeth TRAN is a Kundiman fiction fellow, a Lambda fiction fellow, and the recipient of the Jeanne Cordova scholarship for Lambda fellows in 2017. She was longlisted for the 2020 CRAFT Short Fiction Prize, judged by Alexander Chee. She holds a BA from Rollins College, an M.Ed. from the University of California in San Diego, and an MFA in fiction from San Diego State University. Her book reviews, fiction, poetry, and essays have most recently appeared in *Brickroad, Vien Dong, Little Saigon, Tayo Literary Magazine, Diacritics,* and *Foglifter.* She is a high school English and social science teacher, and a mother of two magical little boys. She lives on the shores of southern California, spending most of her days near the ocean she can't breathe without.

TRẦN Thị Tú Ngọc teaches geography at Hương Khê High School in Hà Tĩnh Province, Vietnam. She has a strong passion for creative writing, and her short stories have won national and regional awards. She is the author of two short-story collections: *Ngụ ngôn tháng tư* and *Linh mộc.*

Vu TRAN is Associate Professor of practice in the arts at the University of Chicago. His fiction primarily concerns the Vietnamese diaspora in America and the ongoing and inherited effects of displacement—specifically its muddling of memory and the self, of domestic and interracial bonds, of the Vietnamese as well as American identity. He is the author of the novel *Dragonfish*.

VĂN Xương is a veteran and often writes about Vietnamese soldiers fighting in the American War in Vietnam. He lives in Quảng Trị, which is also the setting of most of his fiction. He is the author of two short-story collections: *Hoa gạo đỏ bên sông* and *Hồn trầm*.

Christina VO is a Vietnamese American writer whose work explores identity, culture, and belonging. Born in the U.S. to Vietnamese refugee parents, she embarked on transformative journeys to Vietnam in her twenties that deepened her connection to her heritage. Her diverse professional background includes working for international organizations such as UNICEF and the World Economic Forum. A graduate of the London School of Economics and Political Science and the University of North Carolina at Chapel Hill, Vo's writing delves into themes of self-discovery and cultural roots. She currently resides in Santa Fe, New Mexico, and is the author of *The Veil Between Two Worlds* and co-author of *My Vietnam, Your Vietnam*.

VŨ Cao Phan was born in Khánh Hòa, a coastal province in Central Vietnam. His story "War's End" won the First Prize for Short Fiction in 1995 and is widely taught in Vietnamese high schools. He holds a doctorate in military art history and lives in Hà Nội.

VƯƠNG Tâm was born in 1946 and graduated from Hà Nội University of Science & Technology. He is a member of the Vietnam Writers' Association and works as a reporter for the newspaper *Hà Nội Mới*. The English translation of his short story "Red Apples" appears in *Other Moons*.

Permissions

Acknowledgments

WE ARE INDEBTED TO ALL THE contributors whose stories are featured in this anthology for granting us permissions to translate, publish, or reprint their works. Special gratitude to Kat Georges and Peter Carlaftes, co-founders of Three Rooms Press, for their ineffable encouragement, support, and guidance. They recognized the value of this project and gave us valuable suggestions and ideas to make this project as best as it can be. During the entire journey, Kat was patient with us, and we cannot thank her enough for everything she has done, including designing the gorgeous cover, to make the book come to life. We would also like to thank Christina Vo for introducing us to Kat and Peter the moment she heard about our book, and our friends Võ Thị Xuân Hà, Dạ Ngân, Nguyễn Văn Tuấn, and Thuy Dinh for connecting us with the authors whose contact information we could not find. And to our copyeditors Arden Gray and Julia Diorio: your meticulous proofreading of the manuscript and suggestions for revision are greatly appreciated. Finally, our deepest appreciation is expressed to our families for their love, inspiration, and sacrifice to ensure us the best life possible. Also, many thanks to Lindsay Tran for her patience and devotion during the course of this project.

Resources

DVAN (Diasporic Vietnamese Artists Network), https://dvan.org/

Nam Phong Dialogues, https://open.spotify.com/show/7BtHUqhDThqo6OUlrncdyt

Vietnam Veterans News, https://vietnamveterannews.com/

Vietnam Society, https://www.vietnamsociety.org/

War, Literature, and the Arts (WLA), https://www.wlajournal.com

Global Village Foundation, https://globalvillagefoundation.org

Saigoneer, https://saigoneer.com/

Vietnam Studies Group, https://sites.google.com/uw.edu/vietnam-studiesgroup/home

Journal of Southeast Asian American Education and Advancement, https://docs.lib.purdue.edu/jsaaea/

The Vietnam Center & Sam Johnson Vietnam Archive, https://www.vietnam.ttu.edu/

Vietnamese American Roundtable, https://www.varoundtable.org/

The Union of North American Vietnamese Student Associations, https://unavsa.org/

Translation Project Group of the Southeast Asian Council (SEAC) at the Association of Asian Studies (AAS)

Journal of Vietnamese Studies, https://online.ucpress.edu/jvs

Vietnam Program, https://www.ssrc.org/programs/vietnam-program/

NORTH AMERICA

Cornell University, Southeast Asia Program

Columbia University, Weatherhead East Asian Institute

University of Oregon, U.S.-Vietnam Research Center, https://usvietnam.uoregon.edu/en/

Indiana University, Southeast Asian & ASEAN Studies Program

Northern Illinois University, Center for Southeast Asian Studies

Stanford University, Southeast Asia Program

University of British Columbia, Centre for Southeast Asia Research

University of California, Berkeley, Center for Southeast Asia Studies

University of California, Los Angeles, Center for Southeast Asian Studies

University of California, Riverside, Southeast Asia: Texts, Rituals, Performance Program

University of Hawaii at Manoa, Center for Southeast Asian Studies

University of Michigan, Center for Southeast Asian Studies

University of Toronto, Centre for Southeast Asian Studies

University of Toronto, Collaborative Master's Program in Contemporary East and Southeast Asian Studies

University of Washington, Southeast Asia Center

University of Wisconsin-Madison, Center for Southeast Asian Studies

Yale University, Council on Southeast Asia Studies

Harvard University, Global Vietnam Wars Studies Initiative, https://rajawali.hks.harvard.edu/programs/global-vietnam-wars-studies-initiative/

EUROPE

Goethe-Universität Frankfurt am Main (Germany), Southeast Asian Studies Program

Humboldt-Universität zu Berlin, Department for Southeast Asian Studies

Institut National des Langues et Civilisations Orientales (France), Department of Southeast Asian Studies

London School of Economics (UK), Saw Swee Hock Southeast Asia Centre

Lund University (Sweden), Centre for East and South-East Asian Studies

SOAS University of London (UK), Centre of South East Asian Studies

SOAS University of London (UK), South East Asia Section

Universität Bonn (Germany), Department of Southeast Asian Studies

Universität Hamburg (Germany), Southeast Asian Studies

Universiteit Leiden (The Netherlands), Southeast Asian Studies Program

University of Oxford (UK), Southeast Asian Studies Centre

ASIA

City University of Hong Kong, Southeast Asia Research Centre

Institute of Southeast Asian Studies—Yusof Ishak
Institute (Singapore)

Kyoto University, Center for Southeast Asian Studies

National University of Singapore, Department of Southeast Asian
Studies

AUSTRALIA

Australian National University, Southeast Asia Institute

RECENT AND FORTHCOMING BOOKS FROM THREE ROOMS PRESS

FICTION

Lucy Jane Bledsoe
No Stopping Us Now

Rishab Borah
The Door to Inferna

Meagan Brothers
Weird Girl and What's His Name

Christopher Chambers
Scavenger
Standalone
StreetWhys

Ebele Chizea
Aquarian Dawn

Ron Dakron
Hello Devilfish!

Robert Duncan
Loudmouth

Amanda Eisenberg
People Are Talking

Michael T. Fournier
Hidden Wheel
Swing State

Kate Gale
Under a Neon Sun

Aaron Hamburger
Nirvana Is Here

William Least Heat-Moon
Celestial Mechanics

Aimee Herman
Everything Grows

Kelly Ann Jacobson
Tink and Wendy
Robin and Her Misfits
The Lies of the Toymaker

Jethro K. Lieberman
Everything Is Jake

Eamon Loingsigh
Light of the Diddicoy
Exile on Bridge Street

John Marshall
The Greenfather

Alvin Orloff
Vulgarian Rhapsody

Micki Janae
Of Blood and Lightning

Aram Saroyan
Still Night in L.A.

Robert Silverberg
The Face of the Waters

Stephen Spotte
Animal Wrongs

Richard Vetere
The Writers Afterlife
Champagne and Cocaine

Jessamyn Violet
Secret Rules to Being a Rockstar

Julia Watts
Quiver
Needlework
Lovesick Blossoms

Gina Yates
Narcissus Nobody

MEMOIR & BIOGRAPHY

Nassrine Azimi and Michel Wasserman
Last Boat to Yokohama: The Life and Legacy of Beate Sirota Gordon

William S. Burroughs & Allen Ginsberg
Don't Hide the Madness: William S. Burroughs in Conversation with Allen Ginsberg
edited by Steven Taylor

James Carr
BAD: The Autobiography of James Carr

Judy Gumbo
Yippie Girl: Exploits in Protest and Defeating the FBI

Judith Malina
Full Moon Stages: Personal Notes from 50 Years of The Living Theatre

Phil Marcade
Punk Avenue: Inside the New York City Underground, 1972–1982

Jillian Marshall
Japanthem: Counter-Cultural Experiences; Cross-Cultural Remixes

Alvin Orloff
Disasterama! Adventures in the Queer Underground 1977–1997

Nicca Ray
Ray by Ray: A Daughter's Take on the Legend of Nicholas Ray

Stephen Spotte
My Watery Self: Memoirs of a Marine Scientist

Christina Vo & Nghia M. Vo
My Vietnam, Your Vietnam
Vietnamese translation: *Việt Nam Của Con, Việt Nam Của Cha*

PHOTOGRAPHY-MEMOIR

Mike Watt
On & Off Bass

SHORT STORY ANTHOLOGIES

SINGLE AUTHOR
Alien Archives: Stories
by Robert Silverberg

First-Person Singularities: Stories
by Robert Silverberg

Tales from the Eternal Café: Stories
by Janet Hamill, intro by Patti Smith

Time and Time Again: Sixteen Trips in Time
by Robert Silverberg

The Unvarnished Gary Phillips: A Mondo Pulp Collection
by Gary Phillips

Voyagers: Twelve Journeys in Space and Time
by Robert Silverberg

MULTI-AUTHOR
The Colors of April
edited by Quan Manh Ha & Cab Trần

Crime + Music: Nineteen Stories of Music-Themed Noir
edited by Jim Fusilli

Dark City Lights: New York Stories
edited by Lawrence Block

The Faking of the President: Twenty Stories of White House Noir
edited by Peter Carlaftes

Florida Happens: Bouchercon 2018 Anthology
edited by Greg Herren

Have a NYC I, II & III: New York Short Stories;
edited by Peter Carlaftes & Kat Georges

No Body, No Crime: Twenty-two Tales of Taylor Swift-Inspired Noir
edited by Alex Segura & Joe Clifford

Songs of My Selfie: An Anthology of Millennial Stories
edited by Constance Renfrow

The Obama Inheritance: 15 Stories of Conspiracy Noir
edited by Gary Phillips

This Way to the End Times: Classic & New Stories of the Apocalypse
edited by Robert Silverberg

DADA

Maintenant: A Journal of Contemporary Dada Writing & Art
(annual, since 2008)

MIXED MEDIA

John S. Paul
Sign Language: A Painter's Notebook
(photography, poetry and prose)

HUMOR

Peter Carlaftes
A Year on Facebook

FILM & PLAYS

Israel Horovitz
My Old Lady: Complete Stage Play and Screenplay with an Essay on Adaptation

Peter Carlaftes
Triumph For Rent (3 Plays)
Teatrophy (3 More Plays)

Kat Georges
Three Somebodies: Plays about Notorious Dissidents

TRANSLATIONS

Thomas Bernhard
On Earth and in Hell
(poems of Thomas Bernhard with English translations by Peter Waugh)

Patrizia Gattaceca
Isula d'Anima / Soul Island

César Vallejo | Gerard Malanga
Malanga Chasing Vallejo

George Wallace
EOS: Abductor of Men
(selected poems in Greek & English)

ESSAYS

Richard Katrovas
Raising Girls in Bohemia: Meditations of an American Father

Vanessa Baden Kelly
Far Away From Close to Home

Erin Wildermuth (editor)
Womentality

POETRY COLLECTIONS

Hala Alyan
Atrium

Peter Carlaftes
DrunkYard Dog
I Fold with the Hand I Was Dealt
Life in the Past Lane

Thomas Fucaloro
It Starts from the Belly and Blooms

Kat Georges
Our Lady of the Hunger
Awe and Other Words Like Wow

Robert Gibbons
Close to the Tree

Israel Horovitz
Heaven and Other Poems

David Lawton
Sharp Blue Stream

Jane LeCroy
Signature Play

Philip Meersman
This Is Belgian Chocolate

Jane Ormerod
Recreational Vehicles on Fire
Welcome to the Museum of Cattle

Lisa Panepinto
On This Borrowed Bike

George Wallace
Poppin' Johnny

Three Rooms Press | New York, NY | Current Catalog: www.threeroomspress.com
Three Rooms Press books are distributed by Publishers Group West: www.pgw.com